Jove titles by Elaine Bergstrom

BLOOD ALONE
BLOOD RITES
SHATTERED GLASS

BLOOD RITES

ELAINE BERGSTROM

JOVE BOOKS, NEW YORK

BLOOD RITES

A Jove Book / published by arrangement with
the author

PRINTING HISTORY
Jove edition / December 1991

ISBN: 0-515-10728-X

Jove Books are published by The Berkley Publishing Group,
200 Madison Avenue, New York, New York 10016.
The name "JOVE" and the "J" logo
are trademarks belonging to Jove Publications, Inc.

PRINTED IN THE UNITED STATES OF AMERICA

10 9 8 7 6 5 4 3 2 1

PART ONE

BEGINNINGS

ONE

Romania, 729

The room had been made for menial human slaves. Tiny and far too warm, it lacked the grandeur of the drafty great hall of the Austra keep or the smaller private quarters kept for the young and beautiful men and women stolen from the Moldavian plains who served the adult Austras' needs for blood and pleasure.

At twelve, Steffen was too young to be admitted to the private rooms, nor did he desire to know all that went on behind their carved doors. No, he preferred to be here with someone his own size and temperament. Though the cramped space of Ion's room should have sent Steffen into a claustrophobic panic, with practice he had managed to fight down the instinctive fear of close places, step inside and remain. Now, after a dozen visits over as many days he could relax and enjoy Ion's more experienced caresses, the young and so-potent passion of the boy's blood, and the magic of doing something so forbidden that he would not dare think of it outside this room lest the Old One read his thoughts and punish him.

Ion had been the first to suggest escape. They had been sitting cross-legged on the stone floor, a map that Denys had given to Steffen spread before them. It showed the world surrounding them. Names like Lombardy and Bavaria and Carinthia rolled around in their mouths like exotic wines as they

3

had planned to leave the keep and travel from one place to another.

Dreams of adventure were wonderful fantasies but Steffen was old enough to know the truth. He would go someday as some of his older kin had already done, but Ion would die here perhaps as a servant alone in this room or, more likely given the boy's beauty, he would soon be taken to the private rooms where he would be used and used again until, with nothing left to give, the adults would draw lots on who would have the pleasure of his kill.

At this time of year no fences or locks kept their slaves from running away. The ice-coated walls of rock beneath the Austra keep maintained the winter prison. If the boys had any chance of leaving, it would be now.

Steffen, who moved across the peaks with the grace of a mountain chamois, could leave easily anytime he wished. Ion, with his human need for warmth and his physical weakness, could not. But Ion, who remembered the time before he was brought to the keep, could recall the old tales and suggested what they could do. "If you share your blood with me, I can become immortal." Once Ion had denied the Mountain Lords' existence. Now he had lived with them long enough that the line between the facts and the legends had become hazy. Now he believed it all.

"That is not true," Steffen had replied for that is what his elders had taught him.

"How can we know what is true and what is not unless we try."

Ion had a point. So they tested the legend, their youthful kisses, more affection than physical attraction, had grown through their sharings into a passion so intense it made them guilty and hungry for more. Now, as he had done each time they met and shared life with each other, Steffen turned to Ion, panting beside him. "Can you feel a change? Are you any stronger?"

Ion, his dark body sheened with sweat, shook his head as always. "No." He had long since given up hope and yet, Steffen knew, they would share blood again. He lay, his long pale fingers twined with Ion's shorter ones, and they said nothing at all until, through the many layers of stone separating him from the world outside, Steffen felt the lethargy of dawn and prepared to leave.

At that moment, Ion's door crashed inward and the Old One's tall form ducked low to come inside. He took in everything with a single sweep of his lightless eyes. Steffen wisely said nothing though he did move sideways, placing his body between his father and his friend.

"Do you desire him so much?" No softness in that question, no possibility of any reprieve.

"Yes," Steffen replied.

"Kill him."

"No!" Spoken word. Mental recoil. He would not obey.

"Then I will."

Behind him, Ion screamed as the first wave of the Old One's mental torture rolled through the boy. Steffen stiffened from their shared agony, silently trying to absorb it or to somehow deflect the mental blow. He wanted to hold Ion, to merge with him and fight his father's attack, but his mind was not strong enough. Perhaps it never would be.

"This is not disobedience but an abomination. Forbidden," his father said, no trace of emotion in his tone.

But not instinct. Had the sharing been counter to his nature, Steffen could not have done it.

His father followed his private reasoning. "It is forbidden," he replied. "Now I will show you why." A long arm thrust Steffen aside and he fell against the hearth, one hand covered with flame. Though he shrieked from the sudden agony, his father did not turn to him. Instead he lifted Ion as if he were a piece of tinder, holding the boy level with his face. Ion had ceased to struggle, hanging limp as a doll in the Old One's hands, his eyes fixed on the Old One's eyes, his mouth a small circle of fear and awe.

A second wave of pain swept through the boy. Steffen, his heart beating at Ion's pace, his body feeling every nuance of Ion's torment, bolted from the room, running down the empty halls and into the pale morning light.

The screams followed him. Miles away he could still hear them ringing through his mind, still feel the pain.

The pain would have been enough but when his mind grew silent, he knew he had been truly punished.

Later, Steffen returned to the little room where Ion lay crumpled and lifeless on the stones. There he sat with his knees drawn tightly to his chest, while the body beside him slowly cooled.

TWO

Cleveland, 1932

Russ clapped a hand over his sister's mouth to silence her whimpers and pinched her hard whenever she tried to get away. At five, she would be no match for his strength but her struggles and the moans of pain he could feel vibrating beneath his palm kept him from thinking too much about how quickly he'd begun breathing and how hard his heart was pounding. Though a crack of light leaked beneath the closet door, the air in their hiding place felt like it had been used up in the endless hours since the ambulance had come and taken Mama away. He could hear his father swearing just outside the door. He knew where they were hiding. His father took perverse pleasure in knowing that they would not hide if they weren't afraid. Now he sat and waited like a mangy hunting tom for the mice to leave their hole. When his sister was silent, Russ could hear his father's heavy breathing, the sound of the bottle hitting the top of the nightstand.

Someone pounded on the door to their flat, someone who kept on pounding for all the minutes it took for their father to decide to answer. Russ listened to the silence, then heard his father start to bellow again with the same rage he had earlier used on their mother.

Russ let his sister go and started working his way around the boxes piled high in front of them trying not to make a sound.

"Russ?" his sister called anxiously.

"Shut up, you little shit. I'm going out."

"Russ, he'll hurt you too."

He'd answer her later, all right. Now he settled for a quick slap before he went to see what was going on. He left the closet door slightly ajar, tiptoed softly to the bedroom door, and watched the men outside.

Pieces of a living-room chair lay scattered around the room; those near the wall were covered with glass from the shattered windows. His father, his white T-shirt spotted with blood, was brandishing one of the chair legs trying to force a taller man in the black silk suit back outside, probably so he could slam the door and lock it and go back to his bottle while he waited for the kids to surface for air. He had no luck, though. The well-dressed man continued to speak softly with an accent that sounded like Grandpa's and refused to budge. Russ noted that even though it wasn't cold outside, the man wore black leather gloves.

Minutes passed until, furious at the standoff, his father swung, aiming for the stranger's head. Russ was ready to turn and run when the stranger ducked, caught the bar of wood, and jerked on it, pulling his father closer to him, against the blade that had suddenly appeared in his free hand.

A quick upward thrust and his father slumped. The man pushed him backward and he fell. The blood that had started dripping down the blade turned before it reached the handle and spread slowly over his father's belly.

Russ was old enough to know that he should run back to the closet and pretend that he had never witnessed this crime, but the blood and the need to know for certain that the nightmare was over drew him forward. He walked to his father's body and knelt beside it as if he were alone with the corpse, as if the killer weren't standing above him wondering if Russ ought to die too. Russ dipped his fingers in the blood, rubbing them together, feeling how slippery and sticky they'd become. Then he rested a hand on his father's chest, and feeling no motion of breath in and out, he began to laugh.

The man vanished. Russ kept on laughing until the police came and took him and his sister away.

THREE

New York, August 1955

Paul Stoddard stood in the lobby of The Arboretum, his newest creation, trying to be as inconspicuous as possible. In the last-minute rush before the reception began, champagne glasses tinkled past on rolling carts, caterers gave quiet orders, a violinist ran his bow over his strings. Paul, in a quiet corner across from the main doors, heard none of these. Instead he watched the expressions on the faces of the afternoon's early arrivals change from whatever ordinary emotion accompanied them here to wonder, to admiration, to delight as they stepped into the three-story lobby, cooled in part by the massive plantings of bamboo as well as by the pale blue tint of the slanting, soaring walls of glass. Watching these first arrivals was a habit Paul had developed over the years, a way of noting the inaudible "thank yous" of the public that would use his buildings long after the politicians and the critics had vanished.

Even now, now when so many of his lights reflected in New York harbor, now when, at forty, he was famous, he was still waiting for some perfect being to make the pronouncement that, yes, he was as talented as he believed himself to be. He knew he couldn't find it from the critics, who he privately despised, or in his own taste, which was after all personal. No, he would see it here, in the eyes of people stepping into his building for the first time.

A reporter in the lobby noticed Paul in the corner. Instead

of interrupting the architect's concentration, he merely observed him and took notes. "Paul Stoddard does not create buildings, he builds glass cathedrals and calls them skyscrapers," the reporter wrote. "Only time will tell if they will stand."

As the lobby began to fill with men in suits and women in their flowing Dior gowns, the reporter joined his fellow writers for the final news conference, calling out the usual questions, noting the unassuming, almost shy replies. During the half-hour conference, no one noticed how Paul Stoddard's eyes were constantly drawn to a petite dark-haired woman across the room and the tall man beside her who, from looks and coloring, could only be one of her relatives, how occasionally the woman would wink and smile with shy, closed lips and he would ask someone to repeat their question.

"What are your plans for the future?" an older reporter called out.

"Stoddard Design has a number of commissions for private developments and two hotels in Dallas. However, much of my time will be spent on the final designs for the Atomic Research Center in New Mexico."

"Given your views on the subject of disarmament, do you feel comfortable building the Center?" someone else asked him.

Paul knew it would be wise to sidestep a political question, nevertheless he answered truthfully, "Research is always valuable, particularly in this field because it will undoubtedly reveal the futility of another world war."

"Do you support the disarmament movement?"

"I've spent twenty years designing buildings. I would hope they're still standing at the turn of the century." He noticed other hands rising, and for the first time, he understood how his idealism could be twisted and used against him. Naming the building that housed his home and office La Paz was natural, for there was an air of deliberate peace in the design. Donating a quarter of the profits from its first year of operations to the World Peace Federation had been too political a gesture. Stephen had advised against it. So had Elizabeth. In this he had imitated Laurence Austra's pacifist stance and ignored their advice. But the years had shown him the value of caution, and though he still donated funds to pacifist movements, he was careful to spread the money thin, hoping many small contributions would escape the notice one large one would bring. Now, as he felt his heart skip, then double beat, he hid his nervousness and deliberately called on a reporter from an architectural trade magazine, knowing the woman would not ask him anything about politics.

The reporter's technical question led to another similar one. Paul continued the conference until the orchestra began to play, then excused himself, explaining that he had to join his guests. Again, caution dictated that he pose for a picture with Bob McCoy, a conservative senator from Massachusetts and one of his late parents' close friends. He stayed only as long as politeness dictated, then left to greet a number of guests, always moving toward the spot where Elizabeth Austra stood beside her cousin Laurence.

Elizabeth had bobbed and straightened her hair and she wore an indigo silk dress she had designed herself, the large armholes and loose sleeves hiding the unnatural length of her arms. Throughout the interview, she had discreetly kept her distance from her lover, letting the photographers snap their pictures and the reporters collect their usual statements. But now that the formal questions were over, she led him onto the dance floor for a slow, awkward waltz. "You must dance. It's your night," she told him and kissed the corner of his mouth.

One dance. One dance was all his aching knees would take, all Elizabeth dared to risk before the reporters would descend on both of them, asking questions Elizabeth would never want answered. "Later," she whispered and left him standing beside the mayor while she joined one of Paul's shy young associates who looked terribly in need of someone familiar to hold on to.

Through the remainder of the evening, she moved on the edge of the crowd, catching Paul's attention from time to time, a small inviting smile on her face.

At ten, the reception would take on a more formal air. Paul noticed Laurence Austra nervously talking to the violinist.

Later, after the photographers were sent away and darkness would make surreptitious photos impossible, Laurence would take his place at the piano for one of his rare public performances. Laurence, cursed with a musical genius he could never publicly reveal, reveled in these rare opportunities. And if the music he played seemed richer and more complex than the usual Austra pieces played by other soloists, those listening would blame the informal setting or the relationship of the pianist to the composer, never guessing that Laurence Austra's compositions had been rewritten to accommodate human limitations, that the young son lovingly playing his father's creation was, in reality, the composer himself.

Tonight he would play "World Harmonics," the piece recently removed from the schedule of the Chicago Symphony because of its alleged subversive nature. Paul thought of the reporters scattered through the crowd and considered asking Laurence to play a different composition, eventually dismissing the idea as paranoia. The choice of music, after all, was a minor offense, one the papers would most likely blame on the idealism of the performer if they noted it at all. Paul decided to let Laurie have his masterpiece. Besides, it was the perfect music for this room, this night.

The party broke hours later and Paul found Elizabeth stretched out on their bed in the penthouse atop La Paz, a bright red kimono barely covering the tops of her thighs, her dark eyes open watching him as he entered the room, inviting him to satisfy the hunger that experience and empathy allowed him to share. He undressed, leaving his clothes scattered on the floor. He was tipsy from the wine, too fast and inept. He began to slide on top of her when she pulled a chilled bottle of champagne from behind the bed and poured it over both of them. He lapped the pool of it that formed on her stomach and sucked the foaming drops from her hair. She got drunk on his blood and they giggled like children while they loved.

Much later, Paul looked up and saw his face echoing in the tiny pieces of glass and he thought of his picture in the next day's papers. His fame had never stopped thrilling him but it made him uneasy as well and he wished he could just plunk a building down on its site—one morning the city would wake and it would be in place without any fanfare when the design was announced or the bid accepted, without any need for the crowd and the wine and the music.

—But this is your night, beloved,—Elizabeth purred in his mind. —And for the rest of it you dance with me.—

Paul slept until the sun rose painting the room in sea mist and rainbows through the patterned emerald skylight. Then, in spite of his lack of sleep, he woke at his usual time and looked down at Elizabeth. Though her eyes were closed and her mind locked in the deep sleep of dawn, she smiled like a child full of mischief.

Yes, yes, Paul thought as he lay awake and waited for the newsboy's light knock on the outside door. *The Austras knew the ultimate secret . . . not merely eternity but eternal youth!*

When he heard the signal that his papers had come, he went into the kitchen and brewed a pot of coffee. Only after he had a cup poured and had positioned his chair so the sunshine from the eastern windows would fall across his stiff knees, did he open the newspapers and read the reports of last night's reception, a columnist's review of The Arboretum that accompanied it. He'd expected the praise for both, that had been clear last night, but he was more concerned with the damage. It was always there, but this time it didn't seem too glaring. Two brief, and glowing, mentions were made of Laurence Austra's playing, none of his choice of music.

And none of Elizabeth.

He expected the last for no one ever mentioned her, but he wondered how they could avoid doing so since she dominated every room she entered. He sometimes thought she had the gift of making herself invisible, like the legendary vampires who could not be seen in a mirror. Yet people had not stared curiously when he had danced at the reception, so the crowd must have noticed a woman—nothing more—in his arms.

She had the power to deal with them, just as she had the power to give him confidence and strength. And health, he mentally added, as he reached into the covered porcelain dish on the table, pulling out an iron pill and two of the long grey vitamin capsules Elizabeth mixed for him. Their relationship made demands on his body, demands that Elizabeth had centuries to learn how to meet. Indeed, though he should have been anemic and prone to illness, he hadn't seen a doctor in years. Sometimes he wondered if he even needed one.

Paul laid the papers aside, the reviews that mentioned Laurence's playing on top of the stack so Laurence could read them when he woke. He had just pushed himself to his feet, intending to rejoin Elizabeth in bed, when he heard Laurence cry out from the guest room, his own bedroom door open. In a moment Elizabeth stood in the kitchen doorway, her expression one of sharp and sudden misery. "What's wrong, Elizabeth?" he asked.

She didn't answer, only pressed against him, trembling.

"Is it Stephen?" Paul asked, with more concern.

Laurence joined them as Paul had been speaking, his expression mirroring his cousin's as he answered for her, "My father is dead."

Charles Austra dead! Unlike Elizabeth and Laurence who thought of themselves and their family as immortal, Paul had a human perspective. Though he had only known Charles Austra for a few weeks, he had somehow always expected to hear this news. And though it had been over ten years since he and Laurence had last seen Charles Austra, he did not question how the two, with their psychic family bond, could know he was gone.

"And something else has happened. Something so wonderful I feel it even through my grief." Elizabeth pushed back, gripping Paul's arms. "Your work here can be postponed for a little while, *oui*? Please, beloved, we must go home. Come with us."

He hugged her again, sharing her sadness, certain she was not the only one who would need him now. "Of course, Elizabeth," he said.

PART TWO

THE WITNESS

FOUR

1

The first memory Helen would recall with the perfection of her newborn mind was Charles Austra's funeral fire. She smelled the coal gas leaking through cracks in the firebrick the instant before the burners ignited, saw the orange brilliance of the flames, felt their heat when she rested her hand against the furnace grate and held it there, held it until she felt something, some pain to equal what she sensed in the handful of the Austra family surrounding her.

The Austras mourned Charles, and though he had died five days ago while giving her life, she felt nothing for him. What had been there—fear, horror, fascination—all of it had vanished with his death. Now she only sensed the perfect order of her existence. She had become the creature she always should have been. She wanted to run, to laugh, to shriek her pleasure to the starry sky, not stand here and pretend that there was anything left of Charles Austra to mourn. She had never believed less in God than at this moment . . . or in heaven, or in hell.

Though she had glimpsed all three at the moment of her rebirth, now only the fire seemed real.

Pale fingers circled her wrist and pulled her hand away from the grate, turning it over, looking down at the blisters forming on her palm. "I have never known the feelings I sense in you now," Elizabeth Austra said, "but I can share them and try to help you understand."

17

Elizabeth bowed her head and kissed Helen's palm, holding her lips there only an instant. She raised Helen's open hand between them. "Watch," she told Helen and they looked together as the blisters shrank taking the pain with them.

And still gripping Helen's wrist, Elizabeth walked with her through the quiet gathering, up the stairs, and into the night.

"Shouldn't you be with them?" Helen protested.

Elizabeth led her up the mountain path, away from the glass house, and into the thick trees. "I am where I want to be, welcoming my new cousin to our home in Chaves." Her lips brushed Helen's cheek and Helen noticed, not for the first time, the Austras' need to touch one another, as if their mental intimacy was not enough.

Perhaps it wasn't. She felt Elizabeth in the brush of that kiss. Her sorrow. Her joy. Her ageless sympathy.

"There will be a blood sharing later," Elizabeth said, repeating what Helen already knew. "It will welcome you into the family. In the meantime, are you hungry?"

Helen moved back a step, not certain what Elizabeth meant. "Yes . . . I don't know," she admitted. "If this is hunger, then I have never been hungry before."

—You've changed—Elizabeth accentuated her mental message with a fleeting smile, exposing her long rear teeth. "And if you're hungry," she added vocally, "that's good. Tonight your joining with us will be all the more powerful."

"I've already shared Stephen's blood. And . . . his brother's."

"And what am I thinking now?"

Helen looked at the woman for a moment. She sensed nothing. She shook her head. "I don't understand," Helen said.

—You sensed nothing when I spoke to you as I do to the rest of the family. I speak my thoughts to you now as I would to a human. I receive as I would from a human. Let me show you the difference. Tell me about Stephen? What is he doing and feeling now?—

Stephen was beside the furnace in the glass house preparing to grind his brother's ashes, mix a portion of them with the melted white sand and lead, and stir them together into glass. Helen sensed his sorrow, his denial, his anxiousness. She asked, "Will I feel you all the way I feel him now?"

"Yes."

Farther up the mountain a deer ran across the path. Helen heard its hoofs click on the stones. In the woods to her right, a fox watched her with cautious curiosity. How could she be anything more than she had already become? Another change frightened her.

"You feel no more fear than Stephen, *oui*?"

"Fear?"

Elizabeth laughed, a sound of seductive sympathy. "He is afraid that you have been pushed into our world too fast and in that he is probably right. He is worried that his brother's death will somehow taint you and for that he is very foolish, *oui*? And above all, he knows that there will be a half dozen of his cousins vying for your attention tonight. He is jealous and that is an uncomfortably human emotion. You should be pleased that you unsettle him. Few things can."

Elizabeth laughed again and started up the mountain. Helen followed until the glass house was only a small piece of the landscape. She smelled the leaves, the needles of the few pines, and the herbs the family had planted as they broke beneath her feet; all blending into the scent of late summer. They climbed until they reached Stephen's house and stood on its catwalk waiting for the others to come. Though they did not speak, did not share thoughts with each other, Helen sensed Elizabeth's calming touch, her quiet support as they waited side by side for the sad work in the glass house to end.

When the doors to the glass house opened and the family began the climb up the mountainside, Elizabeth moved closer to Helen. —After tonight you will never know loneliness— she said mind to mind. In response Helen reached for Elizabeth's hand, not surprised to find her own was shaking.

ll

For the first time in nearly two thousand years, the Austras welcomed someone half human into the family. Though the

words of the ancient ritual were known by all, only Denys
was old enough to recall them firsthand. Though he had long
ago passed his leadership role to his half brother, Stephen,
he led the family's circle now.

They built a bonfire and Helen stood with her back to the
heat of it, facing Denys. He held a crystal goblet in his hands
and sang the inflected words of family sharing in a low solemn tone, *"Ge cres nas gevornes. Cres Aughkstra!"* From
blood we are born, blood of life eternal. He passed the goblet
to her.

Helen repeated, her inflection altering the alien words to
that of one joining the whole, the words of a child at its ten-
year ritual, *"Ge cres nas gevornes. Cres Aughkstra!"*

The crystal rested heavy in her left hand. She raised her
right, palm up, and winced as Denys bit deeply into her wrist.
The circle began to rotate, each member of the family standing briefly before her, taking one deep swallow from the
wound on her wrist, letting the blood from their own similar
wounds drip into the goblet that seemed to grow heavier with
each small addition.

When the circle had been completed and Denys again stood
before her, when all had shared in her life, she raised the
goblet and turned to face the fire. She felt so much a stranger
as she stared through the flames at each of them. Her straight
blond hair seemed such a contrast to their uniform dark curls,
her deep blue eyes so pale when compared to their colorless
black ones. But she was family—one of these eternal, perfect
predators. Long before she had changed, her soul had guessed
the truth. Tilting her head back, she drank, consuming them
all.

She felt the marrying of cells into one perfect union. She
sensed the thoughts of the family around her, not just the
words of welcome on the surface of their minds but the emotions layered beneath them—deep, deeper. And she felt the
hole, the piece Charles had occupied in their collective
thoughts, and at last understood their rage at the terrible loss
that would never dull with time.

But his death, like so many others, brought new life. Their
acceptance of her—human and family—was perfection in it-

self. At the time of her birth into immortality, Charles Austra had shown her the horror of his family's past. Now she shared the bonds of ecstasy. She contemplated each of their lives as she stared into the flames. When they dwindled into coals, she looked past them at the ring of pale faces surrounding the fire. Slowly, she moved around the circle, hugging her new brethren, sharing separately the thoughts of each as she faced them.

In each, she sensed hope, but felt it strongest in the women. A terrible burden had been lifted from them. Their lives would not be needed to save their race. Helen, with her unique human power, could bear children and live.

Forever.

The thought dizzied her. She took an unsteady step forward and gripped Rachel, who was nearest her, for support, then moved from her to Denys.

He raised his hands and stretched between them she saw a gold chain. A crystal teardrop, black as the eyes of her new family, dangled from it. She bowed her head and he placed the chain around her neck. The crystal still held the warmth of the fire that had forged it and, more, a steadying power she would only understand with time.

"*Nus gevornes!*" We are born! Denys chanted, then whispered to her, "Welcome."

Did she sense an invitation beneath the simplicity of that word? Perhaps someday, she thought. After all, their affection had forever in which to grow.

The circle broke into groups of two and three. Helen saw Stephen standing in the shadows at the edge of the trees. She walked to him and he took her hand and led her away from the fire, down a winding footpath. As they moved, their speed increased until she was running, running swiftly behind him toward his home.

—Our home.—

Though he hadn't asked a question, she could refuse. Helen didn't think to be coy or to tease the uncertainty Stephen tried to hide. She wanted him more than she ever had before. She merged passion and assent into one quick thought and was pleased to see Stephen stumble and whirl, ready to catch her.

She hit him without stopping and they fell together onto the twisted thyme lawn that surrounded the house.

"Here," she whispered and lay on her back, staring up at the scattering of stars.

Since the night she first exchanged blood with Stephen, they had shared a mental bond. She would feel his need before they touched; he would sense her demands even when she did not speak of them. But tonight's family bonding let her sense more than Stephen. As Stephen unbuttoned the front of her green cotton blouse, she felt Rachel's quiet passion as she lay on top of Denys, her long dark hair tickling his chest. She became Denys, feeling him harden, his lips brushing the tips of Rachel's breasts.

She merged with Ann and James and Sebastian gliding four-footed up the hill, bringing down a deer in some forest clearing, feeding briefly on its blood and terror, then letting it go. Only life tonight.

She felt the silent laughter as Marilyn ran, pursued by her evening's suitors, laughing still when she let them catch her and pull her down.

She shared the human rapture as, in an empty clearing, Elizabeth lay beside her human lover. Through her mind, Paul Stoddard became part of the sharing, through his blood in her, he became part of them all, and he lay open to the rapture as Elizabeth's face hovered above him, a dark shadow against the stars.

She sensed them all, a dozen minds around her.

And in the distance, too far for even her ears to hear, Laurence played a flute. It flowed through her mind like the family's thoughts.

Lost in them, she felt Stephen undressing her as if she were one of the others and he someone else, felt his hands pushing apart her legs as if they were Rachel's hands pulling Denys deeper into her or Laurence's fingers fluttering quickly over the pipes.

His need, hers, theirs, so perfectly one.

She heard Stephen's laughter, coming it seemed from a great distance. She felt his brief stab of pain as he bit his lip and then he was kissing her, feeding her his blood, forcing her back to him. He hadn't touched her since her changing but it made no difference. He knew her body as perfectly as if it were his own.

She screamed his name as he entered her, mentally kept on screaming it as he kissed her, biting her tongue, their blood mingling as their bodies twined.

She whispered it as, near dawn, they walked into the shelter of their house.

Sunrise was striking the bedroom windows coloring the raised bed crimson and violet, when Helen stretched and ran one delicate hand down Stephen's pale, long-limbed body. "I love you," she said.

Stephen didn't reply. Helen had expressed a human emotion. What he felt was different, less detached. She had become family. He loved her now as he did himself. He conveyed this not with words but with an opening of his mind, a sharing of what he felt.

"I understand," she said, then repeated, "I love you," and kissed him one final time before the warmth of the sun, colored and softened by the ruby window, touched her body. With it came the dawn lethargy, the call to sleep that could be resisted only with effort. She took Stephen's hand. They slept.

Helen woke late in the day, long after Stephen had left for AustraGlass to resume his duties as director of the ancient family firm. Helen's clothes hadn't been delivered yet so she put on one of Stephen's robes and walked through her house.

The sunlight struck the tall colored glass windows, filling the rooms with soothing prisms of light. Helen, aware of the touch of each tiny rainbow on her bare arms and feet and irritated by the brush of the soft fabric on her skin, dropped the robe over a chair. Clothing wasn't necessary here. This was her home. She could do exactly as she liked.

She went into the unused kitchen for a glass of Tarda water, the special mineral blend bottled in their homeland to diminish the Austra need for blood, then wandered into Stephen's workroom on the north side of the house.

The huge room was the only one in the house with clear glass in the windows. These stretched the entire length of the space. In the windows closest to the door, squares of glass were hung from wires, over a thousand tiny samples of color, the range of her lover's creative art. These, the glass-doored case containing unlabeled jars of powder and sand, and a small gas-fired furnace were the only objects apparently in use. The potter's wheel, the loom and the tapestry on it, a few box cameras on a shelf, and an oven whose purpose Helen did not understand were all abandoned and dusty. Stephen hadn't used the room in years, Helen knew, but the time would come when he'd return to these crafts again. Such was the cycle of Austra life.

In the far corner of the room, where a pair of tall windows shed a strong northern light, she found a number of newly stretched canvases of different sizes and boxes of brushes, paints, charcoal, and chalk. A vase of flowers sat on the table beside the easel, a smock was draped across the back of the chair facing it. Helen put on the smock. Its soft cotton felt right on her, perhaps because the clothing had a function beyond modesty. She closed her eyes and drew Stephen into her mind, sending her thanks, receiving his quick response, his pleasure at how easily her mind reached him.

Staring at the canvas, Helen wondered what she should paint. One scene, one emotion eclipsed all the others. Now that she saw it there was no way she could avoid creating it.

She didn't reach for charcoal, only for prints and palette. She saw no need to sketch her work. The entire painting was fixed in her mind as surely as if the lines were already on the canvas.

She began.

A self-portrait—nothing anyone would recognize. She didn't need to be warned to avoid that. Instead her features were distorted, a cubist puzzle of old and new pieces and parts in-between. Confused. Reluctant. Anticipating. Her face through the flames of last night's ceremony. Her feelings from her changing a few days before.

Hours passed. The light began to dim but her new sight did not notice. She finished after dark. Without looking at her painting, she cleaned her brushes and her hands and left the workroom.

She thought she had created something magnificent. She was afraid to look and find the flaws.

On the sideboard in the main room were a bottle of wine and some glasses, kept no doubt for human friends. Without really thinking, she poured a glass. The taste astonished her, the aroma, the feel of the tannin on her tongue. When she realized she was also hungry for conventional human food, she wasn't surprised. Unlike Stephen whose throat was too narrow to swallow solid food and whose stomach would not digest anything beyond the simplest protein, her body was outwardly human. But her soul craved more—life. Life and blood.

And she was hungry in both respects.

She showered, not minding that the house had no hot water. Cold water no longer bothered her and it cleansed just as well. Through the sound of the shower and the silence of her mind, she sensed Stephen had come home.

—It's magnificent!— he told her. His praise held no surprise as if he'd always known she would be capable of this.

Helen dried off quickly, found the robe she'd discarded, and joined him. He sat on a work chair a few feet from her canvas still staring at it. She wanted to paint him as he looked right now, his long legs stretched out, his arms crossed, one hand with its thin, tapering fingers resting on his shoulder. His red cotton shirt and loose black pants were covered with dust and she saw a line of dirt along one pale cheek. He looked no more than twenty. Legally he was forty-one. Actually, he'd crossed a millennium two centuries ago.

"You'll be famous," he said.

"Is that wise?"

"Denys is famous. His paintings are displayed throughout the world. His name changes with the centuries, that's all."

"Is he still here?" she asked, hoping for a fellow painter's critique.

Stephen shook his head. "He only came for the ceremony. It would be awkward if someone recognized him. Most of Chaves believes he is dead."

"Weren't you planning to stage your own death soon?"

Laurence and Ann were already settled into their positions here and Laurence would be named director at the annual meeting. "If it weren't for you, I would never have come back," he replied. Sensing her need to stay with her new family, he added, "When I leave, you don't have to join me."

"I know."

But she wanted to stay with him, wanted it more than her new family or the fragile ties to the old one she had left behind in Ohio.

"Perhaps it is good that I returned," he added. "Laurie isn't ready to assume full director's duties. At least not yet. He is like Denys—obsessed with his art. With Denys it is painting. With Laurie, music."

"Or you with your church windows?"

"With my work—all of it, though the windows are the most satisfying part. I only wish the family could appoint Rachel as the firm's director. She deserves it more than any of us."

"Why can't you?"

"We attract enough attention for the age of our directors. We should not break new ground with sex, yes?"

"Not yet."

Stephen smiled. "Rachel tells me this as well. As soon as we can, we will gladly give her this honor. As for me, I can wait one more year for you to make your decision to stay or to leave with me. When you do, think of what you need, please."

"I promise." Helen stared at the painting again. "Maybe a year will be long enough," she said more to herself than to Stephen.

"Are you through for today?" he asked.

"I have no idea of what I'm going to do next," she confessed.

"Rachel sent a gift for you. Try it on while I wash off today's grime. Then we'll find inspiration, yes?"

"Stephen?"

"There's nothing to fear, no reason to apologize. When the night is over, you will understand."

He makes understanding sound like an order, she thought as she went to their bedroom to open Rachel's package. Inside was a tent dress of deep forest green. The soft cotton knit was lined in the bodice, cut in a deep V in the front with a woven leather belt that gave it a medieval touch. She put on her leather sandals and stared at herself in the mirror.

Tonight she would feed on some unknowing mortal, would steal his blood, leaving him with scarcely a memory. She could understand this, even accept it, if her change had been more dramatic. But outwardly she was still Helen Wells, still nineteen, shy and pathetically nervous. She bit the back of her hand in the fleshy part between thumb and forefinger and her pain was rewarded with only an indentation that quickly vanished. Yesterday, Elizabeth had offered to pull four molars so that the long sharp fangs would grow in their place. Helen had declined the half-serious offer. She didn't want any outward changes, at least not yet.

She looked at her palm, noticing that the skin that had formed over the blisters was paler than the rest of her hand. Would every wound make her less human? Something in that thought troubled her, and as had become her habit, she gripped the black crystal pendant on the chain around her neck. Its power was beyond anything she'd experienced in the pale blue stone her grandmother had given her a few months—a lifetime—ago. That had been part of a family window. This was part of the family itself—Charles Austra's ashes a tie to its past, its tragedies, its glory. And the tip, she noticed, had been made conveniently sharp.

III

They walked down the mountain on a narrow path leading around the glass house, the AustraGlass corporate building, the Colony where most of the workers lived. They continued taking a winding path through the trees to the isolated Portuguese mountain town of Chaves.

They did not speak as Stephen led her through narrowing streets, finally stepping down a flight of stairs into a small, crudely stuccoed café lit only by bare candles on each rough wooden table. Stephen exchanged some words in Romany with the swarthy barkeeper who took them to a seat against the back wall.

"This is as close to an Andalusian cave as you will find in all of Portugal," Stephen said, paying a barefoot girl of not more than ten who carried over a tray containing a carafe of water, a small bottle of wine, stone mugs, and a plate of coarse wheat bread and cheese.

Helen watched her leave, then commented sadly on her poverty. "They live as they choose," Stephen replied. "Her father owns this café. Later he will play the violin and you will know he could possess whatever he desired."

"And he desires this?"

"His family has food, shelter, and centuries of tradition. If you gave them one of our snug comfortable houses, they would break the windows to let in the air. They are as different from the complacent Spaniards in the houses around us as we are. Feel his emotions as he plays, sense the music in his soul, his ties to his family and his land."

"Of course," Helen replied, puzzled at Stephen's vehemence.

Vocal conversation ended as the gypsy began to play. He walked through the tables, gripping his violin with gnarled fingers that seemed to have curved to accommodate the violin's neck, the tips narrowed and calloused by the strings.

Stephen poured her wine, and as she sipped it, the warmth filled her. For the first time tonight, she relaxed, and let Stephen help her weave her thoughts with the old musician's and glimpse the source of his music—his old loves, his travels, his family, his beliefs.

As Helen sat, lost in the magnificence of the songs, desire began to grow. Not for the old man but for the emotions that gave his music its life. The hunger grew with it. She fought it back but it surfaced just long enough for the gypsy to sense it, miss a note, and pause, staring at her, caught by her eyes. She nodded and he walked slowly to her and, leaning against an empty neighboring table, played a soft Andalusian love song.

When he'd finished, he whispered something to her in Portuguese. She didn't know the words but the meaning was clear. "If I were only younger," he'd said.

—When the time comes, give him that.—

Startled, Helen looked at her lover, then back at the gypsy who had turned to play another song for another table.

"Leave a gift for what you take," Stephen said softly. "Then the ones you use remember only what you've given."

Later the old man joined them, sharing Helen's wine and food, telling stories about his children, all but the youngest grown and gone. As the patrons in the café dwindled to a few stubborn hangers-on, he joined Stephen and Helen outside, walking with them to the river that ran behind the café.

"You looked at me so strangely inside. What were you thinking?" Helen asked through Stephen.

"Of a woman I used to know."

"Do I resemble her?"

"No, but there's something about you." His old love's features formed in his mind, and with no real effort, Helen trapped his thought and directed it back to the day he had first made love to the woman under his wagon and the stars. Now he seemed to fall asleep where he stood and Helen lowered him slowly to the ground.

He smelled of sweat and wine but they were only undertones to the heady, perfect scent of his blood; his breathing scarcely a ripple compared to his pulse. She dreamed with him of love and youth and need, then, at the moment when she uncertainly thought she should drink, felt her pendant pressed in her hand. Stephen guided her, showing her where to cut.

At first she gagged, then relaxed as his life filled her. She became one with the man, yet still herself, viewing his life with an artist's eye. She shared his love for his family, his music, these magnificent mountains, the distant barren planes. Her lips shook as she pressed them against the wound. Sucked. Drank. All of it felt so odd, so beautiful she would have kept on forever but Stephen laid his hands on her shoulders and carefully pulled her away. As carefully, she unwound her mind from the gypsy's.

They left the old man sleeping on the riverbank. Later he

would wake and watch the town's lights play on the moving water, thinking of Helen and the vivid dream he'd had of his first love, never guessing that, for a moment, both had held him.

The next afternoon, Helen painted the scene most vivid in her mind—the old gypsy in his café, his twisted ancient fingers on the strings and bow, his young dark-eyed soul surrounded by the lines of age.

In the weeks that followed, Helen painted six more scenes from the old man's life. What critics would one day call the Andalusian Series was complete.

She began directing their late-night hunts, leading Stephen through the dark and silent Chaves streets, her mind moving outward, listening to the motion behind the stuccoed walls, seeking souls best suited to an artist's brush. They would crawl softly through open windows, stealing blood and visions. Helen lived a dozen lives in a matter of weeks, painting their desires and nightmares, their pasts and the futures they feared.

And Stephen went with her, quietly guarding her, watching her become so much a part of her new world yet so human in her enthusiasm. What he never sensed and she never revealed was her obsessive need to touch everyone she met, to open them and store their lives; and her fear that her human mind could not contain this much experience without bursting. She wanted to stop the hunts or at least slow down. She didn't know how. People had become her addiction, a way of holding on to the part of her that was rapidly slipping away.

IV

In the weeks after her changing, she wrote long letters to her uncle and young cousins in Ohio. She described the cities, the countryside, the firm, her work with an aloof and obsessive fixation on details.

Her uncle read them to his children. Carol, older, would sit entranced by her cousin's new life and the descriptions of the people, unfolding the hurried sketches Helen would send so she could later tape them on her bedroom wall. Alan listened more carefully, rarely smiling at anything Helen wrote. He had been closer to his cousin than any of them, and though the boy never spoke of it, Dick knew he missed her. Because Alan was a sensitive child, Dick suspected Alan also had guessed the obvious—Helen never mentioned how she felt because she wasn't happy, at least not yet.

At St. John's Church on Sundays, Dick would sit and, surrounded by the magnificent Austra windows Stephen had created a century ago, he would pray for her. She had moved beyond them all and praying was all he could do.

FIVE

Helen's days were as frenzied as her nights. She painted with an urgency Van Gogh would have admired and by the end of her second month in Chaves had completed a dozen major paintings.

She worked to a disciplined creative schedule. Rising in late morning, she would drink a glass of water and set to work. Hours later, she would break for a single meal.

Most any food would do though she preferred cold simple things the best. She might not have eaten at all but habit, and fear, required it. To not eat would mean one more break with her human past and an end to the unique symbiosis she had with Stephen. Though they hunted together, he could as easily live on her. She enjoyed his dependency and she didn't want to end the bond. She had lost enough of it already.

On cloudy days, she sometimes walked down the mountain to the AustraGlass offices. If Stephen were free, she would eat lunch in his office, though it seemed he was not entirely pleased with her interruption, the merging of his public and private lives. At other times, she would visit Laurence. He made her more welcome as they sat and shared their mutual concerns about the new lives each of them had so recently acquired.

On sunny days, she stayed indoors, unwilling to face rays that had, since her changing, become painful to her skin and eyes and seemed to pull the strength from her body. And there was always food in the kitchen. She never saw the delivery person though sometimes she would sense a presence in early morning while she slept. Later, she would discover fresh rolls or bread on the table, washed laundry neatly folded ready to be put away.

Curiosity finally got the better of her, and Helen pulled herself awake and surprised a girl sweeping the kitchen.

"Oh!" the girl exclaimed when she heard Helen speak. She whirled, fright fading to embarrassment as she saw who stood behind her.

The girl was about thirteen, a little older than Helen's cousin in Ohio. Her curly auburn hair was tied at the nape of her neck. Her complexion was olive, her eyes hazel with green flecks. Already beautiful, someday she'd be striking. "Are you the one who keeps everything so neat?" Helen asked slowly, not certain the girl understood English.

"Yes. I am Hillary Dutiel."

"French and English?" Helen asked, trying to place her accent.

Hillary shrugged, a gesture carrying sophistication beyond her years. "My mother was Portuguese. But she liked the English."

"Well, Hillary, it's early but I think I want some breakfast. Will you have something?" When the girl looked uncertain, Helen added, "I like to know who's taking care of me."

"I must be at school at nine," the girl replied uneasily.

"Well, you have almost an hour. You can finish tomorrow."

"I am sorry. I shouldn't."

She looked so anxious, Helen decided not to push her. "Well then, go. But come back when you have some time and talk to me. Do you promise?"

Hillary nodded and put away the broom and the smock she had used to cover her shapeless brown dress. As she walked past Helen leaning against the table, she brushed Helen's arm, pulled quickly back, and flushed. Her embarrassment had deepened to something not easily ignored. "Good-bye," Hillary mumbled and left without looking back.

After the girl had gone, Helen sat with one stolen vision

in her mind—herself naked on her bed, her body bathed in the rainbows of morning drifting through the room.

She watches me when I sleep, Helen thought. *Am I so attractive even to a child?*

That evening Stephen came home to find her sitting on the sofa, her feet curled under her. One of the firm's old ledgers lay facedown on her lap and she held a pencil and a small notepad. "I can glance at a page and remember every number," she said triumphantly. She had mastered one more Austra power.

He sat on the other end of the sofa, his legs crossed facing her, and motioned toward the bookshelf. "And those?"

"Words are easier. They make sense."

"And how was the rest of the day?"

She hesitantly told Stephen about meeting Hillary and what she'd sensed at the end. He didn't seem surprised. "I always leave before she arrives. I've watched you while you sleep. She won't notice anything unusual."

Shocked by his pragmatism, Helen retorted, "Stephen! She's just a child. I want her hours changed. She can come in the afternoon."

"Then she will watch you while you're awake. Everyone watches you. Why should the girl be immune?"

She stared at him in stunned silence. She hadn't known.

"You are a child yourself. You want everything. Everyone. How can any mortal resist you? You walk into the Austra offices and all work halts until you leave."

"I'm sorry," she said. "I didn't know what I was doing."

"Sorry!" He realized he hadn't explained himself well. He tried again. "This attraction is now a necessary part of your nature. When we are together, I control it for both of us. Your mind is strong. Control will come with time."

"Teach me," she demanded. She didn't blame him or herself. She simply wanted to learn.

"Very well. The glass workers are having a dance in the Colony tonight. I think we should go. Then, if you are able, you should hunt alone."

"Will it be crowded?" Since her changing she had avoided large groups, the commotion of so many minds.

"Before you can control human desire you must feel it clearly. AustraGlass owns the Colony. Many of the family will be there and they will help you if you call to them. I don't believe you will need them."

"And the hunting?" She tried to hide the fear.

He took her hands. "Understand that this is the hardest advice I will ever give you. When I am in exile as I was when I met you, I take my victims where I will and wipe their minds afterward. The danger adds a certain excitement to the act but it is better here that you find a human partner, one who knows and understands your needs. It is more satisfying and far safer than the youthful games we've been playing, yes?"

"You've been enjoying them," Helen challenged without real malice.

"Of course. It's been many years since I've felt this young, or this reckless. Now put on something beautiful while I wash the soot off my skin."

Helen chose the red peasant skirt she'd bought in Cleveland, a loose gold cotton blouse and wide orange sash. She studied the effect in the mirror, noting how the black teardrop hung between her breasts drawing attention to them. She began to tie back her long hair and changed her mind. She looked freer with it down though its white-blond color made her face far too pale. She smoothed some rouge on her cheeks, added lipstick, and decided she looked better.

In the mirror, she saw Stephen behind her and turned to face him. He wore a red satin shirt with a deep V-neck and long loose sleeves to hide the unnatural length of his arms. Usually, his pants were as loose and as comfortable but tonight he had chosen black leather that hugged his calves and thighs, showing how muscled they were, and black boots that accented the length of his legs. Always handsome, now he looked magnificent; as attractive as he dared to be with people who did not share his secret.

"Stephen, who are your willing victims?" she asked in a honeyed tone.

"My secretary. Emma has been raised by our family,

which makes her ideal. We have a friendship, nothing more. The second is our head of corporate security. His blood strengthens our mental ties, which has proven useful more than once. The third is the madame of the brothel in Chaves.''

"Do you pay her?''

"Primarily for her discretion.'' He quickly added, "I haven't seen Amalia since I brought you to Chaves.''

So recently monogamous, yet he had just suggested she take a lover! Perhaps he sensed that she would be jealous if he used another willing woman. In that he'd most likely be right. "Stephen,'' she began, then halted before finding the right words to say. "I want you to know that whenever you do, I will try to judge it by what we are, not by how I've been raised.''

He kissed her on the forehead and said, "You knew this time would come. Most of the Colony knows nothing about us. They think you are a friend visiting from America, which makes you free to do no more or less than you wish.'' Though he tried to hide his sadness, she sensed it as he added, "And whatever you do, I will understand.''

The Colony held their dance in their largest café. Even that was so crowded that the doors were left open so people could dance in the street if they wished. As they approached the café, Helen sensed the size and youth of the crowd. They wore incredible mixes of color, the women's skirts and blouses were accented with lace, their hair tied up with ribbons. She had not been in a group this large since her changing and the laughter and thoughts mingled with the spoken words created a clamor that deafened her. She stopped on the edge of the crowd, trembling. When she called to Stephen, her words were muffled, one more part of the din. He moved closer to her, taking her hand for reassurance, leading her through the dancers and into the café. As they walked through the crowd, Helen felt the silence move out from her like waves from a stone tossed into a pool.

It wasn't that the music had stopped or the conversation ended, but the attention of the players and audience became riveted on her and Stephen. No one else in the room mattered anymore. The strength of their combined desire made Helen giddy and she stared straight ahead because if she didn't, her eyes would dart from one face to another. She felt naked, helpless, violated, and she saw them all, crawling over her, rippling her apart. Her mind responded with a single great —NO!—

The noise, spoken and mental, increased. People still looked at her, but the intensity of their emotion had vanished. Somehow she had made people forget their desire.

She sensed Stephen's approval. "It is instinct. It cannot be taught. Now dance with me," he said.

She didn't know how she had muted her attraction nor how long she could maintain the mental command, but for the moment she felt safe. She and Stephen swayed with the dancers, hardly more noticed than any of the others. When the music stopped, Stephen's secretary came to say hello to her. After their brief conversation, Helen discovered that Stephen had vanished. She sensed him nearby. His presence gave confidence enough.

Helen scanned the crowd and saw Hillary Dutiel on the edge of it, stretching to be taller than she was, looking more anxious than she had this morning. Helen made her way to Hillary's side and asked, "Is anything wrong?" She stood close to Hillary as she spoke and felt as well as saw the heat of embarrassment spread across the girl's face.

Thinking herself safe in the dim, crowded room, Hillary chose to ignore it. "I am looking for Papa," she said. "He promised he would only come here for a little while. He shouldn't have come at all. He's been sick."

"Do you see him?"

Hillary studied the dance floor and the tables, finally concentrating on one dark section. "In the back near the bar," she whispered without pointing. "He's there."

"Shall I come with you?" Helen asked.

"Please. He won't listen to me. Maybe if you talk to him."

As Helen followed Hillary along the edge of the dance floor and through the tables, Hillary's father noticed them coming. He was alone, sprawled at a table in the darkest corner of the room. An empty wine bottle sat in front of him along with an almost full glass.

He was attractive enough for a man twice her age and Helen sensed a certain smugness in the way he watched her. She looked directly at him and brushed his mind. Yes, he would be one of the safe choices. He knew exactly what she'd become.

She returned his inviting smile as she and Hillary took empty seats on either side of him.

"Are you prowling, Helen Wells?" he asked, his voice so soft she wouldn't have heard his words before her changing, the tone of his voice combined with his French accent to make the question sound like a lovers' secret. He held out his left hand, and as she took it, she noticed his right arm was missing. He'd positioned himself in the room so this would not be seen, though in a place as intimate as the AustraGlass Colony, everyone must have known about . . . about. She tried to touch his mind and failed.

"Please don't," he said, whispering close to her ear now so Hillary wouldn't hear. "If we're going to share the intimate details of my life, I prefer to edit them through speech."

She wondered if he always talked so softly. She imagined him when he was younger, whispering to his would-be conquests so they would have to move close to him to listen, close enough to steal a kiss. "You have me at a disadvantage," she said and asked, "You are?"

"Philippe Dutiel." He turned to his daughter. "Hillary, go ask the bartender for another bottle and two more glasses."

"Papa!"

"Go!" he ordered and the girl, flushed and angry, obeyed.

"She's worried about you," Helen said. "She said you've been ill."

"She always worries. It gives her something to do."

"Is her mother here?"

"Her mother died."

"I'm sorry."

"No sympathy, please. I only knew the woman for one night. One night was enough."

"Who was she?" Helen asked.

"Whores shouldn't have names."

Direct. So direct he almost seemed rude. Helen envied him for that. "If you never knew her, why does Hillary live with you?" she asked.

"The woman died early last year. She named me as father. Someone gave the girl some money and sent her to me on the train."

Helen tried to picture Hillary traveling all alone with her grief to a man who, if Helen perceived correctly, didn't care about her. "Do you think you're her father?" Helen asked. Though she saw a family resemblance, she almost hoped he'd say no.

Philippe shrugged, a gesture much like Hillary's. "Probably. She looks like me. Besides, the whore would have made up a better name." Noting Helen's shocked expression, he added, "Though I only used her once, I remember her. She was my first lay after I lost my arm. She laughed when I put on the condom. I was so clumsy. I'd never done it left-handed before. My stump was still raw. There was blood on the sheets from it when we were through . . . and semen where she wanted it least. She swore at me for both the blood and the break. I remember thinking that she deserved her uneasy nights. Thirteen years later, I discovered I had a daughter. How am I supposed to feel?"

"Perhaps thankful. Some people never have anyone to love," she said, an automatic but sincere cliché.

"I destroyed my own family. One was enough."

"She's quite a worker for someone so young." Helen meant the compliment. She tried to picture her niece Carol up at dawn to clean someone else's house. Never!

"She's intelligent enough to know that she ought to go to school and that I can't give her the money." For the first time, Helen detected some paternal pride in Philippe's voice until he added, "I suppose she gets her ambition from her mother."

"Why are you so hard on her?"

"I'll tell you why because you'll probably dig around until you find out anyway. If I were her age and we weren't related,

I'd be all over her. As it is, I have trouble thinking of her as a relation, let alone my daughter.''

Helen noticed Hillary returning with the wine and moved the conversation in a different direction. ''Have you been that lonely?'' she asked.

''I'm a romantic. I have dreams. Do you pity me, Helen Wells?''

''I don't know,'' she said. ''Maybe I should. Or maybe I should assume this is some sort of complicated seduction.''

''No, just the truth disguised as a convenient lie. Besides you're the one seducing me. Isn't seduction the Austra game?'' He filled the new glasses, then his own, put down the bottle, and handed one glass to Helen, then held out the second for his daughter. Hillary refused to take it, staring at him with stony disapproval. ''That's good wine,'' he bellowed. ''Show some respect for your French blood!''

A few faces at other tables turned to see what the commotion was about, then returned to their own conversations. Hillary, her eyes filling with tears, lifted her glass, tasted the wine, and shuddered. Apparently satisfied, Philippe turned his attention back to Helen.

As Helen sipped her wine, her control began to weaken. The din in the room increased. The bodies added to her confusion. She noticed their scents, their heartbeats, her own desire. She put down her glass too quickly and it fell, spilling the wine. She didn't care. Panicked, uncertain, she began a mental call to Stephen, then halted, understanding. She could handle this problem herself. All she had to do was leave the café and stay away until her head cleared. ''I'll take Hillary home,'' she said, surprised at how evenly she could speak. Phil drained his glass and grabbed the bottle. ''I think I'll call it a night myself,'' he said and followed the two women outside.

Stephen had heard the beginning of Helen's cry, merged with her thoughts for a moment, then withdrew. Her courage, her independence, made him strangely sad. No matter how the night ended, Helen would never be completely his again.

He wove his way around the edge of the dancers, pulling

Emma onto the floor, hiding his concern. Alex Massier was here. There were others in the crowd who also knew Helen's secret. Any would be safer than Philippe Dutiel. The anger in the man troubled him, as did Philippe's long-standing dislike of him. He dismissed the worry, thinking that he probably wouldn't wholly approve of any independent choice Helen made. He wanted so much to control her and now he tried so desperately to let her go.

As he watched Helen leave with the Dutiels, he thought it strange that he no longer wanted another woman. Coming home each evening, he would find a new surprise in paint on canvas, would share whatever joys and frustrations her work and his had brought, or just sit without need of speech and hold her. He did not cherish these things any longer; rather, he expected them.

Perhaps it was habit that made him so possessive of her. Yes, that must be what made her different from the rest of his family. He never considered romantic love. Familial love—that he knew—but centuries of experience had convinced him that he was incapable of any other.

SIX

1

The Dutiels' cottage lay on the edge of the Colony. It seemed older than the rest of the buildings. Someone had remodeled it, adding the modern necessities pouring time into finishing the old beams and floors, repairing the plaster, and sealing the cracks in the outside wood. But that had been done years ago and the house once more showed neglect. There were new cracks in the plaster, windows in need of repair. But everything a child could do had been done. The worn fabric in the furniture had been sewn, the floors and woodwork sparkled.

Hillary, clearly unaccustomed to being up so late, said good night immediately. Helen was about to do the same when Paul thrust a glass into her hand, spilling some of its wine on her skirt. She went into the kitchen to dab water on the stain and Phil followed her, politely keeping his distance. "Don't go just yet, Helen Wells. Enjoy the silence first."

"The silence?"

"I saw how you looked when you came into the café tonight, like you were standing under an icy waterfall. Take a break from the burden the Austras have thrust upon you. Forget your work and all their lessons. Be young for a while. Be irresponsible."

For the first time that night, Helen glimpsed the man Philippe Dutiel had once been and she smiled. "I suppose you're good at that."

42

"Good! I used to be a master of irresponsibility. Then I acquired a daughter. Thank God her disease isn't contagious." He drained his glass and poured another, walked into the next room and sat on a chair arm.

He looked at Helen standing in the kitchen doorway, at her disapproving expression. "You're a lot like Hillary, you know. No wonder she's so infatuated that she talks about you constantly. I think she just wants to be an adult too soon while you're trying to be a thousand years old."

Helen put her glass next to the sink. "I think I'd better leave," she said coldly and started to walk past him.

He grabbed her wrist and she stopped midstride. "Let me go!" Helen ordered, strengthening her words with a simple mental command. Neither worked. Instead, he pressed her against the wall and kissed her. She wanted to push him away but pity stopped her, then something more, much more.

She saw herself through his eyes, felt his mind open to her. He was awake. He knew what she was, yet he wanted to give. So perfectly right; so clearly what human partners were for.

Half-formed instincts warned her to leave. There were other possibilities and any would be better than this man. She didn't want to share his bitterness, to devour his pain.

"If you must go at least do me the honor of staying for one more drink," he said and smiled.

She rested a hand on the side of his face. She wanted him—blood, need, soul. As she kissed him again, she sensed the joy deep within him buried beneath losses far more complex than his arm. She would touch that joy and make it surface; this would be the gift she left him tonight. As she knelt beside him, she tried to convince herself that she need do no more than she had done before.

"No tricks, Helen Wells," he said. "Just promise me that."

He kissed her again and she was rocked by a passion whose purity astonished her. Every carefully ordered vision she had given the others would only be a distraction now. She devoured his need for her and found it inexplicably growing. At last, convinced that she would destroy him completely if she continued, she pulled away. He looked less damaged than puzzled by her sudden recoil.

"Enough," she whispered when he asked what was wrong. His blood seemed too potent, a heady addictive drink she could consume until there was no life in him left to give.

Well after midnight, she left Phil sleeping in his bed and padded through the four small rooms of his cottage, reveling in the efficiency of her new night vision as she roamed through the dark. Hillary slept in a narrow room off the kitchen. A woman's photograph was tacked onto the wall above her bed. A crucifix hung beside it as if this juxtaposition could give rest to her mother's soul. Hillary moaned in her sleep and mumbled something in Portuguese. As Helen had done with her cousins not so long ago, she moved to Hillary's bedside, intending to give a consoling brush of her hand on the girl's back, a calming mental touch. At the last moment, she pulled back, not wanting to startle the girl, but let the mental bond form.

And folded slowly to the floor, her legs pressed against her chest, her arms hugging them, as if by protecting her body, Helen could somehow shield her mind from the abuse and the evil she shared. Sold and used and sold again. No wonder Phil was attracted by his daughter. His instincts told him what the girl had been too ashamed to admit.

It would be so easy to feed on Hillary, to merge with her and dull the sharpest edges of her memory, but Helen's instincts warned her back. There were feelings she must not touch—magnificent in their intensity, poisonous in their pain.

"You become what you take," Stephen had warned. He hadn't needed to say anything at all. Helen left Hillary with one quick mental suggestion, then silently retreated from the room, from the house, from the town, and walked slowly up the mountain toward home.

Even before she crossed the low stone wall separating the private Austra estates from the rest of the AustraGlass property, she sensed Stephen waiting for her. She adjusted the belt on her dress, ran her fingers through her tangled hair.

Concealing her thoughts as best she could, she walked into the house past where he sat waiting. She reached out to touch him, then pulled back. Touching would strengthen their bond and she only wanted to hide.

He stood and walked to the open door and looked out at the trees and sky, his long arms stretched above his head, fingers hooked into the molding. Her spider. Her web.

Helen fell into a chair beside the oak table and buried her face in her hands. "I'm so sorry," she whispered.

"Don't," he said harshly without looking at her. "Don't ever apologize for what you are. Especially not to me."

"You expected it, though. You wanted to hear me say I was sorry."

"Tske!" He hissed the denial in his own language, then sat on the table beside her, reaching down to pick a piece of leaf from her hair. "You should be smiling, laughing, telling me how much you enjoyed him. You did enjoy him, yes?"

"Yes . . . no. I don't know. There's something so sad about him."

"What you should have felt when you met him was need. What you should have received was life. None of the rest was necessary."

"Even sex?"

"He didn't force you. He could not."

"Couldn't! He knew. Do you think there was any way to avoid what happened?"

"He's good at arousing guilt. And pity, yes?"

"I never thought about myself; I wasn't raised to think about myself," she said honestly. "But I have to be that way now, don't I? Cautious. Secretive. Alone."

"Yes. But you have the family. I brought you here to learn from them."

"And now they make it harder for me. I feel like I have a dozen extra people inside of me and every one of them is giving me different advice. That would be confusing in itself but I don't even know who I am." She felt her anger rising, took a deep, calming breath, and went on. "Once you were my teacher, and while I resented being treated like a child, I always understood what you wanted. That isn't true anymore.

Now you don't state things clearly and when I do what I think you're suggesting, you get angry."

"Not at you. Never you. I only find it infuriating that I must teach you the very things that will draw you away from me."

"How can you be so sure?"

"Because my family cannot live on one another. And what we take from the humans we use binds us to them so tightly we no longer wish to be intimate with one another. Our mental ties are strong but our sexual bonds are frail at best. Only on nights when we have blood rituals or on occasional isolated hunts when the lust of the kill excites us do we ever have sex with one another. Then it is magnificent because the passion unites us all."

Helen had already sensed this. Since her changing, Stephen had lost much of his allure. Except for the night of the family bonding, sex had become satisfying but mechanical, as if they had shared fifty good years together. She didn't want to accept this truth especially when, at the core of it, lay some incredible contradiction she could only glimpse. "And when you have children, what then?" she asked.

"Sometimes a couple will live together for years before the woman conceives but it is a joining for convenience. After the woman gives birth and dies, the children are raised by the father with the help of all of us. That has been our way . . . and our curse." He stood beside her and took her hands. "Until now."

Though she wanted to hold him, the shame of what she'd done was still too strong in her. Knowing it was foolish, she stood and forced herself into his arms. Once there, she relaxed, rubbing her cheek against his black silk shirt, smelling the melange of scents, all the people he had danced with, all the ones who had brushed against him in the crowded café, the unique musky perfume of his skin . . . and overpowering it all the reek of Philippe's sweat and semen on her body.

Though he fought his jealousy, the emotion was too new, too strong, and he could not hide it from her. He gripped her arms when, frightened, she tried to push him away, ignored the stab of her nails in his shoulders as he moved down her body. Her shame turned to anger when, exasperated with her struggles, he pulled her down beside him, trapped her body with his mind, and pushed her limp legs apart.

—Stephen, please!—

—Quiet, my love. This is nothing I haven't tasted before.—

He devoured her shame, her anger, and as her hands clawed the carpet and her back arched and she begged him to stop what he was doing, move up and enter her, she felt him bite—and passion, Philippe's passion, flowed through her and into him.

And all the while, she heard his challenge in her mind. —Where is apology in this? Why should there be guilt in what you feel, in the passion you can force a mortal to give?—

She almost believed him, almost, but the more he forced her to feel, the closer she came to the truth until, furious, pushed beyond even her new endurance, she broke free of his mental hold, kicked him away, and bolted for the door. At the portal, she turned back to him and screamed the reply, "You make me feel guilt. You!" and ran into the comfort of the darkness.

When she realized he didn't intend to follow, she slowed her pace to a walk and wandered through the dense woods of the Austra estates, oblivious to her torn and soiled dress, to the blood seeping slowly down her thighs. Though she did not see another of the family, she sensed them around her, knowing she wished privacy and keeping their distance. And inaudibly weaving through it, she heard Laurie's music as if this place where he did not wish to be had already become his domain.

But not hers. Not yet. And not Stephen's, not any longer. He only stayed because of her.

She returned to their house and found Stephen standing on the catwalk, looking down at the valley below, waiting for her. "I am sorry," he began, clearly uncomfortable with this apology. "I don't understand the emotions inside of me. If I did, I could control them, but, believe me, I have no wish to hurt you."

"I understand how you feel, Stephen. It's not even a new

feeling to you. No, it's too akin to when one hunter steals another's prey.''

"You're not that to me," he said so softly she knew he had never considered her that way.

"No, I am your lover, your almost human lover, and no bloody birth into immortality, no ritual bonding with the family, can change that, not until I have the courage to accept what I have become. I see it clearly now. I understand. In all those years at home I would hear 'No, Helen' and 'Thank you, Helen. You're so good to us, Helen.' And then I became ill and crippled and all the restraints that society orders broke down. I could be independent because no man would ever want to make me his possession. I could try to be famous because I would die young. Then you came and said I could be immortal. I understand this. What I am accepts this. But I wasn't raised to be powerful. Women never are.''

Helen paused before asking, "Stephen, what would happen if I did not live on human life?''

"In time you would forget what it is like to be human.''

"Is that so wrong?''

"My father survives that way. One of our women does also. I understand her decision but I think she has lost too much. People are more than food to us. They are the texture of our lives.''

"And we're their fantasies," Helen said softly, then added, "I'm still partly human. I might not suffer any loss.''

"Even my father can walk among men when he must," he said evenly. He dared not hint what vow he wanted. Her choice must be her own.

She held out her hand and, for the first time, showed him the pale patch of skin on her palm. "If I lose my eyes, what color will they be when they grow back?''

When he didn't reply, she added, "And if I am ever damaged inside, will I lose the human ability you all need so much?''

"You could have children and raise them here.''

"No, Stephen. If I don't go with you soon, our cycles of work and exile will never merge completely. We'll face an eternity of good-byes.'' She smiled sadly and reached for his hand, then spoke slowly in his language trying to inflect each syllable as precisely as the shape of her mouth and throat would allow, "You are my chosen, the one who will be father to my children," then added in English, "my husband, for as long as you desire it."

She sensed the tension draining from him as she made this vow, replaced by an old sorrow. There were no words in his language to describe all of her future with him. "You are my chosen," he began in the Austra feminine inflection, "who will be mother to my children." And added in English, "My wife, for as long as you desire it."

"When we leave, take me to a place where there are no people to distract me and remind me of my past. I want to paint the trees and the mountains and the sky the way a deer sees them."

All the Austra family felt this call to throw off the sham of humanity. To run. To hunt. He hadn't expected to see the need surface in Helen yet.

Helen sensed his thoughts. "It's not need; just desire to discover exactly what I am. Then you can be my teacher again. But first you must give me a little time to be nineteen and healthy and almost human; to make a fool out of myself with Philippe or Alex, with anyone I wish. And to become famous. After I die, I want everyone to remember my name."

He shook his head. "That isn't wise, Helen. Unlike the rest of our kind, you have a past—a real one—and it could endanger you."

"We'll destroy all my photographs and break all but the closest ties. Then I'll be no different than Denys or Laurie. You see, I want my family to inherit my estate. Fame will be my gift to them." She imitated his frequent pragmatic tone, "Works of dead artists are worth more, yes?"

He could hardly deny her this brief moment of recognition, especially since she would never have another like it again. So he ignored his uneasiness and asked, "Can you be ready for your first major show in nine months?"

Understanding what he really asked, she considered her response before answering confidently. "Six. Six, and then it will be over."

11

The next morning Hillary stripped off her nightshirt and an-gled her wall mirror so she could study her body. She looked at it, front and back, with a complete lack of any emotion other than detached loathing. Then she put on her baggy clothes, picked up a pin, and moved her face in closer to the mirror. As she stared at her eyes, she thought of her mother and scratched the pin again and again over one cheek until the scratch bled. Satisfied, she took an apple from the table and headed toward school. Though she tried not to think of how she'd stared at her body in the mirror, her mind kept returning to it. She hoped that whatever unknown need had created that moment of curiosity would never surface again.

Later that day, she received a message from Helen asking that she come to the house after school. There she found Helen in her studio, a large canvas mounted on her easel. "I want you to be my subject," Helen told her, not giving the girl an opportunity to refuse. Then, instead of posing her, Helen sat and talked with Hillary, discussing the girl's life in the Colony and her plans for the future. Through Hillary's hesitant answers, Helen glimpsed more of her past. She wanted to dismiss the girl and begin the painting with Hil-lary's face as it looked now, all hope and quiet ambition, barely showing the horror of her earlier years, but simple beauty wouldn't be enough.

Helen wanted her masterpiece.

As they talked, Helen's mind captured the girl, carefully so as not to startle her. In a moment, Hillary sat, her hands folded in her lap, her eyes closed, her body numb and ordered to stay numb until Helen released her. Helen moved behind the girl, making a small cut on Hillary's shoulder, drawing out the blood, strengthening the mental bond between them.

One year, the last year should be enough.

But it wasn't. Helen demanded more, pulling the child through all the years of neglect and abuse until, shaking, sobbing, the girl broke the bond and fainted.

Helen carried Hillary into the great room and put her on the sofa ordering her into a deep healing sleep. Then she sat in a chair across from Hillary and stared at her, re-forming the bond between them as she began to build the portrait in her mind.

The horror Helen had shared vanished. The pain. Even the guilt. What remained was apprehension. Helen didn't know if she had the skill to paint something so subtle, so terrible, so beautiful.

Helen had never been this obsessed with a single work. Hillary's painting became as much a test of her new powers as her skill. Sometimes she would sit for an hour staring at the canvas before making a single stroke. Weeks passed while she worked on the large painting, layering Hillary's life on the canvas until it matched as perfectly as possible the picture in Helen's mind. When she thought she had finished, she stored the canvas and worked on other projects with the same attention to every small detail.

She stopped only for sleep and food and for those infrequent times when the need for blood and passion forced her down the mountain to surprise a delighted Philippe Dutiel. Now that she had made her decision to leave, Stephen paid little attention to where she spent her nights. As for Helen, she easily rationalized the affair with Philippe. She needed him. When she left here, they would break for good. She told him that, even told him why she would go.

Afterward, they never spoke of it.

SEVEN

1

AustraGlass shut down a week before Christmas. The Colony pensions closed, owners and renters alike going off for a three-week holiday. Hillary left with Jean Savatier's family to act as a helper for their three little girls but Helen was too busy to notice her absence. The Austra family—the exiles and those who worked elsewhere in the world—came home. Intimate friends of the family—those who shared the Austra secret—came home as well. The Colony became freer; the Austra family more open, allowing Helen a brief, bittersweet glimpse of how their shared world ought to be.

On the night before the winter solstice, the only traditional Austra celebration, Paul and Elizabeth held their holiday reception in the only place large enough to accommodate the crowd—the Austra corporate offices that separated the Colony from the estates. The couple kept Helen close to them as they greeted their guests, reminding her that though it was their party, she was the honored one tonight.

The Austra family provided a brilliant contrast to the often staid evening attire of the human guests. There was Laurence in a wine velvet vest and slacks over a richly draped pale blue satin shirt; William, from Italy, in a chestnut jacket lavishly embroidered with gold. Madeline, ignoring all evening convention, wore a peach riding habit. Stephen had dressed in what seemed Austra ceremonial best—steel grey suede pants

and vest and the beaded green shirt Helen liked so well.
Helen had dressed more simply—in an embroidered peasant
skirt and scoop-necked black top. She had French-braided her
hair in a single long plait down her back and the Austra pendant was her own jewelry. It had all the significance of a
wedding ring, she thought, and she felt like a bride as she
stood beside Stephen, shook strangers' hands, and hugged
family members she had not met before. She was amazed at
how, through the often fleeting introductions and the subtle
prying questions that accompanied them, she could simply
touch a hand and feel such empathy.

"You share a bond with them," Elizabeth explained to her
as they walked outside with Paul later that evening. "Many
of them are our lovers. Their blood mingles in all of us,
creating a sort of extended family. Do you see?"

"Yes, I see."

"Why do you look so thoughtful?" Elizabeth asked.

"When I look at you and Paul, I think of how Stephen and
I might have been together had I been merely human."

"Then you would have been born different than you were.
Someone less magnetic, less talented. Someone he might have
never even noticed, *oui*? And I will tell you something else
and it may surprise you—most of our men never have human
lovers in the sense that I have Paul." She affectionately
squeezed Paul's arm. "Of course, they take partners and many
have known the truth about them but it isn't the same as a
lasting relationship. Perhaps this is our way of satisfying our
maternal instincts." She smiled, then laughed, brightening
the conversation. "Paul certainly needs taking care of."

"You do?" Helen asked him with a coy smile.

"Elizabeth tells me that I work too hard. That I worry far
too much. That I often forget to eat . . ."

"And that sometimes his only exercise comes in bed,"
Elizabeth cut in and kissed her embarrassed lover on the
cheek. Though Elizabeth tried to sound light, Helen sensed
the fear. "We don't think about our future," Elizabeth added
in a more somber tone. "That is your luxury."

When they reached the fork in the road that led toward the

Colony, Helen stared down the road, then suggested they return to the party.

"We could walk down to the Colony and force Philippe to come back with us?" Elizabeth suggested.

Helen noticed Paul shake his head. "He's made his choice for tonight," Helen said. "And I have made mine."

With a faster pace than Paul's stiff knee could tolerate, she walked ahead of them toward the tiny colored lights, the soft voices, and the music.

And as she entered through the tall doors of colored glass and saw Stephen already weaving his way through the crowd to meet her, she realized that she really didn't care whether or not Philippe came.

11

As Helen suspected, Philippe intended to spend the holidays alone, a brooding bitter rival of the family who owned his house, controlled his livelihood, and, when he was honest enough to admit it, had saved his life.

He had received his usual invitations and declined them all. When Paul Stoddard visited the afternoon of the solstice, Philippe let him come inside reluctantly. He didn't want to speak to anyone except Helen, but he and Paul were old friends and it had been months since they'd seen each other. "Pardon the mess, the maid is absent," he said with a trace of his old, good-natured humor.

"It doesn't look any worse than your room did in our pension," Paul replied, following the remark with an uneasy laugh.

Philippe rinsed out a glass and poured Paul some wine. "We want you to come to the ceremony tonight," Paul said as he took it.

"We?"

"Elizabeth and I."

"And Helen?"

"She already asked you, didn't she?"

"And our monarch, what does he think?"

"Stephen suggested I talk to you," Paul answered.

"So I did guess right, hmmm? No, I prefer to stay here. Helen will come to me. The Austras survive on their lovers, after all."

"You fool! You can't be Stephen's rival. You'd be better off if you were his friend."

"Would you be his friend if you had to share Elizabeth with him?"

"Yes," Paul answered with no hesitation and added, "someday I will share her with someone. My relationship with Elizabeth has lasted because I accept it. Don't force Helen to choose between you and Stephen. If you do, you'll lose her."

"Go home to your lover, Paul. I'll stay here and wait for mine."

"She won't come. Not tonight."

"I'll wait and see."

Paul had set his glass on the kitchen table and turned to go when Philippe grabbed his arm. "I'm sorry, Paul," he said and added, "Have you ever known me not to make a fool of myself over a beautiful woman?"

"Never," Paul said. He looked at Philippe hopefully. "Is that all this relationship is—you making a fool of yourself again?"

"I wish," Philippe replied. "But the truth is, for the first time in my life, I think, I'm in love, and as I always expected, I made the worst possible choice. And the fact is, now that I've finally attained this miserable state, I intend to wallow in it."

Philippe did. He waited that night with his doors and windows open, sitting in a chair, staring up at the fires on the mountaintop, hearing the faint music drifting down, a melody perfectly suited to the stars and the cold . . . a throbbing chant in celebration of the Long Night.

As, still upright in his chair, he fell asleep, he thought he heard her voice, felt the brush of her mind in his. But it was only the beginning of a dream—erotic and almost satisfying.

Helen had touched him, intending to call to him, to beg him to come. Sensing his stubborn resolve, she pulled quickly back. This was a family ritual, their highest celebration, and she would not be torn away from the family by her lover's jealousy and need. With only a slight effort of her will, she pushed him from her mind and concentrated on the ceremony, sharing the cup as it passed around the circle, drinking the mingled blood of the family, reaching for the hands of those beside her, joining minds with all of them.

Her last sharing had been one of initiation. Now, one of them, she shared the collective family memories, ancient and new, the building of the keep above the Varda Pass, the family exodus, the rising of cathedrals and palaces, the triumphs and the tragedies, her mind sharing each memory, becoming part of the whole. She stored it, every detail, to be recalled and slowly savored on some empty night.

The voices! The faces! The magic of it filled her, until she could no longer contain it. She exploded like the others into a song, rising, falling, dancing with the flames, scarcely noticing when the physical bonds broke and their human loves and friends stepped forward and shared their past.

Later, when the ritual had ended and the circle had broken into small groups, Helen went home. Her mind seemed universal now, a part of the family not quite her own. This was the moment she'd waited for. She pulled out Hillary's painting for one final detached appraisal.

And could find no flaws.

The nude, "The Border of Woman," had an almost universal effect on its viewers. It showed a girl who had seen too much, endured too much, and now tried to hold on to her tattered innocence while being thrust into adulthood by the biology of time. She faced the future as she had the horror of her past—with confidence and determination in her wide-spaced hazel eyes.

Helen hid the painting from Hillary. She wisely knew the effect it would have on the girl but she never anticipated the effect it would have on adults. Men could not help but look at it and desire the woman Hillary had almost become. Yet the body was unmistakably that of a child and her protective modest pose made their desire shameful. The expression was frightened and sad as if the subject knew every emotion she aroused and dreaded them.

Helen was forced to remove it from her London exhibit. The American Gallery that would sponsor her New York show was given a preview look at it along with a number of other paintings. The owners were universally enthusiastic in their reception of the nude, making it the focal point of their publicity.

After the London showing, Helen and Stephen visited Alpha, the Austra subsidiary in Ireland. While Stephen had his final meetings with the Alpha managers, Helen took long walks through the hills, reveling in the cloudy spring weather, the smell of moss, and the sea. From there, they flew to America—to fame, to death.

III

One hope sustained Philippe after Helen left Chaves. She had gone without saying good-bye!

He had braced himself for the eventual heartbreak but not for his wounded pride.

Or his hope.

She hadn't said good-bye, he decided, because she didn't want to leave him. He had to see her, had to beg her if need be to give him more time. She had years, centuries, didn't she? Oh, yes, he'd find a way to get her back.

At night, he would lie awake, waiting to hear the front door opening and closing, the rusty hinge telling him she had returned. Then, despondent, he would recite over and over in his head all the words he'd say to hold on to her.

He would tell her how he never even looked at other women, didn't even think about them. How he dreamed of her on the nights she wasn't with him, found himself stammering like an adolescent when she was. How, for the first time, he even got along with his daughter, pleased at her unconscious imitation of Helen's walk and hairstyle and accent. How, the more passion Helen devoured, the more his desire grew.

He would tell her all of this if only he could find her.
Hillary gave him his first real clue.

The girl had been hired to do a final cleaning of Stephen's
house. She was there when the movers came for the last of
Stephen's and Helen's clothes.

Hillary came home that evening carrying a package Helen
had left for her. A wide green sash circled her small waist
and a bright blue ribbon tied back her hair. The colors were
festive, concealing her loss. "Tell me where her things have
been sent," Philippe demanded.

"Why? So you can make more trouble. I'm surprised Senhor Austra hasn't let you go. He must know about you and
Helen."

"Of course he does. That's why you were told to never
discuss *their* relationship with anyone." As Hillary considered this odd logic, Philippe added, "Have you ever seen me
as happy as I've been these last few months?"

"No, Papa," she reluctantly admitted.

"Would you like Helen to be with us always?"

Hillary grinned, the child showing fully for a moment.
"Really?" she said, and with no further hesitation, Hillary
told him, "The men said the boxes were going to Maine,
then something about an architect."

"Paul Stoddard?"

"I think that was the name."

Philippe smiled. He remembered the Stoddard beach house
well. Paul wouldn't mind a surprise visit from an old friend.

EIGHT

1

Helen Wells's life hung on the flat white panels supplied by a New York gallery. The watercolors she had done before she met Stephen, the more vibrant canvases completed during her changing, and the stunning realism and depth of her latest works were all there for the world to view. If the critics had been as trained in psychology as they were in technique, they would have known that some dramatic change had occurred in her. Instead they merely admired the result.

The show was sponsored by a gallery located on the ground floor of La Paz, Paul Stoddard's finest creation. It was held in the lobby, the great expanses of smoke-colored glass turning the early spring afternoon to evening, the modern elegance of the marble floors and walls a perfect backdrop for her work. The show drew crowds not because of Helen's work but because it included pieces from the Austra private collection. But the critics who came to see the eighteenth-century glass sculptures of Steven Austra, the fourteenth-century wood carvings of Edward Austra, the display of the initial sketch for the west rose of Notre Dame and the accompanying glass samples, as well as the other rarely exhibited treasures, studied Helen's works just as carefully. Unlike the other pieces, Helen's paintings were for sale. And the fact that the show had been sponsored by AustraGlass only meant that the price asked for a Wells painting today would be a fraction of its value in the future. The small "sold" tags began appearing on pieces almost immediately.

As the crowd began to grow, Helen slowly moved away from the front doors to a quiet alcove near the elevator where the crowd did not press so close and where she could watch for the rare friends amid the sea of strangers. She had built the wall around her psychic powers, afraid to touch the guests around her and learn how much they really valued her work.

Paul Stoddard joined her. "You shouldn't be hiding today," he said.

"The London exhibit was so small compared to this. It's frightening," she confessed.

He nodded. "When this building was opened to the public, Elizabeth stood here beside me and showed me the thoughts of the guests entering it for the first time. Don't be afraid to meet your public, Helen. They're the critics who really count. Try now. I'll stay with you."

She looked doubtfully out at the crowd, finally choosing an older woman in a severe black suit staring at an Andalusian landscape as romantic as her past. She entered the minds of a pair of collectors in awe of the wildflowers she had completed during her changing. Excited, she moved on and on. Her work. Their praise. Her self. All melted into a drink more powerful than wine or blood. She fed on it until, dizzied by excess, she lowered the mental wall that held back their thoughts. Only then did she become aware that Paul had moved in front of her, hiding her face from the glances of the inquisitive crowd.

"In the future you might wish to settle for observing *expressions*," he said with dry good humor.

His pale blue eyes and white-blond hair made him seem more her kind than the Austras. He had certainly become her closest human friend in the last few months. "Thank you," she said and kissed his cheek.

When she pulled back, he saw the hint of tears in her eyes and understood. "You made the right decision. Though Stephen will probably not admit it, he needs you far more than you do him."

"I know," she responded, her eyes already scanning the crowd looking for him.

Dick Wells arrived an hour after the exhibit opened. He should have been in town the night before, but as the chief investigator in a complicated murder case, he'd had to testify at a trial this morning before catching a flight from Cleveland to New York. He'd come alone. After the tragedies surrounding Helen's changing, Judy Preuss might never be able to relax in the company of Stephen Austra. His children, Carol and Alan, seemed to have mercifully forgotten much of the summer and he didn't wish to bring them and remind them of it. He'd thought of staying home as well but Judy had insisted he come. "Family is important," she told him. "Don't break the tie because of me."

He'd hugged Judy and thanked her. Yes, he had wanted to come. He liked Stephen and he loved his niece and he did not wish to lose touch with either of them.

Dick glanced at the program he'd been given when he'd arrived. He had a frugal nature—to him a numbered print was extravagant—and the four- and five-figure prices being asked for his niece's paintings amazed him.

Then he saw the nude of Hillary Dutiel and for the long minutes he stared at it, he forgot the crowds around him, or that he was tired, or even that his niece had painted this. He felt the same awe he did in St. John's Church, surrounded by Stephen's windows, and he understood. The Austra family could walk into people's minds, record their souls, and, through their work, make those souls immortal. The program noted this piece was not for sale. That was only right for something so priceless.

He noticed Helen on the other side of the lobby doors, talking to a group of guests. She wore a sleeveless green empire silk dress that crisscrossed over the bodice, then fell into long straight folds to just above the floor. Her hair had been arranged in tight curls that framed her face and head like angel's hair and fell down her back in a soft unruly mass. Some trick with her makeup made her eyes look larger than he'd remembered, her cheekbones more prominent, her lips more sensuous. Yet, she had an air of innocent excitement as if she were younger than her twenty years and this her debut or her first dance.

Stephen was beside her, his dark curls a striking contrast to her white-blond ones, her complexion already approaching his pale ivory hue. They made a handsome couple, Dick thought, amazed at how normal he still considered them. Even when Stephen had told him the truth about the Austra family, it had taken hours to convince him of it. How easily they hid!

Then Helen saw him and motioned him over. He was conscious of the eyes watching his niece as she hugged him and kissed his cheek. There were a few women here more beautiful than Helen but men and women did not look at them the way they did at Helen or even at Stephen. The Austra power, the Austra health, drew mortals to them like mayflies to an eternal torch.

As Helen stood beside him, she confessed one human weakness. —Stay close, Uncle— she said to him telepathically. —I feel like I'm for sale with the rest.—

Dick appeared momentarily startled, then, knowing she was showing off, responded with a chuckle and said softly, "If that concerned you, Helen, you never should have worn that dress. I think you'll survive without me. Besides, it looks like a new line is forming to meet you."

He had intended to begin walking through another section of the display when he saw a tall, white-haired man in his sixties farther back in line. With an experienced policeman's eye, he scanned the gallery noting the three armed men in the crowd, their shoulders holsters carefully hidden under full-cut jackets, and, with irrational relief, the guards at each of the show's exits. Even without the security, Raymond Carrera, undisputed head of organized crime in northern Ohio, could only be here to buy. Not certain how Helen would react to the man, he stayed close to her as Carrera walked over to her.

When Carrera took Helen's hand, she sensed the blood on his conscience, the power of the man. She wanted to recoil but held her control perfectly, enough to smile when he introduced himself and complimented her on her work, to thank

him as he said, "I would have bought a picture as an invest-
ment. I think now that I will keep it in my collection forever
to remind me of your face."

Carrera's eyes shifted sideways, meeting Dick's. "I'd heard
this young woman was your niece, Captain. It made me cu
rious. She shows great talent. You should be proud." He
nodded politely to both of them, then turned and walked toward the center of the lobby, one of his guards a few steps
behind.

Helen watched them go, barely aware of Stephen and her
uncle moving closer to her. "He's facing federal charges soon.
I wish I could admit what you probably just learned as evidence for the prosecution," Dick said in a low tone.

"What I learned would make no difference, Uncle," she
replied, certain somehow that the man wouldn't live long but
that his presence here would one day have a tragic impact on
her life.

Her expression grew so troubled that Dick asked, "Are
you all right?"

"I think so." Helen watched the men walk away, inexpli
cably wondering about her strange surge of emotion. Carrera
only made her feel sad and somewhat wary, but his sandy-
haired bodyguard projected such evil she could almost see
the blood on the marble floor where he had walked. Dis-
mayed, she pulled her eyes away from him and took the hand
of a young man who had been waiting to speak to her with
eyes fixed on her face, fighting the desire to reach out and
stroke her white-blond hair.

Later she noticed the bodyguard studying the nude, an expression of avid interest on his face. In spite of her earlier
misgivings, she entered his mind and pulled back immediately. For him, this painting was less art than pornography.
The girl's body excited him, the pain in her eyes even more.
He sensed Helen watching him and looked past the painting
at her. He had eyes like a white wolf's. Ice-water blue. Predatory. Ruthless.

Though he'd made no threat against her, she almost wished
he would. Something tangible would be better than this vague
feeling of uneasiness, this strange, terrible desire to destroy

him for no reason save the harsh instinctive warnings his presence evoked. She watched him weaving through the crowd, always the appropriate distance behind his boss, until Carrera made his choice, arranged the sale, and left.

Two of the armed men Dick had noticed earlier left with him, a third, a wiry brown-haired man in his early forties, stayed behind.

"One of yours?" Dick asked Stephen.

Stephen chuckled. "One of yours. He's with the FBI. But I don't think he's here on business. Shall we inquire?"

"You can but you won't get a straight answer unless you drag it out of his mind."

"I think you're wrong. Come with me." Stephen made his way through the crowd with Dick on his heels. The man saw them coming and looked at Stephen with friendly recognition.

The three moved to a quiet corner where Stephen introduced Dick to Gregory Hunter, then commented, "I didn't think you'd be here today, Gregory."

Hunter laughed. "I notice Laurie isn't here yet. After last night, I'm not surprised. As for me, the boss rang me out of bed at ten. I wasn't awake enough to figure out if he phoned to chew me out for fraternizing with the enemy or to congratulate me on how well I do it."

"The enemy?" Dick asked.

"AustraGlass is not an American company, Mr. Wells. That's enough to make it the enemy these days even if their new director weren't such an avowed pacifist," Hunter said with a trace of bitterness.

"Have you thought about the offer we made you last night?" Stephen asked.

"I could hardly turn it down considering how sick I've gotten of Washington. But I think I'll have to remind Laurie far too often that old habits die hard."

"Been with the Bureau long?" Dick asked.

"I started a year after the war ended. They like war heroes at the Bureau." Hunter wasn't bragging, simply stating a fact he hardly seemed to support. The agent looked at Stephen.

Dick sensed a private exchange, then Stephen excused himself and moved through the crowd toward Helen.

Hunter turned to Dick and said, "The champagne and the noise is a little thick for my hangover. Would you like to join me upstairs for a couple of beers? New York's playing Cleveland at Dallas. It ought to be a hell of a game. Who knows, by half-time Laurie may even be moving."

Dick glanced around the lobby. The minks and feathered hats on the women, the three-piece hand-tailored suits on the men, and the brief snatches of conversation he'd overheard made him feel both underdressed and uneducated. He couldn't visit with his niece here. He didn't even want to. He nodded, and as they walked to the elevators, he asked, "What's upstairs?"

"Paul's penthouse. You haven't seen it? Well, just wait until you see the pleasure dome that New England puritan built for his ladylove."

Hours passed. Helen signed invitations for admirers, answered questions for critics and reporters, laughed with strangers. She felt exhausted, not physically for she was never really tired anymore, but mentally. The noise hurt her ears. Too many perfumes competed for her attention. As soon as the crowds began to thin, she took an elevator to Paul and Elizabeth's penthouse and looked out the slanted smoke-tinted windows, feeling the press of the masses on the streets far below her.

Stephen had been right to take her directly to Chaves. She wondered if she would ever be comfortable in cities as Stephen obviously was. She wandered through the apartment, discovering her uncle asleep on the bed in one of the guest rooms, one of Paul's imported beers on the nightstand, the TV turned to *Dragnet*. It reminded her of the usual Saturday evenings at home when she, Dick, and her two younger cousins had their dinner in front of the television watching Officer Friday get his man, both Carol and Alan intent on the action, amazed that this was what their father did for a living. He never enlightened them about the usual boredom of his job, instead he would tell them he was careful. He wanted them prepared for the worst.

She had intended to wake her uncle and talk to him but decided against it. She thought of how quickly their worlds had divided and wondered if she would ever see the rest of her human family again.

Night fell, the stars—God and man-made—switched on. Stephen came upstairs with Paul and, sensing her sadness, held her. She buried her face against his neck, smelling the elusive musky scent of his hair, feeling his patient concern. "No more shows. No more interviews. It's over," she said.

Stephen did not question her change of plans. If she didn't leave now she never would. "I'll cancel everything. Then I'll need only a few more days to make our final arrangements."

A fleeting smile touched only her lips. "I don't want to wait here."

"My cottage on the Maine coast can be opened two weeks early," Paul suggested. "At this time of year the place will be deserted. I can call the caretaker in the morning and let her know you'll be arriving."

"Maybe your uncle would go with you," Stephen added. "He told me he took a week's leave. I don't think he likes New York very much."

As she considered this, Helen frowned. "I guess I would like the company. I'll ask him in the morning." She moved away from Stephen and walked toward the hallway. "Make whatever plans you like for me. Right now I don't care to hear them. Good night."

In a moment a bedroom door closed somewhat too hard.

"It's hard to give up a life," Paul commented.

"Especially now. But she wants a family so much she'll probably have twins within a year."

Paul laughed. "Why not triplets?" he asked.

Suggesting triplets had been a joke but Stephen replied seriously, "We discussed it. Triplets would make too dangerous a delivery."

"You really have a choice?" In all his years with Elizabeth, she had never told him this. He found it unbelievable.

"The women do though only to a degree. Mistakes do

happen, usually single births. They're tragedies in a way. The mothers die and we gain but a single child when our numbers are already so few.''

''Will Helen be all right?''

''Her grandmother's delivery was difficult. So was her mother's. They survived. There is a clinic about twenty miles away from our house. It's equipped for most emergencies. Food will be a more annoying problem. James didn't give much thought to grocery stores when he chose the location.''

''Maybe you should take up farming and buy a cow to milk.''

''Cows require too much effort. I might try goats.''

''Well, milking is easy anyway.''

''Is it? I never had to learn. How did you?''

''Phillipe Dutiel took me to Brittany just before the war. His parents had a dairy farm.''

''When will the boat be ready?'' Stephen asked, changing the subject. He did not wish to discuss Philippe Dutiel.

''It's in the water,'' Paul said. He sat in one of the chairs, kicked off his shoes, and stretched his legs out on an otto-man, unbending the stiff right one more slowly than the left. ''If there's one thing I've learned in all our years together, old friend, it's never put off one of your requests.''

II

The next morning, Helen and her uncle caught a small commuter plane to Bangor, picked up a car, and drove to the coast. The day was brilliant, the spring sun beating down on the farmland around them. Dick loved the warmth of it on his arms and legs but sympathized with Helen. His niece wore a dark, long-sleeved coat with the collar turned up, a hat to hide her face. She sat with the back of her head pressed against the passenger window, screening out the worst of the rays, her dark glasses reflecting his face on the occasions when he glanced at her.

She should have been happy, he thought. Hell, after her reception in New York, she should have been ecstatic but she hardly spoke at all. Her passivity concerned him. It implied she was somehow unhappy or at least confused. He had always thought of her as a daughter and, like any good father, wanted only the best for her. If his feelings had been any less pure he could never have let her leave home without a struggle. "That was quite an affair yesterday," he finally said.

"I suppose. Money opens doors."

"Opens them early, you mean. You would have been successful anyway. Stephen just speeded up the process."

For the first time since they started the trip, Helen smiled. "Isn't that ironic?" she said.

"Damn it, girl. If you're going to run off with some foreigner who has cat's teeth in his mouth and a thousand-year employment record, he might as well have money."

Helen laughed and squeezed his arm. "I'm sorry," she said. "I don't want to give you the wrong impression. I've just had too many hectic days and yes I do still get tired."

Even through his shirt and jacket, he felt aroused by her touch, a swift stab of lust gone as soon as she let him go. He wondered if she knew what desire she created in him and decided he'd just be careful around her. He began talking, telling her with happened in the weeks after she had gone and how he had finally persuaded Judy Preuss to marry him. "We want you at the wedding," he said.

"Only me?" she asked.

"Yes, Judy said she's sorry. We will be inviting Elizabeth and Paul but Stephen reminds Judy too much of the past. She hopes you both understand."

Instead of replying, Helen pointed to a tavern that served lunches. The place was sandwiched between two larger buildings with one small window in the front. Once inside, Helen chose a table as far from the daylight as possible. Dick ordered a hamburger and a beer. Helen asked for a bowl of soup and some ice in a glass, then filled the glass from a bottle of the cloudy Tarda water she carried in her oversize purse. Without waiting for it to cool, she drained the glass and filled it again. When she took off her glasses he saw how tired she looked, how sad.

"Are you all right?" Dick asked. Realizing she couldn't possibly understand what he meant from his words alone, he rephrased, "Is this change what you expected?"

"Stephen tried to show me what his world was like but nothing could prepare me for how I must live. And the metamorphosis isn't over. It can't be. I feel too human."

"How do you think you're supposed to feel?"

"I don't know but not like this."

"Listen, girl. One of the things I liked most about Stephen as I got to know him was how much he cared about you and the kids. Hell, how much he cared about all of us. After he told me what he was, he started acting like some indestructible prehistoric god. But when I looked past that facade, I just saw a man—a man more sensitive than I would ever want to be."

"I'm not sure I understand what you're telling me."

"I'm saying that you shouldn't try to build a wall to separate what you were from what you want to be. If you do, everything you become will be a lie."

"It already is, Uncle."

"Is it?"

"When Stephen suggested that I ask you to come with me, my first thought was that he was guaranteeing that, should I need it, I would have a willing source of food."

"Overprotective is he?" Dick asked with a straight face.

Helen laughed and leaned across the table to kiss him on the cheek. "I miss you so much, Uncle. All of you."

Dick waited until the waitress set down their order. When they were alone again, he apologized for the lecture and changed the subject. "Now, the wedding will be on August twelfth in Sandusky. Judy's sister will be maid of honor. Corey's the best man. We want you in the wedding party."

Helen shook her head. "Tell Judy that I can't come either," she said, then explained how she and Stephen planned to stage their deaths.

"You're sure that's what you want?" Dick asked when she'd finished. Helen nodded and he went on, "Well, I suppose we can keep in touch somehow. Maybe we can send letters through Paul."

Helen smiled. "More than that. I'll want you to visit us. We both will."

"Then I'll arrange to see you. I promise."

"I thought you'd be the hardest one to tell. I dreaded it and you're making it so easy for me," she said and he sensed her thankfulness in her tone and the quick merging of their minds.

"I never had a choice, not from the day you and Stephen met."

"No, Uncle, you never did." She reached across the table and took his hand, and he was thankful to notice that the sexual charge of her touch had vanished. "The nude is being donated to the Cleveland Art Museum. The Andalusian series has been purchased by the Austra family. The self-portrait will stay with me. Most of the money this sale has raised along with every painting that hasn't been sold is going to belong to you."

"Helen, I can't let you . . ."

"That's my estate. I can't take it with me. Besides, I want to help put Carol and Alan through college. This way I can do it without the risk of anyone knowing what happened to me."

"I suppose we can't tell the kids the truth, can we?"

"Maybe someday. Not yet." She hesitated, then added, "And you'll have to destroy every photograph of me except those taken when I was a child, and all their negatives."

"Damn!" Dick said. "Carol's been keeping a scrapbook."

"What photos does she have?"

"Just the ones we took after you had your hair cut in that stupid shingle. What were you, about fifteen?"

Helen laughed, the first sincerely happy moment of the day, as if apprehension had exhausted her. "Let her keep it. Nobody would recognize me from that."

They talked about the past while they finished their lunch, Helen speaking of last summer's events in a hazy detached tone, as if they had taken place years ago. As they got ready to leave the restaurant, Dick asked her again, "Are you sure you want to do this?"

Helen nodded and put on her coat and hat and glasses and walked outside into the scorching April sun.

NINE

1

They reached the beach house in midafternoon. It had been a harsh winter, they noted, as they pulled up the winding drive. Tiles were missing from the roof, a pine tree had fallen across the road and been recently moved to let cars pass.

The door had been left unlocked and the house smelled of lemon polish and Lysol. As they walked through the main rooms, Helen picked up the phone and heard no dial tone while Dick opened the empty refrigerator and swore.

"We could drive back to town for dinner," Helen suggested, then added with sly good humor, "or I could catch you something."

"Catch?" Dick closed the refrigerator door and stared at his niece, who had suddenly become more alien than she had seemed all day. "Do you do that . . . hunt, I mean."

"Yes."

He tried to picture her face buried in some animal's fur, her teeth biting. He could. That was the problem, he could. "Do you enjoy it?" he asked.

"Yes. The death . . . it's so hard to explain."

"Then don't. I'll drive back to town and get some supplies. If the office is still open, I'll see about having the phone connected. You can get some sleep."

"That would be nice," she replied. Though she wasn't tired, more sunlight sounded horrid. She stood inside the front door and watched the car disappear into the pines, then

71

walked through the long center hallway to the back of the house and out onto the covered deck overlooking the Atlantic.

Paul had rebuilt some of the old terrace. Though it still faced east and south, he had extended it so it jutted out over a sloping mass of dark granite sheets falling steeply to the sea. At high tide the water would pound no more than twenty feet from the base of the deck. Now, with the tide out, there was a rock-strewn beach of rough gravel below, walled in on both sides by the jutting stone walls.

Once there had been steps curving down to the cove but these had long ago fallen into disrepair. Entire sections had rotted away and the top third had been removed altogether, probably to discourage anyone from trying to climb down. She wondered how long these had been abandoned. A few years at most would be all it would take, she thought as she looked up at the louvered roof screening the sun. Snow had apparently drifted on the roof and fallen in one weighty mass, ripping through the louvers and taking out a portion of the railing. Helen, her human experience making her needlessly cautious, stayed well away from the damage.

To the north of the house, the sea had cut a deep bay. She could see a bit of the beach, the long metal pier with the dinghy tied at the end. Gulls bobbed in the bay's protection and Paul's yacht, doomed and waiting, threw a long dark shadow against the water.

The Atlantic seemed deceptively blue, almost tropical in the late afternoon sun but Helen felt the cold wind blowing from it, and sensed how deep and deadly it could be. She heard noises, strange haunting notes in the distant waters, and, wondering if these were whale songs, moved her mind outward, trying to extend it to their source.

She heard a board creak behind her, whirled as a familiar voice said, "Hello, Helen Wells."

She wasn't surprised to see him. Somehow she had known Philippe would come for her. "Did you just arrive?" she asked.

"I've been here for hours. I'm surprised you didn't sense me."

She looked at him coldly. "I didn't try."

He ignored her expression, concentrating instead on how lucky he was to have found her alone. "I came to tell you that Hillary misses you. So do I."

"I've made my decision. I'm not returning to Chaves again. I'm sorry."

His voice rose. She felt his anger as he said, "It's not too late to change your mind."

"No," she said. "You knew I would leave you. I have to."

"But not this soon. Look at Paul and Elizabeth. We could have years together."

"But we won't. I have my duty and I've never hidden it from you." She knew how stubborn she sounded but all she could do was harden her resolve until he understood.

"Duty! You're only nineteen. What are the Austras, some kind of contagious disease? Forget their plans. What do you want to do?"

"What I have chosen."

"And me?"

"I don't know . . ." she lied. "I suppose I would have written."

"Written? Why couldn't you just come to me and tell me good-bye?"

"Because I couldn't bear to face you and feel . . ."

"Because you love me." Now he was sure of it.

"I do," she lied again. Maybe if she left him his pride he would go. She detected danger in his jealousy and her mind reached out, trying to trap his. Her emotions made this difficult and his thoughts seemed fluid, impossible to hold.

Philippe grabbed her, swinging her around to face the sun. Her eyes burned and teared from its painful light. "You love me," he repeated and kissed her.

She froze, unwilling to attract or repel him, trying only to resist the temptation his body offered. He pulled back, hurt and puzzled, and saw the flinty resolve in her eyes. "Damn you," he said as she stepped back. His fingers dug into her shoulder, deliberately hurting her.

She felt her anger as a tiny spark igniting something volatile inside her. Her mind, as strong as any in the family's now, trapped him, forcing him to let her go. As he did, she pushed him back, intending to turn and run, run until she no longer felt his anger or pain. It seemed she had given him nothing more than a small shove yet she saw clearly that his feet left the ground. He landed unbalanced on the edge of the terrace, and fell back against the damaged wooden rail that cracked and broke. The stub of his amputated arm flailed wildly as if he tried to grab hold with his missing hand. Then he fell over the edge and was gone.

Helen's mind, still linked with his, felt him fall and hit and die. She felt his soul scream its protest at this sudden severing with life. A wave of emotion engulfed her and she wailed at the intensity of it, sensing in a way she could not yet define the tiny echoes inside her.

Dick Wells returned an hour later and found his niece crouched in the hallway, wrapped in her coat, shivering, seemingly sightless. He pulled the coat back, looked at her hands and arms, seeing nothing, then realizing that he wouldn't, not anymore. Her clothes were still clean, though, so he scanned the hallway and looked into the empty rooms. Then, as he was returning to her side, he noticed the broken railing on the terrace. He walked to the edge of it and looked down, seeing the body on the rocks below. He went inside and knelt beside Helen.

"Is he dead?" Dick asked.

Helen's only reply was to tighten the ball she had made with her body. Dick assumed she was in shock and decided not to ask her any questions. The death would have to be reported but not yet, not until Helen was able to face the police. He tried the phone. The line was still not connected but he'd been assured service would be on before the end of the business day.

He sat beside Helen, holding her, until the phone rang. When Dick answered he asked the operator to connect him with Paul Stoddard's office in New York City.

Later, after he'd carried his niece upstairs, placed her on a bed, and covered her with a blanket, he followed Stephen's suggestion and called the local police. They arrived quickly, an ambulance and doctor soon after. The team worked with surprising efficiency, the ambulance crew retrieving the body while the sheriff asked Dick the expected questions.

The lies were surprisingly easy for Dick to tell and his position as a captain on the Cleveland police force allayed any suspicions the sheriff might have had. Dick said he assumed the body had been there when they'd arrived. Helen had discovered it while Dick went back to town. No, Helen was not able to answer any questions at this time. The sheriff suggested the doctor took a look at her. Dick wasn't sure if an examination of Helen would reveal any physical oddities but he didn't know how to refuse such a logical request.

He needn't have worried. The doctor never even touched Helen. Instead, he got as far as her door and found himself unable to enter her room. Rationalizing his strange reluctance to go near her with a desire to let her have her rest, he contented himself with noticing what he could from a distance. He decided that her shock couldn't be too great because her color, though pale, was normal and her breathing even. "I'll stop back later if they need me," the doctor told the sheriff when he returned to the kitchen. He gave Dick his telephone number and, looking puzzled, left.

Stephen arrived at the beach house three hours after he'd been called, setting what Dick was certain had to be a travel record. Though it was well after dark, Stephen drove without lights and garaged his car before coming inside.

During the time it took for him to arrive, Helen never moved. He went to her without a word, kneeling beside her bed, softly calling her name. Helen woke with a start and wrapped her arms around Stephen's neck. Dick saw his friend close his eyes and stoke Helen's hair until her shudders subsided and she relaxed in his arms. "I want to leave here," she said in a small, pleading voice.

"Soon," he replied, then added, "go back to sleep."

She responded by holding him tighter. When Stephen stretched out beside her on the bed, Dick decided it was wisest to leave them alone. He went downstairs to the kitchen and pulled a warm beer out of the bag on the table. As he drank it, he put away the rest of his groceries, then went and waited in the one room in which he felt comfortable, the one that faced the road instead of the sea.

Stephen joined him a half hour later, standing beside him at the window, looking out at the winding drive and the trees.

Minutes passed before Dick asked, "Do you know what happened?"

Stephen nodded. "An accident," he said. "Helen didn't know anger would give her such strength."

"She pushed him through?"

Stephen nodded again and Dick asked, "Why?"

"They were lovers in Chaves. He wanted her to return with him." Stephen went on, describing what he could of the last few minutes of Philippe Dutiel's life and how Helen had felt him die.

"No wonder she's in shock," Dick commented. "It must have been horrible."

Stephen shook his head. "Glorious. You look confused, Richard. You shouldn't be. You know that we live on emotions as well as blood. His death would have been an incredible attraction. That's what shocked her."

"The doctor said the man died almost instantly."

"An instant is enough. She will remember it perfectly forever," Stephen reminded him. "And she had another shock. Her terror and revulsion woke the lives in her. She's pregnant."

"Lives?" Dick asked.

"Twins. So far I am certain that one of them is mine. The other is most likely family as well but with a weaker mind. I will know the truth in time." It seemed that Stephen spoke as if he should have anticipated this problem, that if only one were his, he would blame himself. "It's better than blaming her or a dead man, yes?" Stephen added, not caring if Dick minded this reading of his thoughts.

Paul Stoddard and Elizabeth Austra arrived later that night. On the way, they'd stopped in town where Paul identified the body, made arrangements to have Philippe returned to Chaves for burial, and took responsibility for notifying Hillary of her father's death.

As soon as they arrived, Elizabeth went upstairs to be with Helen, and Paul joined Stephen and Dick. He stood in front of the fire Stephen had started in the living room's fireplace, letting the warmth flow through his legs before taking a seat. He appeared exhausted, sad, and, Dick thought, a little guilty. Perhaps that was natural. Stephen had told him that Philippe and Paul had been old friends.

"I told the sheriff we would be picking you up tomorrow," Paul told Stephen. "I said that Helen enjoyed sailing and a day at sea might help her recover. I asked if it was too early in the year."

"And his response?" Stephen asked.

"To be careful. He said the winds are dangerous this early in the season, particularly close to the shore."

"Well, the current won't be our problem."

"The explosives have been planted. When you turn on the radio to call for help, you'll have forty seconds to jump. Will that be enough?"

"Much more than I'll need. Helen can't go with me, not now. We'll have to risk someone seeing her." Stephen didn't elaborate, nor did Paul ask. Her shock alone would be reason enough.

Stephen waited until Elizabeth joined them before spreading a Maine road map on the table. He pointed to a crossroads a few miles from the ocean. "I'll meet Elizabeth and Helen here one hour after the yacht explodes."

"I'm not going until you agree to two things," Helen said, walking stiffly into the room. Stephen looked up from the map, surprised by her presence and the resolve of her tone. "I won't go unless you agree to have someone tell Hillary the truth—about how her father died and about us."

Stephen glanced at Elizabeth who nodded her approval. "All right," Stephen replied.

"And I want her supported until she can live on her own. I'll pay for it."

"I'll make the arrangements for her care," Paul said.

"And let me provide the support. It will arouse too much suspicion if the money came from your estate."

"That will do," Helen said and looked down at the map. "Someone should see us—both of us—go out to the boat, shouldn't they?" she asked in a soft voice as if her demands had depleted most of her strength.

"It would be a good idea," Dick said and added, "The sheriff should get Helen's statement first. Otherwise there will be too many questions about the accident." Dick turned to his niece. "Will you be up to giving one tomorrow?" Helen nodded and Elizabeth added one more suggestion.

As he sat and schemed with the others, Dick found himself enjoying the plotting. It took his mind off the day's tragedy, and as he watched Helen fighting her lethargy, he thought that, given time, she would be all right.

The sheriff talked to Helen the next afternoon. She sat composed and thoughtful, looking far younger than her years in a dark green sundress. She answered the questions evenly, shuddering only when she lied about how she'd discovered the body. Afterward the sheriff took her and Stephen around to the dock. He gave them a friendly warning about the current close to shore and watched them row to the yacht before driving away. Had he stayed he might have seen the yacht veer close to the cliff beneath the Stoddard beach house so Helen could swim to shore where Elizabeth was waiting to help her make the difficult climb up to the deck.

Then the two women sat, their minds merged and separated from their bodies, following Stephen's progress north from the bay. An hour after dark, they broke with him and drove to the rendezvous in Stephen's car. No one had seen it so no one missed it.

Minutes after they'd turned onto the main road, the Coast Guard received a frantic Mayday from the Stoddard yacht. The crew of their cutter saw the explosion four miles out.

The bodies were never found.

The deaths of Stephen Austra, one of the foremost glass artists of the twentieth century, and Helen Wells, a promising young painter from Ohio, made news across the world. No pictures ran with the stories because there were none to print. Their obituaries even made the front page in the Cleveland morning paper. That afternoon, it was moved to page two to make way for a second auspicious death. Vincent Carrera had died of a cerebral hemorrhage a few hours after returning to Cleveland from his meetings in New York.

His last act had been to hang the Helen Wells painting in his office on the wall facing his desk. "The sand and the sky remind me of the hills in Sardinia," he told his son. "A man should always remember where he comes from."

II

Carol Wells cried at her cousin's service and later, harder, after she heard a workman had come from AustraGlass to repair last summer's damage to the windows in St. John's Church. She had gone to St. John's, not certain what she was expecting, but definitely not the old Portuguese worker who only stared at her with a puzzled expression while she looked at the window, numb and grieving for everything she had lost.

Not caring who saw her, she turned and fled, riding her bicycle home, dropping it in the front yard, running inside the house, closing the door to her room behind her. She lay stretched across the bed, sobbing, when her brother came in and put his hand on her back. "It isn't true," he said. "They're not dead. I know."

Carol looked up at him, wide-eyed in disbelief. How could he say such a thing now?

"It's a lie," he repeated.

Carol wanted to hit him, to lash out and make him feel some kind of pain. He was so stupid! She started to turn over, intending to grab his wrist and push him away when a sudden and seemingly adult insight came to her. Alan was too young to understand this tragedy so he simply denied it. If Carol had never seen her mother's body in the casket, maybe she would have made up the same kind of story as Alan's.

She relaxed and pulled her brother down on the bed beside

her. "They're somewhere together," she agreed, drying her eyes, struggling to keep them dry, thinking that at least what she'd just said wasn't really a lie.

Alan knew for certain that his cousin and Stephen weren't dead because he dreamed of them almost every night. Although he often tried to speak to them, he always failed. But after he'd shared brief vivid pieces of their life together, he knew they were hiding somewhere far away, somewhere only his mind could take him.

He didn't know why they were hiding or how he was able to see so vividly the places where they lived. He didn't question their truth or tell anyone because nobody would believe him.

III

Telling Hillary Dutiel that her father had died was difficult for Rachel Austra. Telling her how he had died was even harder. But, to Rachel's surprise, explaining where Stephen and Helen had gone, and why, was simple because Hillary already knew most of the important facts.

"My mother told me that Senhor Austra was a young man when she met him. When I came here he was still a young man. I was curious. I listened to stories the glassworkers tell. I thought that if they were true, then perhaps Helen was the same sort of creature as him."

Rachel smiled, closemouthed. She had only told Hillary that Stephen and Helen did not age like normal people. She had not explained why, at least not yet. Now Hillary was explaining for her.

Hillary continued, "One night when Helen . . . had sex with my father, I pretended to be asleep and then I tiptoed to his door and I watched. I saw her cut him on the shoulder and swallow the blood."

"Did you tell anyone?" Rachel asked, alarmed.

Hillary shook her head. "I wouldn't. Senhor Austra has always been kind to me, and Helen too."

So the girl had simply known she must keep her knowledge

a secret! Rachel was stunned by Hillary's intelligence. "And so you think they are vampires?" Rachel asked.

"No! Those things are evil," Hillary insisted.

Convinced the girl was ready to hear it, Rachel told her the rest of the Austra story—how they lived forever, why blood and the emotions carried in it sustained them, even the family's own conjecture that they originated someplace other than earth.

"Where do you come from?" the girl asked without the slightest trace of fear.

"We don't know. Francis—the oldest of our race—has no memory of a time before earth."

"Why are you so much like us?"

"We aren't. Not inside."

"But Helen is."

"Helen is different from me as well as from you."

"Where did she come from?"

Rachel could tell the girl the details of Helen's strange creation but that wasn't what the girl had asked. Rachel, who could give her no answer, shook her head and said nothing.

Hillary timidly reached for Rachel's hand and studied it, the long fingers, the hard, pointed nails, the soft, unmarred skin. Hillary began to cry and Rachel hugged her. "What's wrong?" she asked.

"Papa's dead," the girl replied, holding Rachel tighter.

"Don't worry I'll take care of you, I promise."

"You don't understand. I always took care of him."

As Rachel helped the girl unpack her clothes in the guest bedroom, she understood that she was the worst possible choice to be Hillary's guardian. The girl needed responsibility rather than security. Rachel, the family caretaker, couldn't offer it, and with so much to do now that Stephen had gone, she hardly had time to think of who might.

There were so many problems occupying her mind. Michael, assigned for the first time to Alpha in Ireland, was having a difficult time adjusting to the conservative Irish culture. Ann and Laurie had settled into their roles perfectly but still needed assistance understanding the responsibilities that accompanied them.

And Rachel, the only one of the family who stayed in one place as long as she was needed, was the only one with the knowledge to help. At least she didn't have to worry about makeup anymore. No, the shapeless spinster Rachel Austra who had guided the glass house through Denys's term as director had died a decade ago, and a younger cousin of the same name moved into her house. A change of hairstyle, of accent and mannerisms, and no one but those who knew would associate the new Rachel with the old.

The ruse was hard, harder even than exile, but Rachel never wanted to be anyplace but where she was needed.

No, Hillary did not belong with her. They were too much alike.

TEN

1

French-Canadian Stephen Audet and his American bride crossed the border near Niagara Falls following an extended honeymoon. They rented a single room in a small town on the St. Laurence near Montreal. Though Stephen always dreaded the loneliness he felt when he was away from his family, Helen's presence was a comfort and the children growing inside her gave him hope.

But she would no longer touch human life.

Even when they hunted game in the hills north of town, she would pull away at the end, letting him devour the full strength of the death agony, afraid to feel even a hint of the attraction she had felt when Philippe died.

But death was a part of what she had become, she had to accept it, had to understand. Stephen did not want her to know how concerned he became when he considered the passivity with which she faced her future. Though she ate solid foods voraciously, she grew thinner and, Stephen noted with alarm, her skin took on a ruddy hue, a sign of stress in his kind.

He thought of the other Austra women, conceiving, letting the life growing in them drain their own, then dying before they ever felt their infants in their arms. Denys had been a child when the last half-human woman had been bonded to the family. That had been over two thousand years ago. Perhaps Denys had misunderstood the process—even Austra children made mistakes. Perhaps Helen was different, closer to the family than the other woman had been. Stephen could only hope that Denys's memory would prove true. If it didn't, then Helen could die. To lose her now, when he was isolated from his own, was something Stephen could not endure.

He thought that if he revealed even a hint of his doubts to Helen, they would magnify through her into real fear. Their lives seemed to have merged completely, their minds and bodies bound by the children growing inside her.

So Stephen revealed nothing, gave no advice though he knew he had to force her to accept her needs. He began taking her places where she would be tempted—nighttime cafés, dances, walks through the crowded streets. And wherever they went, he would break down the wall she built around her, heightening the desire of those around them, making her feel it, want them.

Without a word of reproach, she stopped going out altogether. And she did not question where he went on the nights he left her alone.

Finally, more bored than curious, she followed him, trailing him to a dim and quiet block. There, he waited in the dark passageway between two buildings. When a man walking a dog reached the center of the block, Stephen stepped into the light. Helen heard the exchange, the mechanical greetings of two strangers, saw the man's hands flutter nervously as he followed Stephen into the shadows of the passage while the small dog stretched to the end of its leash, standing guard in the empty street.

Human eyes could not see what she saw now—the man, frozen by her lover's mind, his head tilted back, waiting. And a human mind could not sense the desire she felt flowing into Stephen from that young, anxious man and through Stephen into her.

An invitation! He wanted her to join him! Helen turned and fled.

When Stephen came home, he found Helen standing on the balcony of their second-floor room, gripping its decorative iron railing, watching people walking the dark streets, fighting her need, despising what she had become.

"I took nothing but his desire for me," Stephen said. He hung his dark jacket on the back of a chair and stretched out on the bed.

She ignored him, feeling the dark, inhaling its scents, listening to the sounds magnified in the quiet of night. She felt his mind brush her body, insistent as hands. She pushed it away but only with effort. She needed what he offered now. The life in her . . .

She would not think about her children, not now.

"I knew my mother," he said.

She turned and looked at him, confused. "She died when you were born," she said.

"I knew her for months before that. I knew her voice, the way she spoke, the way she sang. I knew her thoughts. Near the end, I even saw her face. And as I was born, I felt her die. Every death I ever caused, every love I ever lost was easier than that first loss."

As he had spoken, Helen had walked into the room, moving closer to him. Now she sat beside him. "But did you accept them?" she asked.

"Some people are old or weak or in pain. Others deserve to die. Those I could accept. Some I have killed and those I have learned to justify. The others, the ones who have been my friends or lovers"—he rested a hand on the side of her face—"not really. But you can bury the grief beneath happier thoughts. The time for regret is over, yes?"

She nodded once, slowly.

"And if healing takes times, use me," he said. "Let me share my strength."

Though she did not want him to think of her as a child, she was no match for him physically, especially not now. Her body, weakened by abstinence, refused to obey her when he raised the black teardrop pendant, used the point to make a deep gouge in his neck, and pulled her to him.

The scent, the taste, so much like those nights in Ohio when she had first begun to change into his perfect eternal lover.

But she wasn't perfect. She thought of it as she drank, then kissed him, as she felt her gratitude shift into lust. She wasn't what she wanted to be—confident, assured, ruthless as any Austra woman.

—I was wrong to push you so hard in Chaves— he confessed. —I thought that I would lose you if I did not force you to change completely. The human part of you made me uneasy, Helen. I confess that it still does but I would not change it, not too quickly. You have so many years to reach the end, yes?—

He meant it. His words consoled her but they were the last ones she wanted to hear.

The next afternoon, he drove her to Quebec City, to a tiny century-old chapel in the center of town. Austra windows— Helen felt their soothing touch as soon as she stepped into their light. This was Holy Thursday, the start of the Easter celebration, and though she had not been in a church since her changing, she knelt with the others, her eyes devoutly fixed on the monstrance and the sacred bread within its golden halo.

And when the priest shuffled from the sacristy to the confessional, Helen went inside.

Though Stephen was curious, traditions were too strong. Helen's confession would be between her and this priest and God. Even so, after the priest gave her absolution, Stephen stood outside and wiped his mind clean of everything Helen had told him. Most sins were so alike that the old priest never noticed the gap.

But Helen felt cleansed, forgiven, freed finally from the past.

And though she was surrounded by accents that reminded her of Philippe, she slowly conquered her grief. Forgetting was impossible. The memory would stay as clear as the moment Philippe died. But she could bury her pain.

And force herself to be happy.

At night, they walked the cobblestone streets hand in hand, inviting smiles from old men and young girls. They rarely spoke to each other, rarely exchanged even a thought, yet they were always physically touching, reassuring each other that the future could, indeed, be everything they expected.

11

They waited in the town until the high Rocky Mountain roads opened, then flew to Edmonton and bought a four-wheel drive truck and trailer. Stephen's furniture had been shipped to Edmonton earlier and they loaded the pieces and drove north and west into the highest reaches of the Rockies. Stephen turned off the main highway onto a road that soon changed from asphalt to gravel and a mile later turned onto a private dirt drive winding through thick trees.

The house at the end of it was smaller than Helen imagined—a single-story cabin dwarfed by the towering pines around it. It had been built in a narrow wooded valley sheltered by snow-topped mountains. The Austra family owned three hundred acres. This wasn't much land, not here, but it bordered the north end of a national forest. The nearest campgrounds were forty miles away, the nearest hiking trails thirty, the nearest town sixteen. "The main roads are always plowed," Stephen assured her, "and the clinic in Dawson is excellent."

This was exactly the sort of place Helen wanted—rustic, isolated. But as she stood beside the truck and stared at the long log structure, so low she thought she'd have to duck to get through the door, she wondered if her request had been the right one.

Stephen opened the trailer, then tossed her the keys. "Go and look," he said.

As she walked closer to the house, she saw that it was partially earth-sheltered, with steps going down to a tall front door. When she reached the bottom, undid the padlock, and pushed the door open, she found herself in a single, apparently windowless room. Though her eyes adjusted immediately to the darkness, she knew she wouldn't like it here. Stephen, who possessed the family's natural claustrophobia, would undoubtedly hate it.

She heard a rustling by the far wall, then the creak of

hinges and saw a thin line of colored light across from the door. Others followed. She ran to the first window, unlatched the inside shutters and pulled it open, then did the same to the rest, following Stephen around the house. When she'd finished, she surveyed the space again.

The single large room reminded her of the main room in their house in Chaves. Like there, this room was dominated by a huge stone fireplace and tall multicolored windows. The floor was of pine planks and dark rough-hewn beams supported the roof and walls.

"James built it in 1920," Stephen told her as they dusted the floors. "Michael used it from 1938 until last year when he left for Alpha to take on Laurie's role."

When the dark wood floor was polished to a rich depth, Stephen brought in the carpets, unrolling the large oriental in the center of the room, the smaller ones in other spaces where they fit. He reassembled the platform for their bed, put the grey suede sofa, the oak table and chairs where she directed. He brought in the music—a small hammered dulcimer, a guitar, and the *naizet*, the pear-shaped stringed instrument that he'd played for her a few months—a lifetime—ago. He brought in their treasures—the crystal cat Charles had made for him, the stemware from Alpha, the etched crystal candleholders Rachel had given Helen as a welcoming present, her self-portrait that they hung above the fireplace. And last he brought in their work—an easel, canvases, and paints for her, a loom and yarn, carving and carpentry tools for him.

When they'd finished, the space looked sumptuous, at odds with the wilderness around them.

Well after dark, she left Stephen building a fire and went outside.

She saw nothing in the growing darkness but trees and the brighter stars. Instinct had told her to come here but it seemed a mistake now, one she would feel obligated to see through.

Then she saw the wolf.

She might have missed him altogether were her other senses less acute but she had heard him breathing in the trees near the door. She froze and waited for him to notice her and run.

Instead he walked closer to her and, when he was a few yards away, sat back on his haunches waiting for her to make the next move.

Helen did what seemed correct, crouching down, one hand flat on the snow-covered ground, studying him.

He had just eaten, she knew; had just killed an injured deer. He was an older wolf, she sensed eight winters in his thoughts, and had recently lost his mate. Spring had come. He would be alone until autumn when the packs formed. The musky Austra scent had drawn him here, and though he had expected to find Michael, not her, he accepted her as well.

She learned all this without any real concentration. She smiled in delight at her power and the wolf, confused by the sudden change in her expression, turned and ran.

Without thinking, she bolted after him, almost touching him as she followed. When he started to climb over the icy rocks, she abandoned physical pursuit, letting her mind chase him, until he traveled too far to reach. She pulled back, hearing his distant howl, hearing it answered from the house, the echoes falling off the mountains around her.

Oh, yes! She had made the right choice in coming here. She was certain of it now, as certain as she had been on the night of her changing when she decided that she belonged in Stephen's world.

The wolf came every day at dusk and sat quietly outside the door waiting. She learned to talk to it, to give it orders as Stephen did, and though it was nobody's pet, it obeyed

If the night was calm, she and Stephen would hunt with it. Stephen's arms were almost as long as his legs and his hips were double-jointed so he could run on hands and feet. His body was immune to even bitter cold and he wore very little, often nothing at all. Helen, restricted to two feet rather than four and her human flesh covered with boots and clothing, struggled to keep the pace.

With practice, she did. Her heart grew stronger, her lungs seemed larger, and her reflexes quickened, making her more surefooted. At last, sensing she was ready, Stephen ordered the wolf back and let her take the kill. She jumped, sinking her small hunting knife in the deer's neck, straddling it, pulling back the head so she could drink.

She felt its heart flutter with fear, its mind trying to fight hers. She held it easily, devouring its life, feeling its fear fading, life falling easily into death.

And she felt her sons inside her, growing stronger with this feast. She could almost see their tiny fingers held out, demanding more. Yes, if this was what they needed she would provide.

On the nights that followed warm summer days, a fog would form, rolling into the valleys, covering the low cottage walls and windows with its damp, lacy solitude. Returning from the midnight hunts, Helen would pass through it, into the cottage where she would lay beside Stephen and listen to the muffled sounds of the world around her.

Invariably she would move closer to him. There were so few choices left her—actually, none at all save to understand what she had become. But she wished, with human impatience, that understanding would strike like a bolt of lightning and she would be at peace with her new life.

Instead, the nights flowed interminably one into another and, she thought ruefully, while full comprehension of her powers seemed years away, she already had too great an understanding of eternity.

Though she desired to be isolated from humanity, she found herself drawn to them even more than before.

She and Stephen became regulars in the Dawson community, hiding behind their aliases. Stephen posed as an author who had ghostwritten a number of travel books for a firm in Toronto and was making his first attempt at a novel. Helen was an amateur artist who wanted to paint landscapes and wildlife. The house had been in the family for years. When Stephen's brother, Michael, had taken that job in Quebec, they decided to move to Dawson and start a family.

Helen met a number of Dawson women through her regular doctor's appointments. They clucked with sympathy over Helen's isolation, gave her experienced advice on her pregnancy, and tried to keep their eyes off her husband. For the most part they managed to hide their envy, though Stephen Audet's looks were the subject of many morning coffee klatches.

The doctor, who first saw her when she was five months pregnant, judged her to be along only three. Austra children grew slowly, even in the womb. When he examined her, he noticed little unusual though her pulse and blood pressure were rather low. She said her blood type was O positive because that was the most common. She could use any type now; why concern him with something rare. When he asked to confirm this, she refused and produced a donor card from a hospital in Toronto. He didn't argue. The woman was healthy and he anticipated no problems. Besides, he always grew tongue-tied in her presence.

While she waited for Stephen to finish his errands, she would often visit the Dawson library, where she requested books from Edmonton after she read what interested her in the town's collection. She devoured history and philosophy and fiction with the same voracious energy she had once poured into her work. She took out books on the culture of the native tribes of the area—the Kaska and the Sekani. Astounded at how quickly her mind absorbed information, she learned French, then Spanish and, of course, the language of her new family.

And at last, when there seemed to be nothing else left to do, she began to paint again—formless brilliant splashes of color that would never be for sale, created haphazardly as if she were searching for the artist she would become in her next public life.

Through it all, she sensed her children waiting, absorbed in the throbbing of their own hearts, her blood flowing through them and the touch of one another.

She painted what they felt in the womb.

In September, when the snow began to fall, Helen's pregnancy made it awkward for her to hunt. Then Stephen showed her how to stand motionless at the edge of the woods, pick her prey, and call it to her. The closer an animal came, the more able she was to control it, until she could stand beside it, hold it frozen with her mind while she drank.

She tried her hand at other mental exercises as well, working jigsaw puzzles of increasing complexity, first picture up, then picture down. When she could work a thousand-piece puzzle in less than half an hour, she began doing them blindfolded.

And as her children grew, she merged her mind with those of the twin boys inside her. Though both were Stephen's, the smaller one had a far stronger mind. At six months, she began to sense his feelings, his contentment, his primitive annoyance when his brother, "the brute" she called him, kicked.

The snowplow came weekly, the driver who did the main road automatically diverting to handle their private drive. AustraGlass would shut down soon and the family, those in the world and those exiled from it, would be assembling in Chaves for their solstice sharing, the yearly bonding of their minds. Stephen and Helen had planned to go but Helen was obviously close to term and, though she tried to hide it, growing weaker day by day.

She slept almost round the clock, finally waking with a start, bathed in sweat.

"What is it?" he asked.

"They sense something has changed. They can't understand. They're frightened."

"They . . . or you?"

She didn't answer directly. "Sing to me," she said.

He had been doing this for months, training her ears to hear the range of his voice, teaching her the language of her new people. Usually he played the dulcimer or the *naizet*. Tonight he let his mind supply the music, holding her while he sang the story of an ancient warlord who loved an Austra woman. He tried to carve an empire for her and returned to her, wounded, to ask her to kill him because he had failed.

Helen watched the song unfold as he sang, saw the tents with their tattered banners waving in the dry desert wind, heard the stomping of the horses of the warlord's men. Helen felt the warlord's shame and the woman's pity as she denied his request, nursing him until he was well, then leaving him alone with his dreams of conquest.

The story took hours to tell. When it was over, afternoon had turned to night. Helen lay with her head resting on Stephen's shoulder, her body close to his, sharing his warmth.

He lit a fire and fixed her some tea.

"Why do you think humans take such pleasure in war?" she asked him.

"Because their only immortality is through history. That is the moral of the story I think. She had no need of the warlord's gift." And he had chosen this tale, to impart to her through legend a confidence he could hardly feel.

Helen winced. "What's wrong?" he asked.

She laughed. "The Brute is just making his presence known. I think we should name him Richard, after my uncle." She sipped her tea. "I feel so strange tonight, as if I'm being emptied and filled all at once."

Let it be the human half taking control, he thought. *Let it be nothing more than that.*

III

Rachel arrived on New Year's Eve bringing boxes of books, gifts from the family, and Hillary Dutiel. They flew up from Edmonton on a ski-plane and borrowed the postman's spare truck to make the drive. Stephen hadn't asked them to visit and he didn't want them here, especially when Rachel made it clear she had come to act as midwife. No, he wanted Helen safe in a hospital, surrounded by nurses and doctors who knew nothing of the Austra family and would not consider it tradition to snap the neck of the mother's corpse after the children were born.

If Helen hadn't been close to her delivery, Stephen would have dispersed his rage in a solitary week-long hunt. Instead he stayed, avoiding Rachel and Hillary as best he could in a one-room cottage.

That evening, after Hillary had fallen asleep in a makeshift bed near the kitchen stove, Rachel pulled a folder from her suitcase and handed it to Stephen. "This is the first historical meeting you've ever missed. I knew you would want to see the report as soon as possible. I also brought last year's report for Helen to read.''

Helen put down the novel she'd been reading and joined the two at the table. ''Historical meetings? What are they?'' she asked.

While Stephen paged through the more recent report, Rachel explained to Helen that Historical Projection was the Austra-Glass department responsible for all the family's long-range planning. Experts in politics, sociology, and science worked year-round on annual reports that they presented to the family at the end of the AustraGlass winter shutdown. ''Outside of the solstice sharing a few days earlier, this meeting is the most important annual family event,'' Rachel concluded.

''And I hadn't even given a thought to it,'' Stephen admitted. ''Incipient fatherhood has altered my priorities, yes?''

''And after the twins are born, they'll change again. Austra-Glass must move its headquarters out of Europe within thirty years to as isolated a spot as possible. As we expected, this may be our final move. This area is judged most suitable. The family would like you to find a site. Paul will be sending specifics.''

''We can't conduct business from the wilderness,'' Stephen objected.

''You raised that point last year. The department has repeated their recommendation and suggested that the corporate offices locate in Edmonton. By the time AustraGlass is ready to move, Edmonton will be as modern a city as Toronto. We can have our offices there and our production facilities and the family estates here in the mountains. Paul intends to design a completely self-sufficient family headquarters capable of holding four hundred. He has drawn up a list of site specifications for you to follow in your search.''

''Four hundred! The family only numbers seventeen,'' Helen interrupted.

''Nineteen with the twins. We also have friends. Friends have families and we need life to survive,'' Stephen said.

''One thing the report makes clear is that the future is getting ever more complex,'' Rachel added. ''We don't know that the worst will happen, Helen, but if it does we will need total isolation from the rest of the world.''

"And if the world evolves for the better, Denys would love to manage a wilderness resort," Stephen interjected.

Rachel smiled. Helen didn't. She considered the life in her, the world they would enter. "Isn't there some way we can stop this from happening; maybe someone we could warn?" she asked.

"No one would listen and to try would only draw attention to us. That would be the most dangerous course of action we could take. No, Helen. It's best to prepare and hope that our refuge will never be needed." Stephen rested an arm across her shoulders. She leaned against him, looking down at a timetable for the spread of nuclear weapons across the globe.

Later, after Rachel had changed into dark knit pants and a shirt and disappeared for a night's run, Helen made herself some hot chocolate. When she came back from the kitchen, she saw Stephen with the report open on his lap, staring into the fire. She sat beside him, waiting for him to share his thoughts.

She knew he was thinking of something else when he asked, "Would you like Hillary to stay with us?"

"Oh, yes, but I didn't think that you would want her here since . . . ." Her voice trailed off. She felt oddly embarrassed.

"Then you are aware that she desires you, yes? If she stays, you'll have to face that."

"We all will," Helen said. "I still want her here."

"Good. I'm going to be gone a great deal after the twins are born. You'll need help and company and there will be times I'll want to take you with me." He fingered the black pendant she wore and she knew he was thinking of Charles as he added, "We won't give up, Helen. No matter what happens I'll find a place for us and we will survive."

Helen stretched out, resting her head on his legs. Her children were silent tonight, waiting. She heard a sound outside, a musical voice calling, felt Stephen turn to face the door. "Shall we join her?" he said.

"Of course."

He helped Helen up and they opened the door to a rush of moonlight and wind-driven snow. A few yards from the house Rachel stood with a deer beside her, shivering and wild-eyed

with fear. —You need your strength.— Rachel conveyed to
Helen. —Come. Feast.—

Helen, unconcerned by her bare feet, took a step forward,
then felt a moist heat flowing from her. She looked down and
saw the liquid running down her legs, the blood and water melting the snow. Her knees buckled. Stephen caught her as she fell.

Through Helen's labor, Stephen found himself pacing like
any expectant father while the women did the work. He had
believed the Dawson clinic would be best but he knew, as he
felt Helen's waves of pain wash over him, that she would have
died there. She might die anyway, he thought privately. He
didn't dare go near her, didn't dare take her hand for fear she
would sense his doubt and weaken further.

At last, exasperated at his uselessness, Rachel ordered him
from the house and he sat outside, running his long fingers
through his hair. They were hard, tensed, ready to take on
the enemy he could never control. He looked up at the stars,
thankful it was night when Helen would be her strongest.
He'd professed to a score of religions in his long life. Each
had its own deity. He prayed to the sum of these now,
"Please, there are so few of us left. For the sake of my
family, don't let her die."

As he said it, the thought of living without her struck him
fully. His hands began to shake as an emotion, new and pure,
surfaced from somewhere deep within him. Were he able, he
would cry now, not from fear or sorrow but from the exquisite wonder of it.

Later, after five pints of blood, one of them from Hillary,
brought Helen's bleeding under control, after the two little boys
were washed and wrapped in blankets and resting in their cradle,
after Stephen and Rachel hunted silently, letting death renew
their bodies, he lay beside Helen, sharing her dreams.

—I love you,— he told her and he knew that the words had
never held quite this meaning before. He felt her acceptance,
her response.

—Of course.—

Together their minds moved out, embracing their children.

PART THREE

THE INSTRUMENT

1958

ELEVEN

1

Dick Wells was forty-one when he learned he was about to die.

He supposed there wasn't any way for a doctor to break the news gently and he preferred the straightforward approach. He'd had to tell others the same sad news throughout his career with the Cleveland police and, before that, during the war. *I'm sorry*, Dick would say to the wounded. *Is there anything you need to tell me?* Somewhere beneath the honest sympathy of the words in a place only he could touch he'd felt a mean self-righteousness. He was alive and someone else was dying.

"I'm sorry," the doctor said.

Yeah, Dick thought. *Yeah, he probably was.*

In two days Dick would celebrate his third wedding anniversary. As he drove home after the follow-up exam, he recalled that he deliberately hadn't told Judy that the physical the chief had ordered had been anything more than routine. At the time, he hadn't wanted anyone but John Corey, his old partner and now chief medical examiner for the city, to share his worry. Now he decided to wait a little while before telling her the truth and wondered how long he'd be able to hold out.

He thought of his family—of Carol, ready to start her sophomore year at St. Joe's High School, of Alan, who was about to skip fifth grade and seemed on his way to getting a math scholarship to Case, of how Judy would have to raise children that were only hers by marriage.

Not that she wasn't up to it. The fact was, once she knew the doctor's verdict, she'd take charge of everything. Judy was always willing to take charge of his problems at the first sign of any weakness on his part. Competence was one of her most charming vices and he was glad she was so capable but he'd be damned if he'd let her manage his death for him.

Now, if he ignored how anxiously his heart beat or the tight bands of tension across his chest, he felt fine. He'd wait a week, put together some plan before he gave her the news, something to inspire confidence that though his body was fading, his mind was as sharp as ever.

Well, if this wedding anniversary would be his last, he'd make it as special as possible. There was a little Spanish restaurant south of town that Judy adored. The food was terrible and he always suspected the lights were kept low to hide the bugs crawling along the baseboard but the place did reek of atmosphere and the owner hired a violinist on weekends. Dick decided to make reservations for Friday. Though it was more than a tradition that he gave her flowers on their anniversary, this time he'd arrange to have them delivered to their table.

As he drove home, he remembered the first time he'd sent her any. After Stephen had taken Helen to Chaves, Judy had refused to return his phone calls—all of them—and he'd finally sent a marriage proposal enclosed with two dozen roses. He'd stood outside her apartment that night waiting for her to come home. She'd arrived balancing roses and vase in one hand, her briefcase and purse in the other. Water from the vase had spilled leaving dark stains on her bright blue blouse and purple skirt. She hadn't said a word as he followed her inside and convinced her that no one would ever understand what had happened to her the way he did, could ever love her the way he did. Though he had a well-trained memory, he did not recall half of what he'd said but apparently it had been enough—and now their marriage wouldn't last nearly long enough. Purple, bright blue, red. He wanted a bouquet

wild and colorful as the woman herself and decided to order
them in person.

He'd brought Judy flowers from the shop on Payne Avenue
before. Though he didn't like its new owner, force of habit
and an open parking space drew him back to it. As he crossed
the street, he noticed the shop's door hanging half open and
approached it with instinctive caution.

Beyond the reflection in the florist's window, he saw the
owner backed against the wall behind the register. His attacker had a gun pressed under his chin, one hand gripping
his shoulder. Robbery didn't appear to be a motive. The young
assailant was well dressed and this shop didn't do much business in midweek. Though Dick wasn't sure exactly what was
going on, he assumed he had to act fast. He pulled his gun,
kicked open the door, and leveled it at the attacker.

"Police!" he yelled, then, "Drop it."

Instead of obeying, the assailant swung his own gun toward
Dick. In the moment before Dick fired, he saw the man's
hands shaking, the sweat on his face, the painful hunger in
his eyes. As Dick's bullets hit him, the man fell backward,
cracking the glass of the cooler, staining the roses and white
carnations behind him with his blood.

Dick raised the man's head just enough to pile some of the
florist's bags underneath it, dialed for an ambulance he knew
would arrive too late, then phoned the police. Afterward, he
turned his attention to the florist. The florist's knees had
buckled and he lay in a heap behind his counter. "You know
him?" Dick asked.

"Christ, yeah. I'm surprised you don't." Dick stared at
the unconscious man while the florist continued: "That's Peter Carrera."

"Dominic Carrera's son?"

"Yeah. Domie couldn't handle the kid's habit so he cut
him off. Word got out that anybody who supplied Pete would
be out of business permanently. I used to sell to him. He
tracked me down." The florist pulled open a counter drawer.
In the back were cellophane-wrapped packets of what looked

like heroin. "I would of sold to him again if you hadn't come in. You gonna arrest me?"

Dick nodded and the florist replied, "Good. A couple of years in jail will give Domie time to remember it wasn't me who shot his only kid. As for you, your future ain't worth shit, not anymore."

Dick laughed. He couldn't help himself. Life could be so damned ironic.

Judy knew about the shooting before Dick came home. Corey might have called her or maybe one of her friends on the force. She greeted Dick at the door with a hug, then sat beside him. "Are you all right?" she asked.

Dick nodded and gave her a few details she might not have heard from the stoolie at the station. "The florist has decided to trade everything he knows about Dominic Carrera for full-scale police protection. It's the break in their investigation that the crime unit's been praying for. They'll put Carrera away for a long time."

"When?"

"If everything goes right, they'll arrest him in the next few weeks. Once he's in jail nobody in that organization will touch me."

"In the meantime, what about us?" She sounded as if his paycheck were going to be late or he planned to take an unpaid leave. Brave, like always.

He hoped she wouldn't become suspicious when he gave her the chief's order. It wasn't like the chief to tell one of his officers to cut and run, but since Dick would probably be quitting work soon anyway, the chief had ordered him to take a paid leave. Dick left out the chief's rationale when he told her he had the month off. "I thought we might take the kids to Boston to visit your folks. Maybe we could leave them there and take a side trip to New York. Paul and Elizabeth are always offering to put us up."

"Your fall vacation's coming."

"Do you want to go to Canada?" For the last two years, he'd spent a week with Stephen and Helen every autumn. He always asked Judy to come. She always refused but these were different circumstances.

"No. I want you to take Alan when you go." Sensing Dick about to say no, she added, "He's more levelheaded than Carol. He'll keep their secret. Stephen told you last year that you could bring him, didn't he? And Alan would love to go."

"You sound like they're . . . well, normal people."

"They're *not*. That's the point. Listen, Dick, I know Carrera. I met him when I worked for the *Press*. If he can't reach you, he'll go after Alan. I want you both in the safest place you can be."

"What about you? You can't stay here."

"Carol and I are going to stay with Elizabeth and Paul. I called her while I was waiting for you. We can leave in the morning. There's a flight to Denver leaving about the same time. From there you can catch a plane to Edmonton. There's even enough time to wire Stephen and have him meet you."

"You have this all planned out, don't you?"

"I want you safe, that's all."

"Protected once again by the predatory beast?"

He sounded so bitter that Judy frowned. "What's the matter?" she asked.

Last time he'd been in this much danger he and Stephen had been partners in the fight. Now Dick was just a potential victim. "Nothing," he lied, then added the truth, "it's just that a month seems like such a long time."

"It is but those trips north are always good for you. If we go to my parents' place, you'll spend your time worrying about every stranger on the beach. This way you'll be able to relax. Considering how well you've been sleeping nights, you need it."

"I won't even know when I can come home," he complained, his resistance already crumbling.

"I'll buy the Cleveland papers every day. I'll send you a telegram as soon as Carrera is arrested. We can even tell Corey how to reach me. The medical examiners always hear all the newest gossip."

Dick was too tired to fight. Besides, what Judy said made perfect sense for more reasons than she knew. Helen was

Dick's niece. She couldn't come here to say good-bye, he'd have to go to her. And after he was gone, well Alan and Helen had always been close. But, as he reluctantly agreed, he thought the last people he wanted to see now were immortal and psychic. How long would it take for Stephen to sense his self-pity and discover the truth?

The family spent the night in a hotel by the airport. Maybe it was just the room and the fact that they had checked in under an assumed name that brought back the past. Dick and Judy didn't speak of it, not even after the kids stopped giggling and fell asleep in their adjoining room. Instead they made love with an urgency they hadn't felt since they'd first met.

In the morning, Dick woke to the brush of Judy's fingers on the four long slashes Charles Austra's nails had made on his body. He wore those scars as he did the one on his thigh where he'd been stabbed a year after he started on the Cleveland police force or the cut on his stomach where the surgeons had opened him up to remove the German bullets he'd taken during the war. The marks of his jobs. He pretended to be asleep as Judy's fingers moved down his side, following the lines from thigh to shoulder. Though Dick's first wife had died ten years ago, he still loved her and always would. He had no right to be jealous of the dead.

They went their separate ways from the airport. Carol and Judy left first, then Dick and his son walked quickly to their own gate. Dick waited until they were in the air and Alan had stopped pressing his nose against the window glass before beginning, awkwardly, to explain in as vague a way as possible who they would be visiting.

"I know," Alan said before Dick could finish. Then he told his father all about his dreams. He described Stephen's house, their land. He even knew the names of their children and the nearest town. The details convinced Dick that his son had somehow shared his cousin's life. For the rest of the flight, Dick considered how this bond could be possible and why, of all of them, only Alan could accomplish it.

Distracted first by the need to explain where they were going, then by his son's strange revelations, he didn't notice the late arrival who sat behind him on the plane to Denver or think anything of the second late passenger who caught the connecting flight to Edmonton. Dick and the second man even exchanged a few words at the Edmonton airport while Dick and Alan claimed their bags, threw them in the back of a brown pickup, and drove away in the company of a black-haired young man with a face no one would forget.

The man caught the first return flight to Denver. His accomplice had learned Wells was headed for Dawson. He had the license plate of his host's truck.

Enough. He'd been paid to trail, not kill. The killing would be left for someone younger and more capable, someone who would not fail.

II

During the three-hour drive from Edmonton to Dawson, Alan said very little. He sat between Stephen and his father, clutching the carry-on bag holding his books and chess set along with the box of chocolates for Helen and the blocks that he'd bought for Helen's babies at the Denver airport. Stephen and his father didn't say much, either, and Alan stared out the window at the trees and the mountains. He'd never seen mountains except in pictures. Those had always been sunlit, and shown from a distance. Here, close up on a grey and rainy day, they looked huge and frightening. When they drove through narrow passes, he craned his head to look nervously at the rock walls, waiting for them to fall and crush the car.

Stephen rested a hand on his knee. "Don't worry. I've made this drive a hundred times and they never move. Your father told me at the airport that you have dreams about Helen. Tell me about them."

Alan did. Somehow he remembered more about them now than he did on the plane. He could even see some of the dreams in his mind. When he'd finished, Stephen said, "You missed your cousin a great deal, yes?"

"Sure." Alan tried to turn his attention back to the mountains. He felt embarrassed and thankful when Stephen didn't ask him anything more.

They reached the house late in the evening. It was everything Alan remembered, and as he hugged Helen, he stared past her, openmouthed, at the lamplit room inside. Then he saw Hillary, and for a moment he forgot the rest.

He'd dreamed about her too, but she had seemed the least real of any of his visions—a beautiful, quiet creature on the edge of his nights. He flushed as they were introduced and, after a quick "hello," stared at his shoes.

"Would you like to see the babies?" Helen asked.

Anything, the boy thought. *Anything to get me away from her.* Not that he didn't want to be near Hillary but she made him feel so terribly awkward, little, and dumb.

"Hillary, take Alan in. And pull Dickey out of his father's loom."

Dickey had taken advantage of everyone's absence to crawl out of his crib and, with feet and hands on the floor, waddle out of the nursery to explore everything he wasn't supposed to touch. His brother, Patrick, woke as he left. Smaller and far less mobile, Patrick had a mind capable of instigating more trouble from his crib than Dickey could ever conceive of causing on his own. Now, with a wicked knowing smile, he led his duller brother on.

Dickey ripped at the threads of the loom, breaking a few, tasting some of the others. Hearing Hillary coming, he gripped the most colorful skeins tightly with his long-fingered hands. With effort, Hillary pried his fingers away from the yarn, then picked him up. "Chair!" he declared. Hillary immediately sat him down on a potty chair next to the stove. He stood, turned and peed standing up, exactly as he had seen his father do, then grinned triumphantly at Hillary, displaying four tiny teeth on the top and bottom and two longer ones in the back of his mouth.

"Good boy!" Hillary said, and carried him back to the nursery. Alan, the flush deepening and spreading from his cheeks to his entire face, followed.

Hillary set him down next to his brother on a thick feather mattress in a large carved wooden crib. They immediately joined hands, then the two naked, long-limbed infants stared up at Alan with huge, prying eyes. They looked alike though far from identical. Though both had their father's pale skin and loosely curled hair, one was larger than the other and his hair was grey rather than black and shone like polished silver in the candlelight.

"Hello, Alan Wells," the smaller one said in a singsong voice that seemed to be an exaggeration of his father's accent.

Alan gaped at the pair. "How—how old are they?" he stammered.

"Twenty months though they look much smaller. The big one with the yarn in his fingers is Dickey. The smaller one is Patrick. He's been causing all the trouble today, isn't that right?" Hillary purred the last words and began stroking Patrick's stomach in a widening circle. Then she seemed to realize where her hand was moving and pulled quickly back, giving the infant a sharp look as if he'd somehow been responsible.

Patrick responded to Hillary's retreat by biting Dickey's hand. Dickey wailed in a high piercing screech like the sound of an angry blue jay and pounced on his brother. The boys immediately became a twisting knot of arms and legs, rocking the crib with their battle.

"Come on," Hillary said and began to leave the room.

Alan didn't want to leave the boys alone. Their fight looked too lethal. He stayed by the cradle, staring down at the twins who battled like a pair of Tasmanian devils. He wondered what would happen if he tried to separate them and not at all sure he wanted to find out. He wished now that he'd brought them crayons and coloring books instead of wooden alphabet blocks. They'd probably use the blocks as weapons.

Hillary stopped at the door and motioned for him to follow. "It's all right to leave them. They can't hurt each other,

not really." After they were both in the main room, she closed
the nursery door, making certain it was latched.

Stephen and Alan's father had just brought in their suit-
cases. "The twins are fighting again," Hillary said to Stephen. "I think they're frightening Alan."

"I'll toss them outside and let the rain cool them . . ."
Stephen noticed Alan's horrified expression and stopped midsentence. His smile vanished for a moment as he closed his
eyes. In the nursery, one of the twins gave a quick "yip" of
surprise, then both boys fell immediately silent.

Alan stared with wide eyes at the door, then, searching for
some semblance of the usual, walked over to Helen who was
boiling water on the stove.

"Do you still have the dog?" Alan asked her.

"What dog?"

"The one you call Wolf."

Helen glanced at Dick. "You haven't told him very much
about us, have you?"

"I thought it would be better if Stephen did. I wasn't certain how he'd react."

"If that's true, why did you bring him here?" Stephen
asked.

"A sudden emergency. One I really didn't want to discuss
in a wire from Western Union."

—Not you and Judy?— Helen questioned privately.

Dick shook his head once, slowly so his son wouldn't notice. "As soon as the coffee's ready, I'll explain," he said
aloud.

They all sat around the table, Alan and Hillary drinking
mugs of hot chocolate, Dick slowly sipping his coffee as he
described the shooting the day before.

"Is there a chance you were followed?" Helen asked when
he'd finished.

"There's always a chance," Dick admitted, "but it's slim.
We were out of the house less than two hours after the shooting. Carrera will assume the force followed usual procedure
and has us hidden somewhere under police protection."

"So why didn't you send the family east and stay for the fight?" Stephen asked.

"I don't handle organized crime." Dick noticed Stephen's puzzled look and added, "Besides, I didn't want to pass up the opportunity for some extra paid vacation."

"And to bring Alan, yes?"

"He's ready to know all of this. But I think you should be the one to tell him."

"As you wish." Stephen slid down the bench until he sat across from the boy. Alan was just finishing his chocolate, his head tilted back, when he froze and the hand holding the mug slowly lowered it to the table. Alan sat so still he hardly seemed to breathe as he stared, expressionless, at Stephen.

Not a word was spoken but Dick knew that Stephen was conveying a great deal to Alan in private. Stephen finished some minutes later with a quick toss of his head and held out his hand. Alan immediately joined hands with Stephen while wiping the chocolate mustache from his mouth with his other sleeve. Then he stared at Stephen, a frown growing on his face. "Would you show me your teeth?" he finally asked.

Stephen grinned, revealing rear fangs long and white as those of some great cat.

"Can I feel them?"

"Yes."

Alan walked around the table and stood in front of Stephen. He touched the tip of his index finger to the end of one long tooth and jerked his hand back. "They're sharp!" he exclaimed.

"They have to be. They're how I live." Stephen patted the bench and Alan sat down between Stephen and Helen.

"Is it always that easy with kids?" Dick asked.

"It depends on the kid." Stephen hugged Alan, saying as he did, "Now we must understand your dreams, yes?"

"Yeah," Dick answered for his son. He wanted this mystery solved.

"I've considered everything I know about situations such as these and only one thing makes it possible. He has family blood in him."

"Not possible!" Dick retorted, uncertainty making him angry.

"I think I know," Helen said. "He has my mother's blood. Remember, Uncle. After Carol was born she donated blood for Mary."

"Jesus! That's right. Helen, you must have been eight or nine. I'm surprised you remembered."

"I recently went through a difficult delivery myself," Helen reminded him.

"Do you dream about Alan?" Dick asked Helen.

"Sometimes. I assumed they only showed how much I missed him. Apparently, though, we were contacting each other."

Dick asked Stephen the same question. Stephen replied immediately and with some annoyance, "I never dream."

"Never?"

"Not the pleasant way your kind dreams. Ours are a kind of delirium that comes with stress or grave mental illness. They aren't pleasant. I suppose the closest I ever come to dreaming is at the movies. The lights dim. The images flash and for as long as I sit there, I am not in control of what I see."

That explained Stephen's fascination with and terrible taste in movies but not Alan's talent. "But if his mind somehow comes here, shouldn't you at least feel his presence?"

"He has no power to make his presence clear. My mind is stronger than Helen's. Perhaps if he dreamed about me, I would sense him but he does not," Stephen explained.

"But shouldn't he be dreaming about all of you?"

"No," Stephen answered. "The family has a yearly blood sharing to strengthen the psychic bonds between us. Alan's ties to us would be far too weak. Then, of course, we must consider Alan's resolve. He wanted to contact his cousin, so he did."

"I always knew you'd be the first to know," Helen told her cousin with a friendly wink. "We have books on dreams. Would you like Hillary and me to show them to you?"

"Oh, please," Alan replied and followed the women to the bookcase on the far side of the room.

Dick watched his son kneeling next to Helen, his fair skin and dark hair making him resemble Stephen's sons. "Can you change him the way you did Helen?" Dick quietly asked Stephen.

"No. I am sorry."

"Don't be. It was just something I figured I should know."

Stephen glanced at him and Dick sensed the unspoken question. He shrugged and shook his head. The wall, he thought, had begun falling down. He assumed the worst when Stephen told him privately, —It is late. We'll wait until Alan is asleep and then speak more of this, yes?—

They moved the twins' crib out of the nursery into the main room so Dick and his son would have some privacy. After Alan had gone to sleep and Hillary retired to her loft above the kitchen, Dick sat on the sofa beside his niece, watching Stephen pace in front of the fire, waiting for the confession to be pulled from him.

Stephen sat in a chair beside Dick and looked at him sadly. "I do not pry into the minds of my friends, Richard. Whatever problem is troubling you is yours to keep. No, I wish to speak to you more about Alan." He hesitated as if uncertain how to explain, then said, "For his sake, I did not tell the full truth this evening. As his father, you should know."

"He's not in any danger, is he?"

"No, if there were any physical problems stemming from his mother's transfusion, they would have surfaced by now. But the sharing of our blood is forbidden and with good reason."

"Go on."

"When Alan accepted what I am so easily, it may have been his own inclination or it may have been because I wanted him to accept me."

"I don't understand the difference."

"I didn't try to control him but it may have happened anyway. Our blood in him binds him to us. It causes a subtle kind of slavery."

Dick considered this, then commented, "I don't like the idea of my son being controlled by anyone. On the other hand, I don't understand why your customs prohibit it. I'd think slaves would come in handy sometimes."

"We do share blood, but only with our victims, particularly those whose wills are troublesome and strong. It tightens our bond with them and enhances the pleasure of the kill so much so that a thousand years ago we had ritual bloodlettings and forced our victims to drink. But we prohibit sharings with friends and lovers for our own protection. Our minds are"—he hesitated, groping for words to describe concepts the family accepted as so natural they did not need names— "linked with our bodies. This allows us to move our minds out of them, to . . . extend as Helen calls it . . . and to return to them. We share our blood with one another to tighten the psychic bond between us. But now Alan is part of us as well. We will feel the loss when he dies; not as painfully as when one of our own is destroyed but enough that we will know. And because he shares this bond with us, we are responsible for him. Think of it as a form of . . . relationship."

"We're related anyway," Helen reminded him.

"So we are," Stephen agreed. "And, so you understand, we would never try to control him unless our own lives demanded it." Stephen's voice hardened as he added, "Now I wish to discuss your reason for being here. If you had told me the truth before you came I would have insisted that you stay away. I have children. I am concerned for their safety and I do not like the threat you bring with you."

"Stephen!" Helen exclaimed.

"This needs to be said, my love, for all our sakes."

"He's right," Dick cut in. "Everything happened so fast, I wasn't thinking."

"Yes, you were, Richard. You assumed that I am a killer and I will kill for you."

Even that hint of anger in his friend brought back memories Dick wished he could forget. "You asked the same of me once," he said.

"And now, as I did then, I will make our position completely clear. If Helen and I were using our own names, I would take you to the Dawson authorities and explain why you are here. But if I do that now, I risk too many questions.

So understand that whatever happens, we will be completely on our own.''

"I understand. I'll go in the morning," Dick said stiffly.

"We want you to stay, Richard. Besides, if someone knows you are here, your leaving will not stop them from coming if only to find out where you have gone.''

"I suppose," Dick admitted.

"So what must concern us is how soon your killers will act if they followed you.''

"They'll make their move within a few days. Otherwise, they might lose my trail and Carrera would take it out on them.''

"And when they 'make their move' as you say, how will they do it?''

"They'll send someone into Dawson first to ask a few questions about you. If you're hiding as well as you were in Cleveland, you'll look like an easy mark but one they'd just as soon avoid if they can. Is there any time you regularly go to town, maybe to drive Hillary in to school?''

"She studies at home but we do go into town every Tuesday afternoon. Either Hillary or Helen goes shopping while I take a course in auto mechanics at the Dawson high school. We're away from the house about four hours.''

In spite of the seriousness of the discussion, Dick chuckled. "You don't like having any gaps in your education, do you? Anyway, this tight a schedule is good. Tomorrow's Friday. I'll take your supplies list and drive into Dawson and make my presence known. Are you up to skipping a couple of classes?''

Stephen agreed and Dick went on, "Then for the next two weeks, start into town like always, drive about halfway, then turn around and come back. If the killers don't show up by then, they never will.''

"Good. I'd like you to enjoy at least part of your stay here. You need it, yes?''

Dick sighed. "God, yes.'' He stared into the dying fire. He wanted to tell Stephen why he had almost stayed away this year and why he had really brought his son but this was a time for strength and confidence, not confessions of weakness.

—When you're ready, Richard, you will tell me, yes?—

Dick looked across the table at Stephen and nodded slowly. "Before I leave," he said. He owed Stephen that much. He watched the flames consume the rest of the wood, so lost in his own problems that he didn't notice Stephen and his niece leaving the house until he felt the cold draft circling his feet, saw the flames grow and die as the door opened and shut.

As he got undressed and slipped into a sleeping bag, he heard a distant familiar screech answered by the howling of a wolf. His son rolled over and grabbed his hand. "Is Stephen here?" Alan asked in a frightened whisper.

"Yeah," Dick lied.

"Good."

Alan slid closer to his father, his breathing growing deeper and more even as he went back to sleep. Once his son's admitting more faith in the strength of someone other than himself would have gnawed at Dick. Not anymore. If Stephen had asked him to go, he would have tried to leave Alan behind.

TWELVE

1

If ever sons could claim to have been molded by their fathers, it was the Carreras.

Raymond Carrera's father had been a fisherman on Sardinia. He had hobbied at politics, eventually becoming elected mayor of Bosa. His only progressive move had been to give his oldest son a large sum of money and send him to America a few years before the First World War. When the village discovered they'd been robbed, they hung Carrera's father in the town square. After Raymond learned of this, he stopped writing his family, quit college, and took a job managing a restaurant. In two years he had saved enough to send back every penny his father had stolen. He went to law school, finishing in the year Prohibition started. His legal career was short but remarkable. He represented the most powerful Mafia family in Ohio, marrying the boss's only child when he was twenty-seven, taking over the family's operation when his father-in-law died five years later.

That same year, a series of murders stunned the quiet fishing town of Bosa. When they ended, everyone responsible for Joseph Carrera's killing had died.

Dominic's mother died soon after he was born. His father remarried within months and Dominic was raised by his stepmother. In her care, Dominic grew into a pudgy, sullen child, ignored by his father. Raymond's second wife had three daughters before Raymond bought an annulment so he could

115

marry again. His third wife gave birth to a son when Dominic was fifteen. A healthy baby, it died in its sleep when it was five weeks old.

That night, Raymond Carrera almost killed his firstborn but Dominic admitted and denied nothing. Even when his jaw was shattered and his arm hung useless at his side, Dominic stared dry-eyed at his father, refusing to say a single word.

One of Raymond's men took Dominic to the hospital. Raymond Carrera never mentioned the incident to his son but Dominic's defiance must have earned him some measure of respect because, soon afterward, Dominic started learning the family business.

Their main sources of income then had been real estate and alcohol. When Prohibition ended, the family moved into other legitimate enterprises financed by income from prostitution, gambling, and loan-sharking. Though Raymond would have preferred to keep his son out of the illegitimate enterprises, he had no choice but to expose Dominic to all of it and hope the young man had intelligence and caution to balance his temper. He needn't have worried. Dominic Carrera's life was directed by expediency and his guiding principal was to never question the necessity of doing what worked. Had he been born to a more respectable family he might have become a lawyer or a politician, one of the conscienceless community leaders who might never commit illegal acts nor support good ones unless their careers dictated they do so. As Raymond Carrera gradually gave up control of his enterprises, Dominic added drug importing to the line of family businesses. The Carreras prospered, and by the time Dominic Carrera moved into his father's office, it was more powerful than it had been at the height of Prohibition. Among his wealth, Dominic Carrera could include a number of union leaders, two precinct captains in the Cleveland police, a state representative, and a U.S. Senator with his eyes on the presidency. Not a bad deck of cards, and Dominic knew, if he used them sparingly, he could play them for years.

But Dominic did not have an heir he could trust. He'd vowed not to repeat the mistakes of his father and raised his

only son, Peter, with all the attention limited time allowed
him to give. When he realized his attention should have included stronger discipline, he sent the teenager to a military
school. Peter was expelled three months later for drinking in
his dormitory and, while intoxicated, breaking his roommate's nose with a chair. When he came home, Dominic
forced him to dry out, then got him a job at one of the family's legitimate businesses, a spaghetti house on the near east
side. Close enough to downtown to be respectable, the restaurant also catered to a walk-in crowd that bought their drinks
at the bar and picked up their supplies from a drug distributor
running a quasi-independent operation out of Carrera's store-
room. When Peter learned of the underground system, he
demanded a cut in goods. By the time Dominic discovered
the shortages, Peter was hooked on heroin and codeine and
had returned to the most dangerous drug of all—alcohol.

The distributor who hadn't had the guts to stand up to the
boss's son disappeared. Peter was forced to go cold turkey.

Nobody assumed he'd be desperate enough to die for a fix.

A small, wiry man, Dominic Carrera made up for his size
with a voice that could be heard in neighboring houses. The
men around him learned to ignore his volume and listen instead for his whisper.

He had whispered when he'd ordered the deaths of two of
his father's closest advisers because he heard they planned on
challenging his control. He didn't bother to substantiate the
rumors before he set his killer loose. Truth wasn't the point.
Dominic Carrera had to earn respect and earn it fast or his
hold on the Cleveland underworld would crumble.

The job was done by a lone gunman while the victims ate
lunch in one of Carrera's restaurants. Dominic made a point
of being on the premises that day, watching the shooting from
the adjoining bar, and immediately calling the police.

Then he sent his killer on two final jobs. The man blew up
Carrera's yacht along with the boat of a small-time smuggler
who'd begun handling a significant volume of heroin on the
east side. Then the gunman waited, hidden near the dock, for
Dominic Carrera and the federal investigators to arrive at the

scene. A Carrera-owned warehouse exploded at the same moment he fired two shots. The first wounded Carrera. The second killed the chief investigator. Carrera, who spent a week in the hospital recovering from the near-fatal wound, was never implicated in either crime. Even so, he acquired a reputation as a ruthless voyeur who had to be present to verify every hit.

And the murderer, the target of a full-scale hunt by both FBI and local police, disappeared.

As a result of the shooting, a plan the gunman had devised, the investigation moved in a different direction, seeking the independent gang trying to move in on the Carreras. Their new focus gave Carrera time to consolidate his authority, beef up security, and ferret out the weak links in his organization. Now, one desperate act by his son and Carrera's own deadly reputation had undone years of careful work.

But his legal problems took second place now. The first was occupied with the man who killed his son. Soon his best assassin would be on Wells's trail. Nobody could hunt so well. Nobody could shoot as accurately. Nobody else could be trusted to do what must be done.

11

Donna Harper never believed she could live with anyone more vicious than her father until she met Russ.

Not that he hadn't been nice enough in the beginning. As a matter of fact, she'd been damn thankful to run into him.

She'd been hitchhiking west to her grandmother's and had gotten dropped off in a tiny town near Rapid City. She'd gone into a restaurant and ordered eggs and a glass of milk with her last bit of change. Her arithmetic had never been good and she found herself a dime short. Donna laid what she had by her plate and started to leave when the waitress called after her.

Donna would have run if there was anyplace to go. The cops would catch her easy in a town this small. If she told the truth about her age, they'd send her home. If she lied, well, they probably had vagrancy laws. She decided to bluff it. "That's all I got," she admitted to the waitress.

"Look, if I'm short at the till, I got to pay for it. You'll have to see the manager. Lou!" the waitress called into the back room.

A man walked up beside Donna, moving so softly she didn't hear him coming until he slammed a quarter down on the counter. "Keep the change," he said, and winking at Donna as if they'd planned this scene together, he followed her outside and grabbed her arm. "You with somebody?" he asked.

"No."

"You live around here?" he asked.

"No."

He pointed to her knapsack. "That all the luggage you got?"

She studied her rescuer. Though he might be as old as her father, he looked like a kid drifter—his lean build, dirty blond hair, jeans, and check shirt letting him fit in anywhere, his accent impossible to place. And his face—well, it was the sort of face no one would look at twice except for the eyes. Though they were a cold, flat blue with an evenness that gave hints of danger, they crinkled at the edges as if he always smiled. He also smelled of after-shave, the spicy friendly kind she'd always liked. Even though his grip was so tight it hurt, she stared at him and nodded.

"Need a lift?"

She wondered what would happen if she said no and decided to avoid the risk. "Where you headed?" she asked.

"Anywhere's better than here, ain't it?" he answered. They walked around the side of the building to an old Chevy wagon. He pulled her knapsack out of her hand and dumped it behind the seat next to a leather suitcase and a sleeping bag. Donna got in the front, wondering if she had made a mistake and not certain how to get out of it.

They crossed the border into Wyoming and left the highway, pulling onto a dead-end dirt road. He reached into the glove box for a bottle. "Have a drink," he said.

"I'm a minor," she responded.

He grinned. "So I figured."

Donna tasted it, coughed, then forced herself to swallow one gulp. Maybe it would calm her down a little bit, help her think. "What is this shit?" she asked as she looked at the unfamiliar label.

"Armengac," he said. "French brandy."

She read the label, noting the importer. "You from Cleveland?" she asked.

He buried his hand in her long hair, forcing her to look at him. "Listen, girl. Don't ask where I'm from. Don't ask why I'm here. Don't even ask my name and we'll get along just fine."

She stared at him, real fright showing for the first time in her eyes. In response, he twisted her hair. She gave a low sob of pain and he kissed her, then crawled over the seat, pulling her after him onto the mattress.

Donna never had a chance to determine if what followed was rape or a mutual agreement, if she should fight or just let him have his way. It was over too fast. When he handed her the bottle again, the brandy tasted better, its warmth filling her, helping her relax. "Here's the deal," he said as she pulled on her jeans. "I'll take care of you for as long as you want me to. When you tell me you want to leave, you go. OK?"

She refused to agree to anything. "You broke my zipper," she replied instead.

He swung the car around and drove into Newcastle, parking in front of a women's clothing store. "What size are you?"

"Size five."

"Wait here."

As soon as he was out of sight, she opened the passenger door, got out, and pretended to stretch her legs. There were people all around her, a police station on the corner. All she'd have to do was grab her bag, go to the station, and report him. They'd pick him up if not for rape, then for sex with a minor. Then they'd send her home and her father would beat the hell out of her.

To Donna an unknown danger was always less threatening than a certain one. She got back in the car.

He came out a few minutes later carrying a shopping bag filled with packages. "Go on, look," he told her, laying the bag on her lap.

Inside were jeans, shirts, a sundress, panties, and a pair of pink baby doll pajamas with a white feather trim. Donna didn't thank him; after all, she was worth more than a quarter. "What can I call you?" she asked.

"Russ." He didn't ask her name. For the next few weeks she would be known simply as "girl."

She'd expected that Russ lived in his car or had a hovel somewhere, a place matched with his personality so his spread near Buffalo surprised her. The ranch house was on a gravel road rising into the Bighorn Mountains with only four other houses on the street, the nearest at least a quarter mile away. He dropped her dusty bag in its spacious foyer and led her through the living room past blue vinyl couches and glass-topped tables to the kitchen with its long dining counter. He opened two beers and took her out back to show her a pool and patio with a built-in barbecue surrounded by a high wooden fence.

Even when Donna didn't have a place to stay, she managed to sponge off and wash her hair every day. Now she stood on the patio, amazed to the point of speechlessness by her good fortune. He took off his clothes, then methodically stripped her and tossed her in the pool, diving after her. The water was warm as the womb, and for the first time since she'd met Russ, she relaxed. After the swim they had sex on a chaise longue, then lay back and baked in the late afternoon sun. Later they grilled steaks and Donna had her first good meal in days. Those hours were the only pleasant ones she would ever have with Russ.

The abuse started the next morning. Eager to display her domestic skills, she'd gotten up early, put on the pink pajamas he'd bought for her, and made breakfast. She hand-squeezed the oranges for juice, cooked French toast and bacon, and arranged place settings on the counter. To fill the time until he got up, she cleaned the living room, putting all his books and magazines into neat piles on the glass-topped coffee table. Afterward, she turned on the radio, so low that Russ wouldn't be disturbed, and began to dance.

Once she had dreamed of being a dancer but that had been years ago in the better times when the family had money and she could afford to dream. The memory hadn't faded. Not yet. Maybe never. She still danced when she was happy and she knew how well she danced, how beautiful she looked in her grace—like Loretta Young in her flowing gowns rather than the dull-haired little creature she saw each morning in the mirror. She whirled around the room, wrists crossed above her, her bare feet brushing silently over the ivory-colored rug until the song ended and she slowly folded forward like a flower closing for the night.

Russ came into the room, wrapped in an old flannel robe. "Where were you?" he growled.

Donna jumped to her feet and brushed the lint off the feathers on her pajamas. "I cooked. I made . . ."

"I can get my own damned food. I want to wake up with you next to me."

Russ might have meant that as a compliment but it didn't sound like one. He grabbed her arm and yanked her off the high stool, dragging her down the hall into the bedroom, pushing her back on the bed. He crawled in beside her, not touching her at all. Donna tried to hide her tears, wiping her nose on the edge of the sheet because she didn't dare ask him to pass her a tissue.

Later, he got up and left her. She stayed in bed another half hour before she tapped the courage to get dressed and leave the room.

Russ was in the pool swimming laps. A dirty cereal bowl sat on the counter. He'd had some of her orange juice, that was all. She began scraping the dirty dishes and stacking them by the sink when she abruptly doubled over the trash can and started to sob.

You're a survivor, she reminded herself. *You've survived worse before, you'll get through this.* After rinsing her eyes at the sink, she soaked the dishes, then peeked out back. Russ was still swimming his laps in the small pool with an energetic crawl that made him look like an animal pacing a cage. Now was her chance to find the phone. She'd call her grandmother in LA, explain what she'd done, and ask for help.

As she looked for the phone, she realized that she hadn't noticed the street name or house number or memorized the license plate of the car. She could call the operator, ask them to trace the phone number. Then what?

Her stupidity didn't make any difference. Russ didn't have a phone; not in any of the rooms, not even in the bedroom closet or the one in the spare room, empty except for a few storage boxes.

"What are you doing, girl?"

Donna whirled. Russ stood in the doorway dripping water from his bare body onto the hardwood floor. "Looking for sheets," she replied, thankful she'd learned through her years at home to be a quick, experienced liar.

"I don't have spares. Besides, the ones on the bed are still clean."

"Not after last night." She gave him a seductive look and though his lips smiled, his eyes looked ready to kill.

"You stay out of my stuff, you hear?"

"Yeah. I hear."

He moved closer to her and unbuttoned her blouse, pushing it off her shoulders, cupping her breasts and letting them fall. "I suppose I won't have to teach you a lesson, not this time anyway."

"No, Russ. Never." She shook. She couldn't help it. In the last few minutes her danger had become clear. No one was looking for her. No one knew she was here. He could keep her here as long as he wanted, do anything to her, even kill her and no one would ever know. In response to her fear, she saw his penis harden. When he pushed down on her shoulders, she knelt and did whatever he demanded, no more.

The doors and windows all had deadbolts and Russ had the only key. Donna would have broken a window or scaled the back fence and ran but she never had a chance. He was with her every minute of the day and every time she'd get up at night he would wake and wait for her to come back. Over the next week she watched their food supply dwindle, laying her hopes on the day he'd have to drive to town. Then she'd take her chance and leave.

The waiting took its toll on her. She drank too much, forgetting to be wary. One day she woke late and realized vaguely that she was alone. She wanted to stand but went back to sleep instead, rising when the setting sun was slanting in the windows. She staggered into the kitchen, saw the half dozen bags and stacked canned goods on the counter. Too numb to hide her emotions, she watched Russ bring in another pair of bags from the wagon, and thinking of the weeks he must be stocking up for, she began to cry.

He stood in the door. "Not happy to see me?" he asked.

"No, Russ. I'm just sick, that's all."

"You bitch. You slept the whole day, didn't you?" He didn't even bother to look at her or wait for a reply, just walked past her and began putting the cans away, filling the upper cupboards.

She should play it cool, she knew. Apologize and be more careful next time. She should but the ruse wouldn't work anymore just like it hadn't at home. She wished she had her brother's baseball bat so she could use it on Russ the way she had on her father, one horrible but oh-so-satisfying thud the revenge for all her pain. She grabbed the scotch bottle, held it next to her, and waited until he'd reached up to put the flour on the top shelf, then swung, hitting him as hard as she could on the side of the head. The bottle broke and she struck one more time, cutting his neck. Not waiting to see how much damage she'd done, she ran as fast as she was able out the front door.

He caught her at the road, pulling her down on the gravel, dragging her by her feet back into the house. She screamed all the way but there was no one to hear her or maybe someone did and didn't care.

For the rest of the day, Donna learned that Russ was as much a master of pain as he was of fear. She wished he'd beat her the way her father did, with closed fists and open rage. There was something almost innocent in that compared to the way Russ managed to bruise every part of her body and do no real damage. No, the damage would come later, getting worse day by day until he killed her. She was so convinced of it that she didn't even react when he told her this, then untied her ankles from the footboard of the bed and raised her knees so he could enter her.

I am a survivor. A survivor. I cannot forget that, she reminded herself, repeating it in time to the pumping of his body above her.

He cut off her alcohol; probably, she thought, because it dulled the pain. He kept her handcuffed to the headboard at night and during the day when he didn't feel like watching her. The rest of the time, she had the run of the place. She cooked, did the laundry in the narrow utility room off the kitchen, swam with him, talked with him when he asked her to talk, shut up when he told her to. And through it all, she was conscious of his eyes on her, of his unchanging even expression as he sat and chain-smoked and drank.

Sometimes he'd watch her every move, self-consciousness adding to her torment. At other times, he'd ignore her, reading books, magazines, everything he could get his hands on, with the same brutal speed with which he swam. Donna never knew smart people could be as rotten as Russ. She wondered if smart people let themselves be beaten. Maybe that's why he picked her. She'd been dumb enough to let herself be grabbed.

Though she knew it was probably useless to try to escape, she kept a sharp eye out for weapons, hoarding everything that could possibly be used that way behind the hamper under the bathroom vanity. In the next few days she collected a dull steak knife, a roll of masking tape, his spare Zippo lighter, and a bottle of rubbing alcohol. None of it was lethal, really, but each addition gave her a new reason to hope.

She learned to read his moods, to anticipate the moment when the beatings would start. Then she'd turn off the fear, hide from the pain. She discovered that he enjoyed defiance so she'd fight back when he grabbed her, swallow her sobs when he hit. Her struggles made him want her, her hate made him hard, her hope kept her alive.

* * *

Eight days passed that way. Donna kept track of each of them the same way she noted every detail of Russ's face, every tiny hint of his life, every clue to his past.

Then a car pulled into the driveway. The driver gunned the engine twice and sounded the horn. Donna heard footsteps on the gravel, pounding on the door.

Russ pulled out of her, swearing as he put on his jeans. Donna followed him into the hallway, wondering if she should scream. When Russ reached the foyer and saw who was knocking he came back down the hall, pushing her into the spare bedroom. "Don't open this door, don't make a sound or so help me, when he's gone I'll strangle you."

Donna couldn't tell if he was angry or scared so she crouched next to the door and listened.

"A long time, hey, Lowell?" the man asked.

"Yeah," Russ answered.

"Carrera has a job for you."

The voices grew less distant as the men moved into the kitchen. Donna sat back on her heels wondering if she dared creep down the hall to listen, then decided on a better idea. Russ wouldn't look in on her, she had a chance now to search his boxes and find a decent weapon. She opened the closet door and pulled the top one from the stack.

It held her knapsack. Inside the second were women's hiking boots, jeans, a shirt, a can of hair spray, a pen, and a wallet belonging to someone named Beverly Fields. Confused, she opened a third box and found more clothing and another wallet, this time for Nancy Potts.

"Oh, Jesus," Donna said, understanding finally that she wasn't the first and probably wouldn't be the last.

Mary Evans had been a smoker. Her lighter was missing but Donna found a full can of lighter fluid and a stale pack of Camels in her tapestry bag.

Donna suddenly had an idea on how to slow Russ down for a while. Now would be her best chance to carry it out. After returning the boxes to the closet, she slowly opened the bedroom door, listened to the distant sound of the men, and went into the bathroom. There she pulled out the lighter and the rest of her things. Terrified that Russ would hear her before she was ready, Donna set to work.

The voices grew louder again as the men walked into the front hall. Donna worked, frantic, silent, then waited, listening.

"Have Domie call me at this number on Saturday at noon. I know his voice. He knows mine. We'll talk."

"Just let me give you the details," the man argued.

"No."

"Why the hell not?"

"The price ain't high enough for this job. Tell Domie to call me at this number on Saturday at noon his time. Give him the message."

"All right. I'll tell him. And one more thing, Lowell—get rid of the girl."

She heard Russ laugh, the door close.

Then he came for her. She stood in the center of the bathroom, too nervous to even pray.

He kicked the door open and she attacked. The lit Zippo taped to the can of lighter fluid and hairspray threw a ball of fire that ignited his shirt. As his hands flew up to shield his face, she shoved him back into the hall and ran past him, emptying more of the lighter fluid on him and spilling a trail of it down the dark hall. A thin nearly invisible line of blue flame followed her as she ran. The alcohol-soaked carpet flared around Russ, and with a bellow of anger and pain, he bolted for the swimming pool in the backyard. As he surfaced in the water, he heard the window shatter in the kitchen. He was at it a moment later but Donna had vanished. He ran outside, circling the house, looking for her while smoke began to rise through the hole in the window.

The carpets were in flames, the kitchen curtains burning when Russ realized what Donna had done. He climbed the back fence and, keeping low, crawled into the house. As he expected, Donna was close to the patio door, lying facedown, her body covered by a wet towel. She screamed as he grabbed her, kept on screaming as he lifted her, then pushed her over the fence. She tried to run, but blinded and coughing from the smoke she inhaled, she couldn't find the wind to escape.

"Please, Russ. I only wanted to get away. I'm sorry," she said as he pulled her after him to the front of the house and ordered her into the back of the wagon. She stood beside it naked, her tears making tracks down her sooty face. "Since you're going to kill me, do it now."

Russ was missing part of one eyebrow and he'd need a crew cut to hide the damage she'd done to his hair. He laughed, not the cold, vicious laugh she'd come to hate but one warmer, admiring, sincere. "Nobody ever pulled a trick on me like you did in there," he said. "Do you think I'd kill you after a stunt like that?"

"I heard the man order you to get rid of me."

"That's just one more reason to keep you with me. That bastard ain't telling me what to do."

They heard sirens in the distance. Russ pushed her into the back of the wagon and took off down the road in the direction that led away from town. "What's your name?" Russ asked.

"Donna Harper."

"Well, Donna Harper, we'd better see about getting you some clothes."

Donna wrapped herself in Russ's sleeping bag, rested her head on his knapsack, and considered the last hour. She wondered if she'd live long enough to ever figure Russ out.

Russ's boxes survived the fire, and though the note Donna had hastily scrawled on the top one had been soaked by the fire hoses, it was still readable. By that evening, Russ Lowell's picture was on the front page of every major newspaper in the country. And by that evening his hair was darker and shorter, his car newer. Late Saturday morning, he stopped at the diner in Sheridan where he'd picked up Beverly Fields. No one recognized him as he sat on the stool nearest the phone booth sipping coffee, reading about himself in the paper, and waiting for the noon bell.

"You son of a bitch!" Carrera screamed into the phone as soon as Russ answered. "Three hours the police were here wanting to know where you were, trying to trip me up. Six girls in three years, you son . . .''

"Ten . . . and for you two crime bosses, a drug smuggler, a federal agent, and the police captain who murdered your son. He'll feel the pain, I promise you. He'll feel it . . .'' Russ went on speaking with the lethal confidence Carrera knew he could always trust, giving Carrera the same sound advice he had given the boss's father; suggesting, rather than ordering, everything that had to be done.

Russ left the diner a rich man and a desperate one.

If this job failed, Carrera would kill him. Carrera hadn't said it but Russ knew his future was as simple as that.

III

The guard at the Canadian border had been busy since his shift had started that morning. He had one more hour to go when the new Ford pulled up to the gate. The driver was ready with his license and accompanying identification noting that he worked for the FBI.

While the guard examined the licenses, the driver took off his glasses and cleaned them with his handkerchief. Without them, he squinted and his eyes watered and crossed slightly. "Well, Mr. Winston, is this trip business or pleasure?'' the guard asked.

"That's not important, is it?''

"Not for a report. I was just wondering if you had anything to do with the Lowell hunt.''

"I can't discuss our cases,'' Winston replied in an even tone. He pronounced the "I'' with an eastern "ah'' and the guard, who prided himself on knowing American accents, decided the agent had been raised near Boston.

"Do you think you'll catch him?''

"We're trying.''

"Do you think he's in Canada?''

"We've been after him over two weeks. By now he could be anywhere,'' the agent commented with a weary sigh.

The guard gave Winston some friendly advice about the roads, then waved him on without checking the trunk or even asking if he had anything to declare. A careful man, Winston followed the route the guard had suggested, skirting Calgary, pursuing his quarry northwest toward Dawson.

IV

The phone in the Stoddard penthouse rang a little after two in the afternoon. Judy Wells answered and heard the familiar gravelly voice of John Corey. "I called to give you the good news," Corey said. "Rumor has it that Carrera will be arrested in the next few days. Once it happens and Dick gives him a week or two for the consequences of a police assassination to settle into his small and nasty brain, you can abandon that lap of luxury you've been wallowing in and come home."

Judy laughed. "How did you know I've been wallowing?"

"I called Stoddard Design. After I convinced Stoddard that 'I yam who I yam,' he said he was transferring me to *the* penthouse. Can I talk to Dick?"

"Dick didn't come with me. He took Alan camping."

"With some distant relations? No, don't even try to answer that. Dick never does. When you talk to him, ask him to call me if he wants the details."

"I will but he's just as likely to turn up at the office. He's anxious to get back to work."

"So he's coming back? Good."

"Why wouldn't he?" When Corey didn't answer, she asked with a bit more urgency, "Cor, is anything wrong?"

Until now Corey had assumed Judy knew about Dick's illness. He covered his stupidity with a quick lie. "No . . . no, nothing except that he was upset by the department's shabby support of him after the shooting. How's the novel coming?"

"All right even though it galls me to have to write under a pseudonym."

"Give the world a little time to accept female Spillanes. Besides Chandler Wells is a great name for a mystery writer."

They talked about her book and her weeks in New York until Elizabeth returned with Carol. The girl turned gracefully, showing off her white voile dress, the long layered haircut, the pale blue shoes and purse.

"She had to wear the outfit home. No wonder, *oui*?" Elizabeth said. She unpinned her broad-brimmed black hat and kicked off her heels before joining Judy on the sofa. Judy handed the phone to Carol, paying little attention to her conversation, her eyes sad and unfocused as she tried to make sense out of the lie Corey had just told her.

"I'm sorry," Elizabeth said. "Perhaps I should have asked about the haircut but I've never had a young lady in my care before."

"It isn't that. It's . . ." Judy glanced at Carol, gushing to Cor about her latest trip to Sak's, the fabulous theaters, the incredible restaurants. "We'll talk when the New York girl's gone off to change," she concluded softly.

Later, as she sorted out her premonitions with Elizabeth, it seemed that she'd guessed the truth for weeks. Dick had seem more tired than usual, preoccupied, secretive. He hadn't grumbled about his doctor's appointment. Instead, he never mentioned it at all. And his agreement to take Alan north with him had been an abrupt change of heart.

With Elizabeth sitting beside her, she called the family doctor and asked how long it would take to have the results of Dick's physical transferred to a specialist in Minnesota.

The nurse wasn't surprised by the request. With a little crafty prodding, the woman told Judy everything she needed to know.

For the first time since she'd come here, Judy touched Elizabeth, gripping her as if there was a way to absorb her immortality and share it with the one she loved. But she didn't cry. Tears were a sign of weakness and Judy, who could always be the strong one when she had to be, would fight even if Dick had already given up.

"Men are so stupid, *oui*?" Elizabeth said. "They are so afraid of being helpless that they forget how lonely we will be without them."

Elizabeth, Judy knew, was speaking of Paul as well as Dick. She had seen the prescription medications in the master bath's medicine chest and understood that while Dick's problem was by far the more immediate, they both faced a similar loss. It occurred to her, as she sensed Elizabeth's compassion, that for Elizabeth it would not be the first time nor the last. "What do you do to make them fight?" she asked.

"Nothing. They have to decide that on their own. Don't be too anxious to have him back, Judy. Let him relax for a little while. The trip will give him time to accept what must be done."

So instead of phoning Dawson, Judy sent Dick a letter about Carrera's arrest, then waited for Dick's call.

THIRTEEN

1

For the first time in his eleven years of life, Alan Wells was in love.

It took him two days before he did anything but answer Hillary's questions, one more before he felt comfortable around her, and by then he never wanted to be anywhere but close to her.

Though she was older than his sister and would start college in January, Hillary actually paid attention when he talked, considering his opinions as if he were an equal, even quoting him for a social studies report she'd been writing over the summer on segregation in the American South. "You mean you don't discuss this in your school?" she asked with frank amazement after listening to his reply.

"We pray sometimes . . . for peace in Alabama." After Alan said this, he saw her anger, not at him but at his ignorance, and as she worked he read the articles and books Hillary used as references, absorbing ideas he never would have considered in the more hectic atmosphere of home.

That night at dinner, Alan asked his father about civil rights. His father responded with an evasive reply that Hillary would not tolerate. "I could understand you being neutral if you lived in a dictatorship like the one in Russia. But in America, can't people speak what they believe?" she asked.

"You have to understand my position. Policemen are like

133

FBI agents or government employees. If I take a political stand that runs too far against the majority, I could be fired.''

"Even when you are in agreement with the law?'' Hillary asked, unwilling to believe what Dick was saying.

"They'd think up some valid reason to fire me. Everybody always makes a mistake sometime and the result would be the same.'' Noticing that his son looked confused, Dick added, "Alan, remember when Mr. Lehr lost his job with the fire department? The city didn't even bother to make up a reason. He'd been a member of the American Labor Party for a few years. That was enough.''

"That isn't right,'' Alan said.

"Of course it's not but I'm not in any position to change the way people think. I do what I can and hope that when you grow up, you'll be a just man and do the same.''

Before Hillary could raise another objection, Stephen made a point of changing the subject. Throughout the rest of the meal Alan said very little. Instead he thought about what it would be like to march with the workers in Alabama and Arkansas, to risk his life for a cause. When he was older, he would do this if it still needed to be done.

And for the first time in his life, adulthood seemed too many years away.

The days were more full than he'd imagined. Besides his hours studying with Hillary and reading Helen's books on dreams, he hiked in the woods near the cabin, sensing through Stephen's or Helen's mind the life around him. He touched a young fox that Stephen had somehow called to him and looked into the eyes of the wolf that hunted with Helen. If any of this had happened at home, Alan would have been awed, but here Stephen and his cousin were no more extraordinary than the mountains, the clear icy water that flowed from them and seemed to glow in his cupped hands, the tall narrow pine trees, or the house filled with rainbows from its windows.

Alan enjoyed everything but caring for the twins.

He couldn't help himself. He was afraid of them—the strange way they looked at him, their oversize long-fingered hands, their anger. In addition, their primitive attempts to touch his mind would create static in his head as if his brain weren't tuned to exactly the right station.

But worst of all they talked. Not in the simple, often indecipherable babble of toddlers but with overexaggerated enunciation. It was obvious, though, from the way they usually combined their words that they didn't understand many of them. Bomb, revolution, and chocolate were Patrick's three favorites and once Dickey asked for a "tomato Wednesday" with such seriousness that the adults started laughing, leaving Dickey with his lower lip stuck out and misery in his eyes though, like all Austras, he was unable to actually cry.

"Tomato Wednesday," Patrick repeated and laughed with the others.

Alan didn't even smile. He wished he had the courage to pick up the silver-haired boy and explain but he wasn't sure how to begin. Stephen did it for him, carrying both boys to the kitchen to show them the tomatoes ripening on the windowsill, then sitting them on the counter, holding up a calendar, and silently showing the passing of days, naming them as he did.

"Sunday, Monday, Tuesday . . ." the boys recited in their singsong lilt. They kept it up until, exasperated with the noise, Stephen taught them to count.

The more Alan tried to overcome his fear of the pair, the harder it became to even approach them. "They make me feel like such a sissy," he confessed to his father one night after they'd gone to bed.

"I think the little nippers are jealous," his father replied. "You've taken Hillary's attention away from them. And now that they know you're scared, they're playing with your mind, trying to make you feel more afraid."

"Like dogs that bite you when you run?"

"Sort of. Stephen said this is something they have to learn to do but if they bother you too much, talk to him about it, OK?" His father groped in the darkness, grabbing Alan's shoulders and giving him a hug through his sleeping bag. "I'm sorry you've been so cooped up. I wanted to show you more of this country."

"We have lots of time, don't we?" Alan asked, sounding hopeful.

"Sure. And tomorrow we're driving to town with Stephen. The next day, he and I are taking you climbing."

"I thought we were going to stay close to the house."

"If we'd been followed we'd know by now."

"What do you think Carol and Judy are doing while we're here?"

His father laughed softly. "Running amuk in the Gimbels basement."

Alan listened to the wind rustling the pine trees around the house. He snuggled lower in his bag, burying his nose inside, inhaling his own warmth. "I'm glad you brought me here," he said.

"And I wouldn't want to be here without you."

Late that night, Alan woke and heard Helen laughing in the main room. He cracked open the door and saw Helen sitting cross-legged on the floor, nursing Patrick while Dickey waddled around the room.

Patrick saw Alan first and pointed. Dickey turned his way and pushed his body back on his haunches; bare feet, hands, and bottom planted firmly on the floor. *He sits like a puppy*, Alan thought, and smiled.

"Come out," Helen said. She spoke so softly he didn't know if he heard the words or only sensed them in his mind. He liked it when she spoke to his mind, as if he somehow shared her magic. He went and sat beside her on the carpet, brushing her arm in a kind of greeting he'd come to understand tightened their bond, carefully avoiding any physical contact with the child in her arms.

Helen buttoned her blouse and sat Patrick upright on her lap. "I'm teaching Dickey to walk on two feet. Watch what happens."

She motioned to Dickey to come to her. He stood with his hands on the floor, then his fingertips, then his feet alone. He managed a half-dozen steps before he fell, rolling forward in a full somersault. Dickey giggled. Alan rolled forward, imitating him, then rolled back. Dickey mimicked him exactly, then giggled again.

—Help him stand— Helen suggested. Alan shook his head and she responded, "It's all right. I promise I won't let him bite you."

Alan held out his hands. Dickey, his thin fingers almost as long as Alan's, gripped Alan's hands and he pulled himself up. The toddler's long legs shook and seemed in as much danger of breaking as of collapse. Then, his lips pressed together stubbornly, his forehead tight with concentration, Dickey seemed to will them steady. He lifted one leg a number of times, then the other, let go of Alan's hands, and walked to his mother.

Alan clapped, softly because he knew the boys' ears were sensitive to noise though they seemed to make a lot of it themselves when the urge struck them. He thought he should give Dickey some reward. Food was out of the question since they lived on nothing but their mother's milk supplemented with canned milk from Dawson. Alan could make a badge but he had nothing to pin it on since they didn't wear clothes either. The first time he'd helped with laundry he understood that if clothing wasn't needed, it was best not to wear it. Hand washing in water you had to pump and then heat on the stove was too much trouble. Alan considered everything he knew about Dickey, then walked over to Stephen's loom and pulled a few pieces of yarn from the basket beside it. Working slowly while Dickey watched, he braided the strands together and tied the makeshift bracelet to Dickey's arm. The silver-haired boy beamed with pleasure, sat down next to Alan, and fingered his gift while Patrick scowled.

"Why is Dickey so much stronger than his brother?" Alan asked, hoping that Patrick understood him.

"He isn't. He just has the stronger body. Patrick has the stronger mind."

"Will it always be that way?"

"I don't know. We named Dickey after your father, you know. Stephen thinks that he will take after your father in size too. If so, he will be bigger than the men in the family, less thin and very powerful. As for his mind, we'll have years to see how strong that becomes.''

"And what about Patrick?''

"He'll probably take after his father.''

"Or his uncle,'' Alan commented. Contrary to what his father believed, Alan remembered Charles Austra all too well.

"If Patrick knew how interesting you were, he wouldn't be so angry about having you here,'' Helen said. "Why not let his mind into yours for a while and show him where you live and what you do with your friends.''

"That's not interesting, not at all.''

"It is to children who've only lived in a cabin in a forest. Try it. Show them.''

Encouraged by Helen's coaxing, Alan let her merge his mind with the twins. He showed them his house and his toys. He recalled his school, the rows of desks, and the tall stern nun in starched black and white who pounded his knuckles with a ruler when he talked out of turn during class. He took them to Mass at St. John's, sharing not just the windows their father and uncle had made but also the sounds of the singing, the smell of the incense, and how sick it always made him feel. When he finished and opened his eyes he felt as if he had been asleep, and somehow ordering his dreams. Patrick stared at him wide-eyed, almost smiling, then deliberately pointed to his wrist.

"Should I make him one?'' Alan asked Helen.

"He held your bond all by himself, I think he deserves one,'' Helen responded.

Alan chose different colored yarns. "Your brother's are red and gold because those are effort colors. These are blue and green mental colors.'' What he'd just said made him feel self-conscious and he started to laugh. Then he saw Helen's approving expression, shut up and tried to look serious.

"That's good.'' Helen rested her hands on her children's shoulders and Alan sensed her explaining this to them. "I told them they will collect these. They understand.'' She stood and picked up Patrick. "It's nearly dawn. Let's put them to bed. Then I'll have to go out for a while.''

"To hunt?''

"To hunt."

Alan slowly held out his arm, wrist up, looking frightened, hopeful.

"No, you don't understand. It's not a chore, it's . . . magnificent. And I like the rain." She hesitated, then asked, "Are you sleepy?"

He heard the excitement in her question and answered, "Not anymore."

"Good. I want to share a hunt with you."

Helen waited until Stephen came home, dried off at the door, and slipped on a brown satin robe. Then, with only a mental warning, she was gone. Alan, lying on the couch, seemingly asleep, smiled at the wonder of the frosted night.

Helen looked at the ground and Alan saw the long ice crystals beneath her bare feet break and re-form. He saw the world around him distinct as early evening, the frost-coated ground glittering in the quarter moon. He saw the wolf glide, silent and smooth as a ghost, from the trees, felt the air on her bare legs as she ran through the woods, the heat of the deer, the soft light fur of its belly as she brought it down.

Though the deer had run from her, it was not terrified of Helen. She had fed on it before and it knew her scent. But the wolf meant death and it shook as she held it and drank.

Life. Flowing. Filling. Warming.

And he had offered her his wrist!

—Alan, I don't need your gift. But I wanted you to share this. It's my gift to you.—

She let the deer loose, watching it disappear into the forest, giving it a long head start before she pulled the mental leash off her hungry companion and walked slowly through the trees toward home.

Later that morning, Dick found his son covered with a blanket, sleeping in front of the fire wrapped in his cousin's arms. He had an expression of such wonder on his face that Dick left him undisturbed and returned to bed. He waited until he heard Hillary talking to Alan in the kitchen before he got up again.

Alan never told his father what happened that night. Dick never asked. Alan was old enough to have his secrets.

ll

Dick Wells had never learned patience, and at this point in his life, he didn't care to change. In three weeks, he'd read every book in the cabin, absorbed the last two Austra annual reports, played cards with anyone who would join him, solitaire when no one would, and scanned the Edmonton paper looking for some mention of Carrera or the investigation in Ohio, some indication of when he could go home.

During that time, Stephen scouted the area around the cabin and made unscheduled trips into Dawson to see if any strangers had shown up in town. Outside of the usual itinerant trappers beginning to arrive for their winter hunts, no one had come through. Finally, Dick stopped waiting for the killer to come. He wanted his last trip to Canada to be a good one, for his son as well as himself.

But though he told Alan there was no danger, Dick couldn't quite trust his instincts. He kept a wary eye on the road during their drive to Dawson, asked a few discreet questions at the diner where he and his son ate while Stephen had his class. Dick noticed nothing strange. He hadn't been followed. He couldn't have been.

When Stephen joined them, he carried a letter addressed to him from New York. Inside, along with a brief note from Paul and Elizabeth, was a letter from Judy telling Dick that Carrera had been arrested and released on bail.

Now that it seemed safe to do so, Dick phoned Judy. They shared stories about their separate trips, Carol's and Alan's changes. Afterward, Dick made a list of everything Alan would need for wilderness hiking and took the boy shopping for a warmer coat and hiking boots.

The next day, Dick and Stephen took Alan farther into the mountains.

The trip began perfectly. The night's dusting of snow had melted by midmorning, leaving hardly a trace on the frozen rocky ground. They climbed onto the ridge above the cabin, Dick and Alan spreading an early lunch on a sunny outcropping of rocks while looking down on the cabin, its long private drive, and a section of the main road.

Dick joined Stephen on the edge of the clearing where he sat shaded by the surrounding pines, a hat and glasses protecting his eyes from the sun. "A good spot for someone to watch us," Dick said.

Stephen noted Alan trying to lure a chipmunk to his feet with a piece of bread and commented, "At least one man stopped here a few days ago."

"How do you know?"

"His scent. He peed on the tree behind me."

"Should we go back?"

"Not yet. The man could have been a hunter or hiker. I want to see what else I can discover."

After lunch, they traveled deeper and higher into the hills, crossing a rise and beginning a descent that would eventually take them to the flatter country north of the cabin. From there it would be an easy hike home.

"Do I hear a river?" Alan asked.

"With a waterfall," Stephen told him. "You can go on ahead if you like but don't try to cross."

Dick stayed behind to confer with Stephen. "Notice anything?" he asked.

"Not yet. I don't think . . ." He stopped and started to run toward the river. An instant later, Dick heard his son's cry of alarm and followed.

A tree had fallen below the falls, making a natural bridge across the quick narrow stream. In the center of it, a fox had been caught in a spring trap and had somehow managed to avoid falling into the water and drowning. Now it crouched, its eyes glazed with pain, growling as Alan moved slowly closer.

"Get away!" Stephen warned and pulled the boy back. He grabbed a stick and sprang a second trap that had been less than a foot from where Alan had been standing and a third, well hidden by leaves, on the opposite bank. Then he stood over the fox. His hand moved too fast for Alan to follow, his long fingers gripping the animal's muzzle, holding its jaws shut while he examined its wound.

Alan sniffed. Its fur was so beautiful. "Will it live?" he asked.

"No. It won't be able to hunt and it will slowly starve."

"Come on, Alan. We'll climb above the falls," Dick said to the boy.

Stephen waited until father and son moved away before lowering his head.

After the animal had died, Stephen moved its carcass well away from the bank and ripped each trap apart, leaving the useless pieces dangling from their chains.

"There's blood on your face," Dick said in a casual tone when Stephen joined them.

Stephen wiped the streak away. "I think we can stop worrying about the man I sensed, yes? Let's start down. I'll lead."

On the way home, Stephen sprang three traps on the public land and destroyed two more on his own property. Dick guessed the trapper would be furious. He disliked the damage to some man's livelihood but could hardly disapprove. One of these traps wouldn't do any permanent harm to an Austra body but it would probably hurt like hell.

"And snap a toddler's neck, Richard. I've had to destroy traps before. This time I will make certain the trapper moves on."

Dick had intended the short trip to be a test of Alan's endurance. He and Stephen planned a four-day hike and wanted to take the boy. Though Alan had managed the hike well, by the next morning he had a cough and trouble catching his breath. The bronchitis that had plagued him when he'd been a baby had returned. He lay on the couch, wrapped in his sleeping bag, sipping peppermint tea sweetened with honey, melting every time Hillary brushed his forehead.

The girl finally sat on the floor in front of him, her back against the couch, and began reading to him, a strange wonderful story about fur-footed hobbits and magic rings.

Stephen quietly drew Dick's attention to how Alan's hand rested close enough to the girl's back to be covered by her hair. —In ten years he'll be irresistible, yes?— he commented privately.

Stephen sensed only sadness where there should have been pride.

—While we're gone, we'll have that talk— Dick responded when he noticed Stephen's questioning look.

III

Richard's boots crunched on the frozen ground. Stephen's bare feet padded silent as an arctic fox as they wove their way to the highest point of the pass and looked down at the valley spread below them. A river ran quick, cold, and grey through it and on either side of it traces of green defied September's first dusting of snow. The valley stretched ten miles long, eight wide. The rise on which they stood faced south.

No sound should mar the peace of this sight, so Stephen spoke mentally to his friend, —You are looking at the future home of AustraGlass.—

—And its last?—

—Perhaps its last.—

Sure yet not sure. Dick leaned against a boulder and asked, "Does anything really frighten you?"

"Some things. More now than in the past. War, of course, frightens us as much as it does any human. And I fear guns accurate beyond the range of my mind and automatic weapons that can fire faster than I am able to move. But the real danger is exposure and it is becoming increasingly hard to hide. We anticipate as many of these problems as we can. We form plans to deal with them. This is survival. Then we forget about them. This is survival too."

"And if the war you're preparing for actually comes, everything will fall apart. The governments and their weapons will be gone. You'll be safe again."

Stephen laughed. "I'm sorry, Richard, but you have no way of knowing how many times I've been accused of waiting for the end. But I don't." He spread his arms, embracing the trees, the air, the sky. "If I would have to wait a century to sit under these stars again, then the price for security is far too high." He pointed at a great bull elk foraging near the water, then looked sideways at Dick. —Of course we camp here, Richard. Where else?—

Then Stephen was gone, running innocent, careless as the creatures he hunted through the pine-scented autumn air.

Richard dined on venison that night, then sat wrapped in his down bag looking up at the crystal stars, wondering where he would find the strength to start the discussion he had promised.

Stephen sat beside him, dressed only in loose knit pants. He had no need of warmth or fire, and Dick suspected, he only wore the pants out of deference to Dick's modesty. His long-limbed body looked less human when exposed and all the hollows in his triangular face were accented by the sharp shadows of darkness against the fire. His eyes seemed larger than usual, as if they were altered by the night. These changes always seemed to come during their times in the wilderness. Dick wondered if they were deliberate or just a sign that Stephen relaxed up here, lowered his facade. Dick had hoped their differences would make this discussion easier, instead they made it harder. He didn't know how to begin. If he hadn't promised, he wouldn't have spoken at all.

"This week up here is the only time I really see the stars all year," he said, looking at them, then the fire, anywhere but Stephen's face. "I sit under them and empty all the garbage out of my mind and for a little while I know exactly who I am. I don't think there's peace like this anywhere else on earth."

"Then I am glad you came, Richard. You need this time now, yes?"

Stephen gripped his arm and Dick stared into his friend's dark eyes. "You told me you wouldn't pry," he said, as angry as he was amazed.

"I never did. I knew the truth as soon as you arrived. I've seen the look of death in too many people not to recognize it in a friend."

"Then you probably know I didn't want to come here. Hell, I wouldn't have if it hadn't been for Carrera."

"And for Alan, yes?"

Dick nodded. "I had to bring him here. He and Helen were always so close."

"How long does the doctor give you, Richard?"

"Six months to a year. The X rays showed growths in both lungs and the doctor thinks it's spread beyond that."

"I had no idea that what I sensed would be . . ."

"So soon? Surprised?"

Stephen didn't answer. Instead he asked, "Will this trip be too difficult for you?"

"I'll be OK if we take it easy. It's funny, but since I flew up here, I feel better than I have in months so I guess I won't die on you." Dick paused, then, to fill the silence, asked, "You wouldn't like that, would you?"

More than self-pity prompted the question. "No, Richard, I would not."

"Why not? You feed on emotions as well as blood, don't you? You already said death is at the top of your list."

"Not of my friends." Stephen's voice seemed apologetic as he added, "Please, Richard, I didn't force you to tell me this."

Dick looked directly at Stephen, watching his friend's face as he said the worst. "Listen. I didn't want to come here and share the pain but in the last few days I've been hiding more than that. I envy you all the centuries you have coming. Maybe you'll walk on the moon or travel to some star so distant I can't even see it tonight. And if I ever hold a grandchild I'll consider it a miracle. I wish I could make the feeling go away. But all I can do is apologize and hope you understand."

"You use the word envy, Richard. It's a noble emotion when compared to hate. Do you think that how I must live forces me to hide? No, Richard, my need for blood is a little thing beside my immortality. So many times I have wished that I could share my life with those I love or spread it through the world like some miraculous plague. So, if you ask for my understanding, you have it, my forgiveness, yes. But my pity for your pain, never. I am too old to feel it anymore.''

"I don't care about your pity.''

"Then why were you so afraid to tell me this?''

"Because until I confessed it to someone, it didn't seem real. Now you know. Now I have to face it.'' He lowered his head, looking at the fire as he added, "Hell, have you ever known me to be anything but direct? Now look what death has done for me, it has me slinking around.''

"You haven't even told Judy, have you?''

"I intended to, right after our anniversary. Then something more pressing intervened and, you know, I was actually thankful. I could put it off. Corey guessed some of it but, congratulations, you're the first to hear it all.''

"Can the doctors help you, Richard?''

"They want to do an exploratory before starting me on radiation. I told them to forget about any of it.''

"You don't intend to fight.''

"What in the hell for? All I'll get is damn sick and a few more months to be a burden on everybody. Funny how I always figured if I was going to die young, I'd die quick. That's what my job is for.''

"Then why didn't you stay home and let Carrera kill you?''

"And have that bastard think he won?''

"Now a death sentence from a doctor will win instead.''

"Who the hell are you to give me a pep talk for this match?'' Dick retorted.

"Someone who has seen men die because they believed they were going to die, wasting away from the curse of a wizard or a voodoo priest.''

"Modern medicine is not exactly voodoo,'' Dick replied with a quick, sad smile.

"Modern medicine is still discovering secrets healers knew two thousand years ago.'' Stephen paused, waiting to sense the seed of hope in his friend before adding, "You should have gone east with Judy. Elizabeth remembers lost arts. Perhaps she can help you.''

"I don't think . . .''

"Promise me that when this is over you will talk to her.''

Dick started to protest, then abruptly agreed. Though he fought against hope, Stephen knew he wanted to believe—wanted it enough that Stephen's plan might work. If it failed, well, Richard would only hate him a little while.

FOURTEEN

1

Patrick's mind went traveling as it often did when the others were asleep or unaware. Sometimes he would merge with his parents while they hunted or wrestled together on the bed. He especially liked the emotion in the latter, the exertion and satisfaction. But if his parents sensed him watching, Patrick would be ordered out with a painful mental slap. Often they were too preoccupied to sense his presence so Patrick risked the discipline.

He liked Dick Wells's mind too. Dick had a habit the toddler had seen in no one else—he talked to himself inside. He did it all the time but most often when he was angry. Then he'd think words he never said out loud, words Patrick had never heard before. He used some of them only once, when Alan had taken a toy he refused to share and given it to Dickey. Everyone reacted differently. Alan's face had gotten red. His mother seemed shocked, Dickey confused, and his father laughed longer than he'd ever seen him laugh before. "These are words you may think but not share," his father had explained to him, looking at Dick as he did.

So these were private words. Patrick found this so interesting he would sit for hours, stringing and restringing them in his mind, creating incredibly musical combinations of profanity he could scarcely understand.

But he loved studying Hillary best of all. She had beautiful comforting hands, warm strong arms, and a voice almost as pretty as his mother's. Though he didn't comprehend the meaning of many words, he sensed a great deal through others' minds and he knew he had to remain small and weak if he wanted Hillary to stay and care for him. He had tried but in this his body betrayed him and after they went home for the next family sharing, she would leave him and go away to a special school in a place called London.

He knew she was sorry she had to leave but she would go anyway. He wondered if he could go with her with his mind. Since he had no concept of distance or limits, he worked at mental traveling in every quiet moment, trying to extend his range far enough to follow her when she left.

Which is how he came to be awake and studying the ridge on Tuesday morning while the rest of the house slept. He saw a man wearing a dark shirt and pants and carrying a rifle climb onto it. He tried to focus on the man's mind but every thought was nonsense to him.

Patrick wondered if the man was alone. His attention diverted to a sound in the distance and he followed it to a truck parked on the black road and a man working on its engine. Patrick watched the man until he stopped and got into a car parked behind the truck and poured himself a cup of some hot liquid from a red bottle on the seat.

It all seemed so interesting. Patrick wanted to stay and study both men more but he felt Hillary's hand stroking his back and, with a purr of contentment, returned to his body, rolled over, and smiled. She'd touched him first. She loved him best of all.

Later that morning, Alan told Hillary that he felt well enough to watch Patrick and Dickey while Helen drove into town for groceries and Hillary cleaned house. Since Alan had made the first bracelet for Dickey, Patrick had been competing with his brother. They'd each managed to get an extra bracelet in the same colors as before but today Patrick decided to move into the physical shades. He studied Dickey, watching how he stood, locked his hips, and stepped forward, then imitated him exactly. Patrick managed to take four small steps before his hips loosened and his knees buckled and he deliberately fell onto his brother. As had become his custom, he pointed to his wrist. Alan rushed to the basket to obey.

When the bracelet had been tied to his wrist, Patrick waved his arm in front of Dickey, conveying images of his father running and how fast he'd one day go. Then he showed his brother how Hillary loved him best of all. Dickey pouted, ready to start what Hillary called the "dry-eyed wail."

Alan picked up one of the blocks, noted the letter, and held it behind his back. Alan touched his forehead, a sign that Dickey should use his mind and asked, "What letter is it, Dickey?"

Dickey could "see" the letter in one of three ways. He could read Alan's mind. He could move out of his body and look behind Alan's back. Or he could return to the moment when Alan picked up the block and put it behind his back and recall the letter. Any of these would require more mental effort than he had managed before.

Patrick sensed a buzzing in his head and knew that Dickey was trying the really hard way first. Dickey might even get two bracelets for this! Patrick felt Alan concentrating on the letter, giving Dickey as much help as he could. He saw Dickey press his lips together and he seemed about to speak when Patrick said, "D."

Dickey screeched with anger and jumped on him. As they fought, Alan sighed, picked up the magazines that had scattered when the twins started their fight, and rearranged them on the coffee table with the Austra reports his father had been reading on the top of the stack.

Hillary stopped washing the dishes and laughed at the pair, then asked Alan to bring his glass to the kitchen. As he started toward her, a bullet shattered a rear window and imbedded in the floor near the place he'd been sitting.

"Get down!" Hillary screamed and ran to the front door to bolt it. A second bullet smashed into the window enlarging the hole. Hillary leaned against the thickest part of the front door, fighting her panic, thinking of what had to be done. "Stay low, close to the walls," she told the others.

Dickey scurried into the corner and hid in a pile of dirty

sheets and towels. Patrick began to follow, fell and sat, as curious as he was frightened by this sudden danger. Alan slid closer to the protective stones of the fireplace, pulling Patrick with him.

Hillary leaned against the doorframe and considered her options as two more bullets shattered what was left of the window. In the sunlit silence that followed, she heard a car coming up the drive.

She ran to the broken window, slammed and locked the shutters, then risked a quick stretch to pull their rifle out of the cabinet beside it. More frightened then her charges, uncertain of what to do, she nonetheless crouched in the darkest corner of the kitchen, prepared to fire at anyone who tried to come through the door.

A fifth bullet hit something metal outside. Hillary looked out the narrow smoke-tinted front window and saw the driver hiding behind his car, his gun pulled as he scanned the hills above the house, ready to return fire.

She cracked open the door, certain she could slam it shut if she needed to. "Who are you?" she yelled.

The man tossed a leather wallet that landed on the steps. Hillary snatched it up as the man yelled his reply, "I'm Elliott Winston, FBI. I've been following the man up there. Is this where I find Dick Wells?"

Instead of answering, Hillary bolted the door.

"Is he telling the truth?" Alan asked.

"I don't know," Hillary admitted. "But he is firing at the man on the ridge." She peeked out the window, saw the driver run for the protection of the recessed porch, heard another shot. The driver aimed and fired, then fell.

The shots stopped. The man lay on the steps outside the door trying to push himself upright. Hillary saw blood on his shirt and her natural need to help surfaced, overriding caution. She picked up the man's wallet and tossed it to Alan. "Does this look like an FBI identification to you?"

Alan looked at it. "I don't know, I never saw one before."

They both stared at Patrick who was sitting in the center of the floor with his eyes closed, his body rigid with concentration. "Is the man outside going to hurt us?" Alan asked him.

Patrick, his mind drawn to the wounded gunman on the ridge, didn't respond.

"I have the rifle. If we drag the man in and he tries anything, I can shoot him," Hillary decided. She ordered Alan to open the door and pull the man inside.

Alan didn't want to, but he didn't want Hillary to think he was a coward either, so he did as she asked.

The moment the door opened, the man sprang and then he had a handgun pressed against Alan's throat. Hillary, still gripping her rifle, backed away from the door as Alan, kicking uselessly, was dragged inside.

"Where's Dick Wells?" the man asked.

"He's not here," Hillary answered. "He's been gone for two days."

"Where?"

"In the mountains."

"When will he be back?"

"Tonight," she replied, wondering if this lie would help them.

The man swore and his grip on Alan tightened. "Drop the rifle," he said. When Hillary hesitated, he pointed the gun at Patrick. "Drop it or I'll shoot him."

Hillary had met men like this before and she knew he wasn't bluffing. She did as he ordered and glared at him. He looked at her, her eyes and face so familiar, and recalled where he'd seen her before.

She blanched at the look he gave her. "Get the baby a blanket," he told her. She rushed to get one, then wrapped the naked boy in it.

"Leave him," the man ordered. "Now get a pen and paper. I want you to write something down."

Hillary found a pen on the table. She turned to get paper from the desk when he picked up the Austra report. "Here, use the cover of . . ." He saw the firm's name and scanned the room, looking for more clues to this riddle. Then he saw Helen's self-portrait above the fireplace and everything fell into place as long as he didn't try to see any logic in it. "Where's Helen?" he asked.

"She went with the men," Hillary said, praying he wouldn't detect her lie when she should have been more concerned with the truth she just revealed.

Russ picked up both reports, ripped off the last page of one, and thrust them into Alan's hand. "Don't drop them," he said and handed the paper to Hillary. "Write this: 'Stephen Austra, I have . . .' "

"That isn't his name," Hillary interrupted.

Russ looked at the boy on the couch. The resemblance to his father in features and coloring was already startling. "Of course it is. Now write—'I have Alan Wells and your son. I will trade them for Dick Wells at dawn tomorrow . . .' "

"I lied. They're not due . . ."

"The hell you did! Keep writing . . . 'at dawn tomorrow on the road south of Tupper. Drive toward town until you see my car. Come alone.' "

Hillary set it on the table, picked up Patrick, and carried him outside. The boy squinted in the sunlight and held tightly on to Hillary's sweater as Russ ordered Alan into the front seat. The inside handle and lock button had been removed and he used the key to lock Alan in before opening the rear door.

"Put the baby in the back," Russ ordered Hillary.

Hillary understood that she wasn't going but she felt neither fear nor relief, only a sense of duty that made her ask, "Listen, mister. Do you know anything about caring for babies?"

"I don't have to." Russ intended to kill her but her expression reminded him of Helen's painting. Though almost-grown girls could be a problem, he decided to take the risk.

As they drove away from the cabin, Patrick screeched. Hillary clamped a hand over his mouth and wrapped an arm around him. His fingers were hard and curled, his entire body tensed in impotent squirming rage. He pulled away from Hillary and screeched again.

"Shut that kid up," Russ growled.

"He's a baby. He's upset," Hillary retorted.

Russ lashed out, his fist pounding the side of Alan's head. "Now listen to me, all of you. One of you acts up the nearest one to me gets it. Anyone who tries to escape gets shot. If you somehow make it, I'll shoot the others, understand?''

Alan, a hand pressed against his head, nodded. Hillary responded with a soft "yes." Even Patrick was silent, staring intently at the back of Russ's head, trying to understand the trouble he'd caused.

Alan touched two fingers to his forehead, a signal to Patrick to enter his mind. He felt the usual buzzing, then Patrick's confusion and anger as they merged. Carefully, using the simplest terms he could, Alan told Patrick that this was a bad man, someone who would hurt them if Patrick misbehaved. He asked the boy to not talk to Russ. He sensed Patrick resisting this so he added that they would try to get even with the man if they could. Patrick nodded and relaxed in Hillary's arms. Hillary covered his face with the blanket and he slept on the long bumpy drive away from home.

11

Dickey didn't move from his hiding place after the others left. Instead he lay among the sheets in a tight shivering ball of misery and loneliness. When he heard his mother come home he rushed out of the pile, wrapping his arms around her thighs, snuggling close, taking comfort in her scent and the brush of her mind against his.

Helen fought down her fear as she picked him up and cuddled him until his shaking ended, then asked what had happened here.

Dickey didn't have words to explain so he showed her instead—the loud noise of the shots and vague images of how Alan and Hillary had been tricked, how he'd hidden and stayed hidden until everyone had gone, how through it all Patrick had been studying the wounded man on the ridge above them.

Helen's mind, focused by anger, extended. The man was still alive! She changed into a black knit jumpsuit and a pair of thick-soled hiking boots, ordered Dickey to stay inside, and began her climb. As she scrambled with all her newfound speed toward the ridge, Helen deliberately ignored all her options save one—she had to find the children, and if it came to killing, she would follow Stephen's advice. Justification should be easy when her family was in danger. As for strength, it would come, she felt it coming already—more strength than she needed.

Fight down the human emotions, hold them back, she reminded herself. *And whatever you do, don't touch more than you must. Don't feel him die.*

The man lay facedown on the ridge. The bullet had passed through him, the blood on his back already dried by the hot afternoon sun. He'd been unconscious since he'd been shot but still struggled to live. She rolled him over and pulled him out of the sun, then, with effort, ignored her fear and entered his mind. Outrage. Betrayal. Scenes from the recent past. He had only intended to help rob them, to get even for the destruction of his traps, but the man who had paid him to spy on . . .

No! She remembered the killer's face—how she had felt when she looked into his pale eyes one afternoon of her New York reception. And now this monster had her son!

Movement had reopened the trapper's wound. From the rate of bleeding, Helen didn't think he would live much longer. His life called to her and its remnants would give her strength, she knew, enough to do whatever needed to be done. Nonetheless, she ignored this instinct, found the man's pack, and wrapped him in his sleeping bag, then put water and his rifle within reach. Survival was in his hands, not hers. Though she sensed four-legged scavengers waiting for the shadows of nightfall, she left the trapper to the fate he deserved and returned to her frightened son. And if the trapper died, as she believed he would, she would not bury him. He was not her family, nor any longer her kind.

Helen worked throughout what remained of the afternoon as if nothing had happened, unloading the groceries, sweeping up the shattered glass, waiting for the power of the night and the hunt that she knew would come.

At dusk, after she'd nursed the bewildered lonely toddler

who had followed her everywhere that afternoon, she went into the kitchen. A glass of the salty Tarda water did not quench her thirst, the cold soup she began to devour made her gag. Her body demanded life and the strength it gave to sustain her on this quest.

And food was all around her. She need only call and take. As Helen walked up the steep front steps, her mind moved through the woods. Life paused, waiting and dreading the insistence of her summons.

She chose a buck, large and strong, and as it walked into the clearing it smelled the frightening scent of guns and man and shivered in spite of its size and power.

When it moved within reach, her hands shot out, grabbing its legs, pulling them sideways, forcing it to fall beside her. All instinct, she rolled her body on top of it, holding it quiet, cherishing her lover—the life within it.

Its death strengthened her mind, made her body taut, ready for the hunt. It would begin soon. She had no doubt of this. A mother could always find her child.

III

Alan wasn't sure how far they traveled on the twisting roads. They could have been sixty miles from the cabin or less than five when Russ pulled the car onto a narrow rutted drive barely visible from the road.

At the end of it Alan saw a metal storage shed, the remains of a burned-out cabin and a fire pit still smoldering from recent use. Russ tied Alan's hands and feet before dragging him from the car to the flat ground near the fire, then ordered Hillary out of the back. He unlocked the shed door, pulled the sleeping toddler from Hillary's arms, and tossed Patrick to a girl sitting on a sleeping bag inside. Patrick, startled awake, instinctively twisted to land on his hands and feet, and as the girl caught him one of Patrick's sharp nails left a deep scratch on the side of her face.

"Look, Donna, the kid's got claws," Russ said and laughed as he slammed the shed door and locked it. He returned to the fire and faced Hillary. The smile vanished. "Tell me why Stephen Austra and Helen Wells are up here?"

Hillary stared at him, watching his anger grow. He seemed about to explode when she thought of an answer, "They're artists. They're working and raising a family."

"I read their obituaries, girl. Why did they go to so much trouble?"

"They wanted to be left alone."

Russ's anger vanished and he looked at her with a good-natured grin. "You're lying, of course. But you'll tell me the truth, now or later."

As she glared at him, he remembered where he'd seen that expression before. Ah, yes, he'd done the right thing in bringing her here. She flinched and his first swing hit only air. He gripped her shoulders, his fingers bruising her back. "Tell me."

She raised her knee but he was faster and she fell with him above her onto the uneven, rocky ground. The force knocked the wind out of her and before she could catch her breath, he kissed her. Convinced escape was hopeless, she stopped her struggles. Her eyes focused on Alan who lay a few yards away straining on the ropes and she silently begged him to please, please just be quiet and look away.

After an hour, the beating started. Impatient, Russ hit Hillary too hard. She lost consciousness and Russ focused his attention on Alan.

When he heard Hillary start to scream, Patrick twisted out of Donna's arms and beat his body against the door, clawing at its rough wood until it was streaked with blood from his fingers. He stopped after the sounds outside stopped and huddled, shaking with misery, against the door.

Donna slid over to him and picked him up. Using the dim light that leaked through a tiny wire-covered window in the back of the shed, she began pulling the larger splinters out of Patrick's fingers. She didn't notice she was crying until Patrick began licking the tears from her face. The toddler's thin fingers lightly brushed Donna's cheek and she held Patrick tightly. "You poor, scared thing," she crooned, then added to herself, "What in the hell is Russ doing with a baby?"

"I am not a baby, Donna Harper," Patrick declared in his precise singsong voice.

He'd done it so well, she'd never even noticed when he'd stolen her name from her mind! But she hadn't liked him doing it, apparently not at all, because she dropped him and slid quickly to the far side of the shed.

Amazed at her fear, Patrick padded over to Donna and squatted beside her. "I am sorry, Donna Harper," Patrick said. "I would not hurt. He hurts."

"Who?" she whispered, her eyes wide and frightened as she strained to see his face.

"Russ," Patrick told her, then added one more thought from her mind, "your father." Fear and anger had done something wonderful to Patrick. He felt stronger. Smarter. Quicker. He thought of how angry Dickey would be and began to laugh, that high-pitched titter Alan always found so disconcerting.

Donna began to scream.

She was still screaming when Russ pulled her out of the shed, dragged Hillary inside, then pushed in Alan. Alan's lip was cracked, his head bleeding. It smelled wonderful to Patrick and he crouched beside the boy and began to lick the wounds the way he had Donna's tears. "I read her mind," he said happily to Alan.

Alan sighed. He couldn't think of any way to explain why Patrick should not have done that. Even if he could, he wouldn't try to control the child without Hillary's assistance. "Untie me," he asked the toddler.

"I made him stop hurting you," Patrick added. He brushed Alan's cheek with his hand, then crawled behind the older boy and untied him.

Alan's eyes had grown accustomed to the light. He picked up a dirty sleeping bag and covered Hillary, then turned his attention to Patrick's bloody hands. "What happened to you?" he asked.

"Russ hurt Hillary. I wanted to stop him."

Alan pulled out a few more splinters, then sucked on the

wound. The blood tasted strange—like sucking on a copper penny that had been dipped in salt and honey. He spit out a sliver of wood and sucked again. "Does this hurt?" he asked Patrick.

The toddler waited a long time to reply. "No," he said. "No. More."

Alan wasn't certain what Patrick meant. "Do you want me to pull more slivers?" he asked.

—More blood— Patrick replied, showing him what he could not express with words, their bond strengthening, how easy it became for them to communicate when they shared each other's blood.

—What good will that be?— Alan responded and sensed no clear reply. He continued pulling splinters out of Patrick's fingers and sucking the wounds to clean them. The toddler's soft hair brushed his cheek and he held Patrick tightly, too frightened of the truth to ask him anything about Hillary.

Donna paced nervously in front of the fire. Russ had already told her to shut up but she kept on talking regardless of the risk. Actually Donna would risk anything to keep from getting locked in the shed with that monster again. "I tell you, Russ, that little kid knew my name," she repeated. "And he knew about us in Wyoming. About how my father used to hit me."

"A good guess. Considering all the noise he makes, his father probably belts him too," Russ replied.

"Ask him how he knew. And while you're at it, take a good look at him. I know lots about babies and he isn't built like one at all."

Russ put down the Austra report. "All right. If it will make you shut your damned mouth, I'll look at him." He unlocked the shed and pulled the toddler out, kicking Alan back when the boy tried to follow. He took Patrick to the fire and stood him upright. Patrick managed to stand for a moment, then his hips unlocked and he fell forward, flat-handed onto all fours. "Long arms," Russ commented.

"Long legs. Long fingers. Russ, toddlers are pudgy and weak. And they don't talk, not like he does. And when I was in there, he was licking my face. His tongue felt rough. It's not right, Russ. There's something strange about him."

Russ studied the toddler. "What's your name?" he asked after a while. When Patrick didn't answer, Russ looked at Donna in disgust. "Get a blanket and cover him up, will you?"

Donna brought a woven Indian blanket from the car. Patrick shrugged it off. "Aren't you cold?" she asked him.

Patrick shook his head. Russ reached for him, gripping him hard while trying to stick a finger in the boy's mouth to feel his tongue. Patrick retaliated with a deep bite. "Shit!" Russ swore and slapped the toddler hard on his naked buttocks, then tossed him on the ground, holding him down while he pried the toddler's jaws apart and angled the boy's head so he could look at his teeth and tongue. He backed off after a quick glance. Patrick twisted out of his slackening grip, retrieving one of the bracelets that had broken off during his struggle. The toddler held it tightly as he moved away from Russ, a hand on his shoulder, covering a deep gouge one of the rocks on the site had opened during the struggle. Russ pointed at the bracelets. "Ask him what those are," Russ ordered Donna.

Donna did and Patrick responded. "The blue and green ones are mental colors. The red and gold are effort colors. I have six . . . six more than Dickey because I did well."

"Christ!" Russ said as he heard the precise speech of the toddler, then leaned forward watching the child carefully as Donna questioned him.

"What did you do well?" the girl asked.

"I walked with just my feet. I told Alan the numbers on the blocks. I told him what Mother was doing outside."

"So he's smart, so what?" Russ commented, not certain what he'd seen or felt, still trying to deny the obvious.

Donna ignored him. She pulled three pieces of yarn out of the blanket. "Show me the game and I'll make you another bracelet. Lots of them."

Patrick did. He showed Donna everything he could do while Russ sat dumbfounded, watching the two of them. Patrick was proud. He got a dozen more bracelets. And just like he'd promised Alan, he never said a word to Russ.

Much of Russ Lowell's deadly skill came from his intelligence and his mastery of the unexpected. Now, with so many of his careful plans destroyed, he sat and considered his dwindling options.

The kids had finally told him the truth. Dick Wells was in the mountains. He wouldn't be back for days. The trade of Wells for his son, a trade Lowell had no doubt he would eventually obtain, would have to wait.

In the meantime, the kidnapping might be discovered or the family might return and report it.

But would they? He'd wondered about that even before Donna had displayed the toddler's strange mental powers. Now, he had a good inkling of one reason why they wouldn't.

After he locked the toddler with the others in the shed, he studied the Austra global reports. He had no trouble understanding the data or even in accepting it. But the facts astounded him. Where in the hell did they get this information? How much did they have to pay for it? And to whom? Or did they just read minds the way the child was apparently able to do?

How much would this data be worth to a government obsessed with spies and communist plots in the military? In the media? Even in the police?

Enough to buy more than one man's freedom, of that he had no doubt.

Every plan he'd made suddenly became unimportant. He wrote a cryptic, unsigned note for his employer, then shook Donna awake and the two of them drove away, heading for Powder River.

As they pulled up at the two-story rooming house, the largest building in the tiny town, Russ warned Donna, "Not one damned word to Halli about the kid, understand?" He didn't need to be any clearer about which kid. She knew that Patrick had become their secret.

Not that she had any chance to open her mouth. Russ had

pushed her up the stairs ahead of him and as soon as Russ's partner saw her, he ordered her into the bathroom and shut the door. "Hey," she called to Russ. "How long should I stay in here?"

"Until we tell you to come out," the other man said. "Take a bath. And keep the water running."

Donna followed the orders and turned on the tap, then stared out the window at the quiet street below. She saw an older woman walk from the rooming house to the gas station across the dusty street to get a bottle of cold pop from the soda machine. As she returned, the woman wiped her forehead with the side of the bottle.

Donna could call out, beg the woman to help her, and hope that Russ didn't hear. Maybe she could just climb out the window and make it to the ground and get to the police before Russ even knew she'd gone.

And then what? If they caught Russ, he'd probably say she was an accomplice. If they never caught him, they'd send her home. Neither option was a good one. She leaned against the sink and stared at herself in the yellowed mirror. *You're a survivor. You'll be all right*, she reminded herself, then, with a resigned sigh, she took off her clothes and stepped into the tub. She looked down at the old bruises on her wrists and breasts, noticing how they'd faded to dark patches. No new ones had taken their place. Since she tried to kill Russ Lowell ten days ago, he hadn't hit her. Maybe he respected her, maybe he was just preoccupied with the kidnapping, or maybe he guessed, correctly, that for the moment threats were enough.

She turned the faucet down to a trickle and leaned back in the tub, trying to listen to the discussion in the next room. The men were angry, she could tell from their tones, but they kept their voices low. She could make out only a few words. Eventually, she stopped trying and concentrated on washing off the most recent traces of Russ Lowell.

IV

Alan coughed. The motion roused Patrick who slept in his arms. The toddler stretched and, as he remembered where they were, gripped Alan's shoulders so tightly that Alan winced.

"Dark," Patrick commented.

"It's nighttime."

"I am hungry. I want Mama."

"So do I. Can you find her?" Alan asked.

During the long silence that followed, Patrick lay limp in his arms. "No," the toddler finally said and followed that with a long groan of misery.

"Are Russ and Donna back?"

"Yes. They made a fire."

"Was Hillary ever awake?" Alan asked.

"Yes. Her head hurt. She liked talking to me."

Patrick took Alan's hand and placed it over the bracelets on his arm and demanded his payment for spying outside. "Make me one more," he said.

Alan felt dangerously close to tears. Knowing they were useless, he sniffed them back. "I wish I could, Patrick. But the yarn is at home. After we find your mother, I'll make them. Do you understand?"

Patrick's deceptively delicate hand touched Alan's face. "I do," he said. He rested his head on Alan's chest. His breathing slowed and evened as he fell asleep leaving Alan awake, trying to come up with some plan.

Alan lay close to Hillary under the damp sleeping bag and reviewed everything he knew about the Austras. He had thought he was only dreaming of Helen since she had left home but apparently he had actually seen her. He wished he could do that at will and somehow talk to her the way she did to him the night she went hunting.

When she took him with her!

"Patrick," Alan whispered and lightly shook the child until he stirred. "Patrick, I think I can find your mother but I need your help. When we find her, you must talk to her. Do you understand?"

Alan felt a buzzing in his head and the darkness diminished. He was above the shed, looking down at Donna cooking dinner, Russ napping in the car. Without really seeing it, or knowing how he sensed it, he felt Hillary wake and wrap her arms around him and Patrick. Her mind merged with theirs and together they moved higher, in an erratic wobbly spiral that made Alan queasy.

Alan held with Patrick as long as he could, then began fighting the toddler's hold until, with what felt like a pinch between his eyes, Patrick let him go. "But I went far," Patrick protested in a voice far too loud.

"Shhh. Of course you did," Hillary said.

"But you can't go far enough," Alan explained.

"You said I must help."

"And you will." Alan tried to make his explanation as simple as he could. "I dream about your mother but I can never talk to her. You must go with me—in my dream—and when I see her you must talk to her and stay with her in your mind until she finds us."

"No. Dreams are bad."

Alan slapped his hand on the shed floor, let out a long breath of air, and tried again. "Some dreams are bad. This one will be good. I will dream about your mother. When I do, can you go into my mind without waking me and come with me to see her?"

"This is help?"

Alan nodded and Patrick nuzzled against him. —Like this?— he asked.

There'd been only a slight buzzing, certainly not enough to wake him up. "Exactly," Alan said.

Alan rolled over. His head hurt, breathing had become difficult again, and the shed floor was cold against his shoulder. Even so, it had been a long, terrifying day, and filled with need, he focused his mind on his cousin and slept.

FIFTEEN

1

Helen dreamed of them speaking to her—a long way off it seemed but distance made no difference now. Hours had passed while she held Dickey and slept, conserving her strength, waiting for darkness and this calling in her dreams. She woke in the center of the night, powerful, ready for her first human kill.

She doused the fire in the stove and put a squirming, protesting Dickey in the shoulder pack he hadn't used for months. After ordering him to be quiet, she strengthened the bond with her cousin and her missing son. The stars swirled around her as her mind soared toward them, while her body swiftly followed.

Helen reached Russ's campsite an hour before dawn. She unstrapped Dickey's harness and ordered the boy to stay quiet and hidden. When he had done as she asked, she crouched in a stand of scrubby bushes at the edge of the clearing and studied her prey.

Russ had loaded his supplies into the trunk of the car and was just bringing out the children. Alan led, followed by Hillary carrying Patrick and, behind her, a fourth, a girl a little younger than Hillary who seemed as frightened of the man as the others were. Helen heard the man calling the girl's name, the girl answering in a tense even voice. Donna and Russ. Russ . . . the one she would kill.

The rifle Russ carried made Helen nervous. She didn't know how quickly her body would heal if she were wounded so she moved cautiously closer to the car parked at the end of the rutted drive. She would wait until Russ reached the driver's side of the car where he would be near enough to her that she could take him by surprise. Once her hands reached him, he'd have no defense.

She saw the bruises on Alan's face, felt how numb his hands had become in the few minutes since Russ had tied them. She sensed Hillary's fear and her rage grew, narrowed, and focused on the man following the children to the car.

Russ put Alan in the front passenger seat, then walked behind the girls around the back of the car to the other side. Helen tensed, her breathing a shallow pant as she prepared to spring.

As Russ opened the door, Patrick saw her, called to her, and pointed.

Russ whirled and, leaving the back door half open, aimed his gun at her. Smiling, he said her name.

For the first and last time.

The certainty of this awed Helen. She knew exactly how she would strike, wounding not killing, not yet. She wanted him in a way she had never wanted a man before and she felt no pity, no shame, no need to hold back and be anything less than the predator she had become. She sensed all of this as if time had stopped while she gripped her knife and touched his mind, freezing him for the instant she needed to strike.

And she might have succeeded had Hillary not dropped Patrick and grabbed the top of the door, ramming it into Russ's side to ruin his aim.

When the door hit Russ, the gun went off.

The bullet entered Helen's thigh, the pain of its impact pulling her out of Russ's mind, freeing him. With a bellow of rage, Russ slammed the car door and fired again, hitting Helen in the side near her heart. Without bothering to note if she were alive or dead, he swung the rifle toward Hillary.

"No!" Donna screamed and threw herself against him. Russ kicked her back and fired at Hillary, hitting her in the chest. He would have fired again but Patrick jumped at him, his fingers curled, clawing deep gouges into Russ's face and neck. Russ caught him and tossed him into Donna's arms. The toddler's thin arms circled her neck and he looked over his shoulder with cold dark eyes and snarled.

Russ moved back a step. He'd never been attacked so viciously by any kid before and the barrel of his gun shook as he aimed it at Patrick's face. Donna wrapped her arms around the toddler and turned so her body was between Russ and him. "For God's sake. He's just a baby."

"The hell he is! Oh, all right. Give him to me and get in the car."

"No. It's over, Russ. If you force me to go, I'll scream. I'll kick. I'll be more trouble than even you can stand. You said I could leave when I wanted to. That's now, Russ."

Russ had his hand on the trigger, the rifle aimed a little lower than her heart. Slow, certain, agonizing death. Donna didn't even look at the weapon. She kept her eyes on Russ's face. Patrick also stared at him, their expressions perfectly matched.

Russ wanted to kill them both but he didn't. Instead he opened the car and pushed Alan back into the passenger seat, jerked Patrick out of Donna's arms, and tossed him in the back before heading down the winding dirt road. Alan sat beside him looking straight ahead, not even flinching when Russ touched his cheek, holding his hand there as he said cheerfully, "Ah well, you're the important one after all. If you're very good and do everything I say, I'll trade you for your father and you'll be fine."

And his father would be dead. Alan lowered his head to his knees and began to cry as silently as he was able.

Stephen's body would have ignored the wounds Helen received. They might have even healed during the fight, certainly during the time he would have taken to devour his opponent. But Helen's human flesh needed time. She lay facedown on the damp ground, patches of sun beating on her back, its pain hardly noticed among the others—the wound in her leg, the second dangerous one in her chest, the knowledge that she had failed.

Pressing her hand against the hole in her chest, she crawled the few feet to where Hillary lay mercilessly conscious, slowly dying.

"I'm sorry." Hillary struggled for breath and her voice was so soft even Helen had difficulty hearing it. "Russ tricked me. There was blood on his shirt. He . . ." She sobbed and could not go on.

Instincts Helen barely understood told her that Hillary was beyond saving. "No!" she whispered in denial of what had happened, of her fear, of what she knew she had to do to rescue her cousin. She wanted to cry but forced back the human tears and the human emotion that caused them. Later, later she'd give in to that part of her and mourn. —Hillary. I need your help.—

Helen sensed the girl's assent, ripped open Hillary's blouse, and pressed her lips to the wound devouring the blood, swallowing the bits of flesh she sucked in with it, more animal now than Stephen could ever be, more of a beast than anything she had ever imagined. The girl's life coursed through her, the energy in it feeding Helen's mind as they joined in a rush of fear and hope and soared above the clearing and the mountains, moving north and west seeking Stephen.

They sensed him as a point of light shining more brilliantly than the morning sun on the snowy peaks above him and descended, hitting his mind with all the force of their combined fear and pain.

—Death!! Danger!! Home!!—

Then there was only Hillary and herself and the light she remembered from the time of her changing—a different eternity waiting for a human soul. They shared a quick moment, a good-bye, and Helen was alone with the shell of a friend and her sorrow. She gave in to it now, sobbing, oblivious to her own pain, repeating Hillary's final words, "So much was possible."

Helen felt something brush her shoulder and looked sideways at Dickey, squatting beside her, staring at Hillary. "Gone," he said.

"Yes, gone," Helen replied. Instinctively, she pushed herself to her feet and limped toward the comforting darkness of the storage shed. Inside, the healing sleep merged with the dawn lethargy and fell into a coma as profound as the day of her changing.

She was unaware of Dickey unbuttoning her blouse, licking at the wound, then, still unsatisfied, finding her breast. Hillary was gone. Patrick had been taken from him. Dickey had never been so miserable and though he begged, his mother would not hold him.

11

As Russ drove away, Donna had stood in the center of the clearing fighting the conflicting urges to run or to faint. It seemed stupid to do either. *Russ is gone. He won't come back*, she reminded herself.

Dickey brushed her leg. She looked down at the silver-haired boy, screamed, and jumped sideways, then with courage fueled by pity reached for him. He bolted away toward the blond woman who lay motionless with the blood seeping from beneath her. Hillary moaned softly and Donna had decided to do what she could to ease the girl's pain. She'd gone to the fire pit and found a brandy bottle still containing a couple of ounces. As she turned and started toward Hillary, the blond woman began her long slow crawl to the girl.

Donna saw how they looked at each other in shared understanding, love, and pain. She saw Hillary's lips move as she nodded. When the woman ripped Hillary's shirt, Donna thought she planned to help the girl. Though she wanted to go and see what she could do for both of them, she felt fixed on the spot where she stood, as if her feet were planted deep in the hard earth beneath them.

Then Helen began to feed. Donna felt their mental scream, their silent cry for help not meant for her, then an order—primal and instinctive.

Donna ran.

And maybe it was the worst possible choice to make but she couldn't think of any other. "Russ!" she screamed though he was probably long gone. "Russ!" she repeated and ran down the rutted road, stumbling, falling, picking herself up and running again.

Russ had stopped where the dirt road joined the highway and turned sideways in his seat, convinced he'd heard Donna call him.

She ran to the passenger side of the car, saw where Patrick had been tossed, and got into the front seat beside Alan. "Why did you wait for me?" she asked Russ.

He shrugged and turned onto the highway. "Why did you change your mind?"

Donna tried to speak but terror made it impossible. Russ reached over the boy's head and grabbed her shoulder, squeezing until she winced from the pain. "What happened? Tell me."

"The blond woman. She . . ."

"She still alive?"

Donna managed to nod. Swearing, Russ slammed the car into reverse and backed down the dirt road while Alan looked up at Donna. His eyes seemed sad to her, as much from her betrayal as the killings.

At the clearing Russ locked the car and, gun in hand, ran to Hillary's body, so savaged now that he did not bother to check for a pulse. He scanned the area, then checked the storage shed, and in the dim morning light saw the woman inside.

She lay as Dickey had left her, her shirt unbuttoned, her body alabaster pale and smooth as a child's, her breathing even. Russ crouched beside her and studied the bullet hole in her chest. It didn't seem as ragged as it should be nor as deep. Maybe his gun had somehow misfired, diminishing the impact. He laid it down and pulled the knife out of his pocket. He would end it now, personally, cleanly. He unfolded the blade, holding it up ready to cut before wrapping his fingers through the woman's long hair. He didn't need to do this but he wanted to see those eyes open, wanted to see the terror as he made the single killing stroke.

But she didn't wake. Didn't struggle. Unconscious, her body automatically mobilized its final defense, a simple one that hardly seemed strange to Russ at that moment. He didn't want to kill Helen Wells anymore, at least not yet. No, he wanted her for many things and killing was merely the last of them.

As he stooped to pick her up, he heard the distant howling of a wolf and, out in the sunshine, a second closer howl. He looked down at his new prisoner, noting again the odd pallor of her skin, her long slender neck, her incredible beauty, and he carried his prize quickly toward the car.

As he approached it, he saw a shadow moving on the opposite side of it and Patrick Austra pressed against the glass watching something. He warily rounded the front, coming face-to-face with Dickey who pulled on the door handles trying frantically to make one of them open. Russ automatically kicked, intending to send the small boy spinning but Dickey danced out of his way. Russ motioned for Donna to crawl over the seat and hold on to Patrick while he opened the door, then pulled the girl from it before locking Helen inside. Patrick clung to his mother, looking pitifully out the window at Dickey who sat, just out of Russ's reach, staring back.

"You didn't tell me there was another one," Russ said. Donna only shuddered and stiffened, waiting for a blow that never came. "Go get him."

Donna looked at Russ with dull surprise and he gave her a push in Dickey's direction. "Go on. The other one likes you. Maybe this one will come to you."

She took a step toward Dickey. He retreated an equal distance. Another step. Another retreat. The space between Donna and the car grew wider and her choice more clear. She could catch this strange small child so that Russ could kill it and be drawn deeper into his plots of kidnapping and murder or she could take the one chance open to her.

Besides, now he had that woman—that strange, beautiful, frightening woman—so why would he want her anymore? She heard Russ swear and made her decision.

"Run!" Donna whispered and took off after Dickey into the trees, falling flat when the shots started, scrambling to get away from the clearing. Though she immediately lost sight of Dickey, she kept on running until her sides hurt and her legs were weak. Then she doubled over, hugging her ribs, trying to force her lungs to slow their pumping. The trees grew high above her, their branches woven together hiding the sun. The clearing was miles away from the nearest town and she didn't even know which way to go to return it. She'd probably freeze or starve before she found shelter, and with that thought, she remembered the boy, probably as lost as she was. "Kid," she called softly, still afraid that Russ had followed her. "Kid?"

Then she heard a branch crack, whirled and saw a wolf sitting a few yards away, staring at her.

"Shoo!" she said, waving her arms. "Shoo!"

It cocked its head. It seemed to be smiling at her, telling her it wouldn't be frightened away like some toy terrier by a ninety-pound girl, already half dead from exhaustion.

Donna couldn't outrun it nor would her aching legs have the strength to push her up one of the thin pine trees. Maybe an attack would confuse the wolf enough that it would leave her alone. She picked up a stick and rushed toward the animal. It ran until she stopped chasing it, then turned and watched her. Donna caught her breath and charged it again with no better result.

The wolf sat a moment, ran a few yards, stopped and looked back at her. Its intentions seemed clear, and with no idea where she was going, Donna followed it. Even if it took her nowhere, its presence would keep the cougars at bay.

The wolf led her deeper into the forest, then, as if its mission had been accomplished, disappeared into the trees. As Donna stood, considering what to do next, she saw a flicker of motion near the ground, and still holding on to the stick that could hardly be considered a weapon, Donna walked forward as softly as she could.

In the dim light she saw the child huddled against the rotting stump of a fallen tree, clutching a tiny piece of fabric from his mother's blouse. When he saw Donna, he ran to her, wrapping his arms around her waist. Though Donna wanted to push him away, some old memory surfaced in her—of a time when Donna had been a small child, alone and frightened and not at all sure anyone cared for her.

If she ignored the difference between them, this was a

beautiful child. And she wanted to ignore them, to comfort him and herself. She unzipped her oversize jacket, picked him up, and held him close to her. He snuggled against her sweater making a sound like a cat purring softly. She zipped her jacket to keep him warm and ran a hand through his soft curly hair.

She sat on a log, looking at the shadows around her, trying to decide on the best direction to go.

"Dickey," the toddler said. They were the first words Donna had heard in hours and she jumped.

"Donna," she responded with a nervous giggle.

"Home."

Donna choked on a sudden rush of sympathy. There would be nothing left at home for him now. "I'd take you but I don't know the way."

"Home." Dickey pointed in a direction Donna thought was east, wiggled out of the bag, and began walking away from her on hands and feet.

Donna caught up with him, grabbing his arm and pulling him upright. "Dickey, you'll freeze out there."

"Home."

Donna recalled that his mother had apparently arrived on foot and asked, "How far?"

Dickey looked confused and Donna tried a different approach. "How long will it take us to get there?"

She sensed the toddler trying to understand the concept of time, eventually answering, "Night."

Tonight? She hoped he meant tonight. "You won't lose me when it gets dark, will you?" Donna asked.

In response, Dickey took her hand.

Well, Donna thought, no one had tried to eat her, at least not yet, and a trek through the woods seemed preferable to trying to find the clearing where Russ might be waiting to shoot them both. With a quick silent prayer to whoever might be listening, she let Dickey lead her into the trees.

SIXTEEN

Dick Wells had been frying trout for breakfast when he heard Stephen's scream, the sound loud and high, echoing off the peaks around them, saying in a way no words could that Dick had made a fatal error. Though he wanted to shake Stephen awake Dick kept his distance from the creature curled into a tight ball beneath the domed outcropping that shaded him while he slept. Instead he waited for Stephen to join him. When Stephen did, Dick noted how his pale long body trembled as he sat on a log beside the fire. He looked fragile, his drawn face effeminate, delicate. Only his eyes, dark and steady, revealed the full depth of his rage. Since part of it was probably directed at him, Dick said nothing at all as he doused the fire, rolled, and tied his sleeping bag and loaded his pack. When he had finished and Stephen still hadn't spoken, Dick asked, "How bad was it?"

"Hillary is dead. Helen is alive but wounded. That is all I know," Stephen told him.

"It's not too hard to figure out the rest, though, is it?" Dick responded, his voice rigid with hidden emotion. They had Alan, he knew they had Alan, and maybe the twins as well.

Stephen said nothing. Instead he put on a shirt, tied his mountain boots to his belt, and started their return hike at a speed Dick found impossible to maintain. He drowned in the dull pain that filled the space in his lungs where air should

174

rightfully circulate. He ignored it. Fought it. In less than a mile, with his ears ringing and the edges of his sight weaving inward, he admitted defeat. He leaned against a rock and, when he was able, called weakly to Stephen, "I have to rest."

Stephen turned and walked by the slope, his annoyance at having to waste even a few extra moments vanishing as he noted the pain Dick had managed to conceal. He solicitously helped Dick sit, brushing his fingers over Dick's wrist in a brief, probably thorough exam that made Dick feel helpless.

"Will Helen bring the truck to our drop-off point?" Dick asked, not certain he could walk the twenty miles at any speed without collapsing.

"Richard, I received a cry for help not a telephone call. I don't know how hurt Helen is, where she is, or even how long it will take her to heal. We'll go directly to the cabin instead."

"That's at least a three-day hike. Why don't we walk to East Pine and borrow a car?"

"East Pine is completely out of our way and the roads from there to the cabin are far from direct. Now that we're on more level ground I can get us there much faster, yes?" Stephen pulled a length of rope from one of the packs he'd been carrying, then tossed both packs aside. He sat below Dick on the slope and slid backward toward him. "Put your arms out straight over my shoulders, Richard, and raise your knees over my hips."

"Oh, no. You just go on without me and I'll catch up later," Dick said.

"You're the one the kidnapper wants, yes? Now do it," Stephen ordered.

Dick did. Stephen wound the rope around his wrists, his knees, then both their waists, pressing Dick against him. "The terrain is still far from level and the last distraction I need is you slipping off of me," Stephen explained. "Besides, it's best we give you to your assassin alive, yes?" Dick felt Stephen's body shake in a quick, humorless laugh.

"I know what I've got to do," Dick said. "If they have our sons, they'll want to make the trade. I'm ready."

"Of course you are. And after everyone is out of danger, your assassins will be ours."

Stephen arched his back and gave the rope one final tug. Dick winced. "Listen, does the damn thing have to be . . ."

Instead of arguing, Stephen rolled forward onto his hands. *Level ground, hell!* Dick thought as he found himself staring straight down the slope. Convinced they were about to fall, Dick automatically tried to raise his shoulders but the coils made it impossible. He settled for gripping them instead and wondered if they were tight enough. "Should I untie you, Richard?" Stephen asked.

Stupid pride, that's all Dick felt but he wished Stephen didn't have to be so smug in his superiority, waiting for Dick to admit he was exhausted before suggesting this humiliating solution. He was about to say as much when Stephen tensed, flesh hardening to muscles and tendons sinewy and supple as steel cables. They ground into Dick bringing him a stab of an old willed-forgotten memory. The memory intensified as even through three layers of clothing, he felt his body tingle as if he and Stephen were magnetically charged, the human and alien flesh drawn together by forces neither of them could control. Then the memory vanished as suddenly as it had come, forgotten by fear as Stephen began to run.

Dick ordered his body to relax, ordered himself not to pull at the ropes or do anything to break the concentration of the creature moving beneath him. Gradually, he relaxed, closing his eyes, imagining himself on an amusement park ride, then, on flatter ground, in a rocking chair. He felt Stephen touch his mind.

—We're still a few hours from the cabin. Would you like to sleep, Richard?—

—Later.—

The world sped by them. The noon sun that warmed Dick's back probably pained his friend, yet Stephen flowed on, oblivious to its rays, to exhaustion, to the weight of Dick above him. "It's been a long time since you killed a man, hasn't it?" Dick asked.

Dick had meant this as a warning and he did not expect

the vicious anticipation tinging Stephen's inaudible reply. —I can taste him, Richard.—

Later, Dick must have slept because when he woke it was dark and Stephen had stopped in front of the unlit cabin and begun untying the rope. The muscles in Dick's back had knotted and he stretched them out, then let Stephen help him to his feet. He felt a weakness that seemed to have nothing to do with his illness and saw the bloody rip in his sleeve, the bite marks, and the red circle around them. Though he would have gladly shared his blood, being used without being asked angered him. He was about to say so when he noticed how Stephen wobbled slightly, how his eyes were glazed, and for an instant, in Stephen's fleeting grin, just how much he had enjoyed the challenge of that run.

The moment broke as they approached the darkened house. In the doorway, Dick grabbed the flashlight mounted on the wall and played the beam over the room, then went to the table and lit the oil lamps. As the light grew, he noticed the bullet holes in the dark wood floor. He had destroyed the peace of this place and he wondered if he had the power to set things right. Stephen still stood at the door, his expression grim with concentration. "I had expected Helen to be here," he said in a voice oddly flat as if he had just discovered some dry quaint fact. A moment later Stephen walked to the ladder leading to the loft where Hillary had slept.

"Dickey," Stephen called and the toddler immediately jumped into his arms. "Papa!" the boy yelped happily and a moment later a girl climbed down and joined them. Her hair was muddy, her face scratched, and though she looked exhausted, she gripped a knife and eyed them both with suspicion. "Donna," the boy said as he pointed at her.

Stephen held out his hand and said softly, "May I have it, Donna?"

Donna stepped backward away from Stephen, shaking her head. She appeared ready to faint from exhaustion or fear, most likely a combination of both. Knowing from experience that talking would make her feel better, Dick said kindly, "Donna, you can keep the knife if it makes you feel better.

We're not going to hurt you. We know you've been through a lot but we need to know what happened to the two other boys and the women who were here?''

"Listen, I didn't have anything to do with this. Russ took them. I—I tried to stop him . . . Oh, hell! Take it.'' She walked past Dick, handing him the knife as she did so, falling into one of the carved wood chairs, hiding her face with her hands. "He left you a note. I saw it on the table when Dickey and I came in.'' Donna scanned the room and pointed to the paper in the corner where the wind from the door had blown it.

Stephen retrieved and read it. "He used my name,'' he commented, turned it over, and read the opposite side before handing it to Dick.

Dick glanced then at the table where the AustraGlass reports had been stacked and saw that they were gone. "Did Russ take some papers from this house?'' he asked Donna.

"He was reading something yesterday afternoon. And he and his partner had an argument about some company in Europe.'' She glanced at Stephen and, as she'd been doing since they met, quickly looked away, adding, "And you, I think.''

"Even those reports wouldn't be enough to tell Lowell who you were,'' Dick said.

Stephen looked thoughtfully at Donna. "I want you to close your eyes and think about Russ. Try to build a picture of him in your mind.''

Donna did and heard Dick swear. Russ's image vanished.

"So now we know,'' Stephen said softly as he stared at Dick. "When I was young two hundred miles could separate me from my past. Now two thousand isn't far enough.''

"What happened was a coincidence, nothing more,'' Dick responded.

"A coincidence Helen saw coming the evening of her reception. She shrugged it off. So did I.''

"Why doesn't Lowell mention Helen?'' Dick asked.

"He didn't have her when he wrote it,'' Donna responded. "She came later. Russ caught her. Now the dark-haired girl is dead. The blond woman—Helen, right?—was shot in the leg and the chest. It looked bad for her at first but she was alive and . . .'' Her voice rose but she fought down the hysteria, moving closer to Dick and away from Stephen as she described everything that had happened from the time Russ showed up at the campsite with the boys until she ran away with Dickey.

Though Stephen looked concerned, he hardly seemed surprised. "What happened to Helen?" Dick asked him.

"Her human flesh requires time to heal, I think. And Hillary's death was a shock, far worse than Philippe's because, though Hillary would have died anyway, Helen was the instrument. I am certain she stayed with Hillary to the end. They were very close.''

"How long will she sleep?''

"I have no way of knowing. She is unique, yes? But one thing is certain—she chose to go with Russ Lowell. Her instincts are already strong. Had they sensed death in her future, she would not have been able to leave with him.''

"Stephen, she was unconscious.''

"Even unconscious, there are ways to fight. No, he'll be her victim in the end.'' He spoke proudly as if Helen had passed an important test on the road to eternal life, then added, "She won't be sorry when it's done, yes?''

Donna looked from Stephen to Dick, shock clear in her expression. "Forgive me,'' Dick said sadly, "but, Stephen, what do you or anyone in your family know about *maternal instinct?*''

The moment he said the words, Dick regretted them. Dick saw the anger flare in Stephen's dark eyes, noted the effort Stephen required to control it. "Don't ever consider sparing me what I must know,'' he said, his voice perfectly even. Turning to Donna, he asked, "If Lowell ties her later, what might he use?''

"He had some rope and two pairs of handcuffs. He said the cuffs were police issue.''

"How strong would those be, Richard?''

"I've never had anyone break them yet. It's the big guys that try to.''

For the first time Dick detected a hint of fear in Stephen's tone as he commented, "I could break them but he might be able to hold her."

"Well, she has more than strength to work with, right?" Dick asked Stephen.

Stephen nodded, but slowly, as if he weren't sure how effective her mental control would prove to be. "What else did he carry?" Stephen asked Donna.

"A gun and a rifle, his knife, a lot of food and a camera."

Understanding the significance of the last item, Dick paled. "Where did they go?" he asked.

"I don't know. Maybe to Powder River if his partner's still there."

"What did Russ do with the reports?"

"We mailed them. He even waited for the driver to pick up the mailbags."

"Where did he send them?"

Donna shook her head. She didn't know.

Surprised that he should be the one displaying the most outward confidence, Dick said, "Well, Lowell will never figure out all the truth, not if we stop him now. Should we start with his partner?"

"Not yet. Why don't you get an hour's rest, Richard. I'll take Dickey and bring Hillary's body home. You may answer any questions Donna might ask. She needs to know all of it." As Stephen pulled a blanket from the closet, Dickey moved to the front door.

Concerned and somewhat bewildered, Dick said, "You were in such a hurry this morning."

"And we must be cautious now. Hillary was my ward. I don't want her body found. It would raise too many questions and we may not be here to answer them, yes?" Stephen responded coldly and left with his son. A short time later Dick and Donna heard the truck drive off.

"How will he know where to go?" Donna asked.

"Dickey will tell him if he hasn't already."

"Oh." She watched him set logs on the hearth and start the fire. "You're going to want me to stay with the kid, aren't you?"

"At least until one of his family can come."

"That's OK. I can handle him by myself."

Dick went into the kitchen, returning with two beers and a square of cheese. "Do you want me to explain about these people?" he asked as he opened the bottles.

Her human flesh, the beautiful man with the dark eyes had said. "No," Donna decided. "I've had enough weird stuff happen today. Tell me tomorrow."

"If I'm here." Dick studied Donna. She seemed so calm in the face of everything that had happened, as if yesterday and the preceding few weeks had been no worse than all the years before them. Like the girls he'd see walking the night streets when he drove a squad, she'd had to grow up fast. Maybe that's why he hadn't thought twice about handing the beer to a kid who ought to be sound asleep dreaming of her junior prom. "Listen," he said kindly. "Russ Lowell has my son. If you can, I'd like you to tell me about him. Not about what happened today, but about him, how he acts and thinks. If it's too hard to talk about him, I'll understand."

"I want to." Donna stared into the fire. "But I'm scared to even mention his name like if I do, that son of a bitch is going to hear it and come back here to beat the hell out of me again. You're a cop, ain't you? You going to turn me in?"

"That depends. Is somebody missing you?"

"Not the ones I'd get sent back to."

"Then I'll wait until this is over and help you get settled somewhere else."

Since the day Donna had made breakfast for Russ, she had acted her emotions. Now the real ones spilled out and she cried as she told her story, as if this were her confession; her evil, not his.

When she'd finished, Dick sat beside her on the sofa, rocking her slowly as they waited for Stephen to return.

By the time Dick heard the truck, Donna had fallen asleep. He moved away from her carefully so she wouldn't wake, picked up one of the oil lamps, and went outside. Stephen had just taken a shovel out of the storage room on the side of the house and began walking up the hill next to the house. Without a word, Dick grabbed a second shovel and followed him to a clearing out of sight of the road. They dug Hillary's grave in silence, Dick standing beside it while Stephen went for the body. Dickey, who had been sitting motionless beside Hillary's corpse the entire time the men had been digging, followed his father up the hill.

Stephen had wrapped Hillary in a blanket, tying it at the waist and feet with a length of rope and the bright green sash Hillary had been wearing when Russ had killed her. Laying her body on the ground beside the grave, he unwrapped the top of the blanket for one last look at her. Dick raised the light and looked down at the wound on Hillary's chest. The small deep hole a bullet would make had been extended, the skin and flesh ripped outward. He pictured Helen caught in a frenzy of need, digging for the last drops of life. How could she survive this with her mind intact or would it heal with the same perfection as her body?

"Touch her," Stephen told his son.

Dickey who had neither the luxury of tears nor understanding watched his father expectantly as he rested a hand on Hillary's forehead, as if he were convinced his father could bring Hillary back with just a word. Stephen covered the boy's hand with his own, then brushed the wound from which a dark circle of blood still seeped, moistening Dickey's lips and his own with it.

They stood without speaking, but Dick knew by the boy's quick breathing and the intent way he looked at his father that Stephen was conveying a great deal to his son. Then, for the first time since he'd brought her body home, Stephen spoke, making a vow in a tone that managed to be both solemn and ruthless, "The death of those we love is never truly real until we touch and taste it. Now I promise you, Hillary Dutiel, that whatever happens, the man who caused this and the one who ordered it will die."

Stephen spoke with total confidence. He believed he could not fail. Though Dick knew what anger fueled Stephen now, he made the quick unsettling connection that Stephen's grief was a pale imitation of how Carrera must have felt when he saw the body of his son.

* * *

Hours later, Dick was awakened from a fitful sleep by the sound of soft footsteps in the main room. Though it scarcely seemed possible, Lowell might have returned and Dick crouched low, keeping to the shadows as he slowly cracked open his door.

Stephen stood at the near end of the sofa where Donna still slept. His back was to Dick. His arms were rigid at his sides, his fists tightly clenched and pressed against the outside of his knees. Though his head was bowed, Dick could see that the body beneath the black turtleneck and slacks was as tense as his arms.

Dick angled himself so he could get a better look at Donna. The girl was sleeping, soundless and motionless but equally tense, forced to share her nightmare.

Though he should have quietly gone back to bed and gotten whatever sleep he could, Dick remained standing in the shadows watching the silent exchange. When it ended, Stephen relaxed, moved closer to the girl, and ran the back of his hand lightly down the side of her face. As he did, he looked in Dick's direction, acknowledging his presence for the first time. His back was to the fire, his face in the shadows, his dark eyes glittering in the reflected light from the front door. Without a word, he turned and padded silently from the room.

SEVENTEEN

I

The fog that had rolled into Powder River still covered the ground at dawn. Jason Halli buttoned his red flannel shirt and lit a cigarette, then walked to the bare open window and looked down at the hazy street below. Nothing moved, but in a town this size at this hour he didn't expect anything would. He thought he glimpsed someone, a figure beneath the awning of the store across the street, a pale face looking up at him. He leaned out the window and stared into the shadows and saw nothing at all.

His mind was playing tricks. No wonder. In the last twenty-four hours, his plans had fallen apart and his partner had gone insane.

He stretched and winced from a sudden spasm in his back. In the years he'd worked for the Carreras, he'd slept in dozens of cheap hotels but none had made him feel like getting out of the business quite like the mattress in this one.

He turned away from the window and, cigarette dangling from his mouth, pulled his suitcase from under the bed and methodically began to pack, waiting until he was finished before pulling his gun from its hiding place beneath the lower drawer of the water-stained pine dresser. As he surveyed the room one final time, he congratulated himself on his caution. There was no evidence to tie him to the Wells kidnapping, none at all. He'd never even been seen with Russ. He didn't have to run from this crime. He could go anywhere he wanted this time, even straight for home.

Not that Halli was anxious to move to any place but a larger town with a better hotel, someplace where he could shed the bright cotton flannels, put on a suit and tie, and feel civilized again. Though Carrera had immediately posted bail, no one doubted that he would eventually go to jail. Halli would just as soon stay out of Cleveland until the cards were reshuffled and dealt and he knew exactly which players would demand his loyalty and which he should trade it to. He left his keys and last night's rent on the dresser and walked down the outside stairs to his car.

The first doubts surfaced before he'd even left town. What if Russ had left some evidence, some link between them for the provincial police to find? Hell, after the argument they'd had yesterday, Russ might even do it on purpose.

Though Halli had taken the road leading away from Russ's campsite, the need to know became too intense to ignore and he made a U-turn. If anyone was waiting at the site, he'd just drive by. But if it was deserted, he'd take one quick look around, then leave with his mind at ease.

He'd never felt the need to be this cautious before, but the truth was, everything about this job shook him—killing a cop, a goddamn *captain*, most of all.

And for what? Not the money. This job was worth three times what Domie was paying for it. No, it was to keep the respect of a man who was facing five to fifteen in the can.

A suicide run, that's all it had become. And when you're stuck with a suicide run, it pays to be careful.

Halli fiddled with the dial of the car radio and found a single station legible through the mountain static. He switched it off and settled for humming aimless songs from records his father had played on their Edison, songs he hadn't thought of in years.

There weren't any cars at the campsite turnoff and Halli couldn't see any farther down the dirt road. Still, to be on the safe side, he backed down the rutted drive, ready to take off the minute he saw anything suspicious at the site.

He felt pleased with his caution until a truck came up the narrow drive after him. Halli frowned. He'd been watching, making sure he wasn't followed. No, someone must have been waiting for him, assuming he'd come here.

Halli cursed his stupidity, backed into the clearing, and waited. The other driver might think he was trapped, but Halli was prepared. The road widened at the clearing. It would be tight, but even if the driver parked in the middle, Halli knew there'd be enough space to squeeze by on one side or the other. He revved his engine and reached for the shift.

A shadow moved across the passenger side of his car. The window shattered. In a motion too fast for Halli to see, a long arm reached in, turned off the engine, and stole his keys. Halli automatically reached down for the gun on the floor, then froze as he recognized the face in the window, the pale face of the man he'd seen under the awning across the street from his hotel.

Seen and forgot. Until now.

"Get out of the car, Jason Halli," the man said in a voice that had the tone, though none of the warmth, of a sideshow hypnotist's.

Halli felt a quick stab of pain behind his eyes as he forced them away from the man and focused on the truck and Dick Wells just getting out of it. Halli recognized Wells as soon as he saw him. Hell, nobody who should know him could miss him. Wells was practically a department of his own on the Cleveland police force. And he ran it by the book; one real easy to read. Once more congratulating himself on how careful he'd been, Halli got out of his car. What, after all, was wrong with a little talk when they could never pin a thing on him?

"In there," the man said. He even added "please" as he pointed toward the shed.

All traces of civility vanished the moment they were inside. When the man with Wells ordered Halli to sit in the patch of sunlight near the door and Halli refused, the man slammed him to the ground so hard Halli felt his neck crack. He rubbed the back of it as he eyed his captors with defiant suspicion, concentrating longer on Wells's partner. Though the man stood in the shadows, he wore dark sunglasses. Halli had always hated them, how they made it impossible to know what a man was thinking until things had gone too far. "I can guess why you're here but it won't do you any good. I don't know where Russ Lowell went."

"But you saw him?" Wells asked.

"Sure. I met him a few days ago. I told him Carrera had been arrested and that he should forget any agreement he made with anyone in Cleveland." Halli's head began to pound and a sharp needle of pain rose from the nape of his neck. Wells's friend had probably dislocated something the way he'd slammed him down. Hell, the pain must have made him a little woozy or he never would have added, "I told him those were Carrera's orders. I made sure . . ."

The dark haired man cut him off. "You saw Lowell four days ago. You didn't say anything about Carrera's arrest. You met with him yesterday and when you heard his attempt to kill Richard had failed, you ordered him to shoot his hostages and dump their bodies in the hills." The man spoke as if he didn't have the slightest doubt that he was right and Halli didn't bother to argue his lie. His advice had made no difference anyway and he'd never even seen the kid.

"But Lowell didn't listen," the dark-haired man continued. "He's going back to Cleveland. Why?"

"He has some crazy idea that he can have Carrera's charges dropped. He came to my hotel room raving about world communist conspiracies and deals with the FBI. Domie never should have sent him on this job. The guy'd gone nuts living on his own. Look what he did to all those girls."

"But you let him leave with our sons?" Dick said with soft dangerous rage.

" 'Our sons'? I told you I don't know anything about your sons."

"My son Alan. Stephen's son and now Lowell has Stephen's wife as well."

Wells looked at his partner as he said this and Halli sensed that with the first mention of the man's name some sort of agreement between them had just been reached. Halli didn't like the emotion building in this shed. Wells had a reputation for his temper and Halli was getting too old to take the beatings anymore. He eyed both men warily, then concentrated on Wells's partner as he said, "Look, Russ thinks you're someone who died three years ago so I'd say he's crazy. And he's twenty years younger and a hell of a lot bigger than me. I didn't have a gun handy when he showed up, either, or we wouldn't have had any damn discussion. I would of told him to get lost."

"How did Lowell plan on getting back into the States?" Wells asked.

"Hell if I know. Hey, in this business you don't want to know any more than you have to."

"You've been with the Carreras a long time, yes?" the man with Wells interjected. His bossiness made Halli angry. And Halli didn't like it at all when the man moved into the shadows behind him, crouched down, and rested one hand on the back of Halli's neck.

"I don't have to answer that," Halli retorted, his eyes straight ahead meeting the detective's.

"Of course you do," Wells said. "Make it easy on yourself and don't try to lie."

Halli winced from the pain in his head. It had reached an intensity that seemed to cloud even his hearing as he dimly listened to the man behind him say, "Twenty-two years. First for Raymond, now for Dominic."

"How in the hell . . ."

The man behind him continued to speak, the singsong rhythm of his voice becoming more pronounced as he moved from one thought to the next. "You came here a week before Russ. You found this site and thought it was ideal because of its isolation and the shed. This is the place Lowell would have brought Richard if he'd captured him. Lowell carried a camera in his car, yes? Would he have recorded the execution step by step or would a final picture have been sufficient?"

"Shut up, damn it! Lowell's word would have been enough. The pictures . . ." Halli fought to keep from continuing but the impulse to talk had become too strong and he blurted out, "The pictures, all of them, would have earned him a bonus."

"How would Lowell have killed Richard?"

"Jesus, Stephen! We don't have to hear . . ." Wells stopped midsentence, his attention drawn to his partner's fingers lightly rubbing the side of Halli's neck. "Don't get impatient," he warned in an anxious tone Halli didn't understand.

Halli shuddered from the touch, as if these thin fingers were a knife blade or the barrel of a gun. "Just tell me one thing—was Russ crazy or are you really Stephen Austra?" he asked.

"I am."

"I don't get it. What's the point of hiding up here?"

"You'll understand soon, I promise you," Stephen said in a voice so soft it sounded gentle. For the first time since the kidnapping, Stephen's expression revealed all the hunger he had been deliberately holding back. Though Halli couldn't see it, he noticed Dick watching him with pity.

In the next few hours, Halli lost all will to fight. He still didn't know exactly what he faced but he didn't have to. The pounding in his head was enough, the way the questions flowed one into another was enough. Through the hours, he'd managed to slide into the corner of the shed, where he sat with his knees pulled against his chest. Each time Stephen asked a question in his soft, lilting voice, Halli shuddered as if someone had him wired and had switched on the power. But he always answered, quickly, nervously, as if he believed he still had a future and would someday have to face Carrera and confess this weakness. Dick wanted to tell him that he had no choice but Stephen would not have allowed it, and Dick reluctantly admitted, he had no desire to do so.

As one of Carrera's closest advisers, Halli was able to reveal details of the family's crime operation that the combined law enforcement agencies in Cleveland could have scarcely imagined. Then he talked about Russ Lowell, the man's sadism, his intelligence, his crimes. And each new fact about each bloody crime only served to justify and increase Dick's fury.

These monsters had Helen and their sons!

One fact Dick found more chilling than all the others—someone with the Cleveland police had informed Carrera of

Dick's paid leave, his potential independent flight. Of course, Stephen had asked for a name. Halli said he didn't know it. When the pounding in Halli's head forced tears down his face and he still didn't answer, Stephen seemed satisfied.

Without a name, they could trust no one. Stephen's words the night Dick had first arrived suddenly took on a new meaning—they were completely on their own—here and everywhere.

Finally, Stephen repeated the question Dick had been dreading, "Now tell both of us how Lowell would have killed Richard?"

"With fire. A good killer can stretch an execution over hours, maybe even days, though Russ wouldn't have had that kind of time."

"You have done this, yes?"

"I have."

The air in the room seemed to have grown thicker, charged. "I know a great deal about fire, Jason Halli," Stephen said and brushed a finger down the back of Halli's hand. Halli screamed and looked down at the place Stephen had touched as if expecting to see the burn. "A great deal."

Dick left the shed without a word and sat outside, waiting for the sounds he expected to hear. But there was nothing—no screams. No moans. Not even any motion.

Dick recalled the friendly argument over loyalty oaths that he'd had with Hillary. Alan had looked embarrassed at his response and rightfully so. Children didn't compromise. They hadn't yet learned how. But Dick would, hell, he'd do whatever was necessary to hold his son, alive and well, once again. He sat on one of the logs surrounding the fire pit and listened to the birds singing in the late afternoon sun, to the breeze curling through the pine trees, to the chatter of an anxious squirrel on a branch far above him. This was not a time for killing, not even of killers. This was a time he should be making his peace with God.

The air near the ground grew hazy, the lines of the trees less distinct as the shadows of the mountain spread. The sky turned to white, to rose. At dusk, Stephen joined him. He carried a bundle wrapped in Halli's shirt. Though Dick wanted to ask what was in it or take a quick look inside the open shed, he decided he didn't want to know. He looked up at Stephen and one of his hands automatically began to move to the top of the scar running down his side. He pulled it back, embarrassed by what he'd just revealed.

Stephen sat beside Dick. Reaching out he rested four fingers against the top of the long broad slashes his brother's hand had left on Dick's body. Dick shuddered, forcing himself not to be the first to pull away.

Stephen lowered his arm. "The family resemblance is too obvious now, yes?"

"Hell, you don't have to read my mind to figure that out. The way you sat. The way you moved. And when you touched him, all of a sudden I was that two-bit killer and you were your brother. In the last three years, I've managed to force the memory back but sometimes, if I sleep the wrong way, the scar pulls and I dream about him."

"I never asked if you wished the memory dulled or erased. Should I have done so?"

"I would have refused then. I refuse now. Considering what we're facing, Charles's memory is kind of reassuring. You'll make a hell of a partner, Stephen."

Stephen looked toward Halli's car, thinking of the kind of partner he would make. He'd been thorough with Halli, learning everything the man had known about Carrera and Lowell. How they moved. How they talked. Their friends. Their enemies. How they would react in a crisis. The compulsive habits they needed to convince themselves they were still human.

Stephen knew them as he knew himself. His past and their present were so much alike but he and Carrera were in control. Stephen wasn't so certain about Russ. Yet he knew that both men abhorred weakness and respected those they feared. Well, they would learn to respect him soon enough. "Let's go home," he said to Dick. "We'll start our hunt in Dawson tomorrow. If Russ has left no word for us, we will fly to Cleveland and wait for him, yes?"

Dick nodded. He could think of no better plan to deal with the tragedy.

"And when it's over, I will understand if you never wish to see any of my family again."

"You think you're that vicious?"

"You've seen the beast in me, Richard. Before we are through with this hunt, I expect it to be well fed."

Dick had seen the darker side of his friend; nonetheless, he responded truthfully, "Well, I'm ready to help you rip them apart."

"I know. But when we are through, you will think about what you have been forced to do. Then, whatever your decision, I will understand."

ll

The next morning, Donna dressed Dickey so she could drive into Dawson with the men. There, Stephen checked their mailbox. Finding it empty, he and Dick decided to contract a private plane to fly them to the major airport in Edmonton where they could catch a commercial flight to Cleveland.

They all went into the dingy one-room airport that serviced Dawson and the surrounding towns. "I have to call New York," Stephen said to Dick. "Do you want to talk to Judy?"

"I'm tempted to wait until it's over to tell her anything. Otherwise she'll want to be in the middle of the battle and I won't be able to stop her."

Stephen responded with a quick smile, an affectionate comment, "You never could before."

"Yeah, and look what it got us." He took a deep breath and added, "Yes, I would like to talk to my wife."

A pull on Dick's jacket drew his attention to the toddler. The boy had been standing upright at his side, his eyes darting from one unfamiliar sight to another. Now he pointed out the window to a dingy biplane rolling from the storage lot to the unpaved runway.

"I guess that's our ride," Dick said and lifted the boy so he could see the landing better. "Hey, little nipper," he said to the toddler. "When Patrick gets home you'll have a lot to tell each other, won't you?"

At the mention of his brother, Dickey looked up at him and started to grin, then caught himself and remembered to keep his lips together when he smiled. "Good boy," Dick said and put the toddler down so he could take the phone from Stephen.

Their conversation lasted only a few minutes and when he hung up, Dick looked relieved. "Judy took the news pretty well. And she didn't even ask to meet us in Cleveland. That's one of the advantages of having you for a partner," he said to Stephen.

They went outside and got their bags. After Stephen said good-bye to his son, he handed the boy to Dick, wrote two phone numbers on a slip of paper, and gave them to Donna along with an envelope containing a letter and some money. "There should be enough money to see you through any emergency while we are gone. If you have problems with the authorities, the letter explains that we are on vacation and you are visiting to take care of my son. If you need to reach me or need any help with Dickey, phone one of these numbers. Speak to Judy Wells, Paul Stoddard, or Elizabeth Austra, no one else. We shouldn't be gone more than a week. While we're away, take good care of my son."

Though he said the words kindly, Donna sensed a warning. She nodded and, to demonstrate her responsibility, picked up the boy and cuddled him in her arms.

Donna waited for the plane to take off so Dickey could wave good-bye to the men. Then, after much swearing at the heavy spring on the clutch, she made the long trip back to the house.

They reached it by midafternoon. Dickey ran into the house ahead of Donna as if he expected Mother to be home and ready to scoop him up into her arms. Finding no one he sat in the center of the room, his huge eyes desolate with misery. When Donna tried to comfort him, he ran into the nursery, stripped off his pants and shirt with so much force that he ripped them, then crawled into his bed for a nap. Donna, hoping that he'd feel better when he woke, bolted the outside door and lay down on the platform bed Stephen shared with Helen. She smelled a musky scent on the pillows and sheets that reminded her of places far from home. For the first time in months, she closed her eyes and slept without dreaming.

PART FOUR

METAMORPHOSIS

EIGHTEEN

1

Russ Lowell placed three conscious restrictions on his nature—he never picked up a girl anyone would be looking for or one who wasn't a long way from her hometown and he never let pleasure interfere with business. He thought of his girls as he drove east toward home, concentrating longest on Jennifer Potts and how she'd stood dripping wet at the side of the road looking so thankful when he'd pulled over. He'd asked how far she was going, how far she'd come, how many rides she'd had, before he gave any indication, any hint at all that he was more than just some faceless driver she could entice and abandon at the next main crossroads. She'd lasted weeks longer than the others because her terror had been the best until the end when she could not stop crying. He'd taken to gagging her then because he hated the noise of her constant sobs. He hadn't killed her, he guessed she'd choked, but he buried her like the others, far back in the hills where she'd never be found.

And Donna? He hadn't even been looking for his next girl when he ran into her. Then he saw her eyes, and the way she'd been ready to bolt from the diner. She'd been on the run. She'd been running a long, long time. He wondered if she knew that the shots he'd fired at the campsite were just to scare her, that he never chased after her because he wanted her to escape and join the handful of others that he just let go. And he wouldn't even miss her, not now when he had such a prize stretched across his back seat.

When he'd taken Helen Wells, he had ignored all his restrictions. Given what he'd gained, he didn't care.

As he'd been doing for the last fifty miles, Russ glanced in the rearview he had aimed at Helen's face, partly just to look at her but also to try to catch her faking unconsciousness, watching him. But she only slept; hardly breathing, never moving. The boys were almost as cooperative. Alan Wells sat beside him with his hands and feet tied, looking out the window as if everything in the car had ceased to exist. Patrick had nursed from his unconscious mother, then wrapped a blanket around himself and, completely concealed in his makeshift cocoon, had lain on top of her and fallen asleep. Though the toddler had proven to be no trouble at all, Russ considered the boy's intelligence and strength and decided he'd taken too many chances with the woman already.

He pulled the car onto an access road. A quick trip to the trunk gave him the items he needed, and without waking Patrick, he managed to handcuff Helen's arms behind her, closing and locking the door closest to her head before walking to the opposite rear door so he could tie her feet. Then, trying to disturb Patrick as little as possible, he pulled Helen from the car, sat on the ground, and stretched her across his thighs.

Her shirt was still open, milk leaking from one of her breasts. Russ tasted it as his hands moved down her body, under the elastic waist on her pants, lower yet. He didn't want to take her now. No, he wanted her conscious the first time, trembling like the others. But her skin was so smooth, her body so perfect, he'd get acquainted with it while she slept.

As he had when he'd first seen her, he grabbed her hair, pulling her head back. She didn't wake not even when, noticing a metallic glint in the center of her chest wound, he used his knife to dig out the bullet. The wound began bleeding. He tasted the blood as he had the milk, laughing as he alternated between them, relishing what her body had to give.

"Don't worry about what I'm stealing, Helen Wells," he

said, pressing his fingers deep inside her. "You'll have your share of me when you wake. Dream about that."

Russ arranged Helen as she had been, then covered her with a blanket so no passing trucker could glimpse how she'd been tied. His erection pressed hard against the seam on his jeans and every time it faded, he would glance at her in his rearview or reach under the blanket to brush the side of her breast and feel himself harden again.

The wound on her chest healed. As the miles rolled by, he reached back and lifted the blanket often, watching her skin grow, wondering how badly she could be hurt and still survive.

Late in the afternoon, Russ stopped in front of a five and dime on a deserted street on the outskirts of Edson. Patrick still slept on the floor, and after covering Alan and warning him about attracting attention, Russ went inside and purchased two toddler jumpsuits in a three-year size, clean shirts for Alan, and some milk and juice for the cooler. Soon after, he pulled into an empty provincial park, ordered the Wells boy out of the car, untied him, and let him rub the circulation back into his hands. Patrick, who woke when the car stopped moving, got out also, dragging the blanket behind him like a cape, one corner over his head, standing always with his back to the sun so his face was in the blanket's shadow.

"Patrick's thirsty," Alan told Russ. These were the first words he'd spoken since the shooting. He managed to look Russ in the eye as he said them, then quickly lowered his focus to somewhere in the middle of Russ's chest.

"And you're not?" Russ asked with sinister good humor, rubbing the boy's shoulder, enjoying his fear. Alan refused to answer, unwilling to ask Russ for anything for himself. Pride kept him silent. Russ had to give the kid credit for that. With a brief odd stab of pity, he opened the trunk and pulled a box of camp supplies from it and handed the canteen on top to Alan. It slipped through Alan's still numb fingers. Patrick picked it up and gave it back to Russ, laying a hand on Russ's bare arm as he did so, keeping the hand there long after Russ had grabbed the canteen, opened it, and held it out so Alan could drink.

Patrick's touch drew Russ's attention to him, and as he passed the canteen down to the toddler, he again noticed the now obvious differences in the boy's body. "What do you eat besides milk?" he asked Patrick.

The toddler only stared back, his huge child's eyes narrowed in frank defiance. He ignored the question even when Russ repeated it. Without warning, Russ swung an open hand. Though Patrick ducked and moved back a step, his expression did not change. "Just milk and water," Alan answered nervously for him.

"Easy to maintain, huh? Well, Patrick, I have a present for you." He handed the toddler a carton of milk and the clothes bag. Patrick looked at the suits inside—one green, the other blue, took out the blue one and began to put it on. As he pulled up the legs, he paused to wipe the dried blood off his arm. Russ, who had forgotten the gash Patrick had received last night, cursed himself for not buying bandages. He knelt beside the boy and, intending to examine the cut, reached for his arm. With a snarl, Patrick stepped back.

But he moved too late. Russ had already seen the truth.

Beneath the dried blood, the wound had vanished.

Russ spun the boy around, looking at the other arm, seeing nothing at all. He abruptly let the child go and went back to his sandwich, hiding his curiosity for the moment. Patrick Austra and his mother had become riddles Russ had to unravel. He only wondered how much he would be able to discover before he went too far. As he thought of everything he'd learned in his years with the Carreras, the answer became simple after all.

Russ fingered the folded hunting blade he kept in his pocket as he watched the child carefully holding his cup of water, trying to drink the milk without spilling any onto his clothes. A fine line of liquid dripped down Patrick's chin and he caught the drop with one long finger, then licked it, looking at Russ all the time as if milk were not the food he wanted.

"It's too cold," Alan said when Russ asked Patrick what was wrong with it. "He's used to being nursed."

"Well, he's going to have to learn to live without his mother's breast soon enough. He can start now," Russ said, his thoughts still fixed on the wounds that had vanished in hours. A normal woman would not have survived his shots. A normal child would still have a cut on his arm. How far could he go? The question was too serious to be postponed to some more opportune time and he casually pulled out his knife.

The sun had set by the time they'd finished. Russ took the boys to the unlit outhouse, standing with the door open to make sure they left no notes, no trace of their presence behind. Patrick had to strip to use the toilet. As he did, Russ noticed again the odd, beautiful shape of the child's body, how pale his skin seemed, how huge his eyes became, and how they watched him with a look that wasn't a child's look at all.

Hate. And something more.

Hell, that kid knew what he planned to do, knew and gave permission with an emotion Russ could only read as contempt. So be it. The kid would show some fear soon enough.

Russ waited until he had Alan tied and sitting in the front seat of the car before reaching for Patrick. This time the child did not move away and Russ carried him to the picnic table and put one of his hands palm down on the top, mechanically spreading the fingers. Moving so his body was between the boy and Alan's line of vision, he brought his knife down hard with the force of both hands, slicing through Patrick's little finger just below the first joint. The child screamed not with pain or fright but with absolute fury and attacked, a small whirling mass of anger that Russ could not subdue. He did manage to keep the boy at arm's length, though, until Patrick swung with his mangled hand, ripping against the side of Russ's face, tearing at his mouth while he sank his long rear teeth into Russ's arm.

"Damn you!" Russ swore and bit back.

The child's blood, flowing from his severed finger, filled Russ's mouth. Instinctively Russ swallowed, then swallowed again. Patrick, his rage vanishing as quickly as it had come, relaxed and let Russ wrap a handkerchief around his finger and place him next to his mother in the back seat. Russ wasn't sure but it seemed that the woman had changed position. Perhaps her son's pain had called her back to consciousness.

"Come to me, Helen Wells," he said as he started the car. "Come soon or I'll use his agony to wake you."

Though Russ guessed that Patrick had understood at least part of what he'd said, the toddler slid forward, resting his unbandaged hand on Russ's bare shoulder, rubbing his face against the back of Russ's neck.

This wasn't permission, Russ thought. The boy admired him, one predator to another. If he had a kid, he'd want one like Patrick, a future wolf in a world of waiting sheep.

Russ glanced over his shoulder and saw Patrick smiling, his face still pressed against Russ's neck, a hand on his mother's forehead.

Russ drove through the night, the headlights and the dancing ghostly aurora their only light. Eventually, the towns became larger and closer together and Russ, who relied on ignorance as well as fear to keep captives in line, moved the boxes into the car and ordered both boys into the trunk.

Though Alan immediately obeyed—rushed to obey, Russ noted with satisfaction—Patrick hung back.

"I'll hold him," Alan said.

"The hell you will. The kid has to listen to me."

When Russ reached down to grab him, the boy ripped at Russ with his fingers and stuck his teeth into Russ's arm, holding on with all the tenacity of a pit bull puppy on a very large rat. "What the fuck," Russ bellowed and, ignoring Alan's cry of protest, swung the boy sideways against the fender of the car. Patrick, with the breath knocked out of him, loosened his grip. Nonetheless, he screeched as Russ threw him in the trunk beside Alan and kept on screeching after the lid had been slammed shut.

Russ had acted on instinct when he'd included the toddler in his kidnapping. He still wasn't sure how valuable the kid was but he could be the Lindbergh baby and still not be worth the attention his noise would attract. Russ decided to give the kid one more minute, and if he hadn't shut up by then, Russ would kill him.

Silence. Immediate. Revealing.

Russ had reached a decision. The boy had responded. Russ hadn't even tried to tell him; the kid had just known. He recalled the hours by the campfire when Donna had shown him everything the boy could do. He'd grudgingly believed then. Belief was stronger now.

Valuable? Hell, Patrick Austra and his mother might be real treasures if Russ could just figure out how to use them.

Inside the truck, Patrick gripped Alan painfully, pressing his long, thin body against the older boy, displaying a quaking, open fear for the first time since they'd been taken.

"What is it?" Alan asked. Instead of replying, the boy showed him how the floor and the ceiling and the walls pressed down on him, smothering him. "Don't," Alan gasped, fighting for breath. "Close your eyes and pretend you're outside and it's night."

"No," Patrick responded, linked minds with the older boy, and broke them free of the trunk, to hover in the sunshine and look down at Russ stubbing out his cigarette, getting back into the car.

Patrick licked his lips, tasting Russ's blood. This made him feel better in some mysterious way he did not yet understand. He broke the bond with Alan and relaxed as the car began to roll.

Lulled by its swaying, the soft warmth of the sleeping bag beneath him, and the relief of being out of Russ's reach for a little while, Alan finally slept. Patrick stayed awake longer, looking up at the small circles of light coming through the airholes, thinking about Russ, submersing himself in his instincts, sustained by his hate.

II

Finally, Russ drove into a warehouse smelling of diesel oil and decayed fish. He locked the doors behind him before opening the trunk. Huge hooks holding mildewed nets lined the walls. There were pulleys hanging from the ceiling and a number of trapdoors in the floor. As Russ herded the boys to an empty storage room near the back, Alan coughed. He thought he'd heard an echo but the sound was muffled, absorbed by the dampness of the walls.

After Russ locked the doors behind them, Alan's first thought was escape but it seemed impossible. Though there were a pair of windows, they were high in the walls and barred to keep out intruders. Their main purpose seemed to be to shed a dirty grey light on the floor, making the room seem even dingier than it was. As he looked up at it, he saw a grey shape running across one of the support beams throwing down a thin line of dust with its feet. Patrick watched it with interest until it disappeared into a crack in the wall close to the ceiling, then sat beside Alan in the cleanest corner of the room, one where the beams did not cross above them.

Alan didn't know if it was the dampness or the nighttime chill he'd gotten on the trip but he started coughing again. Though he tried to hold Patrick, the toddler slipped from his arms, scurrying on all fours across the room. Sitting with his back to the wall, he eyed Alan warily as if, in his illness, Alan had become the enemy.

"Can you discover where we are?" Alan asked him, not certain the toddler would even answer.

Though Patrick didn't reply, his brow furrowed with concentration, his lips pressed together. The noise of so many machines and the thoughts of all the people on the distant streets confused him. No matter how he tried, he couldn't focus on any of them. He retreated into his body and, with remarkable maturity, sadly shook his head.

"Then take me outside with you."

The boy shook his head more emphatically. Alan understood. The warehouse was safety, shelter, food. Outside, they faced a different kind of danger—the very real threat of discovery.

"Listen, Patrick," Alan said. "We won't call to anybody. We'll just look for clues about where we are. Then, when your mother wakes up, you can tell her. She'll be really proud of you.''

With no real effort, Alan found himself outside, looking down at the warehouse, the empty buildings, the gravel lots. In the distance he could see new piers, boats coming and going in a narrow channel. A gravel road climbed to join a wide paved one where an occasional car drove by. Alan thought *up* and Patrick, anxious to please, obeyed.

Ontario license plates. Windsor Auto Body. Bob's Windsor Diner.

Windsor.

—Now show me Russ and your mother— Alan requested. And he wished he hadn't been so eager to tell her what they knew, wished the success hadn't given him the courage to try to discover what kind of a man had taken them.

Russ had pulled Helen and propped her up against the rear bumper. He knelt beside her on the dirty floor, dipping his fingers in water to wet her mouth and tongue. Though it seemed like a humane gesture, Alan noticed the knife he held in one hand, its tip against Helen's shoulder. He had already made a short deep cut. Now he moved the knife up and down. The cut grew deeper. The blood flowed. Helen never stirred.

Patrick retreated with a whimper.

"It's all right," Alan told the toddler, relying on his age to convey an optimism he no longer felt. "My father will come. So will yours. They'll rescue all of us."

"Mother," Patrick said with such surety that Alan almost believed him. Nonetheless, when Alan held out his arms, Patrick rushed into them, trembling. They held each other until they slept.

When they woke later in the day, Alan felt hot. He'd developed a deep cough and his breathing had become labored. Patrick rested his hand on the side of Alan's face, looking at him with such misery that Alan wondered if the boy sensed some new disaster about to strike. "What is it?" he asked.

"You will go away like Hillary. I do not want to be alone."

"No I won't," Alan told him. "We're in a town. There

are doctors and medicine. Russ needs us too much to . . .
let me get too sick.''

He hoped. But he was hungry and thirsty and shivering
with fever and no one had checked on them to make sure they
were both all right.

At dusk, Alan sensed Patrick merging with him, trying to
contact his unconscious mother. And they tried, tried harder
than they ever had until they touched her. For a moment only
the bond was wonderful, peace and comfort and shared
strength. Then Russ got tangled into the vision and it turned
into a nightmare of pain and blood and the boys fell out of
it, clutching each other, shaking with fright.

Russ stayed. For him this was no nightmare, quite the contrary. Not since the actual event had he ever felt so aroused.

. . . Marc Truzzi sends his men away each night from ten
to twelve. The ones outside go into the kitchen. The ones
who are with Marc everywhere he goes join them. There they
eat a late meal, making obscene jokes about their employer
while dogs patrol the grounds. Upstairs, in his bedroom, Marc
Truzzi hears none of it and if he did, he would not care. No,
happiness made him soft, vulnerable, yet he refuses to abandon his nocturnal patterns. Instead, each night he revels in
his shy old-country bride.

He purchased her from a photograph, the rumor went. He
paid $10,000 to a struggling farmer near Salerno for the priv-
ilege of marrying his sixteen-year-old daughter with the pale
olive skin and the huge dark eyes. She hadn't even looked at
Marc when she'd first stepped off the plane and he had wooed
her for months before the marriage, waiting for the moment
when she would shyly reply for herself—yes, yes.

Now, with the dogs drugged on the ground one floor beneath him, Russ Lowell crouches on the deck outside Truzzi's
window, his face close to the glass, recalling the wedding as
he watches the girl undress.

He had been an usher, one of the men sent to show Carrera's respect for his ally. She had come down the aisle, close
enough to him that he could have touched her had he dared.
She wore eggshell-colored satin styled in a manner that made

her look shapeless as a child and almost hid the trembling of her body.

Her eyes had scanned the crowd looking, he guessed, for a familiar face, apparently finding no one. No one but her husband.

And in spite of Marc Truzzi's crimes, his enemies, his women, she loved him. Russ pitied her then. He pities her now.

Maria. Virgin. Adoring.

Russ has until midnight to make the kill—not his first, but his first that wasn't personal or part of the war—and escape. Though he is impatient he waits for the perfect moment. Truzzi must make no sound, not even a fall. His wife must never scream.

He watches them move in the dim rose-petal light of the sconces, until the woman turns her face away from the window, Truzzi moving above her. Russ carefully opens the window, one foot and then another inside, pads silently across the carpet, the long, thin blade ready. His free hand lowers, pulls Truzzi's head back. One stroke through the neck. Truzzi is dead without a sound and Russ covers the woman's mouth with his hand, holding the bloody knife above her. His orders are to kill her but he holds back. Not yet. He wears a stocking mask and she has not seen his face so maybe not at all.

He waits without moving until she relaxes into a trembling passivity and, humming, he slides Truzzi's body off of his wife, opens his belt and pants, and takes Truzzi's place inside her.

It had been years since he felt such pleasure, not since he was a child and, the oldest and the only boy, had beat his little sister with an electric cord while his father looked on, appraising the discipline he had ordered. Russ hadn't wanted to hit her that first time and he cried and was laughed at for his tears that were of shame not weakness.

Later, when his father was not there to see, he hit her again and again until he taught himself to enjoy it.

He has not cried since. Instead he became strong. Brutal. Psychotic, perhaps, but in the end he created himself. Yes, he knows this and he does not care.

The woman never makes a sound beyond a soft, frightened whimper, even when he is finished and fastening his belt, even when he runs the side of the knife down her body and between her thighs, even when he picks up a pillow and drops it loosely over her face.

"Don't move," he whispers in her ear. "Don't speak."

She has never seen his face. He turns to go.

And hears the pillow being pushed away, the quick indrawn breath before a scream.

All reflex, he whirls, catching her as he did her husband— through the windpipe so she cannot make a sound. Her eyes unfocus, registering a brief instant of terror, and caught by them, he pauses, the moment broken when he withdraws his knife and his face is sprayed with her blood. He smears it across her body, wishing she could respond with a shudder or a sigh or even the warning he had feared.

He looks at his face in the dark window glass and sees his eyes brighter than they should be. He wipes them before the tears could form, thinking that no one would ever know that he had felt this one brief rush of remorse and weakness. He vowed he would never succumb to it again.

Yes, his father and Carrera had made him what he was but he had asked for the change, welcomed the power. In the end, he was responsible; no one else. And he holds life and death in his hands.

And through his reflection, he sees his sister's face, staring at him, twisting like his soul into another face with white-blond hair and deep blue eyes.

The other he had killed.

He looks at the bed. The corpse has changed, grown longer and more pale, the dark hair blond, the blue eyes open, watching him. Her bare legs are apart, her arms raised, her naked body inviting him. He takes a step toward her and she begins to laugh.

She is there dead, there alive in the mirror, there burrowing through his mind, calling him, mocking his passion and his fear.

He brushes the back of his hand across his eyes. He hadn't wanted to kill Maria Truzzi but he had. Tomorrow he would be a made man, one of Carrera's closest allies, bragging about what he had done and how he did it. Tonight he mourns her death and his own.

Only one person sees him cry. Only one person knows his shame.

Helen Wells . . .

As the vision faded, Russ sank into a deep sleep. When he woke some hours after dark, he recalled his dream and her face and her laughter. He unlocked the storage-room door, stole in, and looked down at the two sleeping boys lying close together, wrapped in the tattered blanket Patrick had refused to relinquish. Exhausted by their fear, they did not stir as Russ crouched beside them, pulling Patrick's wounded hand from beneath the blanket, unwrapping the cloth. Patrick's finger was perfect, not even a scar to show where new flesh had replaced the old.

Russ covered the hand and left the room as silently as he had entered it. He lit a cigarette and sat on his cot, staring at the woman on the floor at his feet. Though she was unconscious, he knew she called to him, seducing him with her mind. Yes, more than Maria Truzzi, more than any of the others, he wanted her. Now, he thought he understood why. And as he stared at her, he thought of her son's strange powers and unusual strength and understood how dangerous Helen Wells could be.

During Prohibition, his grandfather had stored whiskey in this warehouse. The base of the building extended above the water and smugglers' boats would pull in beneath it. The trapdoors were used for unobserved loading while the pulleys and ropes hanging from the ceiling made the jobs easier. He tried one pulley after another, finding three that were still intact. After studying the location of each, he picked the one closest to a trapdoor and dragged Helen to it. Taking no chances with her, he looped a heavy piece of line through the rope on her feet and fastened it to a trapdoor handle. Then he lowered a pulley almost to the floor and wrapped the chain of the handcuff around its hook, raising the pulley slightly before unfastening one of the cuffs, swinging her arms above her head, and fastening them again. He slowly raised her until her feet just brushed the dirty plank floor, then tightened the line on her feet. Now, assuming she was strong enough to do so, she could not move up to slip the hook above her or get the leverage to break the cuffs.

Lovingly, as if she were his Maria and this their wedding night, he pulled down her slacks and underwear, letting them hang around her ankles. Cursing the dim light of the warehouse, he took a flashlight from the car and played it over her body, holding the light longest on the pale patches of skin on her shoulders and thigh, the only signs that this morning he had cut her and yesterday she had nearly died. Smiling, he took his knife and slowly ran the tip between her breasts to just above her naval, standing back to watch blood bead. As it began to drip, he moved close to her, only his tongue touching, licking the wound in swift upward strokes so that not a drop of it spilled. Afterward, he sat back on his heels, looking at her in the harsh beam of the flashlight until it vanished.

We're so perfectly made for each other, he thought as he wiped away the dirty smudges the floor had left on her shoulder and face and picked away the bits of sawdust caught in her hair.

So beautiful. So perfect. I can do anything to you, Helen Wells; anything at all, and you will not die.

And when he grew tired of the game, he'd find a way to end it too.

If he had not been so filled with self-satisfaction, he might have detected the soft tinkle of laughter in his mind, the silent sort a young cat makes when it first sharpens its claws.

NINETEEN

1

Dick and Stephen flew from late autumn to the final blaze of Ohio's summer—the crisp mountain air replaced by the muggy, pressing heat of the city. It fell through the open door of the plane, and as Dick walked down the open metal stairs to the tarmac, he had to force himself to breathe. It seemed as if he were underwater, viewing the world around him through a thick haze, foggy and distorted. And the pain he had felt only once since the doctor's verdict returned to remind him that his time, no matter what the outcome here, was limited.

As was everyone's, Dick thought as he watched Stephen walking stiffly in front of him, his wide-brimmed hat pulled low, his head bowed to shield his face from the searing rays of the sun.

An envelope was waiting for them at the airline counter. Stephen scanned a note and pocketed a set of car keys. A short time later they were heading east in a silver-grey Cadillac convertible with a black leather interior that Dick estimated cost at least twice his annual income. The top, Dick wasn't surprised to note, stayed up. "Not a very inconspicuous mode of transit, is it?" Dick commented.

"I learned a great deal from Jason Halli in all those hours we spent together, Richard. Carrera respects wealth and power. When we meet, I intend to be ostentatious in my

211

display of both. Check the glove box. There should be a package for you.''

Dick unwrapped a revolver in a shoulder holster along with a box of ammunition. ''Standard police issue,'' he commented.

''I thought you would want something familiar though I doubt that you will need it.''

On their flights from Dawson, Dick and Stephen had both displayed a kind of stoic bravado that not only hid their concern but kept them from speaking to each other at all. Now, disgusted with the pretense, Dick said, ''You know, I'm content to spend a few hours helping you convince Russ Lowell that he's trapped in the hottest level of hell but if you take out Carrera, the repercussions will be bloody. If he dies, every two-bit hood in town will be trying to take over. I wouldn't care, hell, I'd relish watching the bastards whack one another if it weren't for the bystanders who will be caught in the crossfire.''

''You told me that Carrera was going to jail. All of this would happen anyway, yes?''

''No. Jail will just slow him down a little. As long as he's alive the crooks on the outside will respect him. If they don't, he can order the hits from his cell.''

''What do you want to do, Richard?''

''Find Helen and our kids and get out of here. The law will take care of Carrera and in a few months I'll be beyond his reach.''

''Suppose we destroyed Carrera *and* his empire.''

''Empire?'' Dick snorted. ''I suppose you could call it that. Do you have any ideas for its destruction or do you plan to snap your fingers?''

''Nothing definite. However, we're probably a day or two ahead of Lowell. That gives us plenty of time for plots. Where would you suggest we stay for the night?''

''If you weren't playing dead, I'd say my place. But since your face is too well missed on my block, pick any east-side suburb. Newburgh Heights is good. Nobody should know me there.''

* * *

It had been a long two days and, by the time they checked into a rear room in a motel painted a muted shade of lawn-flamingo pink, Dick was exhausted. He sat on one of the twin beds eating paper-wrapped hamburgers trying to reason with Stephen. Stephen listened intently but refused to alter his plans. He would destroy Carrera. Helen would destroy Lowell. The boys would be safe. Dick didn't like the apparent order of Stephen's priorities though he did not say so. Instead he argued with equally valid concern, "I don't want to be a party to a murder. Even Carrera's."

"Richard, what would happen if we went to the police?"

The question sobered Dick. "This is an international kidnapping. Russ would get word of what we'd done and kill Alan. He'd try to kill Patrick and Helen as well. If he doesn't know what they are, they'd probably be OK."

"He shot Helen. She didn't die. He knows that much, yes? And when he contacts Carrera, I expect him to discuss what he knows. No, I don't think this is a time for me to hide."

"Maybe not from Carrera but you have another problem. Carrera's usual hangouts will be swarming with cops. They'll be spying in windows, listening in on the phones, and some of his closest allies have probably sold out to the feds."

"Sounds like a man desperate enough to bargain."

"So bargain and leave him alone."

"All right. I will try. My hand may be forced, though, Richard. We must find Helen and the boys but I must also recover those reports as soon as possible. Dozens of lives depend on it. You understand this, yes?"

If those reports fell into government hands, AustraGlass might suffer but Stoddard Design would be ruined. Paul Stoddard would have to leave the country fast or face a federal hearing. Someone like Paul would hardly react to either prospect well. "I understand," Dick replied. "There's one other problem. A lot of those cops watching Carrera will know me. Some of them might even know you."

"I can be careful, Richard. Given the circumstances, it's best Carrera not see you at all until some agreement is reached."

"I didn't come all this way to sit on the sidcline."

"I know. But if Carrera reaches you before we know where Helen and the boys are, it will be far more difficult to find them."

Though avoiding a fight ran completely against his nature, Dick was forced to agree. They were still discussing their next best move when, in spite of his anxiety, Dick fell asleep. Later, he dimly heard Stephen moving through the room, then felt the door open and close.

II

Seek. Find. Devour.

The hunt was always the same. The hunger it aroused never changed. It only seemed unique in that for the first time in many years, Stephen hunted a man out of vengeance and he did so alone. He pushed back the loneliness and the rage that followed. It did him no good to think of Helen now.

Recalling everything Halli had told him, Stephen spent the early evening visiting the more popular of Carrera's haunts, finally tracking down his prey in a family-run bar and restaurant whose unmatched wood tables were united by weathered red-check tablecloths and drippy wax candles in wooden holders. The place had an air Stephen understood and appreciated—the decor probably hadn't changed in a decade or more, and if the scents and the enjoyment he sensed in the diners around him were any indication, the place served excellent food. Though Stephen kept his back to Carrera dining with three other men on the opposite side of the room, he had already entered Carrera's mind, eavesdropping on his thoughts.

If the hunt were a simple one, it could be over now. Yes, he could even go up to the table and claim his victim in front of the others. If he let loose any of the rage he'd so skillfully buried, no one could stop him, and when the killing was done, no one would remember his face. But, for the present, Stephen could do nothing. Carrera did not even know the boys had been kidnapped, let alone where they were. No, Stephen could not move this fast. Besides, there were messages to be delivered, a proper way to approach his prey.

Not directly. Not yet.

He looked down at the untouched drink on his table, then at the woman sitting across from him, a sultry dark-haired woman in a white linen who laughed too loud at a joke he told, seeking Carrera's attention. Her ploy worked. Carrera looked across the room. Though he could only see Stephen's back from where he sat, he knew the woman had found a new lover and that was enough. He had ended his discreet affair with her when she'd grown too demanding but the attraction still remained. And the jealousy.

The woman laughed again. Indeed, she could hardly help herself. Dominic motioned to Angelo Volpe to come close so he could whisper, "Call Toni for me. Tell her I'd like to stop over in an hour or two."

Volpe headed in the direction of the lobby and the phone. Stephen, his purpose here almost complete, laid some money on the table and, with the woman's arm linked through his, left through the same door. The woman excused herself in the lobby, and as Stephen waited for her to return from the ladies' room he stopped beside Volpe long enough to pull one simple piece of information from the man's mind. Storing it as perfectly as it had been received, he stood in the doorway to the restaurant and issued a simple command to his prey. Carrera met his eyes, and what should have been the long appraising glance of the old lover to the new one was destroyed by Carrera's irrational surge of fear. Carrera blinked and looked away, wanting to laugh at his moment of insanity. He thought he'd sensed the man calling him by name. Hell! He couldn't have had that much to drink. But things like that didn't exist, only crazy people believed in them.

No one would ever accuse Dominic Carrera of being crazy. Never!

A flash of white drew his eyes back to the doorway where the woman stood talking to the man. He was young, good-looking in an effeminate sort of way. As their eyes met again, Carrera sensed something more, something no one less perceptive would notice—his vision shimmered and he saw dark holes for eyes and fangs in that broad mouth.

Tommy Payton looked up from his plate of spaghetti. "Something wrong, Domie?" he asked.

"Nothing," Carrera responded, pulling his eyes away from the creature in the doorway. *Vampire.* Even the thought seemed to close up his throat and send his mind reeling into confusion and lunacy. No, the word would never pass his lips. Not in this company. Not ever.

With blind certainty, Carrera joined the ranks of so many of Stephen's previous victims—the ones who knew the truth and carried the knowledge to their graves.

III

Toni Domaro tilted her head back against her sofa seat and inhaled deeply on her hand-rolled cigarette, the smell of aromatic Turkish tobacco hiding the spicier scent of the marijuana mixed with it. She always liked to smoke before Dominic came. The fog that descended on her seemed to allow her to put aside the world, to listen more attentively when Dominic talked to her, to be more responsive when he touched her.

They had been lovers for six months and, had he not been arrested, would have probably stayed that way for as long as she remembered her place and acted her part. Toni had learned these lessons early in life. She would not forget them now, not when her future depended on ignoring her pride.

It had been almost two weeks since Dominic had seen her. His arrest had shaken him, she knew, and he now played at being a family man with the same exquisite acting he used to play at being a churchgoer, a businessman, or an art collector like his father. Even so, he paid her rent and sent her weekly checks for the apartment's upkeep so his interest had not entirely waned.

After Volpe had called, she'd changed into a copper-colored satin jumpsuit, one more provocative than usual. The shade complemented the red hair, golden complexion, and light brown eyes she'd inherited from her mother. The deep V-front filled with loosely woven lace revealed most of her breasts.

Having long ago moved past modesty, she was proud of her figure and her looks and how she always managed to appear so much younger than her actual thirty years.

She put out her cigarette carefully, breaking off the glowing tip into the carved marble ashtray on the coffee table, letting the rest burn out. Best not to appear high, especially considering how Peter had died. At this point, Domie would never guess what she'd been doing but she hoped the drug would relax her enough that she could look vulnerable rather than manipulative when she swore to stand by him and asked about her future after he had gone.

She'd quit her job to be available for him, given up her tiny Lakewood flat for this Gold Coast apartment with the tight security Carrera required and rent payments she could never afford unaided. To add to her worries, the police were looking for her, wanting to talk to her about her brother and the murders out west.

Not that she wouldn't mind talking but the truth would sound like a well-planned lie and then they were sure to start asking about Domie. Those were the questions she would never answer, she owed him too much for that.

As for Russ, she thought he'd put the past to rest until two weeks ago when she saw his picture on the front page of the paper.

Toni heard a knock on the door—not Domie's polite double rap or Volpe's obnoxious pound but an unfamiliar faint tap. Still, the guard had let the visitor up without checking with her so it must be someone she knew. She slipped the ashtray into an end-table drawer and opened her door.

The man standing in the hall looked like a gift you would send to a friend distraught over a broken love affair. An expensive gift, she mentally corrected as her eyes swept over the custom-tailored black suit and white silk shirt, the ruby ring on the hand resting against the doorframe. He carried a package wrapped in brown paper and tied with twine. She noted Dominic Carrera's name on it and wondered if Domie had sent her something.

"You are Russell Lowell's sister, yes?" the man asked. His oddly accented voice registered a curious blend of certainty and surprise as if he had just discovered this fact a moment ago.

"My name is Antonia Domaro," she responded coldly. Thinking the guard downstairs had been a fool and let a policeman up, she began to slam the door.

He forced it open and came inside, shutting and locking it before turning to her. "You are Russell Lowell's sister, yes?" he repeated and she sensed something odd in his tone, an urgency that went beyond the emotion a cop would put into his job.

Toni wondered if he was related to one of the victims. If so, he might be a little bit crazy, possibly dangerous. She went on the offensive, "Yeah, I'm his sister. Who the hell are you?"

"That isn't important."

Toni frowned and moved backward away from him, wondering if she could make it to the bedroom and get the gun she kept in her nightstand before he caught her. As suddenly as the idea occurred to her, it vanished taking most of her fear with it. She sat on the end of the sofa and stretched out her legs. "If I don't push the point, you don't have to lie, right? Well, I'm not lying either when I tell you that I haven't seen or heard from Russ in two years. If you're looking for him, I'm sorry but I can't help you."

"I see." The man placed the box on the floor beside her coffee table and sat in one of the high-backed Italian side chairs Domie had purchased for her, the same chairs Dominic had in his own living room, she'd noted with private amusement when they were delivered. "Domaro. It is your married name, yes?"

"Married?" She snorted with disgust. "Domaro was my mother's maiden name. Who the hell would want to admit a relationship to Mark Lowell?"

"Your brother."

"Keeping my father's name wasn't Russ's idea. The guy he works for likes it. You know, a good British name for one of his . . . employees."

"Appearances are important, yes?"

Toni nodded and the stranger looked down and smiled as

if what she told him reinforced something he'd known all along. The gesture made him seem shy and uneasy and she found herself warming to him.

"I've brought a gift for your lover," the man said, pointing to Dominic's name on the cover.

Toni didn't see any reason to deny the relationship. "How did you know?" she asked.

"I have my sources."

"Yeah. Somebody's damn big mouth." She opened the drawer and pulled out the ashtray, but when she began to reach for what remained of her cigarette, he caught her wrist and pulled it back.

"Not yet," he said.

He did not hold her tightly but his flesh against her flesh sent a spark through her. She pulled away, slammed the drawer shut, and sat on the sofa across from him eyeing him warily. Though she detested strangers, particularly those who refused to give a name, she was equally afraid of what she might do if she let her guard down. She was about to demand that he leave when he began to speak in a low flowing voice that relaxed her far better than her Turkish blend ever could.

"Do not worry. I have no intention of harming you," he said. "I only came to deliver the package, but since you are Lowell's sister, please tell me about him."

"What's there to tell. He was a bastard when he was a kid. He's more than a bastard now."

The man responded with a fleeting, tight-lipped smile. "What about his family."

"I'm it. Mama died three years ago."

"And his father?"

Toni frowned and stared at the floor. Even after so many years she did not like to talk about Mark Lowell and what he'd done to all of them. She was saved the necessity of replying by the sound of voices in the hall, the familiar knock on the door. "It's Dominic," she whispered.

The man pressed two long fingers against his lips, a signal for silence, and though his dark eyes were focused on her, Toni had the odd feeling his mind was concentrating on something else. Two more knocks.

"He has a key." No sooner had she said this than they heard the jingle of a key chain, the click of the lock.

Faster than she could follow, the lights went out and she found herself pulled backward into the bedroom, his hand over her mouth. The front door opened. Dominic called her name once, and when she did not reply, he walked through the outer rooms. At the moment she was certain they would be discovered, Dominic swore and left.

Toni took a deep breath, suddenly realizing then that she had been holding hers the entire time Carrera was in the apartment not because of any fear but rather because the man was touching her. She'd become painfully aware of his body, weak and a little giddy from the strength of a desire she thought she'd long ago outgrown. The man loosened his grip but she did not move until he backed away, returning to the living room where he switched on a single reading light and fell into the chair, one leg draped over a carved fruitwood arm. She glanced in the direction of her nightstand and thought of the gun. Hell, Dominic was gone. She'd never get him back tonight so she might as well make the best of what was here.

"Tell me about Russ Lowell," he said when she'd joined him in the living room.

"Look, are you a cop or what?"

Though his voice still remained rigidly polite, she sensed the urgency behind his words as he replied, "I am not with the police. I'm related to . . . a victim. Russ has her now. The police believe that he keeps a woman for weeks. Anything you can tell me might give me a clue on how to find her."

"You hit me good with that one. I couldn't sleep nights if I threw you out now. Look, this is turning into a hell of a strange evening. Let me relax a little and I'll tell you what I can. OK?"

Once again she saw that quick private smile as he nodded his head. "I've never been one to stand between a woman and her vices," he commented.

"Well, you sure as hell were before," she retorted as she pulled out the ashtray.

"Then your lover would have smelled the smoke, yes?"

"How the hell did you know he was coming? Well, I guess I don't care." She took two deep drags, then watched the ash burn out before starting. "I'm almost as beautiful as my mother, I think. She was Joseph Domaro's oldest daughter. She ran away when she was seventeen and came home pregnant and married to Mark Lowell. Their marriage was not a happy one." She giggled at the understatement, surprised at how hard the light marijuana blend was hitting her. "Russ and my arrival didn't do anything to improve it because for as long as I can remember, Mark Lowell beat my mother.

"At first, he was too smart to leave any bruises for Grandpa Domaro to discover. Later, he drank too much and got careless and I guess Grandpa warned him to behave because for a while he never touched her. Instead, he started working Russ over."

"And you, yes?"

"No. He made Russ hit me. It started when Russ was about six and I was three. He'd order my punishment when Mother wasn't home and if Russ didn't do a good enough job on me, the old man would belt him. It went on for years before Mother surprised him at the game. She had a temper herself and I remember that she went for him. When that free-for-all ended, he called an ambulance to take her to the hospital and we were alone with him. We were smart kids. When he pulled out his bottle, we hid in the closet behind some boxes."

"And then?"

"I never saw what happened then, but when we first heard about what Russ had done to those girls, Dominic got really spooked. We met for drinks and I thought I might get his mind off of this mess but he kept wanting to talk about it. After Grandpa saw Mom in the hospital, he went to Raymond and asked him to force some sense into my father. Raymond came to our house in person, that's how important Grandpa Domaro was, and he made threats. One thing led to another and my father died with a knife in his stomach. Dominic said it was self-defense but it might have been planned. You know, good Catholic girls don't get divorced.

"Now I never left that closet but when Russ heard the scuffle, he did. Dominic told me that while Raymond stood over the body, he saw Russ watching him from the doorway with a look on his face that said he'd seen everything. Ray Carrera didn't know what to do. I mean, how would Grandpa Domaro have felt if Ray knifed his eleven-year-old grandson. Some favor, huh?

"I don't know why he left Russ at the scene but he didn't have to worry. When the police came, Russ told them he hadn't seen a thing. Russ went to the Carreras' real estate office the next day. He worked there after school and on weekends. Between whatever Russ did for them and Grandpa Domaro's help, we lived better with Mark Lowell dead than we ever did when he was alive."

"How did Dominic know what had happened?"

"His father told him. He said, 'You can always trust Russ.' The night we got the news, Domie must of repeated that sentence ten times. I never guessed they were that close."

"And he worked for the Carreras all these years?"

"Except for the war years when nobody worked for them but some nasty old men. Ray Carrera was patriotic. He didn't buy deferments for his guys. Russ got sent to the Pacific. He didn't talk about it after he got home."

Toni had said enough, probably more than enough, but the man pressed on in his musical voice, relaxing her and making her want to continue. "After the war, Russ became Ray Carrera's right-hand man. Russ got me a job, a good one, managing the office of a trucking firm. Sometimes, not often, he'd call me and ask that a certain driver get assigned to a certain route. That was his payment, I guess, for getting me the job.

"We hardly ever saw one another. Then Ray died. Three months later, Russ disappeared. I thought he was dead until I read about what he'd done. I can't believe it but somehow I do, you know what I mean?"

The visitor nodded. "And who is Dominic Carrera's current right-hand man?"

"Look, talking about Russ is one thing but . . ."

"Who!"

Toni could actually feel the effort of that command as the

compulsion to respond stunned her like a well-aimed slap. "Domie doesn't talk about business but I think it's Angelo Volpe," she said with disgust.

"You don't like him?"

"If he disappeared tomorrow, I sure as hell wouldn't mourn. Sometimes, when he knows Carrera is coming over, he shows up a half hour or so early. Then he can catch me decked out in something like this so he can sit and stare at Carrera's meat and go home to his family, feeling so self-righteous that he resists temptation. Like I'd put out to that fat slob if he asked. You know what I mean?"

"I do." Throughout the evening, Stephen had felt a growing kinship with Carrera and now more than ever. Toni reminded him of Amalia, the madame in Chaves—practical, intelligent, honest. "Please tell me about Volpe—what he is like and where he can be found when he is not working."

"He's a tall man, maybe six-two and when I was a kid I remember that he used to be solid, you know, the kind of guy that can break somebody in half without even trying? But that was when he was younger and he worked in the packing house and collected bad debts for Ray Carrera. Now he's over fifty and gone to flab. When he's not at Domie's or at home, he's at his brother's tavern. Or at church. When death hits Angelo Volpe, he intends to be prepared. The way he takes care of himself, that's probably wise. Oh, yeah, one other thing—he has a father in a nursing home on the west side. He spends every Friday night with him." She added the details of names and places.

"Is there anyone else particularly close to Carrera?" Stephen asked when she'd finished.

"I only know about Jason Halli. He's . . ."

"Don't bother. I've met him." Stephen hesitated. Toni did not know anything of Carrera's businesses and Stephen had almost exhausted the personal details as well. "One final question—I know Carrera has a real estate office on Mayfair. Does he have another, a more private place?"

"Maybe, I don't know. You know, we've been talking for what, about two hours? And I haven't even asked if you'd like a drink or anything."

"I wouldn't." He stood and patted the side of the package beside the table. "Tomorrow you should arrange to have this package delivered to Carrera. Please do not open it."

Normally curious, she decided to not even touch it. "Listen, do you have to go?" she asked. "I mean, your arrival ruined my plans for the evening. You want to stay and make it up to me?" She stared at him with absolutely no trace of shame.

"Why did you become Carrera's lover?"

"Probably because when you get handed a shit like Mark Lowell for a father you want to glom on to every good opportunity that comes your way. Carrera was the best of mine." She stretched, arching her back as she did so, revealing more of her body than she ever would in Volpe's presence. "Are you sure you don't want to stay awhile?"

The privacy of the wilderness, where he could hunt every day, had spoiled Stephen. Though the life he had taken only a day ago could easily sustain him for weeks, habit made him hunger for this girl. A thousand years ago he would most likely have left her ravaged body for her lover to find. Now, as he stared at her, he considered only two problems: How much would she have to remember? How much must she forget?

Certainly, for her sake, she must never recall anything she had told him, perhaps that she had spoken at all.

Toni grabbed his hand and tugged. Caught unaware, his arm reached its full length for an instant, brushing the top of his knee just before he crouched beside her, sending a strong mental command that she forget what she'd just seen.

His command half worked. Though she still remembered, she no longer felt any curiosity. He silently cursed himself for his chivalry. Though he had been able to use the drug in her system to relax her and exonerate her confessions, it also unfocused her mind, making it harder for him to grasp and control her now.

Well, one dilemma was solved. Only her blood could create the bond necessary to wipe her memory. He would be dining tonight.

"Roll over," he said. When she had, he rested a hand on

the small of her back, rubbing his fingers over the copper satin, then moving his hand slowly up her spine, his mind concentrating on her body, forcing it to respond. She bent one knee, then straightened the leg hard against the cushions. ''For Christ's sake, what are you . . .''

Though she tried to turn over, he pressed against her back too tightly and ran his lips down the side of her neck. Just above the hairline, he bit. Even the scent of her blood could not drown out her perfume. If this were more than a quick simple use, he would insist that she shower.

She began to struggle, believing, he knew from the bond already forming, that he had used a needle to drug or poison her. He held her, feeding her visions of what she wanted him to do until, convinced of their reality by the passion growing in her body, she relaxed and let him control her completely.

He saw no need to hurry, to take or give any less than he would to any other victim. A quarter hour later, while she hovered near consciousness, he sat motionless beside her, oblivious to the room around him as his mind did its familiar work, selectively wiping her memories, filling in the gaps in the ones that remained, mentally reviewing the scene until it seemed convincing and real as any imperfect human memory.

He left her sleeping, the two tiny spots of blood at her hairline, the box on the table and his description as the man who had delivered it the only indication of his presence here this evening.

Downstairs, the guard heard a noise in the service room behind the elevators. When he went to investigate, Stephen walked out the door, as unobserved as when he had arrived.

By the time Stephen returned to the hotel, the sky had turned a pale shade of grey. Pausing outside the door, Stephen ordered Richard into a deeper sleep so he would not wake when Stephen opened the door. Stephen did not want to answer Richard's natural questions now, to plot or plan or justify anything he had done tonight.

Sometime in the course of the evening, Richard had taken off his suit, arranging it neatly on a chair. Now he slept with

the revolver on the floor beside the bed, covered only by a
sheet though the air conditioner made the room cold and dry.
He'd propped an extra pillow under his head and something
about his position and the unevenness of his breathing made
Stephen concerned.

He rested a hand on Richard's forehead and carefully
touched his mind, feeling the dull nagging pain in his chest,
the clumps of runaway cells growing stronger as their victim
weakened.

With all the power his kind possessed, all the centuries
given them, the Austras could never alter the natural course
of another's life. Those they cared for died and their curse
often seemed to be in caring at all.

Though he would try to bargain with Carrera, the man
would not listen any more than one of Stephen's kind would
turn away from vengeance at the plea of a stranger. Then,
released from his promise to Richard, Stephen would give
him the only gift he could—a few months of peace.

He had not killed a man since the beginning of the last
great war. In spite of the increasingly dark Austra annual
reports, he had found the years of peace a comfort, a personal
omen of calmer times. Nonetheless, he warmed to this hunt
and the thought of killing filled him with familiar anticipation.

Soon he would face his prey.

TWENTY

1

Later Carrera would remember that he'd been warned.

The message came while Carrera was eating a late breakfast with his wife and two teenage daughters in a small private room of one of his favorite downtown restaurants. The Paytons and their wives were eating at one table in the main room, Volpe and a couple of the guys at another. Two more were sitting in a car parked close to the door ready to move in if there was trouble. Since his arrest, Carrera had become justifiably paranoid. He knew so much about so many people who didn't have any reason to trust him. Hell, even he'd considered striking a bargain with the feds. The odds were horrible, though. Better to take the fifteen than turn on the guys up the ladder from him. But though he would have preferred to lay low, he was seen in public with his family far more than in the past. He understood the need to look confident before his trial, to build sympathy by creating the facade of an ideal family man. The papers had picked up on this immediately, but instead of exposing the lie, they played along with it, informing the public about the psychiatrists and doctors Carrera had hired to treat his son, the family's anguish and shame when the boy had died.

Carrera's wife would have preferred to mourn her tragedies in private but she understood her duties. She even managed to sometimes feel genuinely content. Dominic had not paid this much attention to the women in his family in years.

While they sat at the linen-covered table eating warm rolls and honey, a messenger hand-delivered the box Stephen had left with Toni. Angelo Volpe knew Russ was in Canada, assumed it had to have come from him, and, following Carrera's orders, immediately brought it to his table. Carrera's guards unwrapped the box and pulled out a sealed wide-mouth urn coated in black lacquer.

Carrera chuckled. Russ showed excellent taste. "Open it," he said, fully prepared to slip the film into his pocket to be developed later.

When the urn was unsealed, Carrera's oldest daughter got a whiff of whatever was packed inside and wrinkled her nose. As the lid was lifted, she ran for the bathroom, vomiting on the carpet in the lobby. Her younger sister looked into the urn and ran after her, screaming. The manager rushed to the back room while a few guests who had recognized Carrera when he'd arrived quietly exited the front. Others craned their heads to see in the doorway to where Carrera sat staring at the head of Jason Halli looking up, seemingly at him, from inside the urn, an expression of perfect terror on his severed head. Carrera, who had killed often and with relish, had never seen a man die in such horror. Never. Oblivious to his wife, to his daughters, to the police mingling with the diners in the outer room, Carrera stood and pounded on the table bellowing a challenge to everyone around him, "Find me the man who did this! Get me the son of a bitch who did this!"

As he stormed from the room, he heard his wife call his name in a soft, broken voice. He began to turn when he saw his daughter standing in the doorway, unwilling to come back in, her lilac dress stained on the skirt, the mascara he'd forbidden her to wear smudged on her cheeks. "Take the pot out the back, Ang," he said to Volpe. He ordered two of the men to escort his family home, then picking up the empty box and carrying it as if it still contained something heavy, he told the others to accompany him to his office.

By the time they arrived there, Carrera had calmed enough that Volpe thought he'd be ready for the rest of the news. "The package came from Toni Domaro," he said in a whisper only Carrera could hear. Carrera, who prided himself on being a family man, had made his lover a well-kept secret. Toni was private, not about business after all.

Russ had left before the affair had begun. Halli hadn't known. But if Halli's murderer knew about Toni, he could know about anything. Carrera looked at the men around him for reassurance, at the bars he'd had installed on his windows, at the gun resting beside his hand. He ordered everyone but Volpe from the room, then said, "Spread the word around, if anyone hears from Lowell, they should tell him I want to talk to him the next time eight at night rolls around. He can call me at the spaghetti place. He'll know what I mean. In the meantime, send a couple of guys over to my house and try to find out how Halli died."

Volpe closed the box containing the urn and what remained of Halli. "That won't be easy."

"We got someone in the coroner's office. What the hell do we pay him for! Call him now!"

11

Will Bowen, an assistant medical examiner for Cuyahoga County, met Angelo Volpe at midnight in Bowen's garage. Volpe had warned him this was not a recent death and Bowen, who lived with his mother, did not want her becoming suspicious by Volpe's arrival or the ensuing smell.

But the decomposition really wasn't so bad and a head by itself was nothing like the torso. Volpe's fastidiousness amazed Bowen. The pudgy, greying man looked less like a gangster than a desk-bound accountant. Bowen often wondered if Volpe fainted at the sight of blood.

The expression on Halli's face was troubling. Bowen stared at what was left of the corpse, recalling where he'd seen corpses with expressions before. "When a man dies, his muscles go slack," Bowen explained to Volpe. "In this case, though, the pain before he died stayed etched on his face. Where did you get this?"

Volpe, keeping details vague, explained while Bowen slipped on his oilcloth apron and went to work.

A quick examination of the neck wound led him to believe

the head had been cut off after Halli died. Bowen examined
the wound, probing it with his fingers, magnifying the cuts,
then called Volpe over to show him what he'd discovered. He
pointed to a darker piece of flesh on the stump of the neck.
"He was cut just below here, not very deep, before he died."

"A knife?"

"I can't tell without seeing the wound but the dark blotch
was caused by blood loss through the cut, understandable
since the wound appears to have been deep enough to reach
the artery."

Volpe went back to his chair some feet from the table and
lit a cigarette before asking, "Could that have killed him?"

"It might have. Afterward, I would guess the person who
decapitated him used a curved, blunt instrument to rip through
the tendons as well as the flesh. When he'd finished, he bent
back the head, cracked the spine, and ripped it off. You want
me to show you?"

Volpe, compulsively concentrating on watching his cigarette
smoke rise, shook his head. "What about his expression. What
do you make of that?" he asked.

"I'm not sure. I'd say the killer is sending Domie a message."

"Yeah. Don't fuck with me. Anything else?"

Bowen noted the coloring of the eyes, then cut a thin slice
of the darkened tissue from the neck. Placing it between two
glass plates, he examined it under the microscope. He wished
he could consult with Dr. Corey on this. Cor was the expert,
not him. But even on his own, Bowen had good reason to
believe that he was right about the cause of Halli's death. "I
want to do some checking around at work. Call me at the
office tomorrow around one, OK?"

"What about Halli?"

"I'm done with him." Bowen rewrapped the head, fit it
into the urn, and thrust it into Volpe's hand. "Nice of your
killer to send a coffin. Throw a wild funeral."

After Volpe left, Bowen went into the house, sat in the
darkness of his mother's lace-covered living room, and
thought about corpses with expressions. He'd only seen one

before and that when he'd just started working for Corey. The girl had been young. She'd been smiling. He hadn't thought anything of it then. In the ensuing three years, his job had exposed him to hundreds of bodies; his position as chief examiner on the night shift to the most brutal murders. Now he knew how unique those faces had been.

The next morning, he went to the library and paged through old issues of the Cleveland papers. The photograph of the victim and the sketchy details of her murder brought back his own memory of the killing and other similar ones that he had not worked on. Dick Wells had been chief investigator. Judy Preuss had covered the crimes for her local paper. For a while the news was full of lurid details, then nothing. Since then Judy Preuss had become Mrs. Dick Wells and the cases had never been solved.

Now he'd heard rumors that Dick Wells and his family were in hiding and Carrera their hunter. The tie was too close to ignore.

Bowen, who had no reason to be at work before three, waited until Corey would be at lunch before going to the office. There, undisturbed, he compared the slide to photos of damaged tissue taken from bleeders. The similarities were obvious. Halli's blood had not clotted.

Enough. When Volpe called, Bowen asked one question, "Was Halli after Dick Wells when he was killed?" Volpe didn't answer and Bowen pressed him, "You want to know how he died? You tell me why he died and maybe I can answer."

"All right," Volpe replied carefully. "We have reason to believe he had gone after Wells."

And if I ever get subpoenaed, you fat old bastard, I'll be sure to quote you exactly, Bowen thought. Concealing his disgust, he said, "Then I can tell you that Halli died from loss of blood, definitely caused by a puncture in his neck."

"How can you be so sure?"

"Three other cases that were similar." Bowen gave what details he recalled, noted the Wells connection to the previous murders, and concluded, "The rumors at the time were that the killer wasn't human."

Bowen enjoyed the long pause that followed his revelation. "Not human?" Volpe repeated.

"Talk to your cops. They'll tell you how hard they laughed. Corey didn't. I remember he was damn tight-lipped about the whole matter."

"Was the murder ever solved?"

"Officially? A pimp committed the first one. The other two were never solved. Off the record? The cases were dropped, forgotten like they never happened. Go. Talk to the cops like I said. They know more than I do."

Volpe did. When he'd heard enough, he took the news to Carrera. He found his boss studying the report that had arrived from Russ in the morning mail. Carrera didn't take Volpe's news well, but his anger was directed at Russ. "The bastard must of known something was wrong but he sends me these and when he calls the office this morning he just repeats his note. 'Read them,' he says. So I'm reading." He held up both reports, then tossed Volpe the older of the two. "Here, you read too."

Volpe sat on Carrera's couch and stretched out his legs.

"Take off the shoes, Ang. That's real leather," Carrera reprimanded. Raymond Carrera hadn't parted with a dime without a fight, a trait somewhat diminished, but still present in Dominic.

Unlike Carrera, Volpe was in the business of collecting information and he immediately saw how difficult some of this must have been to come by. "I could be wrong," he began tentatively, realizing he was treading on unfamiliar ground. "But I think the stuff on our atomic research is secret."

"The company has spies?"

"Yeah, it looks that way."

Carrera tossed a pad and pen to Volpe. "Keep reading. Write down where you think they might have got this stuff."

By the time Volpe had finished the second report, he'd made quite a list. "Maybe FBI, NSC, British Intelligence."

"No KGB?" Carrera asked, his lips curled into an expression somewhere between a scowl and a mocking grin.

What the hell would Volpe know about the NSC let alone the KGB?

"I can't tell," Volpe said as if Carrera had asked the question seriously. "They got a list of their businesses at the back of the report. None of them operate in communist countries so maybe they don't bother to worry about those. Or maybe they're reds. I can't figure them."

Carrera had made some calls on the owners of Austra-Glass. The family wasn't openly involved in politics, and like any smart group of powerful men, it kept a low profile. He'd scanned the list of recommendations and saw them as less political than sound business decisions. If he had access to this kind of information, his family would be ten times richer than it was. "I got some information on their American firms," he told Volpe. "The research company in California is working with silicon chips whatever in the hell those are. A losing operation as far as I can tell. But Stoddard Design in New York City—there's big money in that operation." Carrera pointed to the painting on the wall facing his desk. "That was bought from a studio in a Stoddard building. Before he died, my father told me La Paz was the classiest address in New York City. Stoddard owns it." He leaned back in his chair, satisfaction evident on his face. "I checked him out with some people here. Stoddard also has the building contract for the AEC nuclear research plant in Arizona. They start the second phase of construction in May. You and me, we know construction. How much money do you think they got tied up in that?"

Volpe kept his expression rigid. He didn't want to give any praise to Lowell and he wasn't entirely sure what Carrera meant. "Millions," he responded.

"And Stoddard Design could be a security risk. Maybe even a bigger catch for the FBI than me. What do you think?"

"Could be," Volpe responded carefully, thinking Lowell would be the best trade of all. "What are you going to do?" he asked.

"Wait. We have time. In the last call we got from Halli, he talked about how Russ had gone crazy. The next things we get are these reports and Halli's head. I can't wait to have a talk with that crazy man.''

Carrera noted with satisfaction how Volpe's eyes narrowed. There was no love lost between him and Russ. "Listen, Ang,'' Carrera practically crooned the words, lightening the veiled threat. "If I could of found someone else with the skill to shoot me, Russ would be standing in your place.''

"What I think of him isn't important, Domie. After what he did, you can't trust him with business. Hell, you can't even admit you know where he is.''

The deaths had started well before Russ went west but Ang was right. If the press got wind that he'd kept in touch with Russ, any sympathy the public had for the Carrera family would vanish. "Listen, Ang, when this is over, we'll figure out what to do about him. In the meantime, don't tell anybody anything they don't already know—nothing about the report, nothing about how Halli died, none of it. I'm in enough trouble without people thinking I lost my marbles out of grief.''

Though Volpe still scowled, he nodded and Carrera had no doubt that the order would be obeyed. He waited until Volpe had gone before looking down at the reports on his desk, thinking about Halli's death.

Could the thing that killed Halli be some mindless brute that didn't have the common sense to hide? Carrera didn't think so. No, the killer must be so powerful that he did not need to hide. He thought of the beautiful face he'd seen in the restaurant, the enticing words curling softly through his brain, and he whispered softly, as if afraid to admit his fear even to himself, "Jesus. What in the hell did you send me, Russell?''

TWENTY-ONE

1

During the two-day drive across Canada, Helen often sensed the presence of Russ and the children but had been close to true consciousness only twice. The first had been when Russ had taken the milk that was rightfully her son's, the second when he'd used the knife on Patrick. She'd longed to attack him then and had even managed to throw off her lethargy for a moment. But when she tensed, straining to break the bonds and stop him, she discovered she was far too weak, the ropes and handcuffs too strong. Though she attempted to rearrange herself exactly as she had been, the blanket had fallen off her legs and she'd had no way to pull it back before she'd slipped into sleep once more.

Helen didn't wake again until she felt the point of Russ's knife against her skin. Even then, she did not fear him. The last time she'd felt any real fear was when he shot Hillary, her last human response the tears she had shed over the girl's body.

Though her human flesh would not obey her will, she had expected her mind to sharpen during the ordeal. Austra blood—hers and Patrick's—in Russ should have made him easy to touch but outside of making him sleep more deeply, focus on her or away from her, and occasionally reading his thoughts, she could do nothing to control him. For the most part, he had stayed close to her, occasionally leaving the warehouse but always wise enough to return so quickly that she never had a chance to extend and call for help. Helen sensed that he had more money than on the drive and an appointment of some sort but every attempt to pull details from his mind proved unsuccessful. Each time she failed, she grew more despondent until her powers, like her confidence, seemed to fade altogether.

Through her helplessness, a different kind of anger began to grow. Except for Philippe and Hillary who had been willing to let her share life, she had never been alone with a human victim. Instead Stephen had accompanied her, and what had seemed then like justifiable concern for her safety, now appeared to be covert support. Stephen had lied about her powers, building her confidence, never teaching her what she truly needed to survive.

She focused on this as she hung slowly healing, listening to Russ Lowell moving around her, making plans she could never quite discern, talking to her as if he knew she could hear him. In the last few hours, he had often fixed his entire attention on her, lashing out with violent explosions of nervous energy that must have unnerved his human victims. Now, he sat silently at her feet, chain-smoking, running his eyes over her body. With deliberate precision, he pressed a lit cigarette to the back of her knee until a thin line of blood rolled down her leg. Russ watched it fall, his expression blank, his thoughts as passive. Then, satisfied that she was not yet conscious, he left the warehouse again.

Helen might have been able to stop him from hurting her but she did not want to reveal her growing powers for something as minor as a burn. She settled for the dubious victories of motionless silence and, in spite of the pain, an unbroken bond with his mind. This last was a skill she had mastered too late. She should have demanded that Stephen teach her the more painful points of self-preservation rather than trivial mental games. If she had practiced using powers such as this before the kidnapping, she, Hillary, and the boys would be safe at home, this tragic ordeal long over. She hadn't known enough to ask and Stephen, betrayed by optimism, had never thought to teach her.

Hillary. Daughter. Friend. I still can taste your blood. I

*still can see the world through your eyes as if you were fixed
in time someplace within me.*

Hillary, I promise you that he will never kill again.

She tapped something vital with that thought. For the first
time, she faced her nature without any reservations, welcoming the predatory hunger directed at one creature and one
alone. She wanted to devour Russ Lowell—as coldly, as ruth-
lessly, as painfully as she could. And nothing could stop her—
not Lowell, not even Stephen.

He will never kill again.

As usual, Russ returned quickly, carrying a bag of warm
doughnuts, some juice, and a small bottle of milk for Patrick.
He waved the open bag under Helen's nose as if the smell of
food would accomplish what his occasional pinches, and
worse, could not. "I know you're faking, Helen Wells. I'll
even tell you how I know. I feel you inside my mind. Later,
when I've got the time, I'll make you talk to me." As he
unlocked the back room, he laughed happily because he believed his plans were going so well.

Then he saw Alan.

Helen felt his alarm as he noted Alan's flushed face and
heard the deep congested cough when the boy tried to sit up.
Patrick, who lay close to Alan on the blanket he'd refused to
part with since the kidnapping, didn't even open his eyes
when Russ called his name.

"Is he sick too?" Russ asked Alan.

"He's OK. I think he was up all night." Alan cleared his
throat before responding, and after he got out the words, he
went into a spasm of coughing that left him breathless.

"Here," Russ said, handing Alan the food. "There's milk
for Patrick," he added and left.

"Something's wrong with the kids, Helen Wells," he commented as he locked the storage-room door. Walking past her
without even a glance, he suddenly turned, hitting her hard
in the stomach. Her mind had been fixed on the boys rather
than Russ and the blow surprised her. She reacted with an
automatic grunt and her eyes fluttered open, focusing on his

face, immediately displaying a silent terror she knew he would relish.

"Better. Much better." He took a towel from the camp supplies, ripped off one long strip, and gagged her tightly before leaving again. Though her gag and the extra wall between the storage room and the outside would muffle any noise they might make, she knew he intended to make as short a trip as possible. At least she didn't have to attempt to persuade him to get medicine for Alan. Prudence dictated that Alan stay healthy until he was traded for his father or killed.

As soon as he left, Helen stretched so her feet could take some of the weight off her wrists. The leg that had been wounded was the stronger now and the shoulder where he had shot her the one that did not ache. Her wrists throbbed, her fingers were numb. She hoped the pain would make them strong.

ll

Alan devoured the juice and doughnuts. After so long without anything and with his stomach so queasy from the coughing, he wondered if the food would stay down. Even so, he eyed Patrick's milk with envy.

The room had grown hot, and concerned that the milk might spoil if Patrick slept too long, Alan decided to wake him. Doing so was difficult. The boy had fallen into a sleep far deeper than any Alan had seen before. On the days when Stephen had strung ropes from the rafters so the boys could climb, Patrick would play for hours without becoming exhausted. The mental games had taken more out of him and he would sometimes lay down for an impromptu nap, but never one as heavy as this.

As he shook the toddler, Alan noted how dry Patrick's skin felt, how limp his body seemed, and he reacted with alarm, calling Patrick's name in a low anxious voice until the toddler stretched and opened his eyes.

They had no whites showing, the way Stephen's looked when he hunted, and the small body became suddenly tense as if Patrick had been pulled from some terrifying nightmare. But Alan knew otherwise. Austra children did not dream. "Are you all right?" Alan asked him.

For a moment it seemed as if the toddler's eyes had tiny points of red at their center but they were just reflections of the room's dim light and when Patrick sat up and looked away from the window they vanished. The boy answered Alan in an oddly slurred tone filled with questions, "My mouth is funny. My hands . . ." He left the sentence unfinished as he and Alan looked with alarm at the long, thin fingers curled and hardened into broad-tipped claws. Patrick grabbed Alan's wrist, his nails breaking the skin on Alan's arm. He pulled back and stared at the tiny red crescents his nails had made with avid interest.

—Helen?— Alan called but his cousin responded only with a weak assent and a quick reassurance that everything would be all right. She had problems of her own and Alan guessed they were far worse than his. He decided to try and take care of Patrick himself. "Relax," Alan whispered. "Russ might come back any minute. He mustn't see you like this."

The toddler had been trained since birth to hide. He nodded, his mouth a tight, straight line. The other changes were harder to control but with effort he managed to close his pupils to an almost human size and relax his hands to a toddler's soft, weak appearance.

"That's good," Alan said, then, amazed, asked, "How did you do that?"

"Father taught."

"How?"

"He showed me in my mind," Patrick said.

Patrick's most likely explanation would be to demonstrate. At this moment Alan didn't want it. Instead he tried to distract the boy. "Look, Russ brought you some milk."

Patrick let him go and reached for the pint bottle. After the first swallow he retched and would have spilled the rest if Alan hadn't grabbed the bottle from him. "Are you all right?" Alan asked.

In response, Patrick pulled his lips back in the mockery of a grin. In the few hours he had slept, the pointed second eyeteeth had reached their full length, resembling less an uncommonly long addition to a normal child's mouth than the obvious fangs of his father.

Alan automatically slid away from the boy, moving fast until his back was pressed against the wall. —Helen!— he called, panic giving strength to his thoughts. Patrick echoed to the older boy's fear with a vocal and mental, "—Mama!—"

—I'm here.— She seemed distracted and in pain and Alan almost regretted disturbing her. He felt her mind leave his and saw Patrick calm as she touched him.

As Helen merged with her son, she was rocked by a power stronger than her own and alarmed by the sudden changes in him.

They had happened too soon and in such tragic surroundings!

Austra children weaned slowly, living on milk and blood for months before their fangs grew to their full length. Patrick had given no warning that his body was ready to mature; perhaps his speedy, nearly human growth extended to the Austra powers, perhaps the circumstances had forced the change. No matter, it was done. At home this would be cause for celebration and, in Patrick's case, his first night hunt with his father. Here the changes only meant additional physical traits to hide from their captor, additional needs that would have to be privately met, and one more reason to avoid any outside help for their escape.

She sensed the boys' fear and quickly decided on a way to alleviate it. —Listen, both of you. I need your help. I want you to dream of Alan's father and go to him with your mind.—

—It's too far! We don't know where to go!— Alan protested. He might have to share this tiny room with Patrick but sharing his mind filled him with terror. Patrick hardly looked like a child anymore as he squatted in front of Alan and stared at him with huge, hungry eyes.

—Distance isn't important; that's what the books said. And you found me over all those miles, remember? We're much closer now.—

—Windsor.— Alan tried to relax and explain how they'd discovered it.

—See what you did together, Alan? Windsor is in Ontario across the river from Detroit. If we had a car we could be in Cleveland in a few hours. Your father is probably there waiting for us. Patrick, you call to Alan's father the way you called to me after Russ kidnapped you. Your mind is much stronger now. You should be able to tell him where we are.—

—And if we can't?— Alan asked.

—You tried. You tried together. Will you both help me?—

—I will,— they responded.

—We will— Alan corrected, looking at Patrick, refusing to lower his eyes or think of anything but what they might accomplish. As he felt Helen pulling away from him, he added one more thought, —Helen, I'm sorry that my dad and I came this summer.—

—I'm sorry this happened but not that I found you again.—

As he felt her slowly retreating from his mind, he heard her say, —I love you,— and repeated the words like a goodbye.

All he had to do was dream of his father, Alan thought, searching for confidence. That should be easy since he wanted nothing more than to see him again. He looked at Patrick, noting the shreds of misery still evident on the toddler's face, and held the bottle out to him. "More?" he asked.

Patrick shook his head and pushed the bottle toward Alan. "You. You drink."

Alan didn't try to argue. As he swallowed the lukewarm liquid, it occurred to him that he might need the extra nourishment. But offering himself to Helen who he loved and trusted was an easy thing compared to allowing this unpredictable wild creature to drink his blood. But he would. He didn't see what else he could do. They were, after all, relying on one another. Patrick rested a hand on Alan's knee. Alan put his own on top of it. Neither boy said a word about Patrick's sudden changing. They didn't have to. Their situation, like the bond between them, had just become far more complicated.

III

Russ found what he needed in two quick stops, returning with blankets, some salve for Alan's chest, and a bottle of cough syrup the druggist had recommended. He dropped the supplies next to the place where Alan lay, and after a long look at the toddler sitting beside him, glaring up at him with those dark, defiant eyes, Russ returned to his prize.

He pulled his sleeping bag and a tarp out of the car and began walking across the room to Helen. He had hours to waste until he phoned Domie. There would be no reason to let lust interfere with caution. Of course if he was to get any satisfaction from her at all, he'd have to lower her and untie her legs. Like the boys, she hadn't caused any trouble so freeing that much of her would be all right.

Except the bitch is faking her weakness, idiot, the soft voice of reason murmured.

He could lower her to a sitting position. Her arms would still be tied above her head. His weight would keep her from kicking.

And a twenty-pound baby damn near ripped off half your face. Do you really think this one's afraid of you?

But her eyes were open, watching him. As he moved closer to her, she looked away, her lean body shaking. Everything about her drew him forward, especially the prominence of the pale line where he'd cut her yesterday. Thinking of the taste of her blood, he licked his lips and pulled the knife from his pocket. "You laughed at me!" he whispered, dreams and reality skewed and distorted. "Laughed!"

He had the knife open now. His head pounded and his eyes seemed unable to focus on anything but her and how she waited, so perfectly helpless. He took two involuntary steps toward her then, just as his hand reached for her breast, he forced his mind back to his will and spun on his heel, going outside for a long walk, one that would take him as far from the warehouse as he dared travel on foot.

He returned only when he'd decided on a plan. He focused on it and nothing else, refusing to even look at Helen as he pulled two heavy lengths of rope from the nets and attached one to each of her ankles, then, rather than touch her and risk losing his control, he used them to spin her to face the back of the warehouse. "I suppose you know about the medicine I gave the boy. Can you be thankful, Helen Wells?" He asked this as he threaded the ends of the ropes through separate trapdoor handles a few yards away. He tied each with a slipknot, then spread the tarp and sleeping bag in front of her. He removed the gag. "I don't have to be anywhere until eight. That gives us hours to get acquainted. Let's start with some conversation. Would you like me to lower you a little bit?"

She nodded.

"Then ask."

"Please."

"Better." He abruptly lowered the pulley a half foot, not surprised to see her legs holding her full weight easily, only one showing some minor signs of stiffness. Victims normally rubbed their wrists or flexed their fingers to restore circulation but her hands didn't move and her eyes never left his face. The fear that he'd noted in them earlier had vanished, taking some of his passion with it. But they were adversaries, after all, and soon she would know who was the smarter one here.

He slipped the knots holding her legs. Her feet were pulled forward, her hands taking all her weight again. He lowered her another few inches and again tightened the ropes. Even though he could feel her trying to control his thoughts, feeding him one frantic suggestion after another, each too ideal to ignore, he kept his mind firmly fixed on the plan he'd outlined on his walk and continued the careful balancing of pulley and ropes. Though she tried a number of times, she never had enough slack to reach the hook. In the end, he knelt at her feet and cut her clothes and the shorter rope holding her ankles together. Two final pulls on the slip knots and she was just as securely fastened as before and far more accessible.

He knelt between her legs and ran his index finger down the pale scar his knife had left on her body. "Fear is a remarkable thing, Helen Wells. When people come face-to-face with their nightmares, there's a certain thrill to them. Do you think so?''

Helen only watched him, her eyes locked with his eyes, refusing to look at his body or even the knife he still gripped.

He raised it suddenly, holding it in both hands, its point above her womb. "Talk to me, damn you!" She tensed, pulling at the bonds as he slashed downward, stopping when the point just broke her skin. "Talk."

"Tell me what you want me to say. I'll repeat word for word or perhaps you would like me to show you what I can do?" She replied without any trace of terror, her tone an odd blend of mockery and compliance.

He wanted to ask a dozen questions, to unravel the mystery of her death and hiding but he had hours to spend with her and the questions could wait. He decided he would even let her play with his mind a little, just to test her power. He felt her inside of him—how would he ever explain to Domie about that!—her mind rubbing against his nerves, more arousing than she would be if she were one of his ordinary girls and free to use trembling hands and lips to touch him. He'd wanted to savor the act, to take his time with her but no more. His hands, which had been unbuttoning his shirt, dropped to his pants. He climaxed with the zipper half down. "Damn you!" he bellowed, his fingers squeezing the inside of her thighs, his nails digging through her skin. "Don't you ever do that to me again."

The scent of her blood seemed to fill the room. He held up his red-tipped fingers, and as he looked at them, he thought of Maria Truzzi. Picking up the knife, he made four deep cuts on Helen's chest, smearing the blood across her breasts before falling onto her.

Their coupling was long and bloody and before it was through, Helen had cried out more than once, her body convulsing, pushed beyond endurance, he thought. He sucked the wound until, with his hands buried in her hair, he dared to kiss her, not surprised when she responded. He stayed that way, rocking and rocking, the taste of blood in his mouth, too caught up in the pleasure she so carefully aroused to notice when she bit his lip and his blood mingled with her own.

Moving carefully through him, distracting him with passion, she began to drink.

And his victims exploded in her! She saw each of their faces at the last moments of their lives, their pain and fear as real as her own, devoured and savored by the monster who had destroyed them. As his mind opened completely to her, she understood him finally, fully. Her body responded with a revulsion that tensed her from wrists to ankles. In spite of his weight on her, she felt her body leave the floor as she pulled in one final desperate attempt to free herself and devour him.

He rolled off of her. "Later," he said with a sardonic grin, too obsessed with her face to notice one of her feet carefully push a trapdoor back in place. The wood had begun to rot in the main floor. As she'd responded with what Russ misinterpreted as climax, she had worked one set of hinges loose, her last attempt nearly ripping the door out of its frame. She didn't want Russ to notice it and wasn't even certain it would be more than a hint of how she might escape since that door was linked to her weaker leg.

As Russ lay panting beside her, a brief, vivid memory came to her. She'd been about twelve or thirteen, doing her homework at the dining-room table while eavesdropping on the conversation between her uncle and her father. Dick had been assigned to the hunt for the torso murderer, the madman who left each victim without arms or legs or head. After weeks on the case, her uncle's disgust was evident as he sat in her kitchen talking in a voice slurred by a few too many beers. "The investigators are trying to understand him. They're working on a profile. The bastards! They think he's sane because he hasn't been caught. They think there's some sort of link in the victims because he makes it look like there's one. The truth is he's smart and crazy and there is no motive. He just loves blood."

Her father had responded in a voice too low for her to make out the words but she caught her uncle's loud reply,

"Catch him, hell. When they find him they should shoot him. That's what you do with an animal, after all."

Her uncle, not her lover, had prepared her best for Russ Lowell.

Animal.

She walked into his mind and stayed there, watching as he opened one of the trapdoors and lowered himself into the water, felt the welcome cold wash over her as it hit his body. When he returned, he soaked a towel in the river and began cleaning her off, then wiping her dry. He found a hairbrush in the car and, with her head on his bare knees, began combing out the tangles in her hair, taking care not to pull it and hurt her. When he'd finished, he arranged it over one shoulder, leaving the one with the cuts bare so, as he had done before, he could watch them heal.

After, as the sun on the dark warehouse roof warmed the building, he lay naked beside her, his head on her stomach, his hand on her breast, and slept.

His touch strengthened their growing bond and it occurred to her that she had not fully understood what Stephen had told her uncle a few short weeks ago. To give blood to Russ was useless until she completed the circle and drank from him. Now that she had, she sensed his weakness and saw a way to use it. Her plan would require courage and confidence, perhaps more than she possessed. Her ties to her human past were strong and she knew, in a way that Stephen could never comprehend, that the price of failure would be death.

But she had no other choices, not anymore. She wanted personal vengeance—not just for Hillary or for what Russ had done to her, but for all the women he had used and destroyed. Her rage lay curled, cold, and lethal in the center of her mind, waiting to be set loose. She welcomed it as she stared at Russ Lowell's face and began planning how he would die.

And, heedless of her attention, Russ dreamed as he often did of Maria Truzzi and of all his victims, alive and waiting for his touch.

TWENTY-TWO

1

Men feared Dominic Carrera because he gave them reason to fear. They respected him because he made it unwise to do otherwise. And the temper he had cultivated since childhood had become legendary.

So he wasn't surprised at how nervous Russ sounded when he phoned the restaurant precisely at eight that evening. Nor would Carrera admit that for the first time in years he didn't know if he should be furious or thankful so he settled for being polite. He took the call in a private back room, a phone extending from the storage chest behind it. He had a bottle of cognac and two glasses on the table—one glass half-filled, the second for Toni who was expected in an hour. "You can talk here," Carrera said. "Explain everything."

"You got those reports?"

"Yeah. They came this morning. I read them."

With the relief evident in his tone, Russ detailed how he'd planned the hit and how it had gone wrong. "I took the brat to trade for the father. I grabbed the other kid because I didn't want the people from the cabin to go to the cops."

"An eye for an eye," Carrera commented dryly.

"You didn't ask for the Wells kid," Russ retorted, the speed of his reply revealing a trace of anger. "But while I was in the cabin, I found out that Stephen Austra and Helen Wells were living there."

Last week Carrera wouldn't have believed Russ. Now he merely asked, "You're sure you're not wrong?"

"I saw both of them when I was at that New York gallery with your father. I didn't see Austra so I can't be sure it's him but I got a good look at the woman's face when she came after me for her son. You never forget a face like that. She's gone now . . . along with the girl that was staying with her. That should have been enough to send the people to the police but they never went. They were up there, hiding. I swear it. I tell you, something crazy's going on."

"Yeah, Halli's head for one." Then Carrera told him about the package, how they believed Halli had died, the Wells connection to the earlier murders, all of it.

As he talked, Carrera almost wished this line were tapped. If the FBI got this on tape, his lawyer could have it admitted as evidence of insanity. When he'd finished telling Russ what he knew, Russ upped the ante and described Patrick Austra's physical and mental powers, concluding with an ominous warning, "When I first read the stuff I lifted from the house, I thought they were hiding out because they were communists or something. Now I think whatever's going on is a hell of a lot stranger. If the father's anything like the kid, you have to be careful, Domie. He'll read your mind. He'll try to control it."

Carrera had to give Russ credit. This hadn't been an easy story for Russ to tell, but so far as Carrera could discern Russ hadn't held back any of it. "You said you saw Austra in New York. What did he look like?" Carrera asked. When Russ responded with a description of the man Carrera had seen two nights earlier, Carrera was convinced he had seen Halli's killer. "You know more about this than me, Russell. What do you think I should I do?" he asked.

"Play it safe. When Austra and Wells contact you, you decide on the bargain you want to make beforehand—Well for his son, Austra's kid for whatever you think he's worth. If you meet with Austra face-to-face, don't back down an inch from your position. No matter how right his suggestion seems at the time, don't change your mind about anything until you're sure he's gone and you give yourself plenty of time to think about it. He can't touch you as long as you don't know where I am. If he tries anything, I'll kill the kids. Be sure to tell him that. As for the trade . . ."

"I can handle that," Carrera interjected with some irritation. Russ's advice had become so obvious it seemed like an insult.

"And hide those reports someplace where he'll never find them."

"I know what they're worth, Russell."

"Good."

"And I won't forget to take care of you either. I owe you that."

"Thanks, Domie. And, Domie?"

"Yeah."

"Those girls were nothing, no better than that B-girl Billy whacked over at Fran's."

"So I figured," Carrera said wearily. "Give me two days, then call again. Same time."

Carrera hung up the phone and turned off the ringer before locking it away in the closet. Voices from the restaurant's lounge drifted through the closed door and he heard Toni's among them. Nonetheless, Carrera sat alone, his hand cradling his glass as he considered how to deal with Russ Lowell.

Everyone thought it was so easy for him, like he was one of the vicious dogs played by actors like Cagny and Raft and he could snap his fingers and make somebody disappear and never feel any remorse. Yes, it was easy when it had to be. Revenge could even be enjoyable. Friends were different and Russ had not crossed him. But Carrera sensed something dark and ugly in Russ's justification of what he had done, a rottenness that went far beyond Billy Gerard's rage when the girl at Fran's had given him the clap. He'd walked into Fran's with a baseball bat and beat the girl to death. Everybody expected that kind of thing from Billy; he had that kind of temper. Russ didn't. Maybe the most unsettling thing about all his murders was how balanced Russ had always seemed, how well he'd managed to hide the viciousness inside him.

Well, one thing was certain—Carrera wouldn't desert Russ,

especially not now. Tomorrow he'd talk to Volpe about everything he'd learned and make plans on how to protect Russ. Tonight he just wanted to forget.

Decision made, Carrera opened the door, motioned Toni inside, and locked it behind her. She wore a strapless white sundress that laced up the front. Her eyes were oval and slightly slanted, her tanned skin dark as her hair, and as she padded toward the table, he thought of tigers in the snow. She poured them each a drink, then sat on the edge of the table, her knees spread, her skirt hiked over them. Underneath the dress she probably wore nothing at all.

He took the glass she held out to him. "Do you remember anything more from the other night?" he asked.

She shook her head. "Every time I try, I get a headache and believe me, Domie, I'm out half a bottle of aspirin from all the trying. I think I got drugged or something."

"Maybe a pale-skinned man, thin, with dark curly hair?"

She rested a hand on the side of his face, one long nail scratching behind his ear. "Hey, you sure you want me to get that headache now?" She accentuated the suggestion with that odd crooked smile that made him so crazy for her and tilted her head up, waiting to be kissed.

II

Russ expected to be gone for at least three hours. Helen knew this long before he left.

But though he could keep her from calling for help, he could not silence her mind. In her years of solitude, she had learned to lure deer from the woods, foxes from their dens. As for people, since her changing she'd had her choice of them. An end to this might be easy after all.

She started as soon as Russ had gone, her mind following her hearing in an expanding circle of awareness. A quick mental scan of the surroundings revealed few choices for rescuers. Much of the area hadn't seen constant use since Prohibition and the buildings kept up since then had fallen into disrepair during the recession. The new docks closer to downtown had turned this region into an urban ghost town, abandoned and empty.

She sensed a pair of drunks sleeping off an early evening bottle in a storage shed on a nearby pier. Waking them would be difficult and she continued the search until, near the edge of her range, she found two children, hardly older than Alan, fishing off a concrete pier.

She sent them no more than a suggestion that they explore the old warehouses. The girl was intrigued by the sudden thought of adventure and began talking her little brother into it.

"Ma said we're not supposed to go there," the boy complained stubbornly, using his parent as a scapegoat for his fear.

"Well, she'll never know."

"Yeah, she will. She always knows." The boy stared at the long evening shadows the buildings threw over the rubble heaped between them. Things lived beneath those heaps of rusted metal beams, things waiting with sharp claws for him to get too close.

"Rats and bats and spiders, oh, my! Rats and bats and . . ." the girl teased in a singsong Dorothy voice.

Their argument could take time, and time, Helen knew, was precious. The girl dropped her pole on the ground and began walking toward the buildings. "Oh, fuck!" the boy yelled after her, hoping even the swear would make him sound older, hoping even more that the word that his sister loathed worse than peas in cream sauce would make her turn back. A kick in the shins would be better than this adventure. Even the bar of soap Mom would make him lick after his sister told on him would be nothing compared to those buildings. "Fuck . . . fuck . . . fuck, Carrie," he screamed as loud as he was able. "Fuck . . . fuck . . . fuck."

Though she just kept walking, her shoulders shook. Oh, hell, she must be giggling!

The boy hated the old buildings but he hated being alone out here even more. He ran after his sister, just fast enough to close the distance between them.

And as they walked closer to the warehouses, the boy noted

that only one of them had a new lock and a sturdy enough door to hide some magical treasure inside.

As the pair approached, Helen felt her first misgivings. They were too weak to use one of the scrap metal bars piled beside the building to pry off the padlock. The sight of her would send them scurrying for the police whose questions would be more than awkward.

And yet, they might be the only chance she and the boys would have for escape.

Trust your instincts, Stephen had told her.

But were these concerns true instinct or only doubts—and how was she supposed to know the difference?

III

Soon after Russ left the warehouse to make the call to Carrera, he stopped for a paper and scanned it for word of the murder and kidnapping. Seeing no mention of either, he decided to take the risk of phoning Carrera from downtown Windsor rather than driving twenty miles or more to a pay phone in a different town. Besides his ignorance about his hostages' mental powers, smaller towns had nosier operators and he didn't want to risk anyone listening in on this call. When he'd finished talking to Carrera, he stopped at a liquor store for a couple of bottles of Crown Royal for himself and the woman. He even grabbed a magazine, a chocolate bar, and some chips for the Wells brat, and since he couldn't think of anything fancy Patrick might eat, he bought him a hula hoop from the display by the counter. Damn, he felt like celebrating! The conversation with Domie had gone well. *Better* than well. Domie had understood, had *believed*. Domie was going to take care of him. For the first time since he let her go, Russ found himself missing Donna. At least she knew how to fake a good time.

Well, there were other good times and one of them was trussed and waiting for him back at the warehouse. As he stood at the counter while the cashier tallied his bill on a piece of white butcher paper, he added one final item—a pound slab of garlic-flavored summer sausage. Now that he had time, he decided to do a little investigating and see if there were any traditional weak spots in Helen Wells's nature.

As he drove down the hill toward the river, he saw a pair of children running down the street away from the warehouse. He waited until they were out of sight before driving inside, then carefully studied the lock. So far as he could determine, it had not been touched. He knelt beside Helen and took off the gag. "Did the kids out there see you?" he asked.

"No."

"How do I know you're not lying?"

"Because if the police come, you will kill the boys and me and yourself," she said in a clipped even tone.

"I'm glad you understand my priorities," he commented.

"Of course you intend to kill me and Patrick anyway."

"Just you . . . eventually." Russ expected to see some alarm in her expression as he gave his reply but Helen might have still been unconscious for all the emotion she revealed. He tried to hide his disappointment by delivering the food and presents to the back.

Patrick fingered the red hoop delicately, looking up at Russ with a solemn expression that made him dizzy. Though Russ hadn't expected any thanks, he'd figured the gifts would bring a little relief from the tension, but if anything, it had increased. As he walked back to Helen, he shrugged off his uneasiness. This was the first time he'd handled a job this big without help. He had nobody for cards, nobody to swap lies or get drunk with. The loneliness might just be eating at him but he sensed a change in the warehouse, a definite shifting of tone that unsettled him as if everyone was smugly awaiting the sniper's bullets in his chest. He checked Helen's bonds carefully, running his fingers over every link in the handcuffs before he sat cross-legged beside her, unwrapping the sausage and uncorking the bottle. He used his knife to cut a slice of the sausage, waving it under her nose, disappointed by her almost amused reaction.

"Want any?" he asked.

She shook her head.

"How about a drink?"

"No."

"Anything?"

"Water."

He wedged his knees under her shoulders and lifted her head before uncorking a canteen. As she drank, he commented, "Carrera says Wells and your lover are in Cleveland now. I'm supposed to call him back in a couple of days and see when we make the trade."

"Am I included?"

"The Wells brat is. So is your son. I told Carrera you were dead. After I take the boys to Cleveland, I'll come back for you."

"The trip will take some time," she commented.

"Don't worry, I'll figure out a way to deal with you while I'm gone. I think I've done a pretty good job so far." He poured another drink, corked and rolled the bottle across the room. "I don't want to have too much, you know. I got to keep my head around you. Besides, I got to make the booze last." He dipped his finger in his glass and moistened her lips with the whiskey. "You sure you don't want a drink?"

She coughed. Even the smell of it made her sick. "Yes."

"No drink? Not even blood?" He pressed hard on her forehead, forcing her head back, his face only inches from hers as he told her how Halli had died. Then, without repeating his question, he cut his arm in the soft spot above his wrist and let the blood drip onto her lips. He gave a grunt of pleasure when she opened them so the drops would fall onto her teeth and tongue. He gradually relaxed and let her suck the wound, running a hand down the side of her neck, feeling the ripple as she swallowed. "You're so damned beautiful, you know that," he whispered.

She understood the message Stephen had sent her. She no longer needed to hide. —Of course I do— she replied.

Her words in his mind; somehow Russ wasn't surprised.

TWENTY-THREE

1

As was his custom, Volpe picked up his father on Friday afternoon at a west-side rest home. From there they drove to New Central Market where Volpe double parked in front of the fruit stalls outside the building and helped his father walk the sawdust-covered concrete aisles past women carrying babies and brown paper shopping bags. The old man, who had been partially paralyzed by a stroke, leaned on Volpe, stopping often to greet friends at the meat and vegetable stands, bitching as usual about the food and his roommate at the nursing home and how nobody in the family but his Angelo ever came to visit. Volpe didn't correct him, but in the last year and a half, the old man had feuded with every other relation. Volpe suspected that his father spared him only because if they fought there'd be nobody to drive him to town. After the walk, Volpe took him to supper at the Greek place across from the Market, then to Friday night confession and back to the home. When he returned to his car after helping the old man inside, Volpe found a stranger leaning against it, waiting for him.

"I want you to take a message to your boss." The stranger spoke with an obvious, though not quite placeable, European accent.

Even though his Friday night schedule had long ago become routine, Volpe was surprised. "Stephen Austra?" he asked, recognizing the man from the description Carrera had given. When Austra nodded, Volpe continued, "We expected you to call the office."

"So the FBI could eavesdrop, yes?"

"You and Wells probably know more about that than me," Volpe responded. Though Austra hadn't made a move toward him, the stories Volpe had heard unsettled him as did the unwavering stare of the man's dark eyes. Only a few weak street lamps shed light on the quiet tree-lined boulevard and the houses were set well back from the road. Volpe felt painfully vulnerable.

"I am looking for Russ Lowell. Do you know where he is?"

Volpe shook his head and opened his car door. In the Ford's dim courtesy light, he could see Austra's eyes narrow in what seemed like anger. Though Austra appeared unarmed, Volpe's vague uneasiness intensified into real fear. "I'm sorry," Volpe quickly added. Wanting nothing more than to end this lonely encounter, he pulled a grocery bill from his pocket and scribbled a phone number on the back of it. "This is a clean line. You call me tomorrow morning at ten."

"I want to talk to Carrera personally."

"I'll see what I can do. Call me tomorrow." Volpe dug his keys out of his pocket and got into his car. As he reached down to put the key in the ignition, he dropped the ring and had to maneuver his huge body around the steering wheel to grope on the dark floor for them. When he sat up and looked out the window Austra had vanished without even the sound of footsteps to hint on his direction.

Volpe looked up and down the street for some sign of a car but there was nothing. Not certain if he was more relieved or nervous by Austra's sudden departure, Volpe sped away, relaxing only when he reached the heavy evening traffic on 25th Street. Even then, he cautiously headed through the empty flats and across the low Cuyahoga River bridges looking in the rearview and over his shoulder. Seeing no one following him, he got on the Shoreway and drove to the east side.

11

Volpe was so easy to follow.

Stephen traveled without lights, extending his mind to keep track of Volpe, often letting Volpe make a number of turns before speeding up to close the space to a few blocks between them. He would not have followed Volpe at all but their brief mental encounter had proven fruitless. Volpe did not think in terms of addresses or names. With the familiarity of someone who had lived most of his life in a few square blocks of city, he probably didn't know street numbers at all.

Stephen became aware he was being watched from the time he'd crossed the invisible boundary into Carrera's neighborhood. The Cadillac didn't sound like one of the familiar cars so shades moved up a few inches, windows suddenly opened, and one old woman, oblivious to any threat from the street below, craned her head out a window and watched him drive by.

He had called this Carrera's empire and he had been correct. These streets were as much Carrera's domain as AustraGlass was his. But Stephen felt safe in Chaves, hardly fearing even exposure, whereas Carrera's empire was an unsettled one, the monarch himself uneasy.

He waited until Volpe had parked his car in a narrow alley and been let inside before pulling up in front of Carrera's private office above a darkened bakery. Not wishing to surprise the men on guard downstairs, he knocked on the front door. As he did, he sent a quick mental order that the men inside open it to talk to him. A moment later he entered and the dim inside light went out.

The upstairs room was sparsely furnished—a desk, six chairs, and an overhead light softened by a milk-glass globe. The windows and shades were closed for privacy and protection so a small air conditioner kept the room cool. Carrera, facing the door, was just beginning a game of gin with Volpe when Austra joined them without a knock or word of warning. Carrera looked up at him, and though Stephen knew he'd been startled, he did not show it. Instead he slowly lowered his cards and asked, "Stephen Austra?"

"Yes, Senhor Carrera. That is my name." As he had with Volpe, he maintained a distinct Portuguese accent. He chose it because he wanted Carrera to treat him as a foreigner, one who perhaps held power elsewhere. He certainly held no power here.

They looked at each other across the table, Carrera's eyes raised, Stephen's, almost benevolent, as they looked down. Neither man spoke so Volpe nervously commented, "I don't know how he followed me. He didn't even have a car."

Carrera knew. Stephen felt him resisting the odd tugging in his mind and settled less for control than for following his adversary's thoughts. Carrera sent Volpe downstairs to check on the guards. Volpe returned quickly, pale and shaking. "Jimmy's dead. I don't see a mark on him. Red is alive but . . ." Volpe fell silent. He couldn't begin to explain what had happened to Red.

"Men like that are expendable," Stephen said coldly. "Men like Halli are harder to find and men like you, Senhor Carrera, are irreplaceable. Please, for your sake, keep your hands on the table."

Close up Austra seemed even more delicately built than he had at a distance, with hands whose sole purpose seemed to be to display rings like the ruby rock on his middle finger. Nonetheless, Carrera decided that Austra had issued a warning, not a threat. The distinction between these seemed oddly sharp, and unquestionable. "You killed Jason Halli?" he asked.

"I did."

"Why?"

"He gave some ill advice to Russ Lowell. He ordered Lowell to kill my son. Family to me, as to you, is sacred."

"I am pleased you understand this, Mr. Austra. It makes our bargaining so much easier."

"There is no bargain. I am here to demand that you give me Alan Wells and . . ." Stephen hesitated, then, realizing Carrera thought Helen dead, merely added, "and my son."

He watched Carrera's eyes widen as the compulsion to obey

hit his mind. Carrera forced his gaze to move to his hands, speaking calmly, reasonably, as he responded, "You'll have your son in time, I think. As for Wells—one less cop in the world, who can argue with that?"

"I sometimes agree with you. Small men given power often take advantage of that power, yes?" Stephen answered dryly, pleased to see that the analogy was not lost on Carrera. "But you see," Stephen continued, "Captain Wells shot in self-defense and killed a son who, by all accounts, has been a disgrace to your family. If you went to prison, Senhor Carrera, and your son had sat at that desk for even a few short months, how much of what you and your father have built would be intact in a year? In two?"

Carrera whitened. But Stephen was more intrigued by Volpe's nearly imperceptive nod, the man's strong, shocked thought, *Who the hell is he to give such blunt advice?*

Carrera reasoned along similar cautious lines, and in spite of his rage, he answered with carefully controlled calm, "I never expected my son to sit at this desk but I wished him alive and well, giving me grandsons to carry on my name. Dick Wells took this from me."

Knowing that organized crime rarely retaliated against police doing their duty, Stephen responded, "He only surprised what he thought was a robber."

"If he'd been working I would have left him alone. I checked around. That bastard had the afternoon off."

Stephen knew that Carrera distorted the truth. He had to kill Richard. An audacious murder would be the last display of power by a bitter, almost-broken man. Stephen could force him to agree to let Richard live but Carrera would see through the mental control as soon as Stephen left him alone.

"My son was sick." Carrera's voice rose a notch, the excuse sounding less like a father in grief than a spoiled child's whine. "Every patrolman in the area knew it and they had a number to call if Peter caused any trouble. All Wells had to do was back out of that shop and flag down a patrol car and this meeting would not be necessary. Do you understand?"

Instead of waiting for a response, Carrera charged ahead, "Besides, I hold the boys, Stephen Austra. So all you can do is listen. I will exchange Alan Wells for his father, don't try to argue any more about that. As for your son, you can have him back when all federal charges against me are dropped.''

"That's impossible!''

"You listen to me. I don't know why a dead man is sitting across from me. I won't even ask you to explain. Instead, I am giving you a gift, Stephen Austra. I am leaving your game, whatever the hell it is, intact. I have your reports locked away in a safe place. If you don't help me, I'll hand them over to the feds and trade my way out of prison. I'm sure the government would be interested in them, particularly since Stoddard Design is one of your firms.''

Stephen considered this impassively. So much so that Carrera knew he had surprised his adversary. "Why do you prefer to bargain with me?'' Stephen asked.

"I make this deal with you. You do your half, I do mine, and we're even. With the sons of bitches in the FBI the demands would go on and on and in the end we'd both get left with nothing but a lot of enemies and no place to hide. I figure that the firm that collected the information in those reports must pay their contacts damned good money. Spread some more of it around now.''

Carrera studied Stephen's reaction to this, unaware that Stephen had no contacts, at least not in the usual sense. "This may take some time,'' Stephen responded carefully. "The boys are young. They should be with their families. Would you consider releasing them in exchange for Richard and a postponement of your trial? You have my reports so you are in a position to cause me a great deal of difficulty should I break my part of this agreement.''

Russ might make a mistake. The kids might be found. Better, Carrera decided, to play it safe and avoid the risks. "An indefinite postponement? All right, you have three days to arrange it.'' Carrera scribbled a phone number on a slip of paper and slid it across the desk. "Rumors won't be enough. When my trial's postponement is officially announced, call this number and I'll tell you the time and place of the trade.''

"Very well. But there is one more item I want included in this exchange. I want Russ Lowell."

Again, Stephen noticed Volpe's nearly imperceptible assent and, as quickly, Carrera's response, "You have your people. I have mine. If mine cause trouble, I handle it myself."

"He killed my ward. And my wife. He had no orders to do so. That makes my revenge as personal as your own, yes?"

"No!" Carrera's fist hit the desk. He started to rise, then, with a sardonic smile, fell back in his seat. "You can go to the police, if you wish."

Their traditions were years apart, Stephen realized. Perhaps Ray Carrera would have understood the rules powerful families in Europe had followed for centuries. But too much competition and too many deaths had destroyed the old ways here. All that remained were power and greed, a facade of underdog respectability, and a loyalty fierce as passion and just as fickle. Nonetheless, for Helen's sake, he tried one final time.

—Give him to me! —

Carrera's eyes widened and he appeared somewhat stunned as he said "No" with more certainty than he had a moment before. "However, I would consider handling the matter myself," he added, thinking of Halli and unwilling to condemn Russ to an end like that.

"If you won't make him part of the exchange, I ask that you not harm him."

Carrera understood. "You'll never find him," he said.

"I found you, yes?" With only a slight pause for emphasis, Stephen went on, "I also need some information from you. I have not followed your case. I need to know which judge is hearing it, who is prosecuting, and so on."

As swiftly as Carrera listed the names, Stephen absorbed and stored the information, then responded with a reasonable mental suggestion Carrera immediately echoed, "You might think of other questions too. You meet with Volpe here tomorrow at one."

"Not here. Someplace more public please," Stephen responded. He recalled a stop he'd made with Helen a few years before. "There is a restaurant in the downtown train station. It is called Harvey's, I believe. Is it still in operation?"

"Yeah," Carrera said. "Ang can meet you there. Is that OK, Ang? Ang?"

Volpe sat frozen, staring at the empty wall. "What in the . . ." Carrera began. Then he saw Austra's eyes fixed on him, two hard circles of darkness pulling at his will. "You can't change my mind," Carrera said, though he sounded less certain than he'd been a moment ago.

The reply came softly, a lilting whisper deep within him. —I don't intend to try. Come with me.—

Carrera followed him down the narrow back stairs, leaving the office door open behind him to light the way. At the base, he stopped and waited until the harsh fluorescents of the bakery flickered on. Jimmy lay on his back, his feet toward the door, his hand still holding a gun as if he'd tried to do his job even past death. Carrera moved closer to him. Volpe had said there wasn't a mark on him but Carrera's more discerning eyes noted a swollen crescent-shaped bruise on his neck. Someone had kicked him hard enough to snap his spine.

As if the silence had been deliberately maintained, he suddenly noticed a ragged breathing and followed the sound to inside of the counter. There Red huddled in the corner beneath the cash register, his eyes wide and unblinking. As Carrera approached him, Red began making a soft, keening sound with every exhale as if a scream were trapped in his throat, struggling to get out.

Carrera forced his eyes away from Red and breathed deeply, letting the familiar scents of yeast and anise restore some of his balance. He looked directly at Austra and asked, "What happened to Red?"

—Less than what happened to Halli before he died. Far less than what I will do to you if any harm comes to either of those boys.—

Carrera might have turned and fled but the only escape was toward Austra and he didn't dare move in that direction. "We made an agreement," he said stubbornly. "If anything happens to me, those boys will die."

"I am aware of this. I merely wish to make a point to you

alone. I will make these trades with you. You have my word on it. But you have taken responsibility for Russ Lowell. So if anything happens to my son or to Alan Wells there will be no place you can hide from me and no mortician will be able to wipe the agony from your face when I am done. Remember that.''

Carrera's concentration was fixed on Austra. When something brushed his leg, he looked down at Red whose fingers were convulsively flexing, trying to grab on to him. An instant later he forced his eyes back to where Austra had been standing but the man had disappeared as if the night itself had claimed him.

Carrera rushed to Jimmy's body and pried the gun out of his hand. Its weight made him feel more secure and he went back to Red and knelt in front of him. ''What did Austra do to you?'' he asked.

Red looked vacantly beyond him, eyes fixed on nothing. Yet he must have heard because he took a long, deep breath. As Carrera leaned closer, ready to hear any reply, Red screamed out his entire breath, took another, and screamed again.

Carrera pulled back, his arms covering his ears as the screams went on and on.

What if Red became sane enough to talk about what he'd seen tonight? What if his men discovered what kind of a monster stalked him? Deliberately, Carrera aimed the gun at Red's chest and fired, pulling the trigger long after the chambers were empty. Silence, magnificent and comforting, surrounded him and he stared at the blood spattering the white walls and glass counter doors.

A creak on the stairs drew his attention to the back door of the bakery where Volpe stood, a slip of paper in one shaking hand. ''You kill Red?'' he asked.

Carrera nodded. ''I couldn't leave him like that.''

''I saw Austra leave. I got the license number on his car. We could make some calls. That Caddie won't be hard to track down,'' he suggested.

''Go ahead. But I only want him watched.''

''I don't want to meet him tomorrow,'' Volpe said.

"Damn it! You'll do what I tell you!"

Volpe went back to the office and slumped into a chair, covering his face when Carrera joined him. "I don't want to go the way Halli did," he moaned.

As he said Halli's name, Volpe's hands began to shake once more. Carrera responded fast. "Austra's going to come through for me. He doesn't want to but he can do it." To Volpe, he must have sounded elated but the truth was something more unsettling—relief.

Russ had warned him, diplomatically, it seemed now. When Carrera had felt the tugging at his mind, he'd responded logically. Every time he felt the urge to agree with Austra, he asked himself who would benefit from the agreement. If it was himself, the idea was a good one. If not, Austra was controlling him. The simple plan seemed to have worked.

"I know what you think of Russ but if it weren't for him we'd both be dead right now. As long as Russ has the kids Austra can't touch us. There's no reason to worry, understand?"

The power Carrera sensed in Austra made him want to respond with a display of his own. "And one other thing, Ang. We're going to give Austra a taste of what we can do if he tries to cross us. Get ahold of Willie in New York. Ask him to find out what Stoddard's building now and slow construction down, better yet have him stop it if he can. Tell him, I'll call him at home tomorrow night. In the meantime I guarantee as much as it takes."

The orders given, Carrera rested his face on his hands. "Russ," he whispered softly to himself, sustaining the "s" in a sound less a hiss than a sigh. Stella, his older girl, had just turned seventeen. If Russ hadn't proven to be more a killer than Dominic had ever suspected, he would have made Russ his son-in-law. His father had suggested the match a couple of years ago knowing that Russ was smart enough to ask for advice when things got over his head. Dominic had been prepared to guide him from prison. Now Peter was gone, Russ was as good as dead already, and the best Domini-

could do was avoid serving the time until he found the right man to take his place.

"Domie," Volpe said, resting a hand on Carrera's shoulder. "You all right?"

"Yeah."

"Domie, what will we do with the bodies downstairs?"

"We handle it ourselves." As Volpe reached for the phone, Carrera asked, "Did Austra look human to you?"

"What?" Volpe began to laugh, then realizing Carrera was serious, he added, "Sure."

"Then how in the hell did he get in here without us ever hearing a sound?"

III

When Stephen returned to the hotel, Richard was waiting for him, sitting in the desk chair he had moved to an inside wall, the revolver in his lap. He appeared to have been fighting sleep for hours. "Did you see Carrera?" he asked.

"I did."

"And?"

"He doesn't know where Lowell has the children or even where we can find him."

"Damn it! How can he not know?"

"They talked by phone and Lowell would not tell him. Intelligent man, yes?" Stephen's expression reflected the frustration in his tone.

"Yeah, sure. Are Helen and the boys all right?"

"Carrera believes the boys are. Lowell told him that Helen is dead. I thought it best that Carrera continue to believe it."

"Continue! You didn't demand that he return her as part of any exchange?"

"No, Richard, I could not. Lowell would only lie when asked about her. Then negotiations would become a matter of his word against mine. Days would pass while we resolved this. I want the boys safe. Helen can take care of herself."

Dick thought it best to not push the lack of logic in Stephen's final remark. "I get the point," he said. "What do we do now?"

"I'm sorry, Richard. As I feared, he knows what I am and he knows how to fight my control. So I did the only thing I could—I agreed to the trade. The terms are difficult. I'm not sure I can meet them."

"It's not just me?"

"You for Alan. Patrick in exchange for an indefinite postponement of Carrera's trial."

"You can't do that!" Dick's tone implied that Stephen could but should not.

"He read the firm's reports. He understood their value and demanded I have the charges dropped completely or he would take them to the FBI. The postponement is a compromise. I don't know how to comply with this demand. Can you think of anyone who could help us?"

"At this point in the investigation, even Hoover couldn't help you."

"Then what could we do, Richard?"

Dick considered this a while, then said, "Carrera's facing ten to fifteen years if the prosecution can make every charge stick. With time off for good behavior his term will be closer to six. For a guy like him that's no time at all. I think you can deliver better charges than theirs, yes?"

IV

The next morning, twelve Laborer's Union workers did not report to the Stoddard construction site. By afternoon, the project had lost an equal number of electricians and independent plumbers as well. After a quick call to Stoddard Design, the construction foreman sent the idle drywallers home.

Paul Stoddard calculated the losses of a lengthy slowdown. The financial ones hardly troubled him, but Stoddard Design had a reputation for always finishing buildings on schedule. The owners of the twin high-rise apartments had relied on this and started leasing one tower for January.

If the slowdown went on for any length of time, Paul would assure the owners that Stoddard Design would take responsibility for the tenants, even putting them up in hotels if necessary. That would appease everyone but himself.

* * *

Early that evening Elizabeth visited the site. She returned to the penthouse after midnight and discovered Paul and Judy waiting up for her. One shoulder of her red dress had been ripped, a fingernail was broken, and a thin streak of blood dirtied the back of her hand.

"The workers are being paid to stay away. The slowdown is related to the kidnapping," she told them. "When that's settled, this will be also. All the firm need do is wait a few days."

"We can work around the men who don't show. I'll check the schedule tomorrow."

"You were up at six, beloved. Stay home tomorrow and let someone else handle it."

"No!" Paul began, then, recognizing her concern, added, "I'll try to get home early, I promise."

Try. Promise. Elizabeth turned her back to him and poured herself a glass of ice water from the wet bar. She wasn't thirsty, she simply didn't want to look at him and think about how easy it would be to make that small subtle push and force him to slow down. It would be such a little thing—and such an immense betrayal. When she turned back, he was standing at the hall door. "I'll see you in bed, Elizabeth," he said and left without saying good night.

Elizabeth sat in the white brocade chair across from Judy, kicking off her heels and folding her legs under her. "Did you hear from Dick today?" she asked.

"No. I don't expect that I will any more than Paul will be home early tomorrow. Is he all right?"

"You've known him far longer than I have. Has he ever not taken things too seriously?"

"Is that all?"

"All? Judy, when he has these unforeseen setbacks, I feel the years pulling away from us. Tomorrow he'll be washing down aspirins and vitamins with quarts of coffee and perhaps, because he made a promise, he'll come home at five instead of six. No, his work habits aren't all of the problem, only the worst of it." She stared out the window at the city, then finished her glass. "I think I'll scrub off today's work and join Paul. There are other ways of relaxing, *oui*?"

"What happened to you tonight?"

"One of Vario's hoods got pushy. He won't try forcing himself on a woman again." She watched Judy's eyes widen and her lips turned up slightly as she added, "Not for a very long time."

TWENTY-FOUR

1

There were cops parked on Volpe's street when he was ready to drive into Cleveland for his meeting with Austin. They were always there, watching him with the same avid interest they had devoted to Jason Halli before his disappearance and were still devoting to Jimmy Bova, the Paytons, Joey Kelley, and some others known to be high in Carrera's organization. The cops drove Volpe crazy if only because their presence and the insults they called out when he passed them exposed him to questions from neighbors too naive to mind their own business. "I sell real estate," he told a father of one of his son's friends, trying to put just the right amount of indignant exasperation in his tone as he added, "This is the stupidity we get for our taxes."

The cops' presence made Volpe almost regret moving to Cleveland Heights. Almost, but not quite. He didn't want his kids playing on the streets with boys who worshiped Dillinger and Capone and who supplemented their allowances running deliveries for the guys, getting slowly drawn into the neighborhood web. And he didn't want either of them worshiping some future Carrera the way he had, seduced while still in grade school by the presence of so much power in a person lacking the strength or intelligence to truly wield it. Hell, Carrera had even supported his move, agreeing with him when Volpe had told him how good it looked for the real estate firm to have their chief agent living in a ranch in the suburbs.

Now, after weeks of overt surveillance, Volpe's indignation wore thin though his skill at eluding the police had improved. It took him less than five minutes to ditch his tail and he managed to arrive at the terminal restaurant early. Though he noticed Davey Payton and his nephew sitting at the bar—sent, no doubt, for his protection—he didn't speak to them as he waited for a booth near the back of the restaurant to be cleared and set.

As he followed the maître d' to the table, Stephen Austra caught up with him. Though Volpe should have expected it, he was surprised to see Dick Wells joining them. Though still as big a man as Volpe had been in his youth, Wells looked thinner than Volpe remembered with deep grey circles under his eyes. Probably not sleeping well, Volpe decided, and sympathized. This vendetta had been Carrera's doing, not his, and he had never supported it.

At the booth, he somehow found himself with his back to the entrance. He never liked sitting where he couldn't see who was approaching and now the two at the bar couldn't see his face or get the signal if he was in trouble. Wells was probably more paranoid. He certainly seemed to be as he sat in the corner, shaded by Volpe, shielded by Austra, his eyes sweeping the bar with the instinctive skill of someone used to thinking of himself as a target.

"Are the Paytons with you?" Wells asked him.

"In a way," Volpe admitted. "But I didn't ask them to come."

"Nice of your boss to watch out for you."

"Yeah, he's real thoughtful that way." The waiter came by and they ordered. Wells had a drink with his meal. Austra only requested black coffee and as he sipped it, he stared at Volpe with curious intensity. Volpe couldn't help himself. He kept thinking of everything he and Carrera had learned from Russ and stared back, trying to decide if any of it could be true.

Not human?

The idea was laughable, absolutely hilarious.

He actually chuckled at the thought, and as he tried to force himself back to a deadpan expression, he stopped breathing.

No pain in his chest warned him of a heart attack. He didn't feel as if he were choking. He simply forgot how to inhale.

His hands clutched his throat as the room began to spin. He was dimly aware of Wells and Austra helping him to his feet and dragging him into the men's room, of a loud knocking on the door and someone asking if he was all right. He managed to pull one deep breath but before he could call out the man went away and his throat closed again.

His heart began to race—from fear? Exertion? He leaned against the cold white tile wall and began to slide toward the floor when Austra straddled him and pulled him to his feet. Austra's hands pressed him back against the wall and Volpe stared blankly into Austra's eyes as if their dark centers were the only thing standing between him and death.

Then they pulled him down into the darkness of a closed coffin or a hasty makeshift grave, and for what seemed like eternity, only his nightmare was real.

He tried to pray but the words eluded him. He tried to feel remorse and discovered what he'd always suspected—salvation was not something he could buy from a priest on his deathbed. No, it had to be earned throughout his life.

And he had failed.

Hell opened for him. As he fell to a rush of heat, he tried to scream but the only sounds he heard were the echo of the agony rising to meet him and a distant, steady thumping like a hammer at the slaughterhouse coming down hard on the side of some doomed animal's head.

He wanted to present his case, to protest the verdict and the sentence, but when he tried he had no way to speak.

No breath.

Then everything grew black again, and in the distance he heard someone calling his name, splashing water on his face, beating him on the back. His eyes opened to the glare of the white-walled lavatory and focused on Dick Wells. "You all right?" Wells asked, leaning over him.

Volpe nodded and, when he was able, said, "Thanks."

"Thanks? Don't bother. I was thinking that if anything happened to you, my son wouldn't survive the night."

Volpe dried his face with the towel on the roll, then looked at himself in the mirror. He had a scratch over one eye and he wasn't surprised to see how flushed he'd become. "Where's Austra?" he asked.

"Your friends from the bar were concerned about you. Stephen decided he'd better join them outside."

Both guys were real hotheads. Volpe suspected that they probably didn't know anything about what was going on which would make them all the more dangerous. "We better go sit down," he said.

"You're sure you're OK?"

Volpe's shirt had stuck to his back. He smelled like he hadn't bathed in three days but he felt wonderful because his eyes were open and he had a brandy old-fashioned at the table waiting for him. "Yeah," Volpe said.

"Hot peppers," Wells commented.

"What?"

"You have hot peppers in your salad. My mother used to warn me, 'Never eat hot peppers. They can close up your throat.' Come on. Let's go."

The two men found Austra sitting at their booth with the Paytons. The pair looked far more cozy than they ever got with outsiders and Volpe wondered if they really gave a damn about him. After a few quick questions concerning Volpe's condition, the two men returned to their places at the bar. Volpe pushed his salad aside and canceled the rest of his order.

They discussed Carrera's case for a while. Wells and Austra seemed less interested in asking questions than in giving Volpe reassurance that a postponement would be announced, possibly as early as the next day, and in setting up a face-to-face between Austra and Carrera to discuss specifics of the trade.

As Volpe headed up the long white-walled tunnel from the train station to the sunlit Public Square, he began to walk faster. He felt younger, more alive than he had in years. And if he had been aware that his future had been ordered—compulsion and inclination perfectly matched—he might not have even cared.

Volpe rushed through his meeting with Carrera, managing to grin when he gave Carrera the news that destroyed every chance he had of leaving Carrera's grip in the foreseeable future. Carrera pulled a bottle out of the drawer along with two shot glasses and poured Volpe a drink. The schnapps went down easily, the mint soothing Volpe's sore throat, the alcohol making him oddly light-headed.

He supposed he had his own reason to celebrate. After all, this was his day of expiation.

As he turned onto his street, he drove close to the plainclothes officers staking out his house, softly calling a single request, "Arrest me."

"What?" the nearest officer said, not certain if Volpe had made a request or issued a challenge.

"Take me in. Do it now," Volpe responded. "I don't want my family to see me go."

The officers had enough sense to put on a good show, waving what looked like a warrant before they took Volpe away.

He wouldn't speak to any of them, waiting instead for Jacob Hamlyn, the special prosecutor assigned to Carrera's case. Then, along with insisting on immunity as Hamlyn had expected, Volpe made a stranger request. "They'll be other guys coming in, don't ask me how I know, I just do. But we're dead men, all of us, if Domie gets suspicious. Take the heat off of him. Postpone the trial and don't set a new date."

"I'll consider it. Want to talk?"

"Yeah. But not about your case. Other things."

The next morning, Davey Payton made overtures to another plainclothes officer, not the kind of self-incriminating revelations Volpe had made but enough to convince Hamlyn that he should take Volpe's request seriously.

II

By noon, a pair of plainclothes policemen disguised as fishermen were combing a wooded area along the Black River near Lagrange looking for a gun that had been used to wipe out a government witness in the Carrera case, a gun Volpe told them had been dumped there just a week before. When they found it, Hamlyn decided he'd seen enough. Following a few quick calls, he made the announcement—Carrera's trial had been put off. No, he wouldn't comment on when it would be rescheduled.

As insurance that Hamlyn wouldn't do an abrupt about-face, Stephen sent him one more compulsive confessor. When the news hit the evening paper, he and Dick phoned the number Volpe had given them.

As they expected, Carrera would not meet with Stephen again. But they had assumed Carrera would want to make the exchange of Wells for their sons in a private place, one where they'd have the advantage of the deadly Austra strength and speed.

But Stephen would be denied the slaughter, at least for a while. Carrera was too well informed to make so obvious a mistake.

"We do the switch tomorrow afternoon at three-thirty on the southeast corner of the Public Square," Carrera told Stephen. "You come as far as the Arcade just off the square, then send Wells on foot alone from there. The boys will start walking as soon as Wells does. Anybody crosses us, we'll shoot Wells and both kids."

Dick, who had been listening in on the conversation, took the phone from Stephen. "How do we know you'll let them go?" he demanded.

Carrera chuckled. "Of course I'll let them go. I have no use for them anymore. As for their silence, given the circumstances I don't think they'll talk to anyone. And tell Austra not to bother with another midnight visit. I won't know where your boys are until four-thirty tomorrow, Captain Wells."

"Now hold on. . . ." Dick began, but Carrera had already hung up.

Dick slowly lowered the receiver, his face rigid with shock. "Well, that takes care of any thoughts you might have had about taking on Carrera. Mass slaughter during rush hour is no way to keep your name out of the papers."

"I will find him tonight and learn where he intends to take you."

"Don't. If somebody sees you, Carrera will call off the trade. We can't put our kids in that kind of risk. We'll have to think of something else."

Stephen paced. Dick wasn't sure if it was affection for him that made Stephen so furious or the fact that he was being denied his victim, at least for the moment. Most likely, Dick thought with a trace of gallow's humor, Stephen felt a bit of both.

"We cannot allow this to change our plans. Carrera still has the reports, Richard."

"Find them after you have the boys."

"You have given up, yes?"

"I have. Maybe it's even for the better."

Stephen stopped pacing and stared at him, a long unblinking look that had all the warmth of an army inspection. "Do you think your death will be quick, Richard?" he finally asked.

"No," he said softly, but with no less determination to see it through. It would, he reflected, be a hell of a lot quicker than the other one.

"No," Stephen repeated. "Carrera almost understands what I am. He fears me. I've met men like Carrera. Hundreds of them. The questions will start as soon as he has you, Richard. And they will go on and on."

Dick exploded. "Damn you! I'm not your victim, stop torturing me! Wipe my mind clean the way you did Volpe's if you think I'll say anything."

"And I can feel it happening, if you will let me," Stephen went on as if Dick had not spoken. "This is not an easy thing for me to request but it is the only solution I can see—I want a part of me in you, something I can hold on to no matter how many miles come between us. I want to share my blood with you."

Dumbfounded by Stephen's suggestion, Dick sat looking at the carpet, finally responding, "I thought you never do this."

"Except for occasional victims, I never have. Given our friendship, experiencing your death will be an extreme form of self-abuse. I will feel it, Richard, exactly as I do when one of my own is destroyed. If there is pain, I will feel that. If there is fear, I will feel that too."

"And you're expecting plenty of both, right?"

"I think I can reach them before they kill you, Richard."

And claim his victim. After everything they'd been through, could Dick really deny Stephen this revenge? Honesty forced him to admit that even if his life wasn't at stake, he did not want to. "What will you do with the kids?" he asked. "You can't just drag them to the slaughter."

"Where do you think Carrera will take you, Richard?"

"The flats. He owns a number of warehouses along the Cuyahoga."

"Close to town, yes? We'll get a room in the hotel on the square. I'll hand the boys the key, send them upstairs, and get my car." Sensing Dick about to raise another objection, he added with obvious frustration, "All I'm asking is that you allow me to save your life, Richard."

"Before I decide, I want you to answer one question. If some stranger killed one of your sons in self-defense, what would you do?"

"In this era, in the same circumstances as Carrera, I can honestly tell you that I would do nothing. Richard, I am not the predator I once was."

"But you'll kill Carrera?"

"He deserves to die, yes?"

"I'll do it," Dick responded, surprised by his own lack of reluctance. "When do we have to start?"

"A few hours before the exchange. Novelty seems to make the bond tighter."

"Good. I want some time. First I want to call St. John's and arrange to go to confession tonight."

"You will not die tomorrow, Richard."

"Maybe not. But I'm like Volpe. I play it safe." Dick even managed a quick sincere grin. Now that the main decision had been reached, it was relief to be able to arrange the smaller details. "Then later tonight you and I are going to have that talk about death and souls that we've been putting off for the last three years. I thought we'd have it while we were in the mountains. Then Lowell intervened. Now I want to know even more, not just what you believe exists but everything that you can show me."

"And be convinced of your faith, yes?"

"I'll admit that I've been uncertain for years. I'd like to resolve the doubts."

Dick called the hotel operator and gave her the number of St. John's Rectory. As he waited for the connection, he asked, "Would you like to go to church with me?"

An expression akin to pain flashed on Stephen's face. Dick understood. Stephen had lost a friend at St. John's. Though the memory of the murder would stay with him forever, he did not need the reminder now.

"I would, Richard," Stephen said, then asked Dick to make a simple request. "When you speak to the pastor, ask that the east door to the choir loft be left open. The evening light through the rose window will feel wonderful."

"Like home?"

The instant Dick said the words he regretted them. But though the new memories were even more painful than the old, Stephen merely replied, "Yes, like home."

She'll be all right, Dick thought. *She can't have endured this much to have it . . .*

"Nas szekornes, Richard. We survive."

They purchased two nights at the Sheraton Hotel in the terminal, then pocketed their keys and drove to St. John's. Once inside, Stephen padded silently down the dark aisle and up the stairs to the loft.

Dick approached the confessional with dread. Like Volpe, he'd become sick of the killing, and like Volpe, he knew much more would come. He wished Father O'Maera were here so he could explain everything. The new pastor, young and idealistic, would never understand the shades of evil Dick faced. He might have told the truth to a strange priest but he could not bear to do so to one who knew him. As he looked, perhaps for the last time, at the glory of the windows around him, he began to understand that this place would give him as well as Stephen the strength he would need tomorrow. Stephen and his brother had created these windows, giving homage to a god they did not worship, a treasure to a race that might one day destroy them, an offering of hope for their shared world.

The new pastor was waiting for him. He wore blue jeans with the black shirt and white collar, the stole around his neck the only sign of his priesthood. He looked at Dick with concern and sympathy. "Would you prefer the confessional or to sit with me in the sacristy?"

Dick heard the creak of a hinge on an upstairs door and nothing more. He wanted privacy beyond Stephen's polite attempts to not hear. "The sacristy, please," he said and followed the pastor toward the front of the church. At the altar he turned and saw Stephen's head and shoulders outlined in the light at the base of the great rose window. *Trust*, he thought and turned to follow the priest.

"So you have come back?" the pastor said. "How is the family?"

For a moment Dick didn't know how to answer, then the grief of that simple question caught in his throat. He took a deep breath and plunged. "Bless me, Father, for I have sinned . . ." And as the last of the daylight faded, Dick told what he could of the kidnapping, his plans, even the doubts that followed the doctor's verdict. The penance seemed strange, though appropriate, Dick must not think beyond tomorrow until the day had ended. "It is not your decision to live or die, but God's. Now recite the Act of Contrition," the priest concluded.

As Dick said the prayer and heard the final words of the sacrament, it seemed that the power of grace descended on him as something tangible, a feeling he had not experienced since he'd been a small boy first taking the communion host.

As he left the priest standing near the altar and walked toward the door where he'd entered, the priest called after him, "I'll leave both doors open tomorrow." Dick turned back to thank him and saw that the pastor was looking to the shadows beyond him as if he sensed what other troubled soul shared the comfort offered by St. John's.

TWENTY-FIVE

1

In the two days since Russ phoned Carrera, he had left the warehouse a number of times but always returned within a half hour. But now, with the exchange set for tomorrow afternoon, he had to make arrangements to get the boys across the border. The details would take time—he didn't know how long, but Helen was certain, this would be her last chance to escape before he left with the boys. Even before he began getting ready for the trip, she'd found someone to untie her. As soon as he left, she began to call.

Jean Venault was seventeen, athletic with dark good looks and a habit of thinking in both English and French. He'd been returning from a vacation with school friends in Manitoba. His parents had not wanted him to go, but he had pointed out, correctly his mother decided, that a son old enough to attend a college six hundred miles away was certainly able to handle a three-week trip on his own. Though he'd promised to budget his money, his entire plan consisted of sticking forty dollars in the bottom of his clothes bag. On the day before he started home, a problem with the motorcycle drained nearly all of it. Instead of phoning his parents for help, he'd borrowed just enough for food and gas from his friends and rode for twenty hours straight until exhaustion made further travel impossible. With three hundred more miles to travel and a few precious dollars in his pocket, he'd

come down to the old docks hoping to find an open warehouse where he could park his cycle and sleep. He'd discovered only a bare mattress in the shell of a trailer behind a
burned-out fishery. Though he'd parked the cycle close to the
trailer, the drunks who called that trailer home had opened
his gas tank and filled it with dirt and stones.

Now Venault stood beside the cycle, his dark hair beaded
with the growing evening fog, pulling tools from the cycle's
storage bin, cursing his own stupidity and the distant thunder
that threatened rain the minute he began pulling the tank.

A warehouse down the road caught his attention. It had a
recessed door where he could work, and as he pushed the
bike closer to it, he noticed fresh tire tracks in the thin layer
of dirt that had accumulated in front of its doors. If the place
was still used, it might have a night watchman. He could ask
permission to park inside and do his repairs. With luck, he'd
get a cup of coffee and something to eat out of it, maybe even
some gas to get the bike to the nearest station.

Though the outside padlock made it unlikely anyone was
working now, he pounded on the warehouse doors anyway.

—Jean.— Did someone call him? He thought he heard his
name.

—Jean Venault, help me.—

His name!

He walked around to the side of the building and saw the
barred windows. His curiosity had long ago reached its limits
and he parked the cycle close to the wall. Gripping a flashlight, he balanced on tiptoe on the cycle seat and played the
beam through the room until he found a woman lying on the
floor, her hands tied above her. He was no fool. He knew
why a woman would be naked and tied like that.

As he scanned the room looking for the rapist, the woman
turned her head toward the light and her eyes seemed to focus
on his as if she could see his face in spite of the blinding
beam. Jean Venault had never seen anyone so beautiful or in
so much pain.

—Jean Venault, I am alone now. Help me.—

He looked up and down the deserted street and saw no one
who could go for the police. He knew he should make the

long run up to the main road and flag down a car but he sensed this was not the help the woman wanted. Young and romantic, he did not question his impulse when he found a piece of scrap metal and began prying the hasp off the doors. The bar slipped and broke, its rusty edges making a deep, jagged cut on his palm. After wrapping his hand in his handkerchief, he pulled a file out of his tool kit and began sawing through the padlock.

How much time had passed, Helen wondered? How much longer before he freed her? Should he continue his work or go for help? Instinct would not answer Helen's questions, not this time.

II

By the time Russ had picked up the boat, the storm had broken. More show than rain, the choppy waters of the St. Clair and the flashes of lightning made Russ uneasy. He steered the boat as close to shore as he dared, hoping that the old buildings would draw any stray bolts away from him.

The warehouse was located on a sharp outward bend in the river enabling anyone approaching by boat to view the front of the building as well as the rear. Though Russ could not see Venault, the lightning did reveal the cycle parked beside the building. Russ put in at an old pier a hundred yards upriver. Slipping a rope and a pair of handcuffs into his jeans, he grabbed a wrench from the boat's toolbox and, keeping close to the neighboring buildings, moved in for the kill.

Venault was so intent on the work that he didn't notice Russ coming up behind him. Helen, concentrating on holding the man's obsession, detected Russ too late. Though she sent a quick warning, Venault's response only meant that Russ had to hit him twice instead of once before Venault, unconscious, slipped out of Helen's grasp.

Russ dragged the young man inside, then wheeled in the cycle and went for the boat, pulling it into the dock beneath the warehouse. By the time he returned, Venault had staggered to his feet and, dazed by the blow, looked numbly at his surroundings and Helen. Venault reacted only when Russ turned on the cycle's headlight and, knife in one hand, approached him. The Canadian backed away, one hand outstretched in an impotent attempt to ward off Russ's attack.

Russ responded by lowering his arms. Venault, confused, did the same and Russ had him, sinking the blade deep into Venault's stomach, following with a quick upward thrust. The cut was skillfully done, not deep enough to reach an artery nor high enough to touch the heart but just enough to assure that Jean Venault would never leave the warehouse alive.

Russ didn't bother to watch him fall. Instead he spun and faced Helen. "You!" he said, the single word drawn out in an entire breath as he advanced on her. She sensed the full force of his rage, and as she steeled herself for the attack, she heard Patrick's angry shriek, piercing even through the thick closed door. "Tell him to shut up or so help me, I'll kill him," Russ said.

A lie. She knew that Carrera demanded Patrick alive.

A second shriek was accompanied by a loud thud against the door. Though Helen tried to divert his attention from her son, Russ unlocked the door and pulled it open.

And was hit full force by a twenty-pound toddler who, oblivious now to any need to hide, had eyes dark as a hunting cat at midnight and fingers curved and hard. Russ, one side of his face gouged and bleeding, managed to kick the boy away only to see him whirl and advance once more.

If Patrick had been an Austra adult he would have killed or disabled Russ by now but his body was light and weak and far too slow. Russ lunged past him, pulling Alan through the doorway, pressing the knife against Alan's throat, keeping the older boy between himself and Patrick. "Come any closer and I'll kill him, so help me."

Patrick, on all fours, took one step toward Russ, then raised his head. The scent of blood was all around him but, overpowering it, was the welcome wave of his enemy's fear. That he had done this all by himself gave Patrick a thrilling surge of self-confidence and he looked at Russ and grinned, his long cat's teeth drawing Russ's eyes to his face. His mind extended, instinctively trying to trap and paralyze his victim.

Alan felt the unfocused buzzing in his head, even Venault responded with a gasp of surprise. For an instant Russ relaxed his grip, then deliberately tightened it. Alan cried out with pain.

Patrick padded backward and moved closer to Venault. His still-forming senses were drawn to the young man's agony, the scent of his blood caused spasms of unfamiliar hunger deep inside him. Denied the life of his chosen victim, his body's new demands must still be met.

Russ laughed. "You want him, don't you? Go on, you little animal. Let me see you feast."

Patrick stared at Venault lying helpless, shivering in a spreading pool of blood. As Patrick moved a step closer to him, he felt his mother silently warn him back. A few days ago he would have run to her, clinging to her, begging her to help him. No longer. This decision was his, his alone.

"You want him?" Russ taunted Patrick. "Take him. I even cut your food for you."

The words meant nothing to Patrick. Oblivious now to Venault's agony, his mother's advice, or Alan's shocked cry; oblivious to even the hunger inside him, Patrick stared at Russ Lowell. For the first time, he saw good and evil as absolutes separate from himself and his needs, and he sensed in a way he could scarcely understand that he faced the first great turning point of his life. Determined to choose wisely, his mind became a tapestry of Russ's cruelty, his mother's resolve, and Alan's shocked denial. As he moved from one mind to another, he noticed Alan hold out his hand, palm up, offering himself in Venault's place.

There was a willing victim. He did not need to destroy.

Russ used Patrick's moments of indecision to jerk Alan's hands behind his back and attach the cuffs. When Patrick still hadn't moved, Russ sneered, "You little shit. You're just a baby. You don't know what the hell killing's all about." He dragged Alan across the floor and unlatched one of the trapdoors with his heel before risking a quick bend to pull it open. "Come on, Patrick Austra. Get in the boat. We have to go now." When the boy didn't obey, he pressed the knife tighter against Alan's throat, breaking the skin. "Come on.

You do like I say and I won't hurt you, or him either. You have my word on that.''

Without giving any indication that he'd heard, Patrick padded to his mother and, pressing close to her, ran his fingers down the side of her face and opened his mind to her silent advice. —Go with him. Don't let anyone see you the way you are now. You'll be home with Dickey and Father in a few days. I will be, too. I promise you.—

Promises were always kept but he sensed that she was not completely certain about this one. She kissed his cheek and, with a quick mental caress, withdrew from his mind. Patrick, still tensed and ready to fight, walked a slow wide circle around Russ and climbed down the ladder into the hold. ''Move into the room at the front,'' Russ yelled down, trying to keep his voice even, convincing himself that he was still in charge. ''And get back from the door!''

When Patrick had done as he'd ordered, Russ carried Alan down the ladder. Taking no chances when they reached the bottom, he kicked Alan into the hold and locked the door, sliding a bar across it for good measure before returning to the warehouse.

''That's a slave ship, Helen Wells. The hull is lined with sheet metal. The portholes have bars. When guys pull a double cross and run north, we hunt them down and ship them across the lake in it. Don't worry about the boys. Domic's sending them home. Worry about yourself.''

He moved the cycle so its headlight beam would fall across the length of Helen's body and looked down at her face. Though she kept her expression as impassive as ever, she knew with perfect clarity that he intended to shoot her.

He felt so clever about his plan. He had every detail fixed in his mind. He'd shoot the bullets into her chest, being careful not to hit the heart. She'd sleep just like she had before and when she woke, he'd be back here waiting for her.

So would Stephen. Patrick would tell him and he'd come.

Helen didn't want Stephen to rescue her, didn't even want him nearby when she killed this animal. No, Russ Lowell must be hers alone and she saw only one course to assure it.

With every bit of power she possessed, she pushed her alien seductiveness to its limits and thrust herself into his mind.

As she moved through him touching every nerve, he could feel a dozen lascivious hands and lips brushing his skin, caressing, kissing. And when he thought that like the first time he'd come in pants he felt a pressure inside him, holding him back. She had never done anything like this to him before. No one ever had! Panting, he dropped the gun and crouched beside her, untying the gag with shaking hands, kissing her in return. She responded so perfectly that he longed to cut her bonds and feel her willingly move beneath him. With effort, he kept his hands away from his knife and concentrated on the supreme pleasure of her helplessness.

She waited until he was inside her, pounding her with a passion that seemed to have no conclusion. Then as he kissed her, swearing in his mind that he loved her, would always love her, she jerked her head sideways and sank her teeth deep in his shoulder, deliberately hard, magnifying the pain. Confused, still wanting her, he pulled back and looked at her face. Lips, smeared with his blood, turned upward into a scornful smile of victory.

And without a word she made her final, desperate move. She drew on all the rage she had hidden for days and let the beast inside her loose—not at Russ because she had no way of attacking him, but into him. The skilled mental hands departed with a quick painful crack like a whip across his nerves. His prick went slack.

—Come on. Come on. Come on, you sadistic son of a bitch. Come on. Forget the gun. Use your fists, your knife. I'm helpless. Rip me apart.—

Silent laughter filled his mind. Vocal laughter echoed off the empty walls around him. With a low growl, he attacked.

Helen felt the first deep plunge of his knife, the second. No more. She need not have worried about lack of courage. Her body knew what must be done and allowed it to happen, automatically deflecting only a few thrusts, drawing the blade to the places most in need of damage, forcing him to strike again and again, slashing her chest, her breasts, stabbing her bound and helpless limbs, annihilating her body.

When he'd finished, he sat back on his heels, his clothes soaked with her blood. Only her face and head and stomach were untouched.

He held a palm to her open lips and felt no breath. He pressed two fingers against the side of her neck and detected no pulse. He'd wanted so much more than this. So much. One single sob was all he allowed himself before he pulled away and coldly began wiping down the padlocks and the cycle, every smooth surface he might have touched. Then, with one final glance at the bloody mass that had once been his greatest prize, he crawled down the ladder onto the boat and began to cry for all the time she had forced him to destroy.

And her lover, the father who looked so much like his deadly offspring, would hunt Russ down.

Unless Russ stopped him.

III

Patrick had felt the entire attack. Now he lay pressed against Alan, his teeth deep in Alan's shoulder, satisfying the hunger so much misery had aroused. Alan tried to shake him off but the boy only held him tighter.

"Patrick. Patrick, stop!" Alan said in a frantic whisper. He'd even taken a deep breath to call to Russ for help when Patrick abruptly let him go and turned to face the door, sitting motionless, unblinking eyes fixed on it.

"Patrick, what is it?" Alan asked.

"Russ." The boy frowned, trying to make sense of what he'd learned, then settled for repeating Russ's thoughts in a wooden tone that made them all the more horrible, "I don't give a damn what Domie says. I'll kill the fucker. I know where to shoot."

"You?" Alan asked and, receiving no answer, asked again, "Me?"

"Papa," Patrick said, his face still turned to the door.

Alan had no idea how to warn Stephen. They'd tried to call his father for help a dozen times over the last few days and every attempt had failed. As the boat pulled away from the dock and into the center of the choppy river, Alan wedged himself into a corner and tried to come up with a new plan.

Then Patrick was pressed against him, his hands on either side of Alan's face. Assuming Patrick intended to reach his mother, Alan closed his eyes and steeled himself for her agony. But though Patrick had physically matured, he was still just a small child and he'd had enough of the adventure and the danger, enough of the pain. What followed next would have been impossible for even the strongest Austra adult but Patrick, who had not been instructed in what was possible and what was not, used every shred of human power in his soul. Eyes closed, barely moving, he merged with Alan. Drawing on Alan's energy as well as his own, he soared north and west, looking for the clearing, the cabin, his brother, home!

IV

Donna woke suddenly, feeling hot and sweaty in spite of the cold night draft blowing through the house from the open front door. Though she'd bolted it, Dickey must have managed to reach the lock so he could go hunting again.

His father had said Dickey behaved like a normal toddler. Granted, the first two nights had been normal. Then he'd slept for hours until, tired of waiting for him to get up for his night feeding, she'd gone to bed herself. Sometime while she was sleeping, he'd left the house. When she discovered that he was missing, she had stood outside in the frosty night air calling to him, hearing his high-pitched peals of laughter flowing down from the ridge. When she'd gone running after him, the deep growl of the wolf warned her back. On the second night, she called again and only the wolf answered. Each time she'd sat up until dawn, frantic with the worry that he'd get lost or killed and she'd be left alone to face his father's wrath. Both times, he came home at dawn covered with something else's blood, looking wonderfully satisfied.

Normal, hell! With a groan of frustration, she rolled out of bed. Well, his father could never accuse her of not trying to get him back. She pulled on her jacket and went outside.

This time Dickey waited for her at the edge of the moonlit clearing, standing upright with one steadying hand on the back of the wolf. Deep gashes crisscrossed on his bare stomach and she saw scratches on his cheeks. Whatever he'd killed tonight had fought back. Judging from the smell of it as he rushed past her, it had been a pretty nasty beast.

When Donna joined him, he was in the kitchen trying to clean himself off with a damp washcloth. He flinched and refused to look at her though he did cooperate when she pumped water into the sink and bathed him. She changed the water twice before she decided he was clean. By then the wounds had already begun to heal and she didn't even bother to bandage them before she carried him to bed with her. "I'm a light sleeper, Dickey Austra. You move and I wake, understand." She rolled him over so his back pressed against her chest. Holding him tightly, she slept.

And dreamed of Alan and Patrick here and talking to her and Dickey. Patrick looked different somehow, older and stronger, and when she looked at his face she saw that his teeth, like his brother's, had grown. Though she listened carefully, she couldn't make out the words they spoke. Finally she stopped trying. This was her dream, after all, and she was too much in need of sleep to really care.

She woke at dawn and, pleased to see Dickey still motionless beside her, rolled over and closed her eyes again.

Late that morning Dickey's wail of anguish woke her. All toddler now, he sat with his lower lip jutting and eyes filled with angry misery. "Dickey, what's wrong?" Donna asked.

"Patrick changed too!" he whined.

"What?"

"I saw him in the dark. He changed too."

"Like teeth and everything?"

Dickey nodded and buried himself under the blankets. Donna pulled them off. "Did Patrick talk to you?" she questioned. He pulled at the blanket and she jerked it out of his hand, demanding, "Tell me!"

"Not just me," Dickey responded.

Donna remembered.

She found Dickey some clothes and drove as fast as she was able to the nearest phone.

V

This is the way Helen should have been born—with a body as strong as her mind.

No matter, the strength would come now. Unconscious, barely breathing, she felt the power moving through her like liquid fire. Her heart had instinctively slowed, halting the bleeding so the healing could begin.

She had no idea how much time had passed before the first spasms of hunger hit. She had expected them but she had never guessed they would be this potent, this painful. Their pounding reality kept her from focusing on anything but her waiting victim.

—Jean Venault, come to me.— She forced him back to consciousness and repeated, —Come!—

Venault moaned, a sound so soft she could scarcely hear it at all, then began a long slow crawl across the floor. She sensed his will drawing him forward. He wanted to touch her just once before he died.

The attraction that had always been such a nuisance to control had never seemed as important as it did now. Though she sent him more encouraging words, her thoughts were darker and far more frantic. *Slowly, Jean. Slowly. Please don't die before you reach me. Please!*

He lay motionless, collecting his strength, then with one final surge of will forced himself to slide the last few feet, lying on top of her, the day's growth of beard on his face scratching at the raw wounds on her chest. He felt so lovely, so perfectly alive.

—Kiss me.—

He had to move up to reach her face. Her body was slippery with blood and his weakness made it impossible for him to grip her and pull himself higher. He tried once and his wound opened. His soft whimpering echoed from the walls like the ghosts of those who died here before him. He choked the sound back and, in spite of the pain, drew his knees to his chest and pushed, balancing his entire weight on top of her as his lips touched hers.

She apologized as she kissed him, then stole his pain and willed him to sleep. His head lolled backward and with effort she raised hers and tore at his neck until what remained of his blood began to flow.

When life had ended and he lay dead and cooling above her, she continued to drink, trying to fill her body's relentless demands.

PART FIVE

EXECUTIONER

TWENTY-SIX

1

On the way back to the hotel, Dick stopped for takeout from a Chinese restaurant. Later, after he'd showered off the day's stickiness, he stretched out on one bed eating alternately from the containers of rice and chop suey. Stephen sat cross-legged on the other, sipping a glass of the salty Tarda water the family imported from their homeland. He had placed the bottle on the bedside table for he planned to be awake and talking throughout the night.

Their conversation seemed dark to Stephen, filled with memories of his victims and friends as his mind brushed past the cause of each death to describe the moments, those glorious moments when, for an instant, the darkness parted to admit each desperate soul, giving him a brief glimpse of that other eternity.

"And then you turn away?" Dick asked.

"If we seek death, we find her, Richard. We even tell our children a variant on the story of Lot's wife, turned into a pillar of salt because she *saw* too much. We don't really have to warn them; their instinct serves them just as well."

"Show me what you can of it. Please."

Stephen reached out and grasped Dick's wrist, wincing as he saw Dick flinch. "I'm sorry," Dick said. "Old fears are the hardest to overcome."

"I understand. Close your eyes, Richard. Try to let me in your mind."

* * *

It began with a tickle like a faint breeze. As the breeze grew, more of his senses were blown away until all that was left of his body and this room was the warmth of Stephen's hand on his wrist, the comforting presence of Stephen's mind supporting him. No sooner had he grown accustomed to the emptiness surrounding him than some unseen force grabbed him, pulling him down into a darkness so thick it pressed against him. He began to struggle, fighting to breathe, and felt the hand holding him tighten.

—Is this where you bring your victims, Stephen?—

—Yes, but they find no solace in me, Richard. My friends do.—

A pause, how long Dick could not determine, and his consciousness was rocked as if by a wave or gust of wind. A grey line cut the darkness of this strange silent world and dawn rose to meet him. A flash of brilliant white rolled across the emptiness and over him. Had his eyes seen this, he would be blind now, rejoicing forever in the rapture of his last moment of vision. But only his soul saw, only his soul responded with a great rush of joy. He wanted to run after this force and merge with it forever but another's will held him back, wrenching him away, retreating into the darkness that faded and faded into the dim light and grey shadows of their room.

He thought he'd been asleep for a few minutes, an hour at most. Six had passed.

He looked down at his wrist, saw dark bruises on it, and knew that he had struggled to die with the same passion he had always devoted to life. Stephen had his eyes closed, surrendering to the lethargy of the dawn. Though he knew he should also sleep, Dick lay awake a long time, sorting through the questions that came to him.

When Dick woke later that morning, Stephen still lay in the same position Dick had seen him in last, his breathing so slow and shallow that untrained eyes would mistake him for dead. Deciding he might as well get some breakfast, Dick changed into a clean shirt and took the car keys from Stephen's jacket. Before leaving, he carefully lifted one blind to scan the parking lot and saw two men sitting in a car at the edge of the drive where they could view both exits and Stephen's car.

Though he knew Carrera's men were only watching him, the weight of the revolver and the press of the holster against his shoulder and chest were familiar and comforting, a reminder of his position and his mission here.

A maid knocked on a door farther down the hall. Dick called her down and gave her two dollars for breakfast from the next door coffee shop and promised her another three when she returned. She must have assumed she was supplying Stephen as well because she returned with plates of eggs and potatoes, six slices of toast, and a thermos of coffee. Though Dick had intended to eat a light meal, the smell of fresh coffee made him realize he was famished. He'd just started in on the third slice of toast when Stephen opened his eyes and rolled up on an elbow.

"We've got company outside," Dick commented.

Stephen's eyes briefly unfocused, then returned to the room. "They've been out there all night. They'll be sound asleep when we leave. I'll see to it."

"Coffee?" Dick asked, thinking of Stephen's order in the terminal restaurant.

"Only when I must," Stephen responded and poured a glass of his cloudy water, finishing the second of the three bottles he'll brought with him. "You have questions about last night, yes?"

"Questions! I don't know where to start! One thing I can't understand is how you can go so close and not want to see what lies beyond that brightness."

"Death is there, Richard. Our instincts do not allow us to see her clearly."

"But all you have to do is just go forward."

"Believe me, Richard. If death were a simple act of will, my brother would not have needed our help so desperately."

"I suppose we each have our own eternity," Dick commented, the hint of an unvoiced question in his tone.

Mysteries such as God or even the origins of his own people were difficult for Stephen to contemplate. Unlike man who had to come to terms with personal death, Stephen didn't need belief in God or an afterlife to sustain him. However, he did respond with the one piece of faith centuries had forced him to admit, "I have felt souls, Richard. I know they exist. I know they survive. But my people and yours are so much alike that I do not think man was born to die."

"You said it: the soul survives," Dick responded, surprised by the surety in his tone.

"I am not speaking of the soul, Richard."

"Who knows, maybe in a hundred years or so some genius will figure out how to keep our bodies young forever." Dick smiled wistfully at the thought, then added a more realistic observation, "Well, I sure as hell wouldn't want to live with the crowd." He reached for another slice of toast.

"Save some of that, Richard. You'll be famished again in a few hours."

"It's time?"

"Soon."

"Have you done this before?" The question seemed ludicrous. In all those years, of course he had.

Stephen looked at the carpet, his face scarred by an old memory. "Only once."

"Once? Can you tell me about it."

Stephen did not look up. His mind focused on a world long gone as he began. "The boy's name was Ion . . ." He told the story woodenly, as if even after so many centuries, he was afraid to admit what he had felt. "In the end, I rushed down the mountain passes, through the drifts on the plains below, but I could not outrun his agony. My father was deliberately savage. I could tell you everything he did to Ion but none of it was important except how I felt his death. The part of me in him died too. A place of myself was missing." He met Richard's eyes, his face resigned, remote. "It still is."

Dick felt Stephen's mind touching his, the necessary tie between them beginning to form. "Listen, if I'm still alive tomorrow what happens to this bond?" he asked.

"It will remain for as long as you live. And I will be unable to go to a family blood sharing until after you die."

Not giving up much, are you? Dick thought, forgetting for a moment their growing mental rapport. He felt a response— irritation? anger?—and added vocally, "Even if it was only Patrick that they had and even if I were not to blame, I would still do this."

"And even if it were just Alan, I would do this. We're one family, Richard. We made that agreement years ago.

"A final warning, Richard. I understand how you feel about the attraction I cannot help but exude. Over the years we've been friends, I've kept a physical and mental distance from you. I can't do that now. I will merge with you as tightly as I would with one of my own and I will not allow you to change your mind or to hold any of yourself back. You understand, yes?"

"Yeah. You do what you have to do." Dick hesitated a moment, then, pleased that he would have so little time to reconsider the agreement, added, "I don't want to talk about it. Let's just get it over with." He closed his eyes and tried to pull all the conflicting emotions together. He'd rather face Carrera and whatever horrible death was planned for him than this—this potent reminder of an old nightmare.

"Look at me, Richard. You've known me long enough to trust me, yes?"

"I'm sorry." With effort, Dick stared at Stephen, allowing his self to be trapped by the will of his friend. Without moving his eyes from Stephen's face, he took off his cuff links and laid them on the table between the beds, then rolled up his sleeves. His hands moved to the button on his collar but he lowered them without touching it. *Please,* he thought, *not there; touch me somewhere less intimate, somewhere Charles had never touched.*

Stephen was surprised to see tears in Richard's eyes, a sign that his friend had never recovered from the hours of torment that his brother had inflicted on him. That Richard had somehow managed to bury his loathing and remain friends with Stephen was a sign of the justice in this man—and their shared ties. Stephen felt strengthened by the understanding. Ties were of the utmost importance now. Neither wanted anyone to threaten their family again.

As Stephen's mind moved through Richard, he sensed him fighting the invasion. If Stephen hadn't been so desperate, he would have abandoned his efforts but they had so little time. He rejected the idea of numbing Richard completely. He had to be awake and the taking volitional for the bond to form completely. Richard trusted him. Perhaps trust—a pale emotion compared to so many others—would be enough.

He touched that, only that, and felt Richard's complete confidence in him as if Stephen were far more powerful than he actually was. Richard expected a miracle. Stephen merely assumed that he could not fail. Enough, he decided. It would be enough. He knelt on the floor in front of Richard and lowered his head so that, for a moment, Richard could not see his face. With one rear fang, he made a deep cut across his wrist and held it out to his friend.

Like those games little boys play with razor blades and thumbs, Dick thought, seeking reassurance in the familiar as he looked at the cut on Stephen's wrist, the blood welling in bright beads that flowed together and dropped slowly down his outstretched arm.

He hid from his panic, a fear that was, after all, only a memory, and reached for what was offered.

The bond already so tight pulled at Dick. He felt the spark of attraction flare into desire for what was offered, for the creature offering it, for the eternity he could never have.

He thought of Charles Austra, he could not help but think of him now. That thing in Charles Austra that had wanted to die, that had all its will directed to that end, had been no more able to accomplish it than Richard could cheat the end coming for him.

For the first time he knew exactly how Charles must have felt and he pitied Charles and himself. Since the doctor's verdict, he had not displayed any emotion save anger. He did now.

He cried.

—Richard?—

He felt Stephen pulling him closer, and his own lips, pressed to the wound, sucked harder, a demanding child seeking life.

It coursed in him, a rush of warmth and enduring passion!
As he surrendered completely to it, Stephen lowered his head
to the back of Richard's neck and began to drink, completing
the circle of give and take.

Dick felt himself weightless as if his body were no longer
a part of this act. As he lost all sense of time or place, even
the simple constants of up and down blurred. He knew where
he was from moment to moment only, then forgot, as the
nightmare from his past, in so many ways so similar to this,
was also forgotten.

Hours after they began, the phone rang. Though they knew
it must be the desk giving them their arranged call, they did
not move to answer it.

When they broke, Dick considered life the way he did
God—Eternal. Now.

And it went on forever.

II

As he fixed his shirt and slipped on the jacket, Dick noticed the way the different fabrics rubbed against his skin and
detected the lingering welcome scent of Judy's perfume. Stephen sat cross-legged on the other bed, appearing more sub-
dued than he had been since this ordeal began. "Do you need
anything before we go?" Dick asked.

It took several seconds before Stephen responded with a
slow shake of his head. Surprised to discover that he was
hungry, Dick turned his attention to the remnants of breakfast. Though the toast had long ago become dry, the butter
greasy, Dick spread a thick layer of jam on it and ate it in
slow, careful bites. He thought he'd never tasted anything
quite so interesting before.

The unique pleasure of these simple things had nothing to
do with imminent death. Rather, he perceived the world
through two minds. It had a sharp new clarity but a distorted
focus, as if life were presented in 3-D and he had forgotten
to bring his glasses.

The feeling didn't diminish as Stephen drove into town.
Instead it intensified. The smell of the exhaust fumes from

the cars around them made Dick faintly queasy, the drivers all seemed to be whispering to him. If Stephen concentrated, Dick would hear their thoughts but Stephen ignored them as he usually did, instead focusing on the ordeal to come. Dick wanted to do the same but everything seemed so wonderfully distracting. Even through his dark glasses, the green lawns, the flower beds, the sky, and the glimpses of the lake revealed nuances of color he'd never seen before. The road stretched forward, an iridescent ribbon of vibrating light and heat. Everything had become new and incredibly alive. No matter what happened today, he would enjoy these moments and he yielded to their strange magic until they reached town.

They parked in the terminal hotel lot, took an elevator to the basement, and cut through the underground train station next to the square. It seemed a better plan than the crowds and the sunlight and the risk of running into some of Carrera's men before the exchange.

They saw a policeman Dick knew standing beside the station news counter, and Dick pulled his hat low on his face as they walked a wide circle around him and into Higbee's department store. On the ground level, they cut through two more stores before crossing Euclid Avenue to the Arcade near the Public Square.

The buildings shaded the afternoon streets and only a few thin bands of searing sunshine still crossed Euclid Avenue. Nonetheless, Dick and Stephen stood in the deeper shadows of the Arcade, scanning the crowded street leading to the square. They identified three men who were with Carrera—one standing at the corner of the square where Dick was to surrender, another in a third-story window of the terminal, and Russ Lowell on the flat roof of a building across the street from the Arcade.

Stephen stared up at the monster who had brought so much misery to his family. This would be his chance, the only one he might have to destroy him. A single mental command would force Lowell to take the few steps forward, the fall to the pavement three stories below. Perhaps he'd live, lying helplessly in a hospital bed, a victim dreading the night Stephen finally decided to come for him. More likely he'd die from the fall. Stephen didn't mind making Lowell's end a quick one; after all, he most likely faced an eternity of pain. But as Stephen moved deeper into Lowell, he felt the obsessive need of the man, then saw Helen as Lowell had left her, the blood seeping from the cuts that crisscrossed her body, and he understood what she had done and why. He might have seen much more had he probed deeper, but then the rage he already had difficulty controlling would override his will and he would destroy Russ Lowell with no thought of the consequence.

He loved Helen too much to let her be any less than one of his own. No, he would not protect her any longer.

His nails dug into his palms, the self-inflicted pain restoring his control. With a quick, deliberate snap he pulled out of Lowell and turned to Dick who stood beside him, red-faced with fury at what they had shared.

—How can you see what he did to her and let him live?— Dick asked.

—Helen is no child. If I destroy him I will lose her, probably forever.—

—What if she can't kill him?—

—The boys will tell me where she is being held. They're coming. Can you feel them?

Dick could, and he saw them first, stepping out of the dark terminal entrance to the intersection on the northeast corner of the square. Patrick wore the suit Lowell had given him and he sat in Alan's arms, his eyes darting from person to person, looking for a familiar face in the crowd swirling around them.

No one noticed Dick walking forward, his expression remote and resigned, his eyes fixed on the car parked at the square, Volpe beside it waiting for him. Some glanced at the ragged boy who walked across the street with silent tears rolling down his face; more at the beautiful dark-haired toddler he carried. Only a few of the shoppers glanced curiously as Dick, waiting for the light to change, gave Alan a quick squeeze on the shoulder before he crossed the street.

No, they were oblivious to the drama taking place in their midst until the shots were fired.

In the joy of seeing his father, Patrick had forgotten to send his warning. Stephen, his mind still linked with Richard's, had fallen to one knee with his arms outstretched to lift his son from Alan's arms. On the edge of his vision, he saw the flash as Lowell's rifle fired and instinctively he moved backward though not soon enough. The bullet intended for the top of his spine hit his jaw instead. Spun by its impact, two more hit him in the back of the head. He felt Richard wrenched out of his consciousness, heard Patrick's shriek of rage, Alan's softer cry. A wave of despair and the distant wail of a siren carried him down and down into the darkness preceding death.

As soon as he'd fired, Russ stepped back from the edge of the roof, dropped the rifle, and walked to the fire escape. He climbed down one flight and through an open window. By the time he reached the car parked two streets over from the square, the faded grey jacket had been replaced by a blue sportscoat and tie and Russ looked no different from any professional man going home to his family after a short day's work.

While Russ made his escape, the crowd that had run from the street in terror slowly trickled back, forming a wide circle around the wounded man, the toddler silently trembling against the blood-soaked shirt and the older boy sobbing openly beside them.

At the square, unnoticed, a car drove off. Dick Wells sat in the rear with his head pressed against the front seat, numb to those on either side of him, the cuffs too tight on his wrists. Three shots. Perhaps three targets. And now he was alone and trapped and no one could save him.

TWENTY-SEVEN

1

Stephen waited.

For the first time in his centuries of existence, death had become an act of will and the pain and fear of certain discovery made him almost welcome it.

But for the first time in a thousand years, bonds stronger than instinct drew him back to life—his love and children.

No, in spite of the consequences, he would not choose to die.

He let his consciousness begin to fade, taking the pain with it, yielding his will to his body and its needs.

Dimly, he sensed someone bending over him, rolling him over. "Damn!" the man swore, his hand on Stephen's wrist, his neck, searching for a pulse. Stephen felt the heat of him as the man began to lower his head toward Stephen's chest, thinking he would listen for the slightest flutter of life, unaware that his own was about to end.

Closer. Closer and he would strike.

"Give it up. Nobody with head wounds like that can be alive. Cover him up and take him to the morgue."

The man moved away and Stephen did not have the stength to call him back.

No food!

Did they lock the corpses in their tiny drawers or would he be free to wake and call—the primitive mind of a bloody ghoul in search of life?

"I'll do the postmortem tonight."

The voice sounded familiar, the thought terrifying. If he could move, he would be able to grip this man, pull him close and feed. But he had not been wounded this dangerously in years and in the distant past they had always buried him and left him to the slow renewal of the earth. Now they would drain what was left of his blood, pump chemicals into his body, cut him open. He would never . . .

No! I survive.

But someone was already fumbling with his arm, a brief stab of pain hardly noticed among the rest, then relief. He tried to focus on the man beside him, to hold him back, but his mind must have been damaged because it didn't work. With effort he managed to move his head a few degrees, an almost imperceptible sign of life, then nothing.

Later, consciousness of a sort returned and his mind moved out to study the brightly lit windowless room. He saw himself lying on a long marble table. Shelves with clear glass bottles covered the wall. Someone probed his neck. He felt a quick cut, a tube being forced into him. They'd have to do the autopsy first, wouldn't they? He moved his head again, trying to show that he was alive, but though the person beside him must have seen, he continued with his work. Then blood began to flow into his body—cold, lifeless as if he sucked the remnants of a day-old corpse. Yet it was blood and it did nourish beyond what he would have been able to do on his own. His heart responded by increasing its beat. His mind grew stronger.

And his body began its relentless demand for life. Soon the need would override all control and he would have no choice but to kill.

The man fumbled at his wrist again. The liquid stopped, then started. The sheet covering him was removed. Fear. He felt the man's fear the way he felt his face re-forming, his mind growing sharper. Soon he would be strong enough to call and feed.

And when he woke would he be beside the corpse of his victim? In a hospital bed? In a cell? No matter. His instincts would take control soon and nothing he could do would alter their course.

"Just lay still. The daytime help has all gone home. We're alone for a while. I'll do what I can for you."

The voice! Stephen knew the voice. If he could only remember. His mind seemed clearer now, clear enough to question. —Why?—

"I'm John Corey. Dick's friend, remember?"

—Need . . . blood.—

"I have more. As much as you need."

—Dead . . . not dead.—

"Dead?" Confusion. Understanding. A sudden surge of delicious fear. "It's all I have except for myself."

—Kill. I must kill.—

He felt the body move away in justified caution, the loss of its heat and scent already troubling. "Does the blood have to be human?"

—Alive.—

"Hold on," Corey said. "Give me a little time. There's a lab upstairs. They keep all kinds of animals. I'll bring a cage." He moved back farther as he spoke, ready to turn and run as fast as his heavy body would allow. Stephen still didn't have half his face. How could he bite? One more step. Another and Corey would bolt for the hall.

But the shape of the room had shifted. The door had become smaller, miles away at the edge of a long tunnel, and he and the body on the table were at the beginning, together, alone. Corey smelled himself—the fear, the alien blood on his hands. He sensed the other—the horrible need that reached out to him demanding to be filled. Ropes whirled around him, cutting off all sights but the body whose hunger could not be appeased with anything but Corey's life.

Something ancient, predatory, merciless, was here with both of them and neither he nor Stephen had the means to hold it back.

Corey took a step toward the table. Another. And halted—frozen, ready for the beast to begin to drink. His heart beat faster as if his body was building pressure, preparing to meet this creature's needs.

He did not know how long he stood, his body the waiting meal, before he lowered his head, turned it sideways, and felt the warm, welcome breath on his neck.

Then Corey sensed something he'd never noticed before: the air currents shifting in the room as the main door into the morgue opened and closed.

Stephen must have sensed it as well because the hold on Corey broke and Corey could see the room as the room always appeared—white enamel and polished marble tables, the huge plain clock on the walls charting the passage of lives, and the door that a moment before had been cracked open now swinging inward.

Will Bowen looked startled to see him, then a bit sad. Corey glanced at the hammer in one hand, the stake and autopsy saw in the other.

Corey was no fool. He had been warned years ago about the risks to himself if he tried to help Austra, even knew enough to hold Austra without blame for whatever his instinct demanded. But this? He looked at Will with frank disgust. "That would be murder, Will."

"He was dead already. You said so."

"I was wrong," Corey replied, knowing how foolish he must sound.

"Were you? Then why is this patient being treated by a coroner instead of upstairs in the hospital with a real doctor?" Will raised the crowbar, ready to strike if Corey tried to stop him from approaching the table. "Come on, Cor. How many people did this thing kill on its last pass through town?"

Corey and Will had been friends for the four years Will had worked for him as assistant homicide examiner. Corey was a family man so Will got the three to midnight shift until today when Corey had pulled rank and sent him home. Though Will was one of the last people Corey would have pegged for Carrera's payroll, he had to be on it. How else could he have known what Austra was? "How much does Carrera pay you, Will?" Corey asked.

Will took another step toward the table. "Just let me finish this and I'll forget you ever said that."

Corey stepped backward, hitting the table. "Carrera asked me once, Will. I turned him down."

"I didn't." Will swung, and though the bar hit Corey, it didn't do the damage Bowen had expected. Stephen had reached out one long arm, grabbing Will's wrist, deflecting his blow, then tightening the grip, dragging Will toward the table. In spite of Will's attack, Corey tried to pull him loose. Then the thing that had been Stephen seized him as well. Corey closed his eyes and, concentrating on his friendship for Dick and for Helen, held himself icy calm until he felt the grip on his wrist slacken enough that he could pull away.

The crowbar fell from Will's numb fingers and Will, shaking, looking to Corey as if he were ready to scream from terror for the first time in his life, was pulled toward the gaping, bloody jaws.

It was too late to find a substitute for human life. Corey knew it even before Stephen used his free hand to rip a hole in Will's neck, his palm under Will's chin, holding back the head so the wound stayed open, dripping into his mouth. With the same detached curiosity that made him so good at his work, Cor watched the shell of Stephen's face move as it re-formed until, able to suck the life from his victim, Stephen pulled Will against him.

And Will was still alive! Mute, hopeless terror in his eyes as they silently begged Corey to save him.

Corey couldn't save anyone, not anymore. "I'm sorry, Will," he said, turned his back on the table, and headed for his desk and the bottle he kept in the back of the lower drawer. He remembered falling into his chair, then nothing.

Corey woke to the sight of a covered body resting on the table. Already guessing who had died, he pulled down the sheet and looked at what was left of Will Bowen.

The crowbar lay where Will had dropped it and Corey glanced down the hall at the open doors, then back at his desk where a small puddle of blood had formed from the cut Will had opened on his head. He sensed the messages left in his mind. The first would be a logical one in more normal circumstances—*call the police*. The second—*make a statement to the press*—seemed less so.

Before he reached for the phone, he made a thorough visual inspection of the body. "Yeah, Cor," he said out loud to himself. "You tell the cops they cut his throat. Fine. Now how do you explain where all of Will's blood went?" Corey looked down at the table. A piece of Will's neck had been gouged away, probably the spot where the teeth marks would have shown. The blood on the floor had vanished, washed down the sewer drain, diluted beyond recognition. Even the marble table seemed meticulously clean. "Well, Stephen Austra, you've survived all these years on a hell of a lot more than luck. I'm betting my professional ass on it." Corey removed a suspicious drop of blood from the edge of the table, rehearsed his story through once, then buzzed upstairs, alerting the building to the break-in.

No, he hadn't seen anything, he told the first officers assigned to the investigation. He'd been working, Bowen had joined him. Someone must have broken in and attacked them. Bowen had probably died while defending himself, most likely from the original murderer. No, he wasn't sure who hit him. But who else would want the victim's body and take the time when they were done to wash the room clean of evidence?

Through his alibi, Corey was constantly aware of the passing of time, constantly praying that Stephen would recover completely and find Dick before Carrera killed him.

After the doctors examined him and a nurse taped the cut on his head, after he'd given a statement to the press, Corey was sent home. Instead of going there, he stopped at a sporting goods store and bought a black knit turtleneck and slacks in slim extra-long. He suspected that Stephen would need them, and though he couldn't be certain, Corey thought he had a good idea where Stephen had gone.

11

St. John's Church with its healing family windows had just discharged the handful of faithful from its evening Mass when Corey arrived. He waited near the back doors until the voices inside died away, then climbed the narrow winding stairs to the choir loft.

Stephen lay on the floor behind the top benches, bathed in the waning light of the rose window, hidden from anyone but those who would know where to look. He heard Corey coming and sat up slowly as Corey slipped into the top pew and sat a few feet from him. Corey thought the missing corpse seemed a bit dazed and decided the healing might not be quite complete. Stephen still wore his own ripped and bloody pants covered with a white lab coat he'd stolen from the morgue. Corey laid the clothes between them.

Corey expected Stephen to ask questions about his presence here and downtown this afternoon but Stephen only asked, "Patrick and Alan, where have they been taken?" Again Corey was struck by how still Stephen sat, how when he talked only his lips moved.

"I sent my musses to pick them up. I hear that Patrick was a real stoic down at the police station. No matter what they asked, he kept his mouth shut. When Judy phoned me this afternoon, she said she and Elizabeth were on their way. They'll probably take the kids to Dick's place."

"That's good," Stephen said softly.

"What about Dick?"

Stephen tersely explained what they'd done, concluding sadly, "Since I came here, I've tried to reach him but I can't. Now that the tie is broken, I can only wait for them to begin the execution. Then I will feel his pain and follow it to him."

"How do you know that they won't just shoot him and be done with it?"

"You made the statement to the news, yes? When Carrera hears of it, he'll know I am hunting him. He will want to learn everything he can about me. He has no one to ask but Richard and Richard will not cooperate."

"Damn you. You should have let them kill him. It would be quicker and cleaner than what he's facing."

"No! I will not allow him to die without a fight. His fight. Mine."

"That isn't your decision to make."

"It became our decision when he agreed to share my blood. Besides his family is not safe until Carrera is dead, yes?"

Corey's silence gave a reluctant agreement and Stephen

commented, "I can't be certain but I believe that Richard is being held in the flats somewhere. They intend to kill him tonight. Carrera will be present. I made sure of this the day we met. How many others do you think there will be?"

"This isn't a time for Domie to get cocky. Two or three. He won't let any more in on what he's doing."

"An easy fight."

"You don't sound confident."

"I'm confident I can kill those men. My only fear is that I will not get to Richard in time."

"Let me help. I've got a station wagon parked outside, an old Chevy that'll fit in real well around the warehouses down there. You can stretch out in the back and give me directions and when we find Dick, we've got a way to get him to a hospital if he needs one."

"Thank you, Dr. Corey. If there's anything you think you need, why don't you get it now? Pick me up at the side door in an hour."

He hadn't moved so much as a finger since Corey had arrived. Corey wasn't even sure if he had blinked and his voice, so flat, so tired. "Listen, if there's anything you want, just ask."

"Rest. Blood . . . no, the hunger gives me an edge, Dr. Corey. At the moment I'm fighting to stay away from you. Don't worry, the windows themselves are a form of nourishment."

"An hour," Corey repeated, suddenly anxious to leave.

Corey arrived at exactly the agreed-to time, bringing a cage containing three very large rabbits. Stephen eyed them with a hint of amusement, then stretched out in the back and pulled the heavy cover over his head to shield himself from the setting sun.

Corey headed down the hill from Baltic Avenue, driving the narrow road across the low drawbridges to the warehouses by the river. To avoid any suspicion, Corey kept to the main roads, stopping sometimes on side streets so Stephen could stretch his mind farther, calling and getting no answer.

An hour passed. Two. Corey heard Stephen mumbling in

the back. Given the situation he was probably swearing from frustration but the odd combination of inflection, guttural consonants, and occasional sibilant hiss made the words sound like some primitive incantation. He shared Stephen's concern and forced himself to drive slowly so as not to cross an area too often. Only the rabbits relaxed, curling together in the corner of their cage, their noses buried under soft paws.

The sun set. The cars all went home and Corey pulled into a dark alley. "Why have we stopped?" Stephen asked.

"Carrera's no fool. There'll be men watching the roads. They're sure to notice us if we keep moving. Better to stay still. Besides, if you look ahead you'll see the main road from town to the flats and the bridge that leads to this side of the river. You close enough to reach the drivers?"

Stephen looked over Corey's shoulder. "I am."

"Then we sit tight and see who shows."

Stephen moved the rabbits into the back so he could sit beside Corey. "You know Richard better than I do, Dr. Corey. What is he thinking now?"

"He's scared. But he knows he can't allow it to break his concentration so he seals it up."

"I showed him what he must do. He has to let the emotions loose to call me."

"Old habits die hard."

"I considered those." Stephen rested his head on the dashboard and continued the call.

TWENTY-EIGHT

1

After the shooting, Volpe had dropped off Wells and two guards then went back to the real estate office to tell Carrera what Russ had done.

Carrera might have listened to Russ's excuse, might have even thought of a way out of the mess Russ had created if Russ had faced him after the shooting. Now, with barely a moment's thought, Carrera decided on his last use for Lowell. No matter what the legality of the act, even the rumor that he had been responsible for Lowell's execution would make him the country's man of the hour, a phenomenal change from his lowly status a week ago.

Certain that he would be safer with Austra dead, Carrera called Bowen from a pay phone and ordered him to assure it, then concentrated on finding Russ. After they arrived at the real estate office, he sent Volpe to get dinner from the kosher deli on the next block then set to work making calls on a phone he assumed to be tapped, trying to track Russ down. Enough time passed that he and Volpe were still in the office for the evening news broadcast, headlining the story of Corey's attack, Bowen's death and the theft of the sniper victim's body.

Carrera snapped when he heard the news. With a bellow of rage, he picked up his beer bottle and threw it across the room at the Wells painting. A tear ripped through the landscape like a twisting fault line and the painting fell onto the table below it. Accustomed to Carrera's outbursts, Volpe gripped the arms of his chair and said nothing as he waited for the tirade to end. When it did, Carrera pulled two document-sized envelopes from his desk and addressed them. "Come on," he said. "After we make a couple of stops, we'll go have a talk with Dick Wells."

Volpe knew Wells wouldn't talk. Carrera knew this as well but now he had an excuse to let things get bloody. Wells would die without saying a word. Afterward, he and Carrera would get rid of the body together, telling no one where it had been taken. There were wild places in the parks where no one would find it. Or maybe they'd weight Wells down and dump him in the river to rot at the bottom with a dozen other corpses. *They ought to stick alligators in the Cuyahoga River,* Volpe thought, *alligators to get fat on all of Domie's victims.*

He didn't want to go with Domie now but if could think of an excuse to stay behind, he'd call the police and tell them what he knew. Domie would guess it was him who informed and his life would be over, a single whispered order an exchange for all his years of loyalty. No, like it or not, Volpe had to see this final killing through. Resigned, he grabbed his jacket and followed Carrera to the car. Carrera stopped at a house his real estate firm was listing and Volpe stood guard at the front door, smoking a cigarette while Carrera took the Austra reports from a bedroom wall safe and stuck the documents in one addressed envelope. After he sealed it, he slid the package into the second before joining Volpe at the door.

On the drive across town, Volpe tried to justify what would happen tonight but all he saw was the expression on Wells's face when he'd touched his kid on the shoulder. The guy had balls. He shouldn't have to die for killing scum like Peter Carrera. Hell, if Peter was anyone but his own son, Domie would have ordered Peter hit years ago.

Besides, Peter was dead. Why couldn't Domie see that revenge was pointless?

"Three shots in the head," Domie was mumbling as he

wove the car through the evening traffic. "Three goddamn shots and Austra's still alive."

You can't stop a thing like that, Domie. That day in the restaurant, I looked into its eyes and I knew that no one could. Volpe would have said all of this but it would be admitting too much so he concentrated instead on saying nothing at all.

Downtown, Carrera parked in front of the main post office and handed the envelope to Volpe. "Go get some stamps and drop this in the mail."

As soon as he was inside the building where Carrera could not see him, Volpe noted the envelope was addressed to an aid of Senator McCoy's. The word "personal" written in the corner meant that when the reports showed up in a day or two, the aide would hold the envelope until Carrera himself requested it be delivered. If Carrera died, the envelope would most likely be forwarded to the senator and the revenge would go on and on. While Volpe waited in line behind two other late-night customers, he tried to think of some way to save himself. By the time he reached the counter, one came to him, one that was so easy after all.

During the rest of the drive to the building where Wells was held, Volpe fingered the thin length of wire coiled in his pocket. Dominic would ask him to do the killing. Carrera would kill Wells himself but the pleasure of being the actual murderer could never equal that of standing in front of his victim and watching his face for all the time it took him to die. Domie always said that Volpe was so perfect at balancing pain and death. Maybe he was but tonight, Volpe vowed, his hand would slip or his feet would lose their traction on the blood-soaked floor and Wells would die instantly. Volpe owed his conscience at least that much.

No, he wouldn't play Carrera's vicious waiting game—not anymore.

11

The calm descended as it always did in times of danger, wrapping Dick's mind in icy bonds stronger than the ropes that held him now. They'd begun to form on the drive and, by the time the car had pulled into a covered loading dock, his fear had vanished replaced by a detached resolve as if someone else's life, not his own, depended on him tonight.

Even so, he had not been able to stop his heart from beating so hard and fast that it muffled the voices around him. *Could they hear it? Could they see it, pounding through the veins on his temples?* he had wondered as two men pulled him out of the car. He hoped not. He did not want to give them any kind of satisfaction.

The men led him through a building stacked high with empty fruit crates and grocery boxes, down a flight of open metal stairs so narrow they traveled single file into a basement smelling faintly of rancid fat and refrigerator gas. A metal door to an unused walk-in cooler hung open and the man in front of him moved forward to drag a chair into it.

Dick grabbed the slim chance. Swinging his body, he hit the man behind him hard in the stomach with his shoulder. The man fell backward onto the stairs and Dick kicked him in the groin then tried to run past him. The man spun, grabbing Dick's ankle, yanking it out from beneath him, dragging him down the stairs to the basement floor. The second guard slammed the side of Dick's head with the butt of a gun until Dick wisely stopped fighting, forcing himself to barely move as they tied him to the chair.

His body ached but the pain meant little to him. Only the questions he had asked were important. "What happened to my son? To Patrick?" He had not inquired about Stephen's fate. He'd felt a bullet blast through Stephen's brain, sharing an agony that had brought tears to his eyes. Now somewhere something had died so Stephen could survive.

But was Stephen asleep and healing or already stalking his prey? Dick had no way of knowing. Their psychic bond had vanished with the shots.

The two men guarding him told him nothing before they left. The cooler door clicked shut behind them and the bare bulb above him went out leaving him in complete darkness. For hours he sat alone, one more piece of baggage, ignored as the crates and boxes surrounding him. In the outside room,

a radio switched on and Elvis Presley crooned, "Love me
tender, love me sweet . . ." through the thick insulated door.
Dick didn't try to pull himself loose. Even if he managed to
free himself from the chair, the cuffs would still hold him.
So he sat, conserving his strength for the final fight, mentally
calling to Stephen as he waited for the evening news.

The men outside were talking when the news broadcast
began and Dick had to strain to separate the announcer from
their voices. By the time the pair realized he might be listening and tuned the volume down, Dick had learned enough.
The boys were safe. The sniper victim's body had disappeared from the morgue. As he expected, someone there had
died but he never caught the name.

Not Corey, Dick thought. *Stephen wouldn't.*

Idiot, he reminded himself. *Stephen would kill you if his
body demanded it. And choice would mean nothing at all.*

Ignoring what might have already been done, Dick concentrated on trying to reach Stephen until he recognized Carrera's voice outside, barking orders to the men.

The lock slid back with a well-oiled click and Volpe's huge
form filled the doorway. The bare bulb above Dick's head
came on and he squinted at the brightness as he watched
Volpe and Carrera come in and close the door behind them.

Only these two? Carrera might just be cautious. More
likely, Dick thought, he didn't want anyone but Volpe to over-
hear his questions or the answers he might receive.

Stephen had said he would feel Dick's pain. If so, Dick should
experience as much of it as he could before Carrera realized that
he had no intention of talking and killed him. He therefore
greeted Carrera with a jaunty grin completely at odds with his
usual personality. "Lose something?" he asked in a glib tone

Carrera kicked hard, a steel-toed shoe connecting with
Dick's ankle sending a stab of pain up Dick's leg. Dick let
the pain flow through him and out in a silent cry for help.
"Problems getting away from you, are they?" Carrera swung
a fist. Dick instinctively tilted his head to dodge the blow. As
he did, he saw the edge of a table nearly hidden by the stack
of boxes, the corner of a butcher's scale. Suddenly the boxes

around him made sense. He was dying at the source of the city's drug problem—the rumored spot the cops referred to as Cleveland Central High. "You think I killed your son," he said, his voice ice-water calm. "You killed him with your junk long before I pulled the trigger. He was a casualty of war, no better or worse than the rest."

Carrera's eyes glazed with rage. "Hold him," he ordered Volpe. The big man's hands trembled as he laid them on Dick's shoulders, then clamped tight. Carrera pulled two long rags from his pockets and fastidiously wrapped them around his knuckles before he started in.

As the blows began to fall, Dick pictured the pain flowing through him, the steady stream growing to a torrent of agony moving up and out.

The beating stopped in the same calculated manner it had begun. Dick slumped forward, gasping for breath, a cut above his eye and a split lip dripping blood onto his pants.

"That was for getting smart with me," Carrera said. He unwrapped his hands and lifted a trench shovel from the ledge beside the door. A quick twist removed the handle and Carrera pressed it hard into Dick's stomach. "Now we'll talk about Austra. Then you'll die. Why not cut the pain short and tell me what you know?"

"Ask," Dick responded, not surprised at Carrera's disappointed expression.

"Start at the beginning. How did you meet him?"

Dick had no intention of answering but when he tried to think of what he would not answer, nothing came to him. If Carrera roasted him from the toes up, the answer still wouldn't come. All that remained was Stephen's impassive face, his final instructions, and the blood they had shared a few hours before. The act shamed Dick. The shame enraged him. Friendship. Bonds. Lies! That damned bloodsucker didn't trust Dick any more than he trusted anyone! "I don't remember," he said evenly.

Carrera swung low, connecting with the same ankle he'd kicked. The pain swept through Dick, merging with his fury, creating a potent flammable mix that exploded in Dick's mind in a way that the pain alone never could.

* * *

Stephen sensed the rage—faint and distant. He waited for the second blow with long fingers spread on the dashboard, nails digging into the faded brown vinyl. When it came, he spoke through clenched teeth. "Climb the hill, Dr. Corey. We're in the wrong place."

As Corey drove, Stephen forced his voice to remain slow and even in spite of the growing torture he shared. "Up Canal Street. Left at the bridge. Right on Huron." He only revealed a hint of his concern when he overshot and had Corey backtrack.

The blows became faster and Stephen was close enough now to know Carrera's patience had snapped. Only Richard's endurance kept him alive. As soon as he showed signs of losing consciousness, Carrera would stop the blows and he would die.

Stephen made the last move in his calculated bid for time.

—I'm coming, Richard. Talk to him. Tell him anything he wants to know.—

Though Stephen still continued his directions in the same calm tone, a series of long rips grew beneath his fingers. Corey ran the last two lights.

"Stop." Stephen pointed to a four-story building in the middle of the block. The city's soot had darkened the brown bricks, boards sealed the windows. He motioned for silence and, eyes closed, moved his mind through the space. "Richard's there. Volpe, Carrera. Two others on guard. I'm going in."

"I'll go with you."

"No. I may need you to call the police or an ambulance. You'll know if you should."

"They'll kill him if they hear you coming."

"They won't."

Stephen took off his shoes and rather than risk some overlooked guard seeing the car door open slipped out the rolled-down window. He made no more noise than a shadow as he padded across the dark street. At the corner of the building he leapt high, hooking his hands over the second-floor window ledge while his toes dug into the narrow cracks between

the bricks. Dick's pain was stronger now. Stephen tried to
ignore its waves as he inched himself up and pried out a loose
lower board.

In a moment he'd squeezed inside, hands and feet padding
his fall onto the floor. The darkness meant nothing, his eyes
adjusted, welcoming the change the way his body warmed to
the hunt. His hearing concentrated on the sounds two floors
below him—the men on guard cracking jokes about the killing, Richard's stifled cry following the pain of an impatient
blow. Swallowing a scream of rage, Stephen picked his way
through the debris and slowly pushed open the inner door.

When his memory returned with a sudden snap and he
heard Stephen's faint advice, Dick spit out a mouthful of
blood, inhaled as far as his cracked ribs would allow, and
began. After so much forced silence, the first words came
hard. Gradually, the sentences flowed faster. He embellished,
fascinating Carrera and, judging from his expression, terrifying Volpe.

As he went on, one of the guards outside went upstairs to
relieve himself and died instantly in the darkness just beyond
the door. Stephen jumped the metal rail, landing next to the
stairs. Pushing himself upright, he kicked, hitting the second
guard in the midsection. As his stomach split open, he fell
forward into Stephen's waiting arms, a scream frozen in his
throat. One quick stroke and the man's neck snapped.

Stephen stepped over him to the door. It had been too long
since he'd killed an enemy. With tonight's quick deaths behind him, his past cried out for blood.

As he pulled the door open, Carrera spun, aiming his gun
before he recognized the intruder. When he saw Stephen, he
tried to fire. Though his hand shook with the effort, his
muscles would not obey him.

"Untie Richard," Stephen ordered Volpe.

Volpe, relief evident in his expression, did not need a mental command to force him to obey. He worked quickly, standing back as soon as he'd unlocked the cuffs. Dick brought his
arms forward slowly, gauging the injuries.

"Can you walk, Richard?" Stephen asked.

"If you give me a hand." The words were slurred. His swollen lips refused to move.

"Corey's coming down. I want you to go with him."

"No!" Volpe whispered, the soft desperate word seeming so at odds with his huge body and hands. "No. I have something for you. Please." He dipped into his pocket, pulling out a folded piece of paper and a key, holding them out to Stephen.

Carrera knew what they were. "What did you do to me, Ang?" he shrieked.

Volpe didn't look at him. He was noting the changes in Austra—the tensing and curling of his fingers, how dark his eyes had become. Domie couldn't see it but Volpe knew. As soon as Wells left, he and Domie would both die, frozen the way Domie was frozen, unable to move, to speak, to do anyting but give whatever this thing wanted. Scraps of memory of the afternoon in the restaurant came back to him. He couldn't face that hell again. "Your reports," Volpe said. "They're waiting for you at the post office. The box number's on the form. Get them and leave us alone. It's over."

"The hell it is!" With an angry growl, Carrera fired three shots into Volpe's chest. The big man remained standing, looking more stunned than hurt before pitching forward against Dick's chest.

The impact threw Dick sideways, his battered ribs taking one more bruising on the concrete floor. Ignoring the agony, he turned and watched Carrera moving slowly backward until he hit the table. Stephen had allowed Carrera to kill Volpe, now the gun had become useless once more.

Carrera's mind opened to Dick—the feral rage, the instant when he felt his first despair. He'd lost. Completely. Irrevocably. With Halli's expression clear in his mind, Carrera tried to force his finger to pull the trigger, then tried to drop the gun and appeal to mercy but even begging was denied. Carrera's fingers had numbed, only Stephen's will allowed him to still grip the useless weapon, still point it at his intended victim, make the murder to follow justifiable as self-defense.

Pushing himself into a sitting position, Dick turned and

studied Stephen. Stephen's eyes were huge, clouded with need and, Dick sensed through the bond still strong between them, shreds of regret. How many times could Stephen do what had to be done, kill out of expediency, immerse himself in pain and torment and come back civilized and unscathed? Acting on his own instincts, Dick said softly, "Throw the gun to me, Dominic."

Carrera, partially pulled from his trance, glanced at Dick. Logic told him he should not obey but fear dictated otherwise.

"Damn it, Domie!" Dick yelled. "Listen to me. If you don't want to die the way Halli died, throw me your gun."

Carrera managed to toss the weapon. Dick caught it, aimed, and with the quick justification that he only did what should have been done years ago, he fired two shots. Carrera fell backward against the table, scattering the boxes beside it, beyond Stephen's reach before he hit the floor.

Stephen knelt beside his intended victim, dipped a finger in Carrera's blood, and tasted it. His expression was unreadable, his thoughts equally guarded.

"It had to end this way," Dick said.

"I understand why you killed him. Tomorrow I may even be thankful."

The throbbing in Dick's ribs and face and ankle felt wonderful. He was alive and they would heal. One question remained. Dick thought he knew the answer but he had to be certain. "When Carrera started asking about you, why couldn't I remember anything?"

"You hide your pain too well, Richard, but you've never learned to control your temper."

"That's what I figured." Dick pulled the chair closer to him and used it to help him shift his weight while Stephen picked up the gun Dick had fired, wiped it clean, and pressed it into Volpe's hand. Tomorrow Volpe would be a hero. He might even deserve the honor and Dick would see to it that he got his due.

"I hope you weren't too hungry, Austra. I don't have much life to spare," Dick commented.

Stephen smiled and Dick looked up at the long rear fangs

brushing Stephen's lower lip. Then Stephen crouched beside him, stole the worst of his pain, and helped him to stand.

"Lean against me, Richard, and I'll help you up the stairs."

"Lowell's still alive. Are you going after him?"

"He belongs to Helen, yes?"

"Are you going after him?" Dick repeated with a sharper insistence in his tone. If Stephen wouldn't, then Dick would find the strength and go himself. He'd be damned if he'd let his niece face a madman alone.

Stephen looked at him and seemed to be actually considering the idea, as if there could be any debate.

TWENTY-NINE

Helen Wells—her face.
Helen Wells—her body.
Helen Wells—those incredible things she did with her mind.
When Russ Lowell had pulled out of the pier, sobbing
because he thought he'd lost her, he'd never felt such a horrible emptiness. Then he'd heard her laughter faintly in his
mind and thought it a memory like the rest. By the time he'd
reached the private dock near Rockwood, she'd begun whispering to him saying words he could almost discern. He'd
mechanically dumped the boys into the trunk, then shared a
few drinks with the guys who had driven his car across the
border. He left soon after and sent the guys back to Windsor
on the boat.

On the outskirts of Toledo, Helen's whispers had grown
louder, her words clear. —Fool! Did you think you could destroy me so easily? Come back, Russ Lowell. Your vampire
is waiting for you.—

Then she left him with only her laughter and her memory
etched and burning in his brain.

As soon as he reached Cleveland he'd begun hustling
money, driving around with the kids in the trunk, strong-
arming for old debts, emptying his safe deposit boxes, dump-
ing drugs in the car along with the cash. By the time he fired
the shots into Stephen's head, he had almost $80,000 in cash

325

and goods hidden in the doors. He could live well for a year or two on that kind of dough even with all the special precautions he'd have to take to hold on to his magnificent victim and to avoid the hired killer that Carrera would undoubtedly send after him.

Vampire, she'd called herself.

Was she really? No matter. He knew how to handle her. And after what he'd done to her, there was no way she'd wake up in the few hours it would take him to get back to her. Even if she did, there would be no one to hear her cry out or to heed her mental call. He became so certain of her helplessness that he even pulled off the highway at a truck stop where, with locked doors and a gun on the floor beside him, he slept until after midnight.

When he woke, he felt sharper than he had in days. The storm he encountered when he'd neared Detroit didn't phase him. He'd been prepared for trouble at the border but the guards were sluggish, their rain-soaked shirts sticking to their backs as they ran outside and motioned him through with no more than a glance at his forged license.

It should always be this easy, he thought. Maybe, now that Helen's other lover was gone, it could be. Maybe she'd need him the way every creature in hiding needs its front.

He ought to stop for food, he thought. He ought to get a bottle. A carton of cigarettes.

Later. Later. The urgency of her held him. He drove straight to her—his love, his last home.

The warehouse doors were still locked. Russ thought it an encouraging sign, but when he swung them open, and swept a flashlight over the place she had lain, he saw that his prize had vanished, leaving cracked trapdoors beside their frames, a pile of bloody ropes, and a pair of broken handcuffs on the floor.

She had gone! Russ screamed his rage, the long wail of a hungry predator deprived its meat.

Where? He backed out of the dark building. He had money. A car. Domie's men might already be on his trail. He had to go.

"—Russ Lowell.—"

"What?" He heard her voice, felt her in his mind, soft and weak and inviting.

"—Come to me.—"

She could have run. Instead she'd waited for him!

But he was no fool. When he faced her he had better be prepared. He rushed to the car for his gun and went back inside. Playing the flashlight beam across the dark corners, he finally found her.

"Look at me, Russ Lowell. Am I beautiful?"

Beautiful? The word applied to other women, not to her. The beam revealed a naked body paler than he remembered, leaner and more delicate. As shameless as she had been in his dreams, she held out her arms.

He responded with an involuntary step forward, then another. He raised the gun, but though he knew he should fire it, he only stood grinning stupidly while she closed the distance between them and lifted it from his hands.

"Lock the doors, Russ Lowell. I need you and I've waited too long already."

He rushed to do as she asked, then turned wanting to touch her, to kiss her, but she was no longer behind him. He scanned the room with the flashlight beam, saw a pale shadow, and aimed the light at Donna Crawford's face. The beam wavered from his sudden fear and he focused it again, this time on Mary Evans, the short stiff braids and skintight jeans, the cigarette dangling from her pouted lips.

Tricks. His mind was playing tricks. Not enough sleep. Not enough for days. That must be it. He aimed the beam where the figure had been standing a moment before but it had vanished like the first dream of night.

"Russ Lowell."

Her voice. He swung the light across the room—Beverly Fields, her blue parka open, the yellow angora sweater tight across her breasts. He blinked. Nancy Potts. He bellowed and started running toward the vision, his feet slipping on the blood-soaked floor, his body falling over the pile of ropes.

Rolling over, he started to stand.

A board creaked. He aimed the light up at the approaching shadow.

Maria Truzzi in her eggshell satin wedding dress hovered a dozen feet away, her eyes dark and understanding, filled with tears for the life he had stolen.

Russ was the one trembling now as her ghost moved toward him. He tried to slide back but his feet no longer obeyed. "I'm sorry," he said without conviction, as if the words would make her specter vanish. "I'm sorry!" he said it louder now, the apology of a brutish child caught trying to flee. "I'm sorry," he said a third time, almost contrite now. He would have lowered the light and hoped she would vanish but his hands would not move.

The face shifted as it had in his dreams, the hair lightening, the white satin dress slowly dissolving.

Helen Wells.

She knelt beside him, running a hand down the side of his face. "We've waited too long already," she repeated. The light was only inches from her face when she smiled and he saw the long upper fangs, sharp and ready for their first kill.

"Do you like them?" she asked. "I willed them for you."

He began to laugh, the quick hysterical sound of the doomed, as she slowly unbuttoned his shirt.

The sun was just rising when her teeth finally found their mark. Though she'd been famished, she'd taken her time.

A light fell over the warehouse floor. Helen looked up and saw Patrick standing beside the door, watching her, adult enough now to know he must not disturb her.

"Papa said . . ." the boy began, then halted, unable to explain how his father had made him wait in the car until she had claimed her enemy and would be free to allow Patrick to stay or leave.

She touched Patrick's mind and could not discern even the hint of a suggestion there. This decision was hers alone to make.

The world held such barbaric uncertainty. Human, immortal, she stretched out her hand and motioned for her son to come and feast.

THIRTY

His doctor had given Dick three weeks to make a decision.

Two days past deadline, his ankle in a cast, his face still in bandages, Dick sat beside Judy in the doctor's office and said that he'd be willing to do whatever was necessary to hold on to life. His doctor began with a simple blood test, then a hurried series of X rays. What he saw astonished him.

"The growths have shrunk. Spontaneous remissions are rare in cases like this but it appears that your body is fighting the cancer on its own. I would like to redo the bloodwork, though. There's something else we want to check out. Not anything to be concerned about, so don't worry. Now if you'll sign a consent form . . ." Then the doctor stopped speaking because Dick was hugging Judy and Judy was hugging Dick and no one was listening to him at all. When he had his patient's attention, the doctor repeated his request.

"Hell, no," Dick said, and as Judy grabbed the lab report from his file, he limped out of the office.

Judy waited until Dick had gone to bed to call Elizabeth and share the good news. Last week's near tragedy had dulled Judy's unease around Stephen, and as she talked to Elizabeth they began making tentative plans for a joint trip north. She had to visit her husband's namesake, she told Elizabeth, and see if he was as beautiful as his brother.

Elizabeth laughed as she hung up the phone. If Judy

329

thought Patrick was beautiful, Dickey would steal her heart. She felt a spreading warmth inside as she thought of her young cousins, considering them in a manner she would have found terrifying even a few months ago.

Paul had already gone to bed. Elizabeth undressed and looked down at him thinking that what she had suspected had been true all along—the ancient taboo against sharing blood with a human lover, like so many of the Old One's other prohibitions, had been little more than a lie. Tomorrow she would write Ann and Rachel, both of them caught in doomed affairs, and convey the wonderful news.

But tonight she would give a gift to Paul—a full human lifetime, perhaps more. She would form a new bond between them and begin to teach him to control his pain, to monitor his body and stave off those diseases that were already taking root in him.

She sensed her time to conceive was approaching, and though the end of her life still seemed vague and distant, she hoped death would seek her soon. She had said good-bye to too many lovers. Paul would be the last. With luck, she would not live without him very long.

As the weeks passed, Dick continued to feel better than he had in twenty years. Then gradually, so gradually at first that he didn't even realize it was happening, the fatigue returned bringing with it the heavy nagging pain. He made a second trip to Canada at Christmastime; three more the following year. Each time, he would feed on Stephen, taking as much blood as Stephen dared give him. Then he would lay in the bed that had once been Hillary's, listening to his heart work overtime, trying to pump blood that flowed thick as molasses in his veins. When its throbbing subsided, he would fly home to a few more months of health before he needed to make the trip again.

One evening he came home from work and discovered Elizabeth and Paul had come for a visit. Paul looked younger than Dick had recalled, and as the architect stood to shake his hand, Dick noted that he moved with greater ease. "I can visit whenever you like and help you just as well as Stephen," Elizabeth told him.

"Stephen already made the sacrifice. I can't ask the same of you."

Elizabeth stood, taking both his hands. Her warmth filled him as she silently shared her gratitude. "No sacrifice I make can equal what I owe you for what you have shown to my family. I want to help you, do you see?"

Dick understood Paul's sudden health but he didn't want Elizabeth's help. He wanted Stephen; the call of blood.

He lived five extra years. He lived them well.

He died in his sleep. The family sensed how hard he struggled at the end.

EPILOG

I still keep chocolate creams in the cold box. I eat two a day, at night and in the morning, letting them dissolve in my mouth before I swallow. Small luxuries are the hardest to abandon.

Other changes are wonderful. I no longer feel the nagging pain of a human body. It is in harmony now with my mind and my soul. I think that if I had not been prepared for the sudden physical changes, I would have thought I died. Then as now, my body hardly seems to surround my soul at all.

My skin is paler and smoother. And when the winter winds are silent, I climb to the open ridge above the cabin where I can look down on it and up to the stars. The twins are asleep, the children growing inside me rest. I sense Stephen moving silently up the ridge looking for me. I open my mind and call him to me. The shadows of the moon turn my hair silver and our naked bodies to liquid marble. I need not will my body to feel for it feels so perfectly—his hands, his lips.

I no longer regret the human life I have lost.

I would take it from everyone I love.